Cold Quarry

COLD QUARRY

A CODI SANDERS ADVENTURE THRILLER

BRENT LADD

NEW YORK

LONDON • NASHVILLE • MELBOURNE • VANCOUVER

COLD QUARRY

A Codi Sanders Thriller

Published in New York, New York, by Morgan James Publishing. Morgan James is a trademark of Morgan James, LLC. www.MorganJamesPublishing.com

This is a work of fiction. Any resemblance to persons living or dead, or actual events, is either coincidental or is used for fictive and storytelling purposes. Some elements of this story are inspired by true events; all aspects of the story are imaginative events inspired by conjecture. Cold Quarry was a true labor of love. Like life, the writing process is a journey, one meant to be savored, and to me, it's more about the pilgrimage itself than the destination. I learned a ton while writing this book, and I hope it's reflected in the story and the prose. Only you, the reader, can be the judge of the results. Drop me a line if you have feedback or just want to say hi. I can be found at brentladdbooks.com

ISBN 9781631953019 paperback
ISBN 9781631953026 eBook
Library of Congress Control Number: 2020944079

Cover and Interior Design by:
Chris Treccani
www.3dogcreative.net

Morgan James is a proud partner of Habitat for Humanity Peninsula and Greater Williamsburg. Partners in building since 2006.

Get involved today! Visit
MorganJamesPublishing.com/giving-back

Dedicated to my daughter Makenzie—the Codi Sanders of my family.

She seems to be at her best when the trail is roughest.

ACKNOWLEDGMENTS

With deep appreciation to all those who encouraged me to write, and especially those who did not. I want to thank the following contributors for their efforts in doling out their opinions and helping to keep my punctuation honest: Jeff Klem, Natalie Call, Geena Dougherty, Carol Avellino, Jacqui Huntley, Jeff Loefke, and Wade Lillywhite. A host of family and friends who suffered through early drafts and were kind enough to share their thoughts: my lovely wife Leesa, who is my first reader and best critic. And my editor, Cathy Hull.

A special thanks to my publisher, Morgan James Publishing, who helped make this all possible, as writing is only half the total equation. Finally, to Patrick Fitch for the cover design.

As many concepts as possible are based on actual or historical details. Special thanks to the original action hero—my dad, Dr. Paul Loefke.

Some of the information about the Plymouth Mail Truck Robbery came from *Big Bucks*, written by Ernest Tidyman, a worthwhile read if you would like to know more.

Lastly, writers live and die by their reviews, so if you like my book, *please* review it! I thank you in advance.

CHAPTER ONE

(Based on actual events)

AUGUST 14, 1962 – NEW ENGLAND – ROUTE 3 – 4:12 P.M.

Mist pooled on the faded cracked pavement as Red crushed the stub of his last cigarette with his heel. It joined a group of six others smashed into the wet blacktop. He pinched a bit of loose tobacco from the tip of his tongue and looked up. They were late. Every prior surveillance had revealed a ten-minute variance at most, and now, on the day of the heist, the truck was nowhere in sight. He paced nervously, trying not to look out of place parked on the overpass. His companion, Joe, was standing next to their brown Pontiac's open hood looking just as perplexed. If it weren't for the seriousness of the moment at hand, Red would have laughed out loud at his partner's looks. Joe was a large man, at least six feet tall, with wide shoulders and a grim expression. The funny thing was the yellow summer dress and high heels he was wearing. He even had red lipstick smeared across thick uncaring lips and a blonde wig. A wig that must have been uncomfortable, as he

1

kept scratching and readjusting it, as they stood there and waited. He looked ridiculous. This was a broad no one could love.

"What?" Joe said. "You try putting this on, let alone walk in these ridiculous shoes."

"Hey." Red raised his hands in surrender. "You are looking mighty fine from here."

"Screw you, Red."

Patches of August rain slowly began to settle over the New England countryside as the sun raced toward the horizon, ending its failed contest with the clouds for the day. The air was thick with the smell of wet pine pitch and exhaust. Red couldn't take the waiting on top of the Clark County overpass. He felt like a cornered tourist with an illegible map. With every car that passed beneath, he was getting more wound up. He ran his fingers through his rain-slicked black hair and decided they should try driving back and forth to look less suspicious.

"Let's go for a ride," Red said, as he closed the hood.

He and his "date" pulled the Pontiac back onto the road and slowly crossed to the other side.

* * *

"What on earth are they doing?" Thomas said, through a pair of palmed binoculars, his elbows resting on the hood of his green Oldsmobile. Thomas was the brain behind the operation. He had planned every detail down to the minute, but the truck they were expecting was more than thirty minutes overdue. His lookouts were now driving back and forth across the Clark County overpass like two lost Sunday drivers who couldn't find an onramp.

He was wearing the gray pants and shirt of a Massachusetts State Police Trooper and was parked two miles away at the Clark County Road exit, waiting for a signal that had yet to come. And now, he doubted its arrival at all. The damp air seemed to cloak him in a misty straightjacket.

2

He felt unable to move, helpless in his current situation. All he could do was watch and wait.

Thomas had received a tip three months earlier about a decision made by the banks in Buzzards Bay and Hyannis. They decided to save money on their summertime cash deliveries to their main branch in Boston by hiring the U.S. Postal Service rather than an armored truck for the deliveries. It had been a very successful plan, saving almost fifty dollars a week across the busy vacation season in Cape Cod.

He lauded himself as a detail-oriented person. He had a reputation in the business for planning and getting away with some of the more clever crimes in the Boston area. He had carefully calculated the possible haul in the red, white, and blue mail truck at conservatively one million dollars. But as of right now, *there was no stupid mail truck*. He lowered his binoculars and looked over at the man next to him.

Aggie was leaning on the trunk without a care in the world. He flicked at a toothpick in his mouth, moving it from side to side. He seemed impervious to stress or complications. This often infuriated Thomas. He knew Aggie would do his job when and where it was needed and without hesitation, but otherwise, the man had a way of killing time that was more than annoying. But no matter the stress or amount of bullets flying, he was one cool customer.

Aggie felt his boss's stare on the back of his neck and turned to look at him. "What?"

Thomas said nothing and turned his attention back to the magnified view of the bridge in the distance. "Come on," he said under his breath.

* * *

Forty-five mph was the USPS official policy for the recommended top speed. Patrick Schena was nothing if not a rule follower. As a driver for the postal service, he was always on the lookout for drunk or wayward drivers. He was cautious by nature and proud of his perfect driving record.

The problem with the trips to and from Cape Cod was they had become monotonous. Conversation with the guard riding shotgun, Billie Barrett, had long since run its course. He thought about the term: riding shotgun. It referred to the armed man riding next to a stagecoach driver during the early West, as he literally carried a shotgun for the defense of cargo and passengers. Billie had a snub nose thirty-eight in his holster, a modern weapon with less accuracy and stopping power than almost any other gun in the world.

The thought made Patrick smile at the silliness of it all. A few bags of mail would never be worth the trouble, and between the two of them, they had maybe twelve dollars.

The odds of something happening out here on Route 3 were nil. It was a waste of manpower to have a guard on the clock. Patrick glanced down at his speedometer and eased off just slightly, as his random thoughts had led to a slight uptick in their speed. He was looking forward to his upcoming vacation and thinking of visiting family back in South Dakota but had yet to finalize anything. He pulled out an opened pack of Black Jack gum and offered a blue stick to his partner. A quick headshake, and he took the piece for himself. The spicy anise flavor filled his mouth as he chewed.

* * *

After nine stress-filled minutes of watching the highway while driving back and forth, Red pulled the Pontiac back over to the roadside on top of the overpass. He got out and lifted the hood of the car once again. As he glanced down the long strip of black that cut through green fields on either side, he noticed fog starting to roll in. It would only get harder to see cars in the distance. He let out a sigh as a red and white Ford Crestline passed underneath him. Still no sign of the mail truck. Joe stepped out on wobbly feet, still getting used to the high heels. He used the car for support. Red turned to look at his masquerading companion. It was all part of the boss's plan to confuse any eyewitnesses. Luckily for him, he'd pulled the long straw and missed his chance to be fitted for a dress.

"I don't think it's coming," Red said.

Joe looked off into the distance. "Well, you don't know diddly."

Red snapped back to the highway. Sure enough, the red, white, and blue stripes of a USPS mail truck parted through the patchy fog, the squared-off flat nose and large windshield clearly on display. Joe swayed to the edge of the overpass for a better look and Red ran to the opposite side of the overpass waving his hands in the air with purpose.

Thomas lowered his binoculars the instant he saw the signal. It was time. "They're here."

It was all Aggie needed. He hopped up, popped the trunk, and jumped back into the car, firing up the engine. Thomas quickly donned his tunic and cap to complete his State Trooper outfit. They both ducked down and laid low.

* * *

"That, my friend, is a lot of woman."

Billie looked ahead to where Patrick had pointed. On top of the approaching overpass was a large, blonde woman in a bright yellow dress.

"That's more woman than you could handle in a year," Patrick added. "You'd probably have to bring chalk with you just to mark where you'd been so you wouldn't get lost."

The two men chuckled at the joke, but as they drew closer to the bridge, their smiles faded.

"Yowzeer, that is one ugly female." The disgust on Patrick's face was palpable.

"You'd never live down a night with that. It would haunt you."

Patrick nodded slowly. He pushed his eyes back onto the road, away from the frightful sight. He quickly moved back into his lane and was glad to be under the overpass and moving away.

* * *

Thomas lay flat in the back seat while Aggie did the same in the front. He lifted his head just enough to see the approaching mail truck through the back window. He ducked as it passed and then counted silently to three. As if shot from the gates at a horse track, Aggie and Thomas sprang from their car and moved to the trunk. They pulled out several wooden barricades with detour signs and set them across the lane, forcing oncoming cars to exit the highway onto Clark Road. They jumped back into the Oldsmobile and lit out, spewing gravel as they fishtailed back onto the highway. Five minutes later, they blew past the mail truck going eighty-five mph.

Just ahead was a curve in Route 3 along a forested area. It was a place where the two highway lanes were separated by a copse of thickly planted pines, making it impossible to see from one lane across to the other. It was critical to their plan. Aggie pushed the Olds as fast as he dared. Losing control now would be catastrophic. Hanging on from the passenger's seat, Thomas seemed focused on the road ahead.

A faded blue pickup rested by the side of the road, its engine idling. Vinnie sat on the tailgate wondering if the others had been pinched. It had been almost forty minutes since the proposed caper was supposed to go down. He did his best to look natural, but sitting was not his specialty, killing was. He was a dyed-in-the-wool killer of men.

It started with his first job, working as a carny. Vinnie and his partner were part of a traveling Bonnie's Big Top. They starred in a sideshow— Klutz, the 800-year-old mummy. Vinnie had perfected his pitch to passersby with a crazy accent from nowhere. *Come see Klutz. Over eight hundred years old. Some flesh still remaining on the body.* In reality, it was a stolen skeleton from the local college, which they had wrapped in old rags and dried pigskin. The audience had been generally impressed, and they made good coin over the first three cities on the tour. But money changed people. He'd seen it countless times in his short life.

One night, after all the customers had gone home, Vinnie discovered a stash of cash hidden under the mummy's faux sarcophagus. His partner denied having cheated him, but Vinnie could tell when the man was lying. He drove his knife into his partner's heart without hesitation, scooped up the cash, and never looked back.

Vinnie used his newfound killer's instinct to work his way up the ranks of the underground and Mafia in the upstate area, eventually ending up in Boston. Now he was a top-notch gun for hire. You name the target, and Vinnie would give you a price and guarantee results. It had been a very successful formula.

He'd connected with Thomas two years ago on a museum heist that had been very profitable for all. They had crossed paths two other times and developed a strong working relationship. As a killer, it was hard to have much of a personal life, but Vinnie trusted Thomas more than just about anyone.

He fingered the reassuring steel of a Thompson machine gun that lay hidden under his jacket next to him as he strained to listen. He brushed away some of the sporadic rain from his hair with a flick. He could just make out the sounds of tires squealing in the distance. The curve he was parked on made it impossible to see very far, but it sounded to him like game time. He put on his jacket and hid the machine gun in the cab of his truck. Then, in a carefully orchestrated routine, he pulled his truck diagonally onto the highway and parked it.

* * *

Patrick pulled toward the right edge of the lane as he watched a green Oldsmobile blast past his view through the metronome-like windshield wipers of the mail truck. "Someone's in a hurry," he said.

"Probably saw that woman back there," Billie said with a chuckle. The conversation quickly lapsed, and once again they shared the road in silence. Up ahead, the highway curved out of sight. It was getting close to dusk, so Patrick turned on the headlights. The rain had diminished, and he hit the button to kill the wipers. It was off and on; it couldn't make up its mind. Someone should invent a way to make windshield wipers intermittent, he thought to himself, but just as quickly dismissed the thought.

As they came around the curve, he spotted a pickup parked in the middle of the lane. The green Oldsmobile that had just gone past them a few seconds before was pulled to the side of the road. A police officer looked like he was giving the pickup driver a ticket. Patrick slowed. He pressed the brakes as the policeman waved for him to stop.

* * *

Thomas watched as Aggie flew around the curve, tires crying in protest. They'd passed the mail truck and were trying to get into position. The car quickly pulled to the edge of the road just about thirty feet behind Vinnie's pickup parked in the middle of the lane. Thomas jumped out in his uniform and pretended to talk to Aggie in the driver's seat. As soon as the mail truck started to slow, he stepped onto the road and waved for it to stop. The driver barely seemed to hesitate as he pulled the truck to a stop just in front of Thomas.

Thomas moved around to the mail truck's driver side to have a word with him. At the same time, the other two vehicles moved in to surround the mail truck. It was quick and efficient. The hours of practice had paid off. The pickup suddenly reversed right toward the mail truck, braking just inches away from impact. The Oldsmobile pulled in behind the mail truck, completing the maneuver.

Thomas watched as the driver's smile faded to confusion. At that moment, everything changed. Vinnie showed up with his sawed-off shotgun, and Aggie with a Thompson machine gun. Thomas pulled out a Colt 1911 and pointed right at the driver's head. Per the plan, Vinnie did the talking. He was, in Thomas' mind, certifiable, and it took no time for the two USPS employees to grasp that he would shoot them for the smallest of reasons.

"Hands up now, or I'll shoot you where you sit."

Both employees raised their hands in unison.

"Now, unlock your doors!"

The driver squawked, "They're not locked."

The doors were quickly opened, and the two men were pushed to the ground and disarmed. Their hands were tied and they were blindfolded. Once that was done, Vinnie escorted them back to the rear of the mail truck. He took the guard's keys and unlocked the back rolling door. Inside was a pile of sealed mailbags. Thomas and Aggie removed all sixteen canvas bags and placed them in the trunk of the Oldsmobile.

Vinnie tossed both men into the back of the mail truck, got inside, and drove. The heist had taken just under two minutes to complete.

After driving for a little over an hour with several false stops, Vinnie pulled the mail truck over to the curb along Route 128. "Any of you's two move, and I'll let you have it!" he said to the two men inside.

He left his captives bound and gagged, and walked the five blocks to where his car had been parked, whistling a tune as he went.

They stashed the money inside a wall in Thomas's basement, then carefully replaced the wall and moved old storage items in front of it. Red and Joe then drove the Oldsmobile and the blue pickup to a dark alley. Red used five gallons of gasoline to set them on fire and then strolled away with Joe, making light conversation and a few off-colored jokes.

In the end, the gang had all come away clean.

Now came time for the real genius behind the crime—how to not get caught.

CHAPTER TWO

AUGUST 8, 1967 – BOSTON – 8:45 A.M.

Special Agent Daniel Johnson walked up the crowded stairs from the Red Line. The air was sticky and humid with a distinguishing odor—a mix of body odor and garbage. His train was delayed twice, but he would still make it to his office on time. With each step, he could feel his sock pressing against the moist cardboard insert, barely keeping the sidewalk out where his loafers had worn through. He would need to get them resoled and soon. Hopefully, it wouldn't rain before that happened. At thirty-nine, Daniel still had some of his hair and, for the most part, a good attitude. His wife Candice and their two children were at times more of a distraction than a blessing, but he had made vows and was determined to see them through.

As an FBI agent, you had a lot of perks, but money was not one of them. The pay was meager and the hours brutal. Daniel liked the thought that he was essentially above the law, but his tendencies ran toward the straight side of being an agent and there was no profit in that—only honor.

The Sheraton Building at 470 Atlantic housed the field office of the FBI in Boston, a thirteen-story rectangle with a concrete steel and glass makeover.

He blew his nose on his handkerchief as the geriatric elevator operator escorted him to the fifth floor. The man had a perpetual coffee-stained smile set against a loose nicotine-wrinkled face. His maroon uniform and bill-less hat were adorned with shiny brass buttons.

"Morning, Special Agent Johnson."

"Sal."

It was a ritual that had grown no further than a few words. Daniel looked in the mirror of the elevator and ran his hand through his thinning hair. He wasn't happy with the reflection that stared back. He was looking old for his age, tired even, but it had been a long trail to get here. Maybe a trip upstate to do some fishing with his colleagues would help. He'd been invited by Special Agent Withers, a man who seemed to carry the delicate haze of debauchery within a collective bouquet of sweet perfume and whiskey.

Daniel had yet to give him a response. He'd overheard several other agents talking about the trip by the water cooler. It sounded fun.

He moved with robotic purpose through the smoke-filled common area and into his small office. The heavy wood paneling fought against the weak yellow glow of his desk lamp and the small square window on his back wall. His faded rosewood desk held a newer, powered typewriter and a brand new push-button phone. There was a stack of eight boxes in the corner, all from the same case. With a dour expression, he eyed the cold, leftover Sanka sitting in his coffee cup from the night before.

SA Daniel Johnson had been one of the first federal agents assigned to the Plymouth Mail Truck Robbery back in '62. He was tasked to the major crimes division, and it was his job to track, sift through, and pressure the known criminals capable of carrying out such an audacious heist. The bandits had been clever, leaving little evidence, and that alone limited the potential players. Johnson knew that most criminals were fueled by the excitement of a crime and couldn't keep their traps shut after it was committed. That led to their demise in many cases. Even now, five years later, there was no word on the street about the Plymouth Mail Truck Robbery, the most daring heist in U.S. history. Not a word.

At one point, more than sixty postal inspectors, a host of FBI investigators, and hundreds of state and local authorities were involved in the case, creating a competitive vibe that had one agency hiding information from the others. There was even false information leaked in an attempt at one-upmanship. It had been a complete disaster for everyone involved with reports of falsified evidence and forced confessions. The Justice Department raised the reward from $2,000 to $150,000 in hopes of moving the evidence needle. That had the phone operators working double shifts just to answer the calls, all filled with useless information and baseless accusations.

Daniel looked over the few eyewitness reports for the hundredth time. Some of the motorists that had been detoured off Route 3 had seen a state trooper from behind. Others said he was a white male, short or tall, slim or stout. Several reported a large woman broken down on the overpass. It was a mishmash of conflicting information.

The powers-that-be moved to create The Coalition of Law Enforcement Agencies in an attempt to get everyone back on the same page and play nice. Now, all evidence and information flowed to one source. It was progress, but when there was no hard evidence, case files were filled with opinions and conjecture—thirty boxes worth.

Initially, the press was taken in by the heist. It was lauded as a romance crime. No one was killed or injured. The thieves got away with over $1,500,000 in small, unmarked bills, making it the biggest cash heist in the country's history. One of the banks shipping the money claimed that a single $1,000 bill was among the small denominations. It was something the authorities could track, but as of yet, it had not surfaced. It became the red herring of the case.

Newspapers sensationalized the story to the limit, even speculated wildly to get readers to buy their papers. This clouded the investigation and had the police chasing their tails. Daniel would have no part in the circus. He remained focused on known criminals and squeezed them every chance he got. But time and poor results washed away interest in solving the crime. By 1967, there were just a handful of investigators left on the case, SA Daniel Johnson among them.

In the end, there were no convictions, and the money remained unrecovered. It was a stain on the USPS and the FBI.

Daniel picked up a faded clipping from a newspaper headline.

> *William F. White, Chief Postal Inspector was asked if the Postal Department considered it was taking a chance in transporting huge sums of money over back roads without escorts. "That's hard to say," he answered. "If we say yes, we look stupid. If we say no, we still look stupid."*
> —*Boston Herald, August 17, 1962*

He instinctively reached for his coffee cup and took a sip. *Argh.* Stale and cold, just like this case.

He was pretty sure who the players were, but there was just no proof. And in 1967, proof was now required. It was not like the old days when you could just railroad the most likely suspect. Now, there was talk of criminals' rights. They called it Miranda Rights, a swearword in his book. A year ago, the Supreme Court had overturned Ernesto Arturo Miranda's conviction, and now arresting and convicting felons had become much more difficult. At least he could still lean heavy on a suspect and wiretap him if needed. He glanced at the only photo of his family. It was taken years ago, and the smiles haunted him. He could never have imagined the all-consuming requirements of children. They needed this, they needed that, and they even demanded your time. He flipped the photo down, and with it the corrosive thoughts dispersed. He was a committed father, he told himself, as long as it didn't get in the way of everything else.

The brown phone on his desk rang. He pressed the flashing button and picked up the receiver. Daniel answered in a pat response, "Johnson."

He listened to the voice and then hung up, drumming his fingers on the desk. This could go two ways. *Justice must be panicking*, he thought. They were making one last stab at convicting three men. Daniel knew the evidence was thin, but they were being told to move ahead with the prosecution anyway. It was any man's guess what would happen, but maybe lady luck was finally on his side.

The meeting room was a holdout from the police ready rooms. It had twelve chairs and a briefing pedestal in front of a black chalkboard. The wooden chairs were small and uncomfortable with vertical backs that were straight out of the Spanish Inquisition. Daniel found an empty chair and sat stiffly. He looked around. With each month, the Coalition of Law Enforcement Agencies, CLEA, had shrunk. Last week's briefing had only five agents, but today, there were ten.

Keith Boddington was the lead on what was left of the Coalition. He had spent the last thirty years as a postal inspector and spearheaded things once the agencies combined resources. He was an angry man with a face to match, but beneath his seemingly rough exterior, he had a perfectionist's love of details. Every *i* dotted and *t* crossed. He had little need or time for personal grooming, and his disheveled hair and rumpled clothes proved it.

"As you all know," he said to the group, "Justice has committed to one last push on the Plymouth Mail Truck Robbery before the statute of limitations runs out on this case. The trial starts Monday at 9:00 a.m., so let's go over everything one more time just to be sure we haven't screwed the pooch on this thing. If we need to work all weekend to get ready, so be it."

Daniel listened as each agent volunteered his or her information. The Federal Grand Jury, sitting for the Northeastern District of Massachusetts handed down three secret indictments. They charged Joseph C. Tripoli and John J. Kelly, alias "Red," and other persons unknown under Title 18 of the United States Code, section 2114 specifically, with robbing two United States postal employees of $1,551,277, and putting the lives of those postal employees in jeopardy.

Evidence was mostly circumstantial, and they had put almost all their eggs in Daniel's basket. "Agent Johnson?"

Daniel perked up at the mention of his name.

He cleared his throat. "As you all know, Thomas Richards has maintained his innocence and we have nothing to tie him to the crime. Compliments of a little luck on our part, he now claims to know who the parties are behind the Plymouth Mail Truck Robbery. He has agreed to give state's evidence against the ones responsible in exchange for an immunity deal. It is not the most ideal situation, as I'm sure you all agree. But Justice is willing to play ball since we are only days from losing the whole thing to the statute of limitations, and some justice is better than no justice."

This got a mumbled agreement around the room.

Someone asked, "What's the minimum sentence look like?"

And an answer came. "A conviction carries a minimum sentence of twenty-five years."

Keith continued the meeting, going over all the details. Daniel tuned him out. He thought of the lucky happenstance that had presented Thomas to him.

Daniel was literally walking toward his bank when he noticed a man in a guard's uniform walking away from an armored truck. He was carrying a bank bag. In an instant, Daniel recognized the guard as one of his main suspects, Thomas Richards. He pulled his revolver and had the gangster dead to rights.

The brazen man had used some kids with firecrackers and perfect timing to distract the real guards for just a second while he helped himself to a bag of the bank's money from the back of the open armored car they were loading.

Thomas immediately surrendered, and when faced with a sure conviction, leveraged his knowledge of the Plymouth Mail Truck Robbery for his freedom. The Justice Department, desperate for any type of conviction, jumped at the deal. It would be the conclusion to a case that had spent upwards of twenty million taxpayer dollars and 104 years of man-hours with nothing to show for it. *Finally an end, and I'm at the center of it all,* Daniel thought. The contemplation had him imagining a step up in the Bureau and with that, better pay. It was everything he'd been working for. Yes, he would tell Special Agent Withers that he was definitely in for the guys' fishing trip.

On Monday at 9:00 a.m. the trial commenced. Daniel watched from the hallway as the press tried to fill the courtroom. It was chaos. He waited and waited for his man to show, but as the doors to the courtroom closed, there was still no sign of Thomas Richards. Daniel had taken no chances and placed round-the-clock surveillance at the man's house. Though the prosecutor had pleaded with the court to deny bail, the law was the law: innocent until proven guilty. Thomas had been released on $25,000 bail and had been a model citizen ever since. Sunday, Daniel stopped by his house to go over his testimony one last time. Richards named Red, Joe, and Vinnie at the heart of the robbery. Everything was finally lining up. Now, he just needed him to say it in court.

Officer Caldron approached with a worried look on his face.

"He ain't there."

"What do you mean?" Daniel asked.

"I mean, I went into his house, and he's gone."

"Com'on!" Daniel exclaimed, as he ran toward the exit.

Officer Caldron hurried to catch up, calling out, "We had the front and the back covered all night!"

* * *

Agent Daniel Johnson laid his head on his desk. He had a headache that had lasted three days. The aspirin burned his stomach to knots and only dulled the pain. He had gone from hero to zero faster than he could compute. The trial ended, all suspects were acquitted, and his key witness had vaporized. They searched the man's home and confirmed it was empty. In the basement was a chunk of wallboard that had been removed, and there was no sign of Thomas Richards.

A nationwide APB had been issued and turned up nothing. Now the statute of limitations would certainly run out on the unsolved crime, a crime that had romanced a nation. Daniel pondered the meaning of the removed wallboard. Had the money been there in Richards's house all this time? It was a disaster.

He stood and moved for the exit, desperately trying to put it all behind him.

His phone rang, and he decided to ignore it. Maybe he should spend time with the family instead.

As he was exiting the lobby, a girl from the switchboard came running his way.

"Special Agent Johnson?" she called out.

Daniel turned her way and looked up.

"There's a call for you, and he says it's urgent."

"Oh yeah? Who says it's urgent?"

She looked down at a piece of paper she was holding. "Sherriff John Hobson."

Danial let out a deep sigh and a nod. "Can you patch him through to that phone?" He pointed to the phone on the wall of the lobby. The girl nodded and ran off. A moment later the custard-colored phone rang.

"Special Agent Johnson."

"Agent, thanks for taking my call. This is Sheriff Hobson out in Bozeman, Montana." The voice was hollow and distant.

"How can I help you, Sheriff?"

"Well, I was at the Big Bear Diner for lunch, and I didn't think much of it, but there was this guy who seemed familiar to me. Well, no biggie, right?"

Daniel tried not to roll his eyes.

"So I get back to my office, and sure enough, he's that feller you're lookin' for."

"What fellow?" asked Daniel.

"You know, the one that stole all that mail money and then up and disappeared."

Daniel jerked upright. Had he heard right? Was this a credible Thomas Richards sighting? Sheriff Hobson had his full attention.

"Well, I booked it back to the diner, but he was long gone. But just so you know, he was here. I'll swear to it. It was definitely your man."

Daniel took the sheriff's information, thanked him, and ran to his boss's office.

* * *

The Frontier Airlines turbo prop had made good time against the headwind. Daniel stepped out into the glaring sunlight and down the steep steps to the tarmac. The Bozeman Yellowstone International Airport looked like a leftover from World War II, which it was. In 1940, the Civil Aeronautics Administration, CAA, provided training for pilots just prior to the war. The military-style building was lacking in design and amenities. Daniel looked up and was taken aback at the sheer intensity of the sunlight here. The air was crisp and clean with a faint smell of pine and jet fuel. Ranger Calloway from the Mount Edith Rangers Station was leaning on a late model Dodge Power Wagon just outside the terminal. The truck was orange and black with a U.S. Forestry logo on the sides. The Power Wagon was a capable four-wheel-drive pickup that had served the forest service well.

"You Agent Johnson?"

Daniel nodded as he showed him his badge.

"I was told to deliver you a vehicle. Keys are in it."

"I was supposed to meet Agent Klem out of the Boise office."

"Don't know anything about that. Sorry," Ranger Calloway said and then left.

Daniel placed his bag on the passenger seat. He climbed up behind the wheel and looked over the controls. The whirlwind that had taken place to get him here was taking its toll. It took him a second to figure out the vehicle, but he was soon on the road, heading for his destination— the Big Bear Diner. The trees were majestic and the countryside beautiful, but all Daniel could see was his chance at redemption. To bring his witness and his reputation back.

The diner in Three Forks was exactly as Daniel had imagined it. A large pitched-roof cabin-style building made of river rock with redwood trim. There was a red neon diner sign and a large bear out front carved from an impossibly giant tree stump.

Sheriff John Hobson was waiting as Daniel stepped out of his car. He was a tall and lanky man with olive skin and jet-black hair. His face screamed all business, but her had a polite way of going about it. He shook hands with Daniel and gestured to the front door. "Come on in. The coffee here is pretty good, and Cindy can give you more details."

They sat in a booth by the window, and Daniel showed him the mugshot of Thomas Richards he had brought.

"Yep, that's him," Ranger Calloway said, with hardly a glance to the photograph.

A sudden hope filled Daniel's soul. Maybe he could save the case and himself.

Cindy was a forty-two-year-old waitress with a world-weary expression that matched her stained and faded apron.

"Hey, Cin, this here's the Fed I was tellin' you about. Could you tell him everything you told me? Agent Johnson, show her the picture."

Daniel showed her the picture. She took it and examined it like she was a doctor prepping for surgery.

"Yeah, that's him all right. He ordered the scrambled hash and a coffee, sweet."

"Did he say anything or do anything in particular?" Daniel asked.

Cindy shook her head. "Just ate and paid." She looked up at the ceiling for a second, thinking. "But I did happen to notice him leave."

Both Daniel and the Sherriff stared in rapt anticipation. But no more information came forth.

"Well?" The sheriff asked impatiently.

"Oh. He drove a blue Plymouth Roadrunner and took the turnoff for the 287."

"287 . . . where does that go?" Daniel asked.

"Montana City," the sheriff said, "then Great Falls and finally on up to Lethbridge, Canada."

Canada. The word hit Daniel like the slam of an unseen door.

"I could use some help," Daniel said.

"Love to, but my jurisdiction ends right here in Three Forks."

"Understand," he tossed back, as he moved to the small phonebooth by the exit door. With his index finger Daniel spun the zero on the rotary phone and waited. A scratchy voice answered. "Operator."

"Collect call from Daniel Johnson to Boston, Gladstone 2-3675, please."

* * *

The call had gone smoothly, and Daniel's boss seemed pleased with the progress. He promised to start a dragnet around the Bozeman area and called the border crossing up north to give them a heads up. There was still no word on Agent Klem who was supposed to meet up with him. He would find out what happened and get someone there ASAP. Several more agents were going to be flown in from Denver to help out.

Daniel nodded at the information, but he could not wait for support. This man would not escape again.

He pushed his Power Wagon up the 287, a twisty highway that led north into the mountains. It was getting late in the day when he noticed a small handmade sign along the road: Lodging two miles. A little over a minute later, he saw another sign with a one-mile notation.

The Pine Crest Lodge was actually two mobile home trailers that were parked by the side of the road. The seasonal lodge migrated from place to place, depending on the need and amount of customers. It was painted white with a thick red strip down the middle. Parked by the last trailer was a blue Plymouth Roadrunner. Daniel almost slammed on the brakes but managed to continue on past the traveling motel. He waited until he was out of sight and then parked the Dodge on the side of the road.

This was it. After a long, drawn-out case, he could finally wrap things up. He would have to do it all by himself and that meant going against FBI policy, but this surely had to be the exception. It was time to use extreme caution. A chill went up Daniel's spine as he checked his pistol and then started to move along the side of the road back to the lodge. He was an investigator, not a policeman, and had never had to shoot at anyone before. Today, he would take no chances. His heart was racing in the thin mountain air, and he paused to catch his breath. He had left Boston with nothing but a quick call home, but his wife would understand, especially if things went well.

The sun kissed the distant mountains. Soon, the valley would be blanketed in darkness. He could see the Pine View Lodge through the branches in front of him. The two mobile homes were parked end to end. Each trailer had five small rooms and one shared bathroom. He could hear the distant rumble from a generator somewhere providing the remote facility with power. There were three cars parked in front of various rooms, but only one mattered to Daniel, the blue Plymouth Roadrunner. He appreciated the simile the model name represented for a man on the run. The vehicle was parked at the end room of the second trailer. A light shone through the small curtained window next to the room's entry door. Daniel stayed low as he moved stealthily to the door. On closer inspection it was an aluminum and wood affair, much like you would find on a travel trailer.

He took a calming breath and then flung his body. The flimsy hollow-core door buckled. Daniel followed it into the room, gun raised and ready. The extremely cramped room was clad in cheap wood paneling with a single twin bed, one dresser, and a shelf with a lamp. In one corner were three large suitcases, and sitting on the bed reading a paper like it was Sunday afternoon was Thomas Richards. He seemed unfazed as he looked over to the broken entry door.

"I was wondering when you would get here," he said. "I was sure you would catch up to me in Sioux Falls, but when that didn't happen, I started to lose faith."

"It's over, Thomas." Daniel looked at the man who held his future in his hands. He seemed older than the last time he'd seen him. Being on the run must take its toll.

"Perhaps it is, but you can't say I didn't give it my best shot."

"Keep your hands where I can see them. Now, drop the newspaper and slowly stand up."

Thomas did as instructed, keeping his hands raised in plain sight. He had no desire to get shot.

Daniel's nerves were jacked up, as adrenaline rushed through his system. His gun hand shook slightly as he watched Thomas comply.

"Now, down on your knees and put your hands behind your head."

He watched as his fugitive, with his black predatory eyes, knelt to the floor. The man never took his eyes off Daniel.

Daniel moved quickly to round the bed and take control of his prisoner. *This will make everything right back home*, he thought. He just had to take him back to Boston, and he could put the case back on track. In his haste, he didn't realize that the cramped quarters of the small room made it a bit tight to get around the bed. He caught his foot on a metal leg just under the corner of the bedframe. In an instant, Daniel lost his balance and fell.

* * *

When the door burst open Thomas was surprised. He was sure he had left Boston clean. During the whole trip, he'd been very careful with his trail and human interactions. That this Fed had found him was certainly unexpected. He had a gun stashed in the drawer of the nightstand, but he would never reach it in time. So he decided to play it easy. First, start a casual conversation. Second, wait patiently for an opportunity.

Once kneeling on the ground, Thomas watched as the very intense copper suddenly tripped and fell. The room was small, and Thomas remembered doing the same thing earlier when he checked in. The oversized legs of the bedframe were set too close to the edge. At the time, he cursed at the pain in his foot and hopped around for a brief second, waiting for it to subside. Now, he praised the bloody thing, as it had given him his opportunity. One he would not spurn.

Thomas pounced on the fallen Fed and grabbed his gun hand. They struggled in the confined space between the wall and the bed, unable to roll or escape. It was like fighting in an open-top coffin. The man on top owned the advantage, and Thomas was on top. He used his head, fists, and elbows to inflict damage, while keeping Daniel's gun hand at bay. A quick forehead into the Fed's nose and a crunching sound loosened his grip on the gun. Thomas knocked it away and followed with a flurry of punches. The intensity of the fight shifted momentum in his favor, and Thomas finally managed to get a chokehold on his assailant. He watched as the man's eyes bulged, then dimmed and closed.

Thomas used Daniel as leverage to get up from the tight space. He stood over the man and spat on him, as he considered his options.

* * *

Daniel drove the Power Wagon down the dark winding highway, his free hand touching his disfigured nose that had been broken in the fight. He worried what his wife Candice would think once it healed crooked. His children. It was the first time he'd thought of them in some time. He'd been so caught up in this case that he'd put them on the back burner of his life. It was wrong, he knew, but hopefully he could make it up to them. He *would* make it up to them, and his wife, too!

Sitting in the passenger seat was the man he had hunted, threatened, caught, lost, and then hunted again. But now the roles were reversed. Thomas Richards was pointing an unwavering gun at Daniel's belly.

Daniel had awoken facedown on the worn gray linoleum floor of the motel room. His hands were tied behind his back, and Thomas was pointing a gun at him. Within a few minutes, he had been escorted out and down the road to his parked truck. He'd been tasked with loading three heavy suitcases in the pickup bed and then driving north along the 287.

"Why did you leave?" he asked Thomas.

His question was met with silence.

"I mean, we had a deal. You had amnesty. All you had to do was testify, and you'd have been free."

"Free?" The man seemed to seethe as he spoke. "You Feds make me laugh. Free. I'm no stool pigeon, and if I did testify, you think I would be free? I'd be dead in a ditch within the week. For an FBI agent, you ain't too bright."

"So what now, shoot me and drop me in a ditch?"

"I'm leaving that life behind. Besides, I was never a killer, always a planner."

"The master mind behind at least twenty crimes that I know of," Daniel said.

"More like forty but never once proven."

A beat of silence passed as Daniel downshifted for the steep grade in the road.

"No, I'm going to drop you off in the town of Greenville. You can do whatever you can from there."

"Greenville?" Daniel asked.

"A little town I read about in the local paper."

They continued on through the night until the silence was interrupted.

"Turn there." Thomas pointed to a sign that read: Greenville Two Miles.

As the headlights swung to the right, they illuminated orange and white road barricades across the small road.

"Go around it," Thomas commanded.

Daniel did, and the truck easily navigated the small road that wound down through the valley. The thick trees soon gave way to an open area. In the pale moonlight, Daniel could just make out a small town. There were no lights on as if everyone had already gone to sleep.

As the truck pulled into the town, Daniel realized the residents were not sleeping; the town was abandoned.

"A ghost town? You're dropping me off in a ghost town?"

"Sort of," came a sideways reply from Thomas. "Greenville has been recently unoccupied, but it will soon fill back up, and you can tell your tale to whoever shows up."

Daniel looked at the buildings as the headlights illuminated them one by one. The town of Greenville was old-school with clapboard and brick buildings. There were maybe thirty homes surrounding a small main street with several businesses. The headlights flashed across the front of Mott's General Store, barren except for empty shelving and moving shadows as they passed. The ghosts of the missing residents.

"Pull over here. Keep the engine on."

The Power Wagon pulled to a stop in front of a small brick building with a sturdy wooden door. The sign on the wall read: Greenville Jail.

"Step out, Agent Johnson. Nice and easy."

Daniel exited the truck and followed Thomas's gun, as it pointed orders. He opened the door to the jail and stepped inside. The room was small, but clean.

It looked like it had just recently been evacuated. There were a few papers on the floor, but anything of value had been removed. Thomas directed him to the back area where three cells with bars were located.

"The middle one."

Daniel complied.

Thomas took the set of keys that were on a hook just inside the door and locked him in the cell. He then backed away to look at his handiwork. This brought the first smile to his lips in many days. "Don't worry, I'm sure someone will find you in no time," he said. "And by then, I'll be out of your grasp forever."

Thomas took the keys and tossed them into the other room. He stepped up to the bars, just out of Daniel's reach.

"I have a little something for you."

He pulled from his wallet a $1,000 bill and placed it on the edge of the horizontal bar.

"It's the one traceable thing from the Plymouth job I could never spend."

As revelation grew across Daniel's face, his hatred grew.

Thomas just stared at the federal agent, his nod almost imperceptible. He turned and left the building without looking back.

"You won't get away with this," Daniel called out. "I will find you and hunt you down no matter how far you go! I will never stop. You hear me?"

The building was doused in darkness as the Dodge pulled away.

Daniel tried the door for good measure, but it didn't budge. He checked every bar, screaming in frustration. Finally, he sat on the wooden bed, furious at himself. He would never live this down. Locked in a jail cell by a fugitive. It was humiliating. His career was done. He'd be lucky to get a posting as a guard at a laundromat.

Eventually, he decided that nothing more would happen that night, so he lay down on the hard wooden surface and tried to get some rest. He would figure something out in the morning. It was going to be a very long night.

* * *

Daniel woke with a start. Something was wrong. His cell was flooding. The water was starting to cover his bed. He stood up. It was just above his knees. He slogged to the cell door.

Still locked. He climbed to the small barred window in the back and looked out.

The view filled him with terror. As far as he could see was water. The whole town was flooding. He took a quick inventory of his assets. He had a wallet, twenty-seven cents, and his FBI shield, plus the $1,000 dollar bill still lying on the bars.

He called out for help repeatedly. Eventually his voice went hoarse. The reality of his situation hit him. He'd been a fool. Work had been his passion, and what had it gotten him? A watery grave. If only there was some way he could see his family just one more time. A second chance to say he was sorry for being so stupid. They were the most important things in his life, and he realized it too late. If only he could see their faces or even a picture of them one more time. He should have carried one in his wallet. The thought sent a flash of guilt through his body like a high voltage shock.

He leaned against the bars. Tears started to flow until he was sobbing uncontrollably.

CHAPTER THREE

THREE RIVER LODGE, MONTANA – PRESENT DAY – 6:55 A.M.

The sun's morning rays cast a blinding glow off the lace curtains, causing Special Agent Codi Sanders to squint before opening her eyes. Across from her, covered by only a thin white sheet, was the man she loved. Not the romantic definition of love, but the first man in her life, since her father, that she truly cared about. Someone she could spend hours with and not get tired of. This was a first for her, and it was all very exciting. She traced a finger along the silhouette of his body.

It was rising and falling with the soft breathing that comes from a deep sleep. She could just make out Matt Campbell's broad shoulders and narrow waist, his masculine scent. She loved all of his bits and pieces, but most of all she loved his mind. He had a kindness and a simple way about him that contrasted with his incredible intelligence, surely a member of MENSA or maybe even the Triple Nine Society. Codi's heart skipped as she relished the intimate solemn moment. She slid out of bed and padded to the bathroom wearing nothing but wool socks. She had never thought of herself as beautiful, but had never had any problems attracting the opposite sex—or the same sex for that matter. But she was just too focused on her career to take anyone seriously. Matt, however, was a different story. He had come into her life in an unorthodox way that allowed their growing relationship to sneak up on both of them. He was definitely a person of interest.

The wood-paneled and rustic-beamed room looked out to a lazy stream that rippled along its journey. Beyond was a forest of fir and pine that was occasionally interrupted by vertical granite peaks with a few Quaking Aspen thrown in for contrast. It was very picturesque.

Wearing a skimpy bathrobe, she strolled out of the bedroom and into the kitchen, being careful not to wake Matt. She poured herself a cup of hot water and placed a teabag of lemon grass tea inside it. Using the heated cup to warm her hands, she moved to a chair by a large picture window and plopped down comfortably. The view was off the charts. The tranquility and quiet had been a genuine recharger for her. She breathed in the clean air and slowly let it out through her nose.

After solving a case that had spun her up so much that she seriously considered breaking the law to exact revenge, Codi needed this break. Matt swooped her out of D.C. and far away from it all. The couple had made a week together seem like a dream come true, and Codi, for the first time in her life, was looking forward.

After months of much discord between them, mostly job related, a little good fortune was in order. Codi sipped her steeped tea. Outside a speckled fawn picked its way through the clover. It was a magical moment, suddenly interrupted by the buzzing in her pocket. Codi answered her phone without taking her eyes off the precious animal.

"Sanders," she whispered trying not to disturb the scene.

"So how is the wilderness treating you?"

The voice on the other end of the line was instantly recognizable. Supervisory Special Agent (SSA) Brian Fescue was her boss. The boss who had given her two weeks off after her last case. The boss who had promised not to bother her until she got back. The boss who'd better have a really good reason for calling two days before her vacation was over.

After a particularly intense case where he first worked with Codi, SSA Brian Fescue had stepped out of the field and into an office job so he could be closer to his family. He was the driving force behind the FBI's Special Projects division based in the Washington D.C. field office. He recruited Codi and her partner, Joel. Together, they solved several very old cold cases and had become two of the division's shining stars.

"What do you want?"

"Look, I hate to ask—"

"Then don't," Codi parried.

"I promise, I will make it up to you. Besides, you have only a couple days left on your . . . break?" Brian wasn't sure how to describe what Codi was calling it, since she demanded two weeks off and just up and left. "It will take three hours at the most, and you can take Matt with you."

Codi sighed. *How could there be a Special Projects case in the middle of Nowhere, Montana? Ugh.*

Now for the fun part, unofficially deputizing Matt.

*   *   *

The winding mountain road was still damp after a brief downpour, but the clouds had all blown away, revealing a beautiful spring day. Codi drove the rental Ford Explorer, following the directions given by the dispassionate male voice coming from her smartphone.

"The town of Greenville, Montana, population 345, was evacuated in 1967, compliments of our government's eminent domain. Blah, blah, blah. They had built a dam down river, and now the town is known as Greenville Lake, swallowed up and gone," Matt read from a file on Codi's smartphone.

"And they say you can never go home again," Codi said.

"Funny. But you can with scuba gear."

Matt was trying to not get sick while reading from the passenger's seat on the winding road.

"You're probably going to get in trouble for letting me read in on an active case."

"It's a cold case, and besides, Brian said you could come, so now you're my work partner as well."

Matt gave Codi a wry smile at the implications. "Well, you did swear me in."

"Is that what we're calling it now?" Codi said with a mischievous grin, before changing the subject. "What's it say about the dam?"

Matt scrolled through the files. "The contract went to Bortles Grading who subsequently went out of business just before completion. The Bank of the North had the bond, so they had to come up with another three million to complete the project. Almost sunk them as well."

"Case of the lowest bidder getting the job rather than the most qualified," Codi said.

"Most likely."

Matt read on. "Eight months ago, stress fractures were noticed on the dam, and they slowly drained the lake to the halfway point in hopes of repairing it."

"Let me guess. That didn't work."

"Nope. Three weeks ago, they gave the order to drain it all and then tear down and rebuild the dam." Matt added, *"Dam!"*

"You're such a dork. Adorable but—" Codi said.

"Hey, you lobbed it in. I just hit it."

"Wow, a baseball analogy from a science geek."

"I get that from my mom; she was a huge Diamondbacks fan."

They shared a moment of silence as the Explorer slipped through the pristine countryside, bouncing on new shocks and springs.

Codi summarized. "So the dam fails, they drain the lake, and the town of Greenville comes up for air after some fifty-plus years."

"And boom, they find a body in the town and call Special Projects," Matt added.

"Yeah, but a body doesn't necessarily mean FBI. It must be something . . . more."

* * *

The two-mile gouge in the earth looked as if a large kidney-shaped meteor had impacted the ground. Beautiful green forest surrounded the dark brown scar that narrowed further up the canyon. In the middle of the blemish was a hovel of small, dilapidated buildings—Greenville. They parked the Explorer and stepped out onto a muddy impromptu parking lot. There were four other vehicles on site. Two were from the local police, one a state police cruiser, and the fourth was a coroner's van. The first thing to hit them was the smell. Miles of dying biologicals cooked in the midday sun. Algae, lake grass, and fish all rotting on the ground. It was overpowering. Matt almost got back in the car and left.

They each wore jeans and hiking boots as they sloshed their way to a temporary plank walkway that had been set up to allow access along the muddy lake's exposed bottom. The shapes of a once quaint town were clearly visible. With a little imagination you could make out what each building used to be.

"The town is surprisingly intact," Codi said, as they balanced along the wood planks.

"That's because the oxygen level at the bottom of a lake is often very low. It prevents things from deteriorating."

"See, you're already helping," Codi added.

This praise encouraged Matt enough to endure the awful smell. Codi had been there, done that, when it came to smells, and she was managing okay.

The wooden walkway slurped with each step as the muck and slime from the lake's bottom clung to the planks. Codi was the first to see it.

A one-story brick building. It was a sheriff's office, but this one looked like it was plucked right out of an old Western movie and tagged over with a spray can filled with rotting algae. Codi flashed her badge, and they were motioned inside the building by two police officers standing outside using their smoking habit to help mask the stench.

Matt considered taking up the nasty habit just to find some much needed nasal relief.

"Agent Sanders, and this is my partner, Dr. Matt Campbell."

Matt nervously shook hands with the two men waiting just inside the sheriff's office.

"Lieutenant Granger, and this is Officer Paul," the older man said. He was about sixty with a weathered face to prove it. His hair was receding but still had a shiny black shade to it. The officer next to him was much younger. He was struggling with breathing the polluted air just like Matt.

There was a minute of awkwardness, and then Codi extended her hands, palms up. "Sooo?"

"Oh, yeah. It's right in here. A couple of hikers braving the mud and smell discovered the body and called it in. The cell door was rusted shut when we got here so I'm guessing it must be from sometime in the past."

The older man, whose name Codi had already forgotten, led them into the back area that housed the jail cells. There were three lockups separated by rusted iron bars and a narrow access walkway. The once red bricks were now covered with a thick black algae dying in the newfound air.

The middle cell door had been cut off with a torch and set against the brick wall. A perfectly clean skeleton lay sprawled in the middle of the floor. It looked like something you would buy as a Halloween decoration.

"Dead prisoner," Codi said. "I'm not sure I'm tracking why we are here?"

"Sorry, this is why."

He handed Codi a dull piece of metal. "We think he was one of yours."

Codi turned the hunk of metal over in her hands and examined it. She had never seen one before, but it was clearly half of an old-school FBI badge. She handed it to Matt who looked it over with care.

"Half a badge," he said to himself.

"So . . ." Codi voiced as she took in the scene, "what was an FBI agent doing locked up in a jail cell in an abandoned town that was covered in water more than fifty years ago?"

"Good way to hide a crime, if you ask me," the older officer said.

"Exactly." Codi asked, "When was this town flooded again?"

"'67," answered Matt and the officer in unison.

It made Codi pause for a second. "What was happening around here in '67?"

"Nothing but the dam, as far as I know."

Codi pondered the implications, then looked over to see Matt tampering with the crime scene.

"Matt, what are you doing?"

He was using his hand to scrape away the algae on the back brick wall.

"This badge looks like it was ground down, not cut."

Codi immediately picked up on his thought. "Maybe the wall?"

"Exactly."

They both scraped at the wall as best they could. The two other officers in the room watched the bizarre display.

"Check it out," Codi said.

Sure enough, there were faint scrapings on the back brick wall. An A followed by a G and an E.

"He left a message before he died," Matt said.

"Lieutenant," Codi said, "see if you can get someone to help out here."

The man stood with his mouth agape. It took several seconds for him to react.

Codi was proud of her temp partner. He had just delivered—big time.

CHAPTER FOUR

Special Agent Joel Strickman sipped his Peruvian roast with its vanilla-toned sweetness while checking his emails. He absently pulled at his shirtsleeves, as they were riding up his arms. The mind-numbing amount of useless information generated by the government always amazed him. The only benefit was an incredibly robust firewall that thwarted all the Russian dating services and male enhancement ads that seemed to find you even if you weren't looking. Joel typed a reply to someone on the second floor, whom he had yet to meet, regarding a requested search for a known embezzler. He sent the information and trusted it was enough.

His phone buzzed.

"Agent Strickman."

"What are you wearing?" a husky female voice asked.

"What? Wait, who is—?" Joel looked at his phone's caller ID: Codi. "Not funny."

"It was funny to me. So, here's what we have so far."

Joel looked up to see Codi on the phone as she walked into his office.

"Hold on? I thought you were in Wyoming."

"Montana," Codi said, after hanging up her phone.

Joel still looked confused.

"Montana, the state?"

"No, the Disney character."

"Yeah, but what are you doing here? You're not due back till tomorrow night." He realized he was still talking into his phone and put it down, sheepishly.

"Something interesting came up."

Joel was afraid to tackle that statement, knowing Codi had just spent time away with Matt. He sat uneasily, waiting for a further explanation. He glanced at his partner. She was wearing a white collared shirt, navy slacks, and matching blazer. Her trim athletic figure was barely concealed beneath. Her eyes were twinkling with the promise that came with a new case. He'd seen that look many times. It often meant long hours, bad hotel rooms, and second-class travel.

"A case. I'm back here on account of a case. Matt's back in Boston, and I'm here with you."

"Sounds like a fair trade."

Codi looked at him sideways as she sat in the empty chair next to him.

"So, what case?" Joel asked.

"I thought you'd been read in?"

"No. Brian's got me doing research on a . . . never mind. What have you got?"

Codi sat down and updated Joel on her recent field trip.

"So, a possible federal agent dies in a flooding town by being locked in a jail cell?"

Codi nodded.

"I'm betting it has something to do with some kind of fraud surrounding the building of the dam," Joel surmised.

"That's what I'm thinking. Maybe he got too close to the truth. I had the skeleton sent to Quantico for autopsy. Let's see what we can get from this."

Codi held up an evidence bag holding the partial FBI badge. Joel's eyes flared as he adjusted his glasses for a closer look.

The brass was tarnished to a deep black-brown, but the engraved eagle and "Bureau of" lettering, was still visible. On the back was the first three numbers of an identity code, 921. The rest of the numbers were missing. Codi plugged in her phone and showed him the pictures she'd taken of the engraved letters. Joel studied them carefully.

"What's this?"

"It looks like he used this badge to scratch out a message on the cell's brick wall before he died."

"Jeez! You could have led with that."

"What and take all the fun away from this moment?" Codi smirked.

Joel shook his head as he inspected the lettering on the wall. It was hard to make out. Some of the letters were very clear and others were illegible.

"I had a team go over the cell very carefully. We should have a better idea what it says by EOD."

Joel took a pen and paper and started writing down the letters he could make out.

AGE JN NTR K THR CHAR G LT   O E TO M L

"Save yourself the headache," Codi said. "This will all be a lot clearer when we get our next update. Plus, the spacing is all wonky since it was a carving. Let's work on the parties involved in the building of Greenville Dam. I'll take the bank; you take the construction company."

Codi walked back to her office, but Joel couldn't resist a puzzle. He tried to work on the problem Codi had given him, but his mind kept returning to the strange spacing of letters. He called across the hall to her.

"Codi, can I see that picture of the cell wall again?"

"Focus, Joel. We are working up the dam companies. You'll get your chance to solve it once we get the lab results."

Joel's shoulder's slumped, and he turned back to his computer. He took a deep breath and started his search.

In her mind, Codi's first task was to look up the badge numbers 921. Unfortunately, electronic personnel files didn't go back to the sixties, not yet. She picked up her phone and dialed.

"Joel, field trip."

"Where?" Joel asked.

"I have no idea."

* * *

Sterling Riche set his cellphone down on the polished red cedar desk. He rubbed his hands together and carefully considered his next step. He was a man with many options, and choosing the right one was his specialty. A large picture window looked out on an expansive view of the lake. His home office was at times as much of a sanctuary as it was a prison. Two of his workers had radiation poisoning and were dying. He leaned back in his custom red leather Kingston Eden chair. It was not the first time, but hiding the evidence had become . . . problematic. He needed a fix for this particular problem.

After a twinkling of thought, he stood and went over to a map that was mounted to the hand-textured wall. It showed a vast tunnel system running through a mountain. His mountain. A family legacy going back three generations. His grandfather, Tom Rich, had bought the mountain back in the sixties from The Poudrette Mining Company, a family-owned business with a legacy of its own. They had discovered a vein containing a previously unknown gemstone, which they called Poudretteite. The gemstone is a brilliant pink color and is a thousand times more rare than a diamond. In fact, the only known source of Poudretteite was their mountain, located less than thirty-five miles east of Montreal, Quebec.

Sterling's grandfather had slowly expanded the mine over the course of his lifetime, selling to collectors and gemologists. His father took over and had done more marketing than expanding and had slowly raised the price of Poudretteite, making the mine more profitable.

Sterling had done both. Profits were good, but the vein seemed to be running out, and he could see the writing on the wall. All that the family had built could come crashing down.

He pushed his workers deeper into the mountain, and they found something else. Uranium. Not just any uranium, but high-grade, very clean ore.

The problem was that ever since the Russians dismantled half their nuclear arsenal, the price of uranium used in the production of plutonium had gone way down. Plutonium was the result of the transmutation of individual uranium atoms. That made the radioactive element hardly worth the effort to mine. At twenty dollars per pound, uranium was cheaper to leave in the ground. His luck seemed to be running out.

All that changed two months ago when he was introduced to a man who seemed more myth then reality. Julian Drexler.

He was a power-hungry and dangerous individual with connections across the globe. This was a man Sterling could learn from. Drexler had somehow gotten wind of Sterling's discovery and made it his business to know more.

Sterling left the room and headed for his six-car garage. Next stop, the train station. They were to meet at The Powerhouse Café, located in the medieval castle rising up out of the Lawrence River. It was part of the Boldt Castle Museum on Heart Island, Alexandria, New York.

In 1900, George C. Boldt, owner of the world-famous Waldorf Astoria Hotel in New York City, commissioned hundreds of stonemasons and artists to build a 120-room castle for his beloved wife, complete with tunnels, a powerhouse, Italian gardens, and a drawbridge. Not a single detail or expense was to be spared. When Boldt's wife died unexpectedly in 1904, he ceased all work and never returned to the island, leaving the massive complex to wither and die.

In 1977, some seventy-three years later, the property was acquired and a dedicated crew worked to complete the compound. Tourists from around the globe make the pilgrimage to view the magnificent grounds and structures that were a testament to a man's love for his wife.

* * *

Sterling took a sip of his extra dry martini and tried to look unperplexed at Julian Dexler's late arrival to their meeting. He marveled at the lavish grounds and the almost magical aspect of the island estate. The intricate wood-patterned floors and hand-carved ceilings were breathtaking. Every detail had been considered and perfected. He made a mental note of a few things to redecorate back at his home in Montreal.

A striking woman in a brick-red blouse with a modest black skirt and matching high heels flowed in his direction. She sat down in the chair across from Sterling and purposefully folded her hands in her lap. He glanced around nervously and then leaned back in his chair, forcing himself to relax. It didn't work, but he would play it as cool as he could. She never took her eyes off him. They were dark green, almost black-green eyes. She was a coal-haired beauty with strong cheekbones and an enigmatic red smile set against pale skin.

"Hello, Sterling Riche, my name is Dorthia. It is a pleasure to meet you."

Sterling paused for a second. "You don't look like Mr. Drexler," he said lamely.

"Something came up, so I'm here," was her reply.

Sterling pulled his napkin from his lap and dropped it on the table. He stood and began smoothing his custom-tailored vicuna wool suit.

Dorthia could tell it was all for show. She had done business with many men just like him, plus she'd read his dossier very carefully and knew the position that Sterling Riche was in. He could ill afford to pass on this opportunity.

"Before you go, I must say that I have Mr. Drexler's full confidence. Here are my credentials."

She slid a large flat envelope across the table. Sterling looked around to see if he was being set up. There seemed to be no one who looked suspicious or who was even paying attention to them. Curiosity finally won out. He sat back down and peered into the envelope. Sterling's heart jumped once he realized what he was holding.

"A million dollar Eurobond?" he said quietly. Maybe he would stay a bit longer and listen to her proposition.

Ever since the U.S. banned the issuance of new bearer bonds in 1982, the Eurobond was a popular way to anonymously exchange large amounts of money. Current redemptions of bearer bonds have become nearly non-existent due to a 2010 law that relieved banks and brokerages of their redemption obligation. Hence, use of the Eurobond by less legitimate and fringe businesses has shot up immensely.

A young man in a burgundy apron approached the table. "What can I get you?"

"Nothing. I'm not hungry," Sterling said, gesturing to his half-full martini.

"I'll take a bottle of water. And please don't open it. I'll do that myself," Dorthia said.

Paranoid much? Sterling thought to himself as the waiter left with their meager order.

"We have tested the ore you sent us," she said, "and I have to say, we are impressed. As you know, radioactive material is closely watched and patrolled. If ever I were to use radioactive material in an unorthodox way, for example, the major governments of the world could track it all the way back to its source. It tends to leave a difficult trail to cover up. Each mine that produces the ore has an elemental signature or isotopic pattern that is documented and tracked. Cigar Lake Mine: three percent nickel. Grand Canyon Mine: five percent tin. Like a fingerprint."

"Whereas, a new, unknown source of high grade ore is untraceable?" Sterling posed. He was quickly getting the gist of their proposed alignment.

She paused as the waiter placed her bottle on the table. She looked out at the beautiful surroundings. Once the waiter was out of earshot, she said, "I see you understand."

She paused once more to let the moment breathe. Timing and cadence were an important part of the negotiating process, and rushing was never smart. Dorthia leaned in and spoke very softly. "Plutonium is very hard to come by. Plus, it is very expensive to make. That's why it currently sells for 2.86 million U.S. dollars per kilo. Those that can make it, like major governments, guard it with extreme care. The steps required are way over my head. Basically, you have to take U-238, which is what you have in a basic uranium mine, and get it to U-239. That's accomplished by capturing extra neutrons, a fairly complicated process. Then you need to run your U-239 through a series of decays to get it to Pu-239."

Sterling gripped the corner of the envelope, suddenly feeling a bit overwhelmed—*plutonium!*

"And finally, you have either weapons-grade or reactor-grade plutonium, based on how much Pu-240 ends up in the final pot. It's a real pain in the butt."

Sterling took a scarcely controlled sip of his drink, never taking his eyes off the woman.

"We propose to pay you double the going rate for uranium for an exclusive delivery deal of all your deposits. All done very hush hush, of course. Or you can choose to take door number two."

Sterling glanced around him one more time for good measure. Everything seemed normal. If he was being set up, he couldn't tell. "What's to keep me from just leaving with this envelope right now?"

"Nothing. And by the way, you've been clenching your fingers around it; I would say you need it more than I. My employer, however, would have it back by EOD along with your head, so it is of little consequence to me."

Sterling dropped the envelope as if he just realized he was holding a poisonous snake. He dabbed at the beads of sweat that had sprouted on his forehead. "So what is door number two?"

CHAPTER FIVE

VALMEYER, ILLINOIS – NATIONAL PERSONNEL
RECORDS CENTER – 3:48 P.M.

In 1973, there was a disastrous fire at the National Personnel Records Center. It destroyed approximately eighteen million military and federal personnel files. Most of the military files would never be restored, but much of the federal employee files had some type of back-up. The problem was there was little need for these old files, so most of them just sat in boxes or old steel filing cabinets, never to be seen again.

The National Personnel Records Center, or NPRC, was a three-story aboveground building filling almost an entire square block. It was located in Valmeyer, Illinois, and housed over one hundred million documents, mostly military, some going back to the late 1800s. After much effort, Joel had tracked the 1967 FBI personnel files to the third floor, Wing C.

He and Codi walked through the massive complex, their shoes echoing on the hard linoleum floor. A faint odor of mold wafed through the air, like an abandoned library with a yearlong water leak.

44

"*Indiana Jones*," Joel said.

"What is?" Codi asked.

"This place is just like the warehouse in that movie."

Joel was right, the rows of box-filled steel shelves went on and on in every direction.

"It should be right . . . here, Box C-321-a56483." The diminutive employee with a shaved head pointed to a box some ten feet up on a shelf. Joel walked down to a rolling staircase and pushed it into position. He climbed up and pulled out a very dusty box, number C-321-a56483.

Ah choo! He sneezed a cloud of dust in all directions. The airborne particles provoked another sneezing fit. After about six hard, back-to-back sneezes, Codi was starting to get worried about her partner.

They took the box to a nearby table, and their escort left them to it. The box contained a list of all the badge-carrying FBI agents from 1964–1969. It included their birth and employment dates. Joel scanned straight to the badge numbers. They used a five-digit system back then. With the first three numbers they had retrieved from the old badge, 921, they made copies of the pages containing agents from 92100 to 92199. That narrowed their search down to one hundred possible agents. The next task was to find the actual files on these agents. That was going to take some time.

Codi's phone made a funny chirp. There was a video call coming in. She glanced at the caller ID and punched the button. She adjusted the camera, leaning it against a stack of folders, so it took in both Joel and her. On the phone screen was a small image of a woman in a lab coat. Codi pointed as she introduced Joel.

"Sanders and Strickman."

The caller cleared her throat and then replied, "Hi, I'm Doctor Mason, like the jar. I have the report on the human remains you shipped to us."

The doctor was a graying African-American woman in her mid-fifties. She had a round face and a sour expression. Codi thought the woman looked like she'd been indulging in the lab's formaldehyde.

"As you may or may not know," Dr. Mason said, "there are only so many things a skeleton can tell us. Things like gender, age, race, height, and even blood type."

Codi tried not to roll her eyes. She was not good with people who spent time telling you what they were going to tell you before they told you. She decided to hold her tongue and let the woman drone on.

"Trauma seen in skeletal remains falls into three categories. One, antemortem. Two, perimortem. Three, postmortem."

"So, before, during, and after death. Got it," Joel said helpfully.

This made the woman pause for a second as though she had been interrupted. She waited until she was sure Joel was totally done. After an interminable pause, she cleared her throat and continued. "There are a few things that we can tell from the skeletal remains. Mid-thirties, Caucasian, five-foot-ten, male. Had our vic been shot, stabbed, or bludgeoned there would be signs of that on the skeletal remains themselves. I carefully inspected every bone myself and found no sign of trauma. With no soft tissue and no signs of trauma on the bones we cannot definitively determine the cause of death."

Codi leaned back in her seat. *Please get to the point.*

"However, based on the location and other information provided, we would suggest drowning as a possible cause of death."

There we go!

"I have sent a full report to your email."

"Thank you very much, Doctor, this will be a big help in our investigation," Joel said as he finished up the call.

"Okay. We are looking for a thirty-nine-year-old white male approximately five-ten," Joel said optimistically.

"Sounds like just about every agent in the FBI back in the sixties."

Joel realized she was right.

* * *

A blur of greens and browns flashed past. Sterling stared listlessly out the train window. There was a lot to think about. He was taking the train back to Montreal. It would allow him to organize his thoughts after choosing door number two back at his meeting with the inventive Dorthia. I guess it's true what they say, money talks. Now, it was up to Sterling to make the changes necessary to the mine to move into the future—his future.

The Poudretteite Mining Company could last another five years at most. If they sold their mined uranium at forty dollars per pound, they could extend things for maybe another ten. But then what?

Door number two had been a revelation—a chance to sell his ore for as much as one million U.S. dollars per kilo, and he was going to make that happen, no matter what. He processed the steps that would come next. It was something he could do and do well. He smiled at the thought of what the next several months would look like. The woman from the meeting had recommended a man, Dr. Garth Baghdadis, who could oversee the whole operation. Sterling looked at the piece of paper with the man's contact information. He would need to act quickly to secure him.

"Can I get you something?" A cute attendant in the first-class car broke him from his reverie.

Sterling suddenly had an appetite, and he ordered accordingly. This was going to be a very good day, he thought, as he fingered the folded million-dollar Eurobond in his suit coat pocket—very good indeed.

* * *

Juliette Cole lowered her binoculars and slid down in the seat of her car as the silver rental drove by. It had taken nine months for her to regroup and find the people responsible for the death of her twin brother, Dax. She constructed a list and prioritized it. First up was FBI Agent Codi Sanders, followed by her partner, Joel Strickman. Juliette massaged her shoulder absently. She had taken a bullet in the melee that had cost her almost everything. The throbbing seemed to be telling her a storm was coming.

Juliette's life had taken a u-turn when she discovered that she was a twin. Adopted at birth from a mother in the French penal system, she had been raised by a wealthy couple. Her twin Dax, however, had grown up on the streets of Paris and had built a successful turnkey criminal network for those with the means and desire to engage him. From the moment she discovered Dax, it was like two magnets coming together. It was that missing "something" each had been looking for all their lives. They both recognized it instantly, and Juliette took to his operation like a natural. Together they became a deadly duo, perfecting the illegal and immoral work companies and individuals needed but couldn't be associated with.

Dax had marveled at how quickly Juliette had shed her societal norms and adapted to his world. They vowed to never separate; the bond between twins overpowered and trumped all else. It was on a particularly difficult operation that Agent Codi Sanders and her team had gotten involved in Juliette's business. They ruined everything the twins had worked for, ultimately killing her brother in the process. Juliette had not witnessed her brother's death, but as she was escaping from a burning warehouse in a truck, she literally had the wind knocked out of her by no obvious source. In that instant, she knew without a doubt that Dax was gone. Later, she discovered that he had been crushed between a metal fire escape and the building it was loosely attached to. Once she was free of the burning building, it had taken a little luck, but she managed to escape the agents hunting her.

After an emergency operation on the bullet wound in her shoulder by a backwoods doctor, Juliette vowed only one thing—vengeance. Leveraging every asset still available to her, Juliette bounced back. She discreetly made her way to America and into the country's capitol. Locating Codi in Washington D.C. had not been difficult. Public records were just that, public.

The real trick was tracking them to this seemingly random city in Illinois. It required a bit of luck and quick thinking. Juliette spotted her targets exiting the FBI offices with carry-on bags. She made a quick call to the switchboard, impersonating a local law enforcement officer with a critical case that needed Agent Sanders's input. In no time, she obtained her destination city—Saint Louis.

That information, followed by a quickly chartered flight, and she had caught up with her prey as they exited the airport. While the two agents went into a building in the early afternoon, Juliette waited patiently in her rental car across the street under the shade of a tree. Now, her revenge was close at hand, and, even better, it looked like it was going to be a two-for-one special.

The sun dipped behind a building as dusk approached. Juliette watched as her targets exited the building and drove past her vehicle heading back to the city. She put her rental car in drive and followed at a discrete distance.

* * *

Codi drove in silence. The long day had caught up with both of them. The rolling hills and verdant farmland was a nice change—the heartland.

"So, thoughts?" she asked Joel, absently.

"The sixties was a weird time for the FBI," Joel prefaced.

"What do you mean?"

"Here's just one example. You know that sixties song 'Louie Louie' by The Kingsmen?"

"Sure," said Codi and started to sing the lyrics.

She turned onto the interstate heading east.

"Yeah, well the FBI thought it contained pornographic language. You know how the words are kinda mumbled?"

"I guess," Codi said.

"They did this big investigation that lasted two years, only to admit that the song was unintelligible."

"Our tax dollars hard at work," Codi said.

"Oh! Pull in!"

"What?"

"An old-fashioned drive-in restaurant with carhops. When was the last time you saw one of these?" Joel asked.

"Only in the movies," Codi said in wonder, as they exited the freeway.

She pulled their silver rental car into a parking stall that was covered by a curved steel awning, which surrounded a giant, whiskey barrel-shaped walk-up restaurant. There was a small sign indicating they should roll down their windows, leaving about two inches up for the serving tray to hook onto. A young, blond woman on roller-skates glided to a stop next to Codi's door. She was maybe sixteen with cute dimples and a carpet of acne.

"Welcome to Willie B's. What'llitbe?"

Codi and Joel ordered food and drinks, each feeling like they were experiencing a piece of history they might never see again.

The food was satisfactory at best, but the experience, unforgettable.

The Great Forest Hotel was a Motel 6 rip-off clad in faux wood beams. It was attached to a large indoor waterpark and attracted screaming kids and families from across the state. Joel and Codi waited in an interminable queue to check in. The wait included one three-year-old tantrum and two projectile vomits by a pale six-year-old. After a little pleading, Codi and Joel got rooms near the end of a hallway, top floor.

When Codi closed her door, the cacophony of hallway vacationer noise lowered to a dull roar. She poured a mini bottle of Jack Daniels into a plastic cup from the bathroom. The fiery warm liquid went down in one gulp. After the day she'd had, it was a needed relief. She placed her gun and shield on a table and lay back on her bed, contemplating opening her suitcase. Maybe tomorrow. Her phone buzzed indicating a new text. She ignored it.

* * *

Juliette parked her car in the lot across from the hotel. She pulled an H&K USP Compact with a silencer from her gym bag and checked the clip and slide before tucking it in her waistband and pulling her shirt over it. She strolled with purpose toward the lobby of the busy hotel. She was wearing a black, oversized t-shirt with "The Future Is Female" printed on the front. She pulled her cellphone from her stretch ops tactical pants and dialed.

"Great Forest Hotel, can I help you?"

"Hi. This is FBI Director Carol Thomas. I'm looking for one of my agents, Joel Strickman. I believe he is in room three . . . hmm, I can't read his writing."

"Yes, that's 582. Just a minute, I'll connect you."

As soon as the phone started to ring, Juliette hung up. She moved as if she belonged, glancing at the information sign to get her bearings. She took the back staircase leading to the fifth floor, avoiding three security cameras.

* * *

Joel's mind was consumed. Puzzles did that to him, and finding the identity of the dead agent was an enormous puzzle. Some might call it chronic obsessive behavior, but he would dwell on a problem until he solved it. He sipped a cup of coffee he had doctored from the mini kitchen in his room while going through the photocopies of the agent files they had collected. Paperwork and pictures were spread all across his bed. It was weird to still be working with paper, but until they got around to digitizing all the old files, paper it was.

He had two additional piles stacked on his coffee table, a large pile on the left and a small pile on the right. He methodically moved pages from one folder and spread the contents across his bed to inspect. Once satisfied, he returned the contents and moved to the next folder. He was looking for very specific information that indicated a missing or presumed dead designation at the end of an agent's career.

His phone buzzed against the faded table's surface. Joel glanced at the caller ID and stabbed the speaker button.

"Hi, Codi."

"Hey, I just got a text from the forensics lab. They did an ultraviolet and an infrared pass on the wall, and they have more letters for us. I'm sending you the message. You'll see the new letters are in bold. Oh, they also said that this is as good as we're going to get. You'll notice the spacing is a little wonky. It was probably carved in a hurry."

Joel looked at his phone as the text came in. "Okay, thanks."

AGE **TJ**NS NTR **K**ED THR CHAR**D**G **L**TY **LOVE** TOF M LY

He flipped over one of the file jackets and wrote out the message. Immediately, the new letters made some sense to him. The ending: *Love To Family.* Now, for the rest of it.

Codi lay back on her bed and stared at the ceiling. She had managed to remove her shoes, but had yet to attend to her suitcase. With a heavy sigh, she stood and moved to the door, knowing Joel could use her help. She absently collected her room's keycard and left, leaving her gun and badge still on the table. She placed the *Do Not Disturb* sign on the knob and headed down the hallway.

* * *

Once on the fifth floor, Juliette paused to catch her breath. She moved down the hallway watching as the numbers on the doors increased: 570, 572, 574. She kept her head down as she passed a family arguing about where to go for dinner. She stepped up to door number 582 and listened for a second, while removing a small electronic device with a keycard attached by wires. She placed the card in the door's keycard slot and hit a small button on the device. A random series of red lights flashed until they were all green. *Click.*

* * *

Codi strolled barefoot down the hallway, letting a yawn spill from her mouth. She stuffed her phone in her front pocket and looked up to see a woman in all black at Joel's door. In an instant, Codi was alert. Something was off. This was no maid. She quickly realized she had left her gun back in the room. *Argh.*

"Can I help you?" Codi asked flatly.

The woman at the door turned, and in the briefest of moments, both parties recognized each other.

"You!" the woman called out, as she reached for something at the small of her back.

Codi bolted instantly, scanning the hallway for an exit, which was a kill zone at best. There were double glass exit doors about two hundred feet away at the other end of the hallway. She would never make it. The woman she recognized was Juliette Cole from a few cases back. She had kidnapped and tried to kill Codi. It ultimately ended in a showdown that left many on both sides wounded or killed, including the woman's brother Dax. Juliette had driven off in a truck. Codi chased her on foot, delivering a bullet that blew her getaway vehicle apart. By the time Codi got to the scene, the woman was gone. It was a face Codi would never forget.

The first bullet whizzed past her head, followed by the sound of a soft *pfft.* Laundry. It was a small sign on a door, but it screamed "sanctuary," if even for a few seconds. Codi dove through the door as two more bullets embedded in the doorframe, inches from her. She heard the soft *whiz* of the silenced rounds moving in her direction and knew the shooter was in pursuit. That meant Joel was safe at least for now.

She took a second to get her bearings and looked for a solution to her newfound problem. The room was long and narrow. On one side, commercial washers and dryers lined the wall. The other had racks and shelves filled with cleaning products and restocking supplies. The door had no lock, and at any second, a highly-trained killer would be coming through it.

Codi's mouth went dry as she searched for a weapon, anything. There was nothing. On an impulse, she climbed up a small maintenance ladder that was leaning against the wall next to the back of the door. The door suddenly kicked open, just missing the ladder. A silenced pistol entered, followed by Juliette, both cautiously scanning left and then right.

Codi silently stepped barefoot from the top of the ladder to the top edge of the door and launched herself in a desperate attack. The woman seemed to sense more than hear Codi behind her. She spun on her heels, raised her silenced H&K at Codi, and fired twice as Codi flew through the air. The first bullet missed her, but the second caught her squarely in the hip. It spun her slightly off course, but she managed to land on top of her attacker and grab her gun hand. The shock of the bullet's impact would have to be set aside for now, or this was going to be a very short fight. Codi used her momentum to smack her forehead into Juliette's nose. There was a crunching sound followed by a spurt of blood.

Juliette moaned and her eyes promptly watered, making her vision blur. She succeeded in hanging on to her pistol and used all her strength to bring it to bear on Codi. They wrestled and rolled on the floor each trying to exploit the other's weakness.

They traded blows, doing some damage. Juliette flipped over and got on top of Codi. Codi managed to fling Juliette's gun arm against the corner of an industrial dryer and the pistol skittered across the floor with a notable *umph*. Juliette maintained her upper position on Codi and clamped both her hands around Codi's neck. Codi tried to knee Juliette, but her injured hip made her leg sluggish. Juliette countered with a knee of her own.

Codi bucked and punched, but her assailant held firm on top of her. She could feel her strength ebbing, as she struggled without oxygen. White specs flashed at the corners of her vision, and her body spasmed its last gasp. The last thing Codi remembered was looking up at the round door of the dryer. She reached up with her free hand and with all her remaining strength, swung it open into Juliette's face.

* * *

Juliette knew one of her shots had made contact, but Codi's sneak attack from above had surprised her. She focused on trying to get a shot off that would injure or kill the woman. It was force versus force, and sooner or later, something would give. A sudden sharp pain, as her arm impacted with the dryer's edge, sent her weapon flying, but she had used the distraction to roll on top of her victim. Now she had the leverage she needed to end this fight. She fought to get her hands around the woman's neck, and then squeezed with everything she had. She could feel the life leaving her target. Each attempted punch carried less and less power. She gripped the woman's throat as if it could bring her dead brother back to life. Just as Agent Sanders's eyes started to roll back in her head, Juliette was stunned by a wicked blow to the side of her head from the dryer door. There was a sudden shock to her system, and everything went black.

* * *

Codi lay on her side, gulping air like a last place Olympic sprinter. Her foggy mind started to clear, and she squinted around the room. Lying a few feet away was Juliette. She was dazed and trying to sit up. Suddenly, her glazed eyes lasered on the situation at hand. Codi saw Juliette's gun on the floor, a mere three feet to her left, but it might as well be a lifetime away; she would never beat Juliette to it.

Codi did the only thing that came to mind; she jumped up and sprinted for the door. As she rounded the doorjamb, she could hear Juliette moving behind her, scrabbling for her gun. Codi raced down the hallway toward the double glass exit doors at the end. Her hip screamed with every step, giving her a hitch in her stride. The doors were about fifty feet away and closing. With any luck she would make it. Doors to rooms went past, as did the patterned carpet. Codi pushed herself with just one focus.

Once through the doors, Codi realized her mistake. They were not exit doors but rather doors leading to a viewing balcony that overlooked the indoor waterpark. Off to the side was another door with an exit sign and access to a stairwell. The waterpark was a massive affair with a giant curved glass roof that lit an infrastructure of eight slides, four pools, and a kids' play area. There was a giant waterfall in the middle that dumped onto a mesh floor and then drained to the largest pool. Surrounding that was an oval-shaped lazy river.

Codi didn't hesitate. She leaped off the balcony in a freefall to the water below.

* * *

Juliette instinctively grabbed for her gun and aimed it at the blurry figure running from the laundry room. She fired three quick shots but was too slow, still needing time to get her bearings. Her head was reeling from the knockout blow of the dryer door. She stood on wobbly legs and stumbled to the exit. She could feel a trickle of blood oozing from a gash in her forehead. It could wait. She stepped into the hallway just in time to see her target slip through a pair of double doors. Juliette pushed herself forward—half-walking, half-running. Every step brought more clarity and a return of her strength.

* * *

As Codi emerged from the water, a young man with red swimming trunks and a whistle immediately came running. He blew a shrill blast in her direction. One look at Codi's bloody hip, and he turned pale.

"I'm a federal agent," she said, "and there's someone trying to kill me. Get everyone out of here and call 911!"

The young man froze in disbelief. Codi grabbed his arm and pushed him into action. She ran toward the center of the park as three bullets stitched the water behind her. A fourth dropped the young man in his tracks. A pool of blood quickly flowed across the pool's edge and spread into the water. Codi didn't hesitate as she dashed forward. There was nothing she could do for him now.

It took five seconds for the first scream. From there, it multiplied like a virus on a cruise ship. Soon, the entire complex, filled with families and kids, ran for the exits in sheer panic. The sound was reassuring to Codi, as it had not been her plan to put innocents in harm's way. But when you are unarmed and being chased by a highly-trained assassin, sometimes your choices are limited.

Codi chanced a peek over her shoulder as she moved deeper into the complex in time to see Juliette jump from the balcony in hot pursuit. This would give her about ten seconds before she was reacquired. She looked around for a weapon—anything.

* * *

Juliette pulled herself from the pool and glanced at the ground. There was a decent blood trail that moved deeper into the park, away from the dead lifeguard who had inadvertently blocked a kill shot meant for her target. She held her pistol out and followed the trail. This would be most fulfilling, ending the woman who had taken everything from her.

* * *

Joel was humming "Viva Las Vegas" to himself for some unknown reason. He had found an agent whose file matched the profile. Thirty-nine, white, five-ten, and presumed dead or missing. Even the letters of his name fit. Agent Daniel Johnson. He tried different combinations of the other letters, ultimately deciding on a viable message. He stepped back and took the whole thing in. He was close, real close. He had gone from this: AGE **TJNS** NTR **KED** THR CHARDG LTY **LOVE** TOF M **LY**. To this: Agent Johnson Tracked The Richard Guilty Love to Family

"Gotcha." His lips curled up at the ends. *Dang, I'm good.*

Suddenly, an alarm sounded, breaking him from the moment. It seemed to be coming from the entire floor. *A fire?* He quickly gathered his files and papers and hurried out the door. As he exited his room, he looked for Codi, but there was no sign of her. He headed for her room and banged on the door.

"Come on, you in there?"

He noticed a few drops of something that looked like blood leading from the laundry room off to the double doors at the other end of the hallway. He followed them, holding his files close, like a newborn child against his chest.

Once out on the balcony, Joel looked out at the massive indoor park below. It was a water funhouse built for pure entertainment. He started for the exit stairs to the right, when movement caught his eye. A lady with a pistol moved deliberately below. She was hunting someone in the park.

"You gotta be kidding me," he said under his breath. He pulled his gun, turned and sprinted for the stairs.

The alarm sounded throughout the waterpark. A female voice repeatedly told guests to walk to the nearest exit in a calm prerecorded directness. The few guests who had not yet managed to leave, did so without delay.

Water flowed and canned music still played in the now empty and colorful hunting grounds. The entire place was a ghost town. Codi and Juliette appeared. One armed and dangerous and the other a wounded animal. Each with only one thought, kill or be killed.

Juliette moved methodically as she followed the faint blood trail with every sense on high alert. She had been patient and determined to get here, and no one would deny her this moment. The fading trail led under a slide and past a staircase that led to the start of a ride called "The Hurricane." She tracked the drops to the edge of the lazy river right across from the central waterfall. She leaned over to look both ways along the river. Her quarry was gone.

* * *

Codi could just make out Juliette's shape through the curtain of water that formed the central waterfall. She had purposely left a blood trail to the lazy river and then doubled back into the waterfall, careful to clean any new blood drips, before hiding there. Juliette was now only a few feet away. As soon as the woman turned her back, Codi flew through the pouring water, slammed herself into Juliette's back, and they both tumbled into the lazy river.

* * *

Joel, clinging to his stack of files, gun in hand, ran through the waterpark. He took the stairs leading up to the start of a ride called "The Tornado," one that had five stars next to its name. He was hoping he could get a better visual of what was happening from higher up. The air burned with chlorine as he huffed his way up the textured blue plastic stairs. Once on top, he panned the area below. Nothing.

* * *

Juliette had been caught unaware and was unable to take a breath before hitting the water hard. She found herself again in a hand-to-hand battle, this time underwater with very little oxygen in her lungs. She managed to hang on to her pistol, but Codi had a vice lock on her wrist, and there was no way to point it at her. So she did the next best thing and pulled the trigger. Underwater, a 9mm bullet is only effective to about eight feet. It flew harmlessly away, but the concussive blast was immense when contained in water. Codi and Juliette both had the air knocked out of them and were forced to surface. Codi used both feet to kick off Juliette's chest to put some distance between them. She surfaced about ten feet from her attacker and gasped for air. Juliette did the same but quickly brought her gun up out of the water. Codi quickly realized her mistake. She gulped some air, ducked back down, and swam for her life.

Juliette finally had her prey cornered. All she had to do was wait until the woman ran out of air, and the instant she surfaced it would be game over. This was going to be fun. She bounced along the surface of the lazy river's bottom pacing Codi's receding form. She mentally counted down the seconds with a building optimism.

* * *

Joel had never been a fan of heights, but he had no time to think about that now, just react. He'd seen Codi and Juliette appear directly below him and Codi was in real trouble. Holding tight to his files, he jumped into The Tornado's slide feet first. His gun in firing position and his eyes as big as saucers. The sudden drop made him vocalize a high-pitched scream as he slid nearly vertical for the first thirty feet before hitting a turn and being forced to the edge of the slide with three Gs of force. Water sprayed in all directions, but his glasses blocked some of the spray, so he could still see ahead.

Juliette turned to the source of the scream. A man with a gun was hurtling in her direction. She spun around and began to fire at the moving target. As she pulled the trigger, she recognized the man's face. It was Agent Joel Strickman, her initial target, and he was being delivered right to her.

Joel felt three successive impacts to his torso before he could manage to return fire. He emptied his magazine generally toward the active shooter.

The return fire soon ceased as Joel hit the pool at the bottom of the ride, causing his paperwork to fly and giving him an instant water enema in every orifice.

He emerged, coughing and sputtering. There was blood everywhere, but a quick self-inspection told him it wasn't his. Paperwork had saved his life. *That's a first*, he thought.

"What took you so long?"

He glanced over to see Codi in the water across from him next to a facedown Juliette Cole floating on the surface of the lazy river.

"What, me? I just saved your life."

"And it's about time."

Joel was at a complete loss for words, as he stood there with his jaw agape in the bloody water.

Codi smiled, and in a rare moment of sincerity, said, "Thank you."

Joel, still a bit flummoxed, just nodded. He finally found his voice, as sirens approached in the distance.

"Who was she?"

"Juliette Cole, from that case in Europe."

He looked like he'd seen a ghost as the name hit home. She had nearly killed him on more than one occasion. "The twins."

Codi nodded.

"Guess she had unfinished business after we killed her brother," Codi said while painfully climbing out of the water.

Her hip throbbed, and it was going to be a long night once the cops arrived. She looked down at her injury for the first time. The bullet had hit her cellphone in her front pants pocket. She pulled her phone out and lowered her pants to inspect the injury. Her cellphone was destroyed, but it had slowed the jacketed projectile enough that she could just see the back of the bullet sticking out of her skin.

Joel started to look away when he saw Codi lower her pants, but he was concerned, and helping her with the wound trumped his need for partner decorum. Her pink lacy panties were not lost on him. They were mostly soaked in blood. The copper color of a bullet showed in the fleshy part where her hip and thigh met. Codi tried to grasp it with her fingernails and pull it out, but it was stuck.

The pain was high but manageable, and Codi looked around for something to grip it with.

"Joel, I need your help."

"Okay?" he answered with hesitation.

"See if you can get a hold on this bullet and pull it out."

"Can't we wait for the paramedics?"

"Don't be a Jack Wad. It's just a bullet. Pull it out!" Codi demanded.

Joel sighed and climbed out of the water. He dropped to one knee in front of Codi. Her pants were half-mast and she was standing there in fairly revealing panties. This alone made Joel start to sweat. Luckily, the water from the river disguised it. He scratched at a nervous itch and wiggled his fingers trying to get up the nerve. *Wow, she is one beautiful woman.*

"Come on, get to it," Codi encouraged.

Joel gripped the back of the bullet with his fingernails and pulled, but the bullet held firm and his nails just scraped off. Codi winced at the pain but encouraged him to try again. Same result.

"I can't get a good enough grip on it. We'll have to wait for help."

Codi was not a fan of doctors or hospitals and had demonstrated this in the past. Her partner never quite understood it. "Use your teeth."

"What? *No way!*"

"Come on, it'll take two seconds."

"You are freaking nuts, you know that?"

"Don't make this awkward."

"Akwar—" Joel took a deep breath and went for it. He grabbed her by her buttocks with both hands, opened his mouth, and leaned in. He used his tongue to probe for the bullet and then set his teeth to grab onto the back of it. He pulled slowly and carefully. The bullet slid out. Codi moaned at the pain.

The sound of a man clearing his throat interrupted them, and Joel, in a panic, swallowed the bullet. His eyes doubled in size as he looked around Codi's hips to see three policemen, guns drawn. They were staring at Joel on his knees in front of Codi with his hands on her butt and his mouth doing God knows what. Codi, even with her pants down, was undeterred.

"That was very good, Joel," she said with a smile and a wink.

Joel's cheeks reddened as he tried to grasp his situation and the possible lead poisoning that he was getting from the bullet. He pulled his hands from Codi's backside as if he had touched a hot stove.

Codi used her index finger as a plug to stop the bleeding and her other hand to nonchalantly pull her pants back up. Joel turned six different shades of red. He jumped to his feet and tried to stutter an explanation while trying to show the policemen his badge.

"We . . . we're federal agents. I, I was trying to suck, I mean get the—"

The cops seemed as muddled as Joel.

Codi piped up, "Anybody got some super glue?"

CHAPTER SIX

The sun had come up hours ago, but Codi and Joel had just made it to the hotel café for breakfast. It was an IHOP knock-off, and the service was as mediocre as the food. It had been a long night, as Codi and Joel battled the gauntlet of local and state bureaucracy.

Joel sipped his coffee silently as Codi ate like she hadn't been fed in three days. It took her three cups of coffee to revive herself after drinking herself to sleep the night before.

They had found super glue, and her wound was sealed and wrapped. It hurt but was otherwise a non-issue. She had been extremely lucky.

Joel looked forlorn. He had read up on the swallowing of unwanted items and spent most of the night tossing and turning in fear.

"Lead poisoning is no joke," he said.

"You shouldn't believe everything you read on *WebMD*."

64

"It's written by doctors!" Joel shook his head in dismay and took another bite of his waffle.

"It's the Internet. Besides, the bullet was copper-jacketed. I don't think you're going to get lead poisoning. More like copper poisoning."

Joel stopped mid-chew, realizing he had been researching lead poisoning all night when he should have been reading up on copper poisoning. The events of last night still had him jacked up. He took a calming breath and remembered it was Codi who had actually taken a bullet.

"So what about you? Aren't you concerned? You need to take this seriously, Codi!"

"Oh, I am. I made sure to ingest enough alcohol last night to kill any germs," she said, while rubbing her temples.

Joel hadn't thought of that, and suddenly he needed to get himself a drink to sterilize a certain bullet in his stomach. He poked at his food nervously.

An assassin from their past with a vendetta against them was something new. It was totally unexpected and had blind-sided the partners. It seemed there was really no way to prepare for some scenarios. All the training in the world would help, but sometimes, a little luck was required.

Joel looked over his cup of tasteless coffee as he spoke. "I've been meaning to ask you, what's a Jack Wad?"

Codi looked at him, confused.

"You called me that yesterday," Joel said.

The light clicked on. "Look, Joel, I'd been shot, and I needed you to get the bullet out. It just came out of my mouth. Honestly, I have no idea what it means. But it sounds harsh, and that's what I wanted at the time."

"Okay, fair enough. So, since we are being honest, what is it with you and hospitals and doctors?"

Codi continued to chew for a moment, and then put her fork down. She took on a faraway look before speaking. "When I was younger, my father was injured in an underwater explosion that killed two other divers."

"Right. He was an underwater demolition guy for the Navy."

"UDT." She nodded. "He was rushed to the Navel Medical Center in San Diego where he fought for his life. He was making steady progress until a doctor prescribed conflicting medications. It caused a massive myocardial infarction."

She paused for a second before continuing, remembering the moment. "If it hadn't been for the hospital and the doctors, he would have pulled through and been okay. I was there when they pulled the plug. His eyes just . . . closed."

"I'm so sorry, Codi. But not all hospitals and doctors are to blame; they save a lot of lives too."

"I know that, Joel, but I like to do things my way. And for right now, I would like to avoid them if at all possible."

"I think most people would agree with that statement," Joel added.

They shared a moment that was more real than most. Codi finally picked up her fork and dug back into her food, although this time much more slowly.

* * *

Farel Utomo sat next to his fellow workers on the wooden bench, tying his boots. He had come for the promise, the promise of a new life. But lately, he had felt so weak that he started to have doubts. One year and three months ago, Farel had taken a chance and left his native land of Indonesia. Initially, he made his way from Buru Island to the capital, Jakarta, looking for work. The mass of bodies all trying to make a go of it was intense and there was little opportunity for an outer islander. Eventually, he found work as a dishwasher at the Golden Bamboo Restaurant. The pay was so meager that he was forced to sleep under a tree in a raised planter at the Taman Suropati City Park. He made a few friends in his new life and even had his eye on a young waitress named Aulia.

Farel spent most of his rare free time trying to better himself, and when word on the street reached him about an unexpected prospect, he took it. Five years' labor in exchange for a passport and immigration papers to Canada. It was too good to be true. He signed on and boarded the ship that would take him to a new life. The covert ingress into the country had been scary. It started with a night delivery requiring a cold ocean swim to the shore. From there, his group of twelve men was trucked in a small cargo box almost three thousand miles to Quebec. It had been stifling and soon reeked of fear and desperation.

He had undergone three weeks of training, which he was told did not count toward his time served. Once trained, Farel began working and living in the mine. It was a soulless gray place of darkness with artificial air and light. He and the others were each given a small room of their own. There was a communal bathroom and kitchen/living quarters.

Farel was required to wear protective clothing and steel-toed boots. His job was to drive a small tractor that housed a drill-bit attached to the front. Drilling the stone created a lot of dust and was murder on the drill bit. It needed to be changed out frequently as it dulled and then started to bind up. The task required eight pilot holes thirty inches deep in the wall before the explosives team came in and took over. It took a lot of focus, and Farel was proud of his responsibility, especially considering his past.

For his services, he and the other workers received three meals a day and one day a week to relax. They were never allowed to go outside but were provided with a TV and a foosball table in the common room. Farel was grateful to his God and his bosses for this chance. He would prove himself worthy. The only things he really missed were the sunshine and Aulia, but he did his best to follow the rules and was treated fairly.

Each worker had been given a calendar to keep by their bed so they could track the days of servitude. It was very gratifying to mark off the days. Farel was just past the halfway point when his foreman moved him to a much lower section of the mine. The ore was different there. It had a dark gray composition and was actually easier on the drill. They made good progress following a rich vein.

Over the last three weeks, Farel had picked up a cough. It had gotten worse, and now he was feeling like crap. As soon as he finished his shift, he went straight to his bed. He tried to keep a positive attitude, but he was feeling weaker by the day, and his gums had started to bleed. By Thursday, he had trouble getting out of bed, and a medic was called. The man probed and prodded Farel, taking notes as he went. After about ten minutes, the medic helped him to his feet and escorted him to an upper section of the mine unknown to Farel. There were glass doors and windows, with rooms on both sides of the main stone walkway. Some contained very complicated looking equipment, like a science laboratory. The workers there wore white lab coats as they worked with the hi-tech machines.

He was taken to a room with bright overhead lighting. It was a sterile environment with a concrete floor and white walls. There was a small stainless steel table and two chairs. The medic was kind and spoke enough Indonesian for them to communicate. He had Farel sit in one of the black leather chairs, as he did several tests. He asked him questions and wrote down his answers on an electronic tablet in his hand. He took Farel's blood pressure and looked down his throat. Farel was starting to feel hope that they would find what was ailing him and get him fixed. He wanted to finish up his commitment and start his new life in Canada. He had been practicing his English and was starting to understand a few words.

The medic stepped out into the hallway. Farel could see the man discussing something with one of the bosses. There were hand gestures and several nods and shakes of the head. Finally, the boss shook hands with the medic, and then entered the room smiling. Feral tried to stand, but the man gestured for him to stay seated. He sat down in the other chair across from Feral and spoke some words he was not quite familiar with.

"You're gonna be okay, son," he said, smiling.

Feral's lips turned up in hope.

The man drew a pistol and shot Feral in the head.

* * *

Matt pulled the strained zipper on his suitcase. He had twenty minutes to get to the airport that was only ten minutes away. He checked the status on his Uber and decided it was time to head outside. The barracks where he lived had been converted into apartment-style rooms for his team and him. They had been assigned to this base for its security and access to the other technology teams housed there. It didn't hurt to have more than one brilliant mind attacking a problem, and they regularly had breakthroughs.

The time spent in Montana with Codi recently was precious to him. It was exactly what their relationship had needed. No distractions. After their side trip to the abandoned town of Greenville, Codi seemed different. He could see that her wheels were turning with a mystery to be solved. He knew the look and the mindset. It was a trait he also possessed. It served them both well, but second place was no place for him. He made an excuse to leave early and hoped it would allow Codi to focus on her new case without damage to their strengthening relationship, a relationship he hoped to improve. Matt grabbed his phone and sent her an emoji heart with a *Miss U* text. He knew texts and emojis were hollow at best. Nothing beat face-to-face for proper communication, or, more to his liking, skin-to-skin. For now, however, it would have to do. The reply was unusually prompt. *Me2.* It was all he needed for now, and the corners of his mouth reached for the sky.

Matt had been the recipient of his grandfather's work, started some sixty years ago and passed to him through his grandfather's partner. He had gladly taken over the reins and had both completed and enhanced the project. Almost two years ago, their invention was stolen to be used as a weapon, something Matt had never considered. The thieves kidnapped him along with a young GSA agent named Codi Sanders. It ended in a race to stop a madman bent on the destruction of London. Matt and

Codi pushed themselves to the breaking point to stop the man and the weapon. The intense time spent together during that debacle had forged an incredibly strong friendship that blossomed into something very special. But maintaining a high-octave relationship was always doomed to fail. It was the quiet time they had spent together after the case, on a beach in Ireland that cemented their real feelings for each other.

But lately, like most couples, they had been experiencing their share of ups and downs. Their recent trip to Montana, although cut a bit short, was just what they had needed.

It was an encouraging upward trend, and Matt was starting to think about his future. His mind drifted to thoughts of Codi. She was an extraordinary woman. He had never met anyone so determined and driven yet still willing to give. She made time for life and tried to get as much out of it as she could. The woman would shoot you in the head if it was warranted, and she would kill herself to save you if that's what was needed. He let his mind wander to the more primal lizard parts of his brain as he imagined them together. Her firm waist and butt accenting her athletic form. Her amazing breasts that seemed to defy gravity. And her smile that cut right through hi. . .

A sudden honk jerked Matt from his thoughts. He had been standing in the street lost in the moment. The Uber driver in the gray Prius waved.

Matt's mind jumped back to the matter at hand. *Get out of the street and into the Prius.*

He put his luggage in the trunk and climbed into the car. Today, he was off to Arizona for field tests. It was the next stage in the Focusable Cellular Beam Technology development.

FCBT was the acronym given to his invention. It was a machine that broke compounds down to a cellular level before transmitting them through the air. Similar to how helium can pass right through a balloon, the smaller molecules would penetrate the skin. Matt's dream was to be able to fly over a remote village and vaccinate every person in a single pass.

But then Nial Brennan came into the picture. He stole it and renamed it SkyStorm before loading it with a deadly agent and aiming it at London, planning to infect thousands of innocents. That act changed everything for Matt. It deflated his passion for his project and made him a lot more cautious. He realized there would always be bad people in the world willing to do anything to promote their agenda.

Luckily, Codi and her team managed to stop the attack and retrieve his invention. Upon its return, the military took charge. They gave the device the odd acronym FCBT and collected up Matt and his project "for national security sake." They wrapped the whole thing in secrecy and layered it with a giant heaping of painful bureaucracy. Progress since then had been slow but promising. Matt had run several trials with exceptional results, and they were close to wrapping up the testing. It had Matt thinking about what came next.

CHAPTER SEVEN

**WASHINGTON, D.C. – FBI MAIN HEADQUARTERS –
SUB-BASEMENT – 11:26 A.M.**

Codi stepped through the double doors. She was a mess. Four grueling hours in the OPR (Office of Professional Responsibility), a division much like internal affairs for police departments. She moved zombie-like to a vending machine in the hallway and purchased a Pepsi. A small wooden bench next to it seemed to call to her. She plopped down and opened the can. She opened the top button of her blue button-up that contrasted nicely with her charcoal suit. She took a sip of the cold soft drink and leaned forward, elbows on her knees.

They had asked her every possible question and then did it all over again. The committee dug up information from an old case where Codi and Juliette had previously clashed. Codi lost her cool a couple of times at the stupidity of it all but somehow managed to persevere. At one point, the investigative panel spun the information to make it look as though Codi had chased this woman down and assassinated her, and the death of the lifeguard was caused by her actions. The truth seemed to be of little concern to them, especially considering Codi didn't even fire her weapon and had been shot herself. The level of CYA went deep, and she was nothing more than a captive lamb ready for slaughter. If finger pointing were an Olympic sport, the FBI would have one heck of a team.

She took another drink and stretched out her stiff neck. Oh well, what will be, will be, she tried unsuccessfully to tell herself. The truth was, she really liked her job. She loved being an FBI agent and felt like she had made a real difference. She lived by a strict code: If I'm not wanted, I'm not going to be here. Her mind spun with the possibilities of what might be next for her, but she just wasn't ready to let go, not yet. She decided she would fight to stay right where she was.

If this is what happened after you were involved in a shooting on American soil, she was going to have to rethink her whole approach. Shoot first, bury the body and all evidence, and then ask questions. That thought, along with a deep breath, seemed to relax her a bit.

She wondered how bad it must be for Joel, as he was the agent who fired a weapon. And thank God he had. She considered how the whole mess had gone down. It could have ended much differently. Her hip had finally stopped throbbing, and she was able to walk without a limp.

A door opened and Joel, looking much like she felt, walked over and sat down next to her. "Those guys are morons."

"Yeah, next time, just let them shoot me. It'll be a lot less paperwork."

This elicited a small upturn of Joel's lips and a partial nod. "Suspended until further notification," Joel deadpanned.

"Me too. Can I buy you a Pepsi?" she asked.

"What, no beer?"

"Not in this building."

"In that case, Pepsi it is."

Codi stepped over to the machine, swiped her card, and pressed a button.

"In the military, there is a chain of command, and we were expected to follow orders," she said. "In the FBI, there is a lot more thinking and acting on our own." She handed Joel the cola.

"And then a bunch of Monday morning quarterbacks come in with their 20/20 hindsight and judge us."

"Exactly. They weren't there, so they have no idea how things really went down."

Joel just shrugged.

"You wanna get out of here?"

"Absofreakinlutely."

* * *

The Richelieu River moved slowly as moonlight rippled across the undulating surface. Sterling watched as a couple of his workers said a short prayer in a language he didn't understand. They tied weights to two bodies lying on a tarp on the floor of his boat. The men worked in tandem to lower each body over the side and watched as it slipped below the black surface.

Sterling had been frustrated with the loss of the workers. He spent a lot of money and time acquiring and training them. Radiation was no joke, and his entire team was still trying to get a handle on it. They ordered several Demron Class 2 Radiation suits from Amazon, and now it looked like he would need to provide one for each and every worker. He would start the process on Monday. They would need to be careful with the number of suits per order though, as they were probably regulated. The last thing he needed was attention from some government stooge.

Sterling stared for a minute until the water smoothed flat again. He turned without remorse and started his Mazda Nagare Hybrid powerboat. The high-performance boat ran on electric motors, and Nano Titanate batteries gave it rocket-like speed without the noise. The dark graphite shell made it almost invisible at night. A white foam trail was the only giveaway of its presence. They travelled north twenty minutes at a leisurely seventy mph and then docked at the craft's covered waterfront home in Saint Hilaire, a small riverside warehouse he owned with water access on one side and street access on the other. Sterling jumped out of the boat, allowing the two men to tie it up and reset the charging cable. He speed-walked to his yellow SUV and reached for the handle.

"Good evening."

Sterling jumped out of his skin, as Dorthia stepped from behind a delivery truck into the light of a streetlamp.

"*Jeez*. You just about gave me a heart attack!"

"I see you've been busy?" she said.

"What are you doing, spying on me?"

"We have an investment with you now, and I, for one, would hate to see anything happen to it."

"Well, thank you for your concern, but I have somewhere to be right now."

"Miss Rhonda Fortier can wait."

Sterling's face flashed red at the mention of his mistress's name. She was waiting for him in his downtown condo for one of their regular Friday night trysts.

"You have no—"

Dorthia put her hand up to stop him. She knew this would infuriate him, being controlled by a woman, or by anyone for that matter. As a proper narcissist, Sterling Riche was very predictable. She decided to take it down a notch.

"Look," she said, "you are doing a great job for us, and as I said, my employer is the type of man who finds out everything there is to know about a person before going into business with them. That's just how he works. It's not personal. I can get you more workers to replace the ones you have lost, and I can keep our distribution lines open and operational. But you will have to mine and refine our supply. That's on you."

Sterling nodded imperceptibly.

"So how close are we to the first shipment?"

"We have some delays due to manpower and startup unknowns. The radiation thing has been more complicated for my foreman than he anticipated. I'd say . . . three weeks at most.

Dorthia stared at Sterling with unblinking eyes.

"Okay. Three weeks," she said. "I can source better protective clothing for your workers, as well. It wouldn't do for them to lose their false dream of freedom before we're done with them."

Sterling gave no response.

She held the gaze for just a beat too long, then turned and disappeared back into the night.

That woman gave him the creeps. He would have to take her down a peg or two, but that would require careful planning. The thought perked his libido just enough to get him back on track for his rendezvous.

* * *

Codi cracked open an eye. Her head spun and pounded. The sun cast a warm D.C. glow across her white bamboo sheets, accenting her athletic form. She tilted her new bullet-free phone and realized she had missed her morning routine: protein bar, green juice, and an hour in the pool doing laps. She had only recently returned to swimming. It had been a passion of hers that helped pay her way through college. Few people were faster than she was in the water, but after drowning and being brought back to life on a previous case, it had been hard to rejuvenate the appeal. The case responsible nearly killed her multiple times, but it also launched her career with the FBI. It helped refine the tenacity that now pushed her to the finish line on everything she took on. To say Codi was driven was not giving her enough credit.

But not today. Today she decided to roll over and go back to sleep. Besides, after a late night drinking the town dry with her college BFF Katelyn Green, she deserved it. They had met in a Poli-Sci class at University of California San Diego. Now Katelyn lived in D.C. and worked for the office of Senator Hightower from Wyoming. She was outgoing and had been the genesis of several regrets over the years for Codi. But the two had an unbreakable bond that almost always ended with a Tequila shot or three.

Codi's phone buzzed . . . and buzzed.

She finally reached out and clicked it. "This better be good. I was having the most exquisite dream."

"Dream? It's nine-twenty."

"Says you."

"And most of the east coast. Can you manage a three-way at ten-thirty?"

Codi's boss, SSA Brian Fescue had a casual way about him that hid the seriousness of his position and the cases he often oversaw. Codi, and even her partner Joel, had flourished under his tutelage.

"*Augh.* I'm supposed to be suspended," Codi said as she hung up.

* * *

Joel looked agitated in his navy Brooks Brothers suit as he waited in his boss's office. He couldn't quite sit still. Codi, on the other hand, looked like she was hung over, and not just a little. Her hair was mostly combed, and she had managed some deodorant and lip-gloss. It was like being on the outside looking in. She dry-swallowed two Advil and scrunched her eyes, trying to chase off her impaired condition.

The door popped open and Brian entered.

"Thanks for coming in. How are you feeling?" The second part was addressed to Codi.

"I'll live."

"Good. First things first. You have both been cleared in the shooting," Brian said.

Joel let out a giant breath he'd been holding. Brian slid their guns and badges over to them. Codi checked her clip before sliding it back into her holster.

"You would think that after all we've done, they would cut us some slack," Codi said.

"I'm still waiting on my medal from the last case," Joel added a bit anxiously.

Codi and Joel's previous case had put them in the path of a misguided but determined Chinese general with an undetectable nuclear missile. They had played a major role in thwarting its impact on the city of Chicago.

"For us, the FBI way is the only way," Brian said. "Plus, you're on American soil, so we do things by the book here. And Joel, I told you your medal is—"

"Yeah, yeah, I know, in the mail."

The two men shared a matching grin.

"By the book. That should make Joel happy," Codi said, trying to interrupt the male bonding.

Joel's smile faded rapidly with Codi's response. She was always trying to get him to paint outside the lines, but it just wasn't really his thing.

"Okay, so everyone has filled out their paperwork and covered their . . . jobs. What now?" Codi asked.

"Nice segue. First of all, where do we stand on the dead agent?"

"I think I've worked out the message, and we now know his identity," Joel said, and he slid some paperwork over to support his claim. A few of the pages smelled of chlorine and had smeared ink and bullet holes in them.

"Here, let me show you." Joel pulled out a page with the recovered letters. "This is the message as far as the lab can read it."

AGE T J NS N TR KED TH   R CHARD G LTY LOVE TO F M LY

He pulled out another page with doodles and crossed-off lines on it. One sentence stood out at the bottom.

"This is what I think it says."

AGENT JOHNSON TRACKED THE RICHARD GUILTY LOVE TO FAMILY

Brian asked, "Agent Johnson?"

"And who's The Richard?" Codi asked. "Sounds like an egotistical maniac if he calls himself *The Richard*. Maybe you should try that, Joel. *The Joel*. It has a nice ring to it."

Joel tried to get them back on point by ignoring his snarky partner.

"His name is Agent Daniel Johnson. Initially, we thought he was investigating some kind of fraud on the Greenville Dam project. He's from Salem, Massachusetts. He joined the FBI when he graduated Boston Coll—"

Brian interrupted his timeline story. "Just show me the baby, Joel. I don't want to know about the labor."

Joel knew that was his boss's code for *get to the point*.

"Yes, of course."

Joel shuffled a few more pages and continued, "Agent Daniel Johnson was thirty-nine with a wife and two kids. He was one of the major players in a massive task force assigned to the Plymouth Mail Truck Robbery."

"I remember reading about that at Quantico," Brian mused.

"It was the biggest heist in U.S. history at the time and still remains unsolved. They had several suspects, and one of them was about to turn state's evidence when *poof*, he disappeared. The case stalled out just as the statute of limitations kicked in."

"I always thought that was a stupid law," Codi said. "I mean if you're guilty, you're guilty, right?"

"So what about him?" Brian asked.

"He had checked in with his boss at our Boston offices and said he had it on good authority that . . ." Joel looked through his notes for the name, "Thomas Richards, one of the masterminds they think was behind the robbery. The guy who was going to turn state's evidence and then up and disappeared. Well, a couple of days later he was sighted near Bozeman, Montana."

Codi interrupted. "Let me guess, Agent Johnson took off after him and that was the last time he was ever heard from."

Joel nodded.

"I guess it wasn't construction fraud," Codi said. "Sounds more like an inside job. They could have been in on the heist together."

Brian spoke up. "Maybe. But I think this message tells a different story. It seems to me that he was an agent right to the end. It gives his name." Brian pointed to the message on the paper. "Joel, can you change 'The Richard' to Thomas Richards."

Joel did so.

"He gives us the perp. And finally, a message to his family."
AGENT JOHNSON
TRACKED THOMAS RICHARDS GUILTY
LOVE TO FAMILY

"It was straight up murder," Codi said.

The three agents grasped the gravity of the moment.

Brian broke the ensuing silence. "Good work, you two. Keep on this, and let's see if we can put this agent's case to bed and give any living relatives some closure. Now that there is a murder, there is no statute of limitations."

He smacked the desk in a celebratory fashion.

"Oh, almost forgot," Brian said. "I have another body I need you two to check out. I've emailed you the details. Now, get out of here before I take those badges back." He tried to look annoyed when he said the last part, but the feeble threat only worked on Joel. "And yes, the family is fine, so don't ask."

"Wasn't gonna ask."

"Sure."

Codi nodded at the statement as she left his office. Brian leaned back and tried to catch his breath. It had been a non-stop kind of morning. He had taken his current position in the FBI after a crazy manhunt across Europe nearly cost him his life and his job. During that case, he managed to help Codi enough for her to save the day, and himself to save face with the current administration. It had taken him from obscurity to supervisory special agent status. Shortly after, his wife gave birth to their second child, Abigale. He was a committed family man, and when the administration offered him his current position, he was happy to take it. A chance to blend the job he loved with the home life that was important to him.

Family life was always a mixed bag of the unknown. One second, everything was perfect, and the next, utter chaos. This morning before he left, his four-year-old, Tristian, came down with a fever. Abigale, now two years old, had stuck a plastic BB in her ear. Where she had found it and why she determined the best place to keep it was in her ear was still a mystery. The peaceful morning went south quickly. In the end, Brian had been forced to abandon his wife Leila to handle the mess.

His Jamaican heritage was something he was proud of, but he kept the accent well hidden until he got upset. This morning it was working overtime to be heard.

Brian was about three inches shorter than Joel, but he was built like a tank. And his cappuccino-colored eyes seemed to get to the truth no matter how hard someone tried to hide it. He was good to his agents and worked just as hard as they did.

He picked up his cellphone. Time to call the wife for a BB update.

* * *

Joel had his email open before his butt hit his seat. "Would he really have taken our badges back?" he asked Codi.

"Only yours, Joel. What have you got?"

Joel paused a moment trying to decide what to do. "I've got all my eggs in the FBI basket. That's what I've got. I haven't even thought about—"

"*No,*" Codi interrupted. "What have you got on the case?"

"Oh." He leaned in to read the small file.

"Floater."

"Why would Special Projects care about a floater? Seems more like a case for local authorities."

"Ah-ha," Joel said while reading further into the file.

"Is this how the day is going to go? Do I have to pull every answer out of you one by one?"

"Oh, sorry—radiation. The body was irradiated. That's why we're being called in."

Codi leaned back. *Radiation, that's nasty stuff.* This was not how she wanted to start her day.

Joel picked up the phone and called transportation.

* * *

Julian Drexler clasped his hands behind his back as he stared out at the city below him. Toronto was a mixture of the modern West and European classic. The iconic CN tower stretched into the sky before him with its glass-floored revolving eatery, a place many feared to even set foot in. Beyond that was the Great Lake, Ontario, dividing Canada and the United States. The boat traffic was light this morning, the septuagenarian noted, as he pondered a business conundrum. He was a man with fingers in many pies, most of which were legitimate. But his biggest source of income and power had always come from the dark side of his business.

In 1968, Julian left his native country of the United States. He smuggled himself across the border into Canada to avoid the Vietnam draft. That single action set him on a course that would change his life forever. Being a draft dodger and an illegal left him little choice but a life on the streets. He struggled, and one particularly cold winter made him desperate. As they say, desperate men do desperate things, and this was the case for Julian. He tried to rob a man using a pocketknife, but the man resisted, and the ensuing struggle turned deadly as an angry Julian plunged his knife into the man repeatedly. For a peace-loving draft dodger, the hardness that followed never left, and a newly forged life of crime loomed before him. Julian embraced it and turned it into a successful business of crime. Now, he could buy and sell the street criminals, like he once was, at will.

He turned and walked back to his glass and steel desk. Its surface reflected the magnificent view from the seventy-second floor. Julian picked up one of the three revolving burner phones he cycled through daily. He had learned early on that money could buy useful information. That information could then be used to protect oneself or ruin a competitor or make him even more money. This was at the heart of Julian's off-book business. His latest venture, however, had a slight hiccup. Word came to him about a problem in upstate New York. He would need his best man on the job. The voice on the other end of the phone was all business.

"This is Dorthia."

CHAPTER EIGHT

"Champy. This is awesome," said Joel.

"What is?" Codi asked.

"We are headed to a place steeped in folklore, Lake Champlain. There have been over three hundred sightings of a lake monster that lives there named Champy."

"Like the Loch Ness monster?"

"Exactly. There is also audio and video evidence, as well, and a state law protecting it."

"Well, that probably explains the radiation. A radiated mutated creature on the loose. We need to hand this case over to the X-files."

"I don't think that's a real thing," Joel said.

"You mean like your monster?"

"Hey, just because you haven't seen it, doesn't mean it's not real."

"Oh, so I need a little faith?"

"Precisely."

"Okay, but let's start by focusing on our case first. Then we can find your sea monster."

"Sure. Oh, turn right here. Lake monster, not sea."

"I see," Codi said with a smirky glance in Joel's direction. She had been nursing a mild hangover all morning, and it was becoming a regular thing. Waking in the night to images of the man who had tortured her a few cases back was not something she relished, and alcohol seemed to be the only cure. Drink enough and you won't dream.

Codi turned the white Mazda rental car right on South Street. They had flown into Plattsburgh International Airport in New York and taken the rental north on the 87 to Champlain. They passed two cashless tollbooths and crossed a bridge over the meandering Great Chazy River.

The small-town clinic was a single-story home with white clapboard and emerald wood trim. Codi parked the car along a grass-lined curb, and the two agents walked up the cracked sidewalk to the entrance. The trees were filled with fragrant blossoms that worked overtime to overpower the smell of the nearby lake. The door was locked. Several knocks brought nothing but sore knuckles for Joel.

An old, faded blue Ford step-side pickup pulled up behind their rental car, and a tall lanky man well over six-foot-five extracted himself from the truck. He hurried over to Joel and Codi.

"Agents Strickman and Sanders?"

They nodded.

"Sorry I'm late. Got to talking with ole Herb at the Lucky Trout Café. I'm Doc Canter. Pleased to meet you both. Welcome to Champlain, home of the famed Champy."

He shook their hands with excitement. He was so tall, even Joel had to look up to meet the man's gaze. He unlocked the front door with a practiced routine and ushered them inside. "Come in, come in."

The clinic looked just as Codi had expected, with a small waiting room, offices, patient rooms, and a back lab area.

"Sheriff Vance should be here any second. The body is in the back, being kept cold and away from people. I work at the university hospital in Plattsburgh doing radiology and cancer treatments and spend a couple days a week here. The county pays for part of the operation, so we maintain a small morgue in the back. When Cobb . . . er, Sheriff Vance brought in the body, I was asked to do the autopsy. Pretty typical stuff. We get bodies from the lake every so often."

Footsteps on the wooden porch steps alerted them to Cobb Vance, the local sheriff. He entered the waiting room, and introductions were made.

"As I was saying," the doctor said, "pretty typical to get a body from the lake. I started the autopsy just like I always do, and I just happened to look down at my dosimeter badge. You see, I hadn't taken it off when I left the hospital. Anyhoo, I looked down, quite unexpectedly, and the darn thing was maxed out."

Joel opened an app on his smartphone and started taking notes.

The doctor continued. "I called Cobb here. He came over with a Geiger counter, and sure enough, the body was radiating at over a thousand rems of radiation—that's 100 Sieverts (mSv)."

Codi and Joel shared a look.

"So we wrapped him up in a lead-lined body bag and waited for you to get here."

Joel looked up from his phone. "Can you give us an idea of the level of radiation 100 Sieverts is?"

"Our victim would have been dead in less than ten days from this kind of exposure."

"You say, *would* have been dead?" Codi asked.

"Oh, I thought I told you. He was shot in the head. Somebody saved him a lot of pain and suffering."

The sheriff finally had a chance to look helpful. "There was also a broken rope around his waist, so I'm guessing he was tied to something heavy and dumped. He wasn't supposed to end up a floater."

"Can we see the body?" Codi asked.

"Sure. That's why you came all this way. I don't recommend you stay more than a coupla minutes with it, though." He leaned in conspiratorially. "It stinks."

The doc led them to the back room, still chuckling at his joke. He pulled out one of his two refrigerated body drawers. He paused as he looked down and then looked around the room with concern. He opened the second drawer and took on a rattled expression.

"The body . . . it's gone."

* * *

Codi opened her eyes to a new day. She was feeling rough. She had no memory of how she had gotten home and to her bed. Last night's alcohol had not yet completely moved through her system, and her mouth tasted like the inside of a restaurant trashcan. She sat on the mattress edge, waiting for her head to stop spinning and pounding, her lavender bra and panties accentuating her figure. The good news was her hip was all but healed. However, the last few days had taken their toll. She was having trouble sleeping with everything racing through her mind. Though alcohol helped, she needed a better solution, something less addictive. She had regularly taken life on and bent it to her will but a crutch like alcohol was not in her DNA. It was time for a change, something a little healthier.

Katelyn Green had convinced Codi to accompany her to a political fundraiser that had somehow spun out of control. It started with a glass of Champagne and ended with tequila shots and some slow dancing and body grinding with two D.C. up-and-comers so full of themselves, Codi thought they might explode.

Katelyn's curvy figure and carefree attitude got the boys' attention, but Codi's athletic build and genuine charm kept them around. Codi, however, was only playing wing-girl these days, and her attempt to steer Katelyn toward a more promising guy had failed miserably. After an emergency intervention to save her friend from a giant mistake, Codi managed to get them an Uber home. She had no memory beyond that.

She reached for her phone to check the time. It buzzed just as her fingers touched it, giving her a start. It took several seconds before she looked at the caller ID: Mom. With a practiced flick, she sent the call to voicemail. Codi rubbed her temples, trying to process the call. Her mother hadn't been much more than a skeleton in her closet since she left her college degree behind and joined the Marines as an enlisted soldier. Why was she calling after all these years? Codi put her feet to the floor and sat all the way up. She moved listlessly to the bathroom, the call and her hangover weighing heavy on her mind.

Growing up just north of San Diego had been an optimal experience. Though her father's job as a demolition diver for the Navy sent him away for long periods of time, the reverse was also true. When he was in town he was very active in Codi's life.

She had taken to the water at an early age, and her dad taught her to swim and surf almost before she could walk. He took her camping and taught her basic wilderness skills, including gun safety and shooting. Codi flourished, and she soon found that few people were faster than her in the water.

Her idyllic family dynamic came crashing down the day her father passed. The toll it took on her mother could never be quantified. She spiraled out of control. There were many days when Codi was sure her mother would never come back. It forced Codi to stand on her own two feet at a young age and trust in only one person—herself.

She used her natural athleticism and solid grades to earn a scholarship to UCSD. There, she competed in the nationals in both the crawl and the butterfly. It was a fading connection to her father that she fought hard to keep and to prove her worthy of his love.

Codi would never forget the look on her mom's face when she shared her plans to follow in her father's footsteps and join the military. It caused the widest fissure separating them yet. Codi found herself alone, with no support system, forcing her to succeed or fail on her own. Ultimately, it made her a very driven woman with something to prove, pushing her to the top wherever she went. That drive fueled her acceptance into BUD/S, the elite training program to become a SEAL, a goal very few women achieve.

She held her own and was still standing after several trainees dropped out from the intense pressure. It took a conspired effort from the misogynists around her that left Codi's ankle shattered and her dreams crushed.

Eventually, Codi phoenixed from the ashes of despair and the self-destructive behavior that was consuming her. The experience had changed her in many ways. She found there were some things more important than success. She found a softer side and married it to her driven side. It allowed her to appreciate others in a way she never had before, leading her to ultimately accept a job with the General Services Administration, GSA, as a paper-pushing federal agent. She leveraged that experience with a politically charged case and was recruited into the FBI Special Projects division. Her GSA partner, Joel Strickman, had followed her, as they had already made a name for themselves. Even the President knew who she was.

Codi stepped out of her apartment into an unusually humid morning for a D.C. spring. Her headache now dulled, thanks to a couple of Advil, she was eager to hit the pool and do her ritualistic laps to re-group and kick off her day.

* * *

Joel breathed in the rich aroma of his Don Pablo Supremo, a medium-dark roast from Colombia with citrus notes and a lasting chocolate-walnut finish. He looked over at the small Peace Lily that was growing on his desk, then to the bullet that was housed in a small glycerin filled jar. He smiled at the thought of how brave he had been to don rubber gloves and retrieve the keepsake. He tapped his keyboard to wake up his computer and entered his twenty-seven-digit password. The screen popped to life just as he heard . . .

"Hey."

He turned to see his partner Codi standing in the doorway.

"Morning," he said. "How was your weekend?"

"I'm swearing off alcohol and my friend Katelyn. She's a bad influence. So tomorrow I plan to feel pretty good, thanks"

"If you're determined to have an addiction, I recommend caffeine," Joel added.

"Noted. So where are we on the body?"

"That's the real question, isn't it—where?"

"Let me know what you find. I'm going to be massaging my temples and pondering my current life choices in my office."

Joel nodded absently as Codi left.

The body had vanished, and at this point, there was no trail to follow. It was time to shift gears. Joel pulled up the case files on the Plymouth Mail Truck Robbery and started to go through them. There were a lot of files. This would take days. Agent Daniel Johnson had gone after the suspect Thomas Richards and ended up drowned in a jail cell in an abandoned town under a lake in Greenville, Montana. A mystery, to say the least. What happened to Thomas Richards and the money from the robbery? Too many questions. He needed answers. They could wait.

He started a digital search for the missing radiated body. The clinic in Lake Champlain was just modern enough to have a digital footprint. Joel pulled up phone records, billing, and deliveries. He did a deep dive, but after two hours, he had nothing. He leaned back and took off his glasses. He closed his eyes and pondered the situation. After a moment, he picked up his phone and dialed.

* * *

Codi looked at her phone screen; the missed call from her mother displayed. She hadn't left a message. Codi struggled with a decision, to call her back or not.

As far as she knew, her mom was still in the San Diego area, but that was just a guess. She thought back to the last time they had spoken. The words had been harsh and judgmental. It had not been her finest moment. Codi opened up her computer and did a Google search. Janet Sanders, San Diego. A file of information popped up after a bit of same-name eliminations. Codi placed her mouse on the file and was about to open it.

"Hey, Codi! I think I have something."

She moved her hand away, which had been hovering over her mouse, and turned in her chair.

The main room for the Special Projects division was small by FBI standards. It was square, bullpen-style, with nine desks set within tall office cubicles. There was a carpeted hallway down the middle, and Codi's office was straight across from Joel's. Daylight glowed from windows on the back wall where a small glass conference room was housed. Function ruled over form.

Staying seated, Codi playfully rolled over in her chair across the hallway and into Joel's office. Her hair was held back in a ponytail, and she was wearing blue slacks with a grape-colored Henley. Her sunglasses were still perched on her head from the trip into the office.

"I called the clinic," said Joel, "the one with the missing body. Anyway, I got ahold of an intern who works there part-time. He was on call when the body was removed."

Codi's brows stitched together above bloodshot eyes.

"It seems to have all been above board. He sent me a picture of this."

Joel opened the file, which had a receipt. It showed a pick-up order and company name.

"Somebody picked up a body on the fourth at 5:59 p.m. for a company named . . . named CSI."

"Do we know who authorized this?"

"No. The intern I talked to said a call came in about 3:00 p.m., and the paperwork was all in order."

Codi leaned in closer. "Looks like the intern signed for it."

"It was approved by Doc Canter. The only problem is I asked the doctor about it, and he never signed such a document."

Joel brought up another document that displayed two signatures.

"I compared the two signatures, and sure enough, they don't match."

He pointed to two signatures placed side by side on the screen. "The doctor's real signature is on the left."

"Wow, not even close. I don't think people pay much attention to signatures anymore, what with everything having gone electronic. I used to sign my mom's name on grocery checks when I was a kid. The two signatures were nothing alike, but the bank didn't seem to care."

"I hope you didn't put that on your FBI application," Joel said.

"What?"

"Check forger."

Codi looked over at him for a second. "You might be surprised at the stuff that's not on my application. So who signed this signature?"

Joel was turning red as he answered. "I have no idea, but if you look at the time, it's about seventeen hours before we got there."

"Someone's playing us for fools. See if you can find out something about CSI—other than the TV show."

Joel did a quick search and found a promising lead. "It looks like a front or maybe a shell company to me. I'll do some more digging."

Codi rolled back to her office. She ignored the page that was still up on her computer, her mom's file. Her arm felt leaden as she reached for the mouse. Now was not the time. Instead, she headed for the break room for a glass of water and more Advil. She needed a moment to clear her thoughts.

Joel eventually found a website for the company. It was bright and very colorful.

"Got it," he said to himself, as he read the caption. *CSI, Cadaver Services Incorporated.*

The page looked as if it was geared more toward a preschool than a real business. He spied Codi coming back down the hallway.

"CSI. It's a distribution company for unclaimed corpses. Gross."

Joel clicked on the contact tab and found a phone number. Codi plopped next to him in his extra chair, rubbing the tension out of her neck.

"I wonder if they still have our body," Joel said.

CHAPTER NINE

The Maple Grove Strip Mall was at least thirty years old. The faded blue stucco had a gray pallor, and the ivory wood trim was starting to peel. There were no maples, let alone a grove of them, within sight. The 7-11 that had anchored the facility with the most foot traffic had long since been replaced with Woodside Liquor Store. It was robbed with regularity and now employed a full-time on-site security guard.

Joel checked his watch as Codi tested the locked door to suite E. It was five minutes to nine in the morning. The small lettering on the entrance said CSI and nothing more. The mostly empty parking lot said right place, wrong time. The morning sun was just starting to clear the buildings and painted their white rental car orange.

Joel had tried calling several times. The number from the website rang and rang with no answer and no option to leave a message. It was an odd way to run a business. In the end, Codi and Joel road-tripped it up to the

94

verdant rolling hills of Conshohocken, just northwest of Philadelphia. Codi leaned her back against the wall as Joel tried calling one more time. She was wearing her traditional navy pants with a white shirt and a navy coat. She wore her hair down to match her mood. The four-hour drive from the FBI motor pool that began just before five in the morning had left her lackluster.

"I was at a restaurant last night and saw Agent Collins with his wife," Joel said.

Codi tried to ignore the statement, but she could tell that her partner wanted to talk.

"Oh, yeah? Chubby Collins or Angry Collins?"

"Chubby."

"What was that like?"

She had been uncommunicative for most of the morning ride, but now with the sun out, she was starting to wake up.

Joel continued, "I don't know, but they seemed . . . happy."

"That's nice," Codi said without effort.

"I wonder . . . I wonder if that's in the cards for us."

"What, dinner in a restaurant?"

Joel shot daggers at her snarky reply. "Funny."

They stood in silence for a minute.

Codi offered, "I think that whatever makes you happy is what's in the cards for you, Joel. If you will it and work toward it, you can make it a reality. Of course, happiness is not the same for everyone."

"Just like love is not the same for everyone," Joel added.

"Exactly."

Codi supported her head back against the wall and continued, "We all want it in one form or another. Love of money, love of self, love of fame, love from another. Some people even love to share their love with others. But it all adds up to one thing: Happiness comes from getting the love we seek."

"I don't know. I've seen some very unhappy rich people," Joel countered.

"I didn't say true happiness, Joel." Codi turned and made eye contact with her partner. "I think true happiness comes from giving love not getting love."

Their conversation was interrupted as a 1978 shiny, baby blue Cadillac Eldorado Biarritz pulled into a stall next to them. The 425 cubic-inch 8.2-liter engine rumbled to a stop. A short woman about fifty-five years old stepped out of the car and strutted in their direction. She had wide hips and a wide face, which was covered in an excess of foundation and rouge, and eyes holding up a heavy coat of mascara. Her hips shimmied from side to side in her leather pants as she walked. A bright red silk blouse housed large breasts that moved in time with her steps. The only thing that didn't move was her hair. Aqua Net was alive and well.

She smiled through red lips with impossibly white teeth set against a spider web of smoker's lines.

"Are you two beautiful people waiting for me?"

Joel was taken aback by her forwardness.

"We are if this is the door you're headed for," said Codi as she straightened up.

"Well, it must be your lucky day. Come on in, and tell me how I can help you."

She looked back at Joel. "Aren't you just the cutest thing?"

She opened the front door and deactivated the alarm. With a flip of her wrist, she turned on the lights and gestured for them to follow.

"Is, is this CSI, Cadaver Services Incorporated?" Joel asked, still a bit flummoxed from her comment.

The woman stared him down. Her head cocked to the side for a better look. "Dang, you are a cute one."

Codi stifled a smirk and saved the comment to her memory bank. She would use that line on her partner at a later date.

"You betcha," the woman said. "Cadaver Services Incorporated. How can I help you?"

Codi looked down at a small business card holder. She could make out the name Patty McGuire. She pulled out her badge and showed it to the woman. "This is Agent Strickman and I'm Agent Sanders, but you can call us Joel and Codi. Are you Patty?"

"Yeah, Patty, but everyone calls me Fat Pat."

Joel had to ask, "Fat Pat?" The woman didn't seem particularly overweight to him.

"Yeah. Used to be a lot heavier. Went on an extreme diet and lost seventy pounds."

Curiosity got the better of Joel. "Extreme diet?"

"Six months of chemo. Lost the weight and somehow even managed to quit smoking along the way. So far, no more cancer. 'Ceptin' now I'm missing half my liver."

"Wow. Congratulations?" Joel said in confusion.

"Yeah, cancer's a real bite. So, what do you two beauties need?"

Joel explained their situation and Fat Pat quickly caught on. "Do you have the order number?" she asked.

Joel brought up the image of the delivery receipt on his phone and slid his fingers apart to zoom in on the image. He read the numbers off to Fat Pat, and she wrote them down. She then turned on her computer and let it warm up.

"So what is it you do here?" Joel ventured.

"Bodies. We're in the body business, hon. You'd be amazed at the need out there. Colleges, teaching hospitals, labs. The demand seems to always outweigh the supply."

"Sounds like a good business model," Codi said.

"Sure, business is booming," Fat Pat said. "I haven't even had time to update our website or move to new offices."

Joel and Codi shared a look. That explained the bad phone number on the website.

Fat Pat picked up a pair of readers and leaned forward. "00539," she said to herself as she input the last of the numbers Joel had given her. "Okay, here we go. Looks like your John Doe went to the farm."

* * *

Joel could smell it before he could see it. The sweet stench of carrion was in the air. He pulled the rental car into the parking lot and placed his hand over his mouth as he exited their vehicle.

They had dropped off their borrowed car at the Philadelphia FBI offices and taken a short flight down to Knoxville, Tennessee. From there they rented a car and drove out to the University of Tennessee's Forensic Anthropology Center.

The tall red brick building with a gray roof was set off from the rest of the campus and was home to one of the most distinctive studies on the planet. The decay of the human body. Commonly referred to as the Body Farm, it is a vast fenced-in space of corpses all rotting and decaying in various stages and under dissimilar conditions.

The logo on the door was a circle around a human skull in profile with the words, Forensic Anthropology Center. Codi pushed the door open for Joel as he lagged behind. The fresh air-conditioned atmosphere inside was a welcome relief. She watched as once inside, her partner visibly calmed down and started to breathe normally. They were met by an old man in his late sixties. He was spry and had a twinkle in his eyes. His smile parted a nice white Vandyke as he shook hands with Codi and Joel. He was dressed casually in jeans and a light blue collared shirt with the sleeves rolled up. He wore a thick belt with a large brass buckle.

"Dr. Billie Blunt. Nice of you two agents to visit us. We do a lot of work here at the Farm for the FBI, but rarely do we get field agents, mostly lab techs and MEs, that sort of thing, you know. How can we be of service?"

Joel explained about the missing corpse that had apparently been shipped to the facility. He opened a page on his phone and showed Dr. Blunt the paperwork to substantiate his claim. The doctor listened with care and slowly nodded.

"And you don't know who authorized the shipment?" the doctor asked.

"Not that we can find so far." Joel added, "The order was faxed over from a blind number."

"I didn't know people still had Fax machines," Doctor Blunt said.

"I know, right?" Codi quipped.

The doctor scratched absently at his beard.

"Hmmm. Very curious. It is unlikely for us to get a donation that hasn't been fully vetted."

He turned and started walking away. "Follow me. Let's see if we can get to the bottom of this."

Joel and Codi followed him to a back door that opened to a concrete path ending at a wooden gate in a tall wooden perimeter fence. He lifted the latch and led them inside. Codi glanced back at her partner who was now breathing through his shirt, as each step forward increased the intensity of the smell of rotting flesh.

"Do you know much about the Body Farm?" Doctor Blunt asked.

Joel shook his head and mumbled, "No," through his shirt.

The doctor seemed right at home. "The Body Farm is a research facility for the study of human decay," he said. "Since 1987, we have tracked and followed all the steps of decomp, from blowflies to maggots, even the effect of different soil types and temperatures. We have hundreds of bodies all laid out to decompose in different scenarios. It all gets tracked, photographed, computerized, and standardized, giving us a very accurate decomposition timeline. So when a body is discovered in a crime, whether underground, underwater, or even in the trunk of an abandoned car, we can tell how long it has been there, along with many other variables that are critical to solving cases."

Joel was turning a shade of green as they passed body after body, laid out in various stages of decomp.

"Hey, Karl!" the doctor called out.

An impossibly tall African-American man angled over to the group. He was bald with hunched shoulders and a dead gaze that belied his shining smile.

"This is Karl. He keeps me organized."

Introductions went around, and the doctor briefed him on their situation.

"He went into the swamp," Karl said, looking at the paperwork on Joel's phone.

"Ah, you are in for a real treat, the swamp. Come on, let's see if we can fish him out."

Codi followed Doctor Blunt's lead, but Joel was fearful of what kind of *treat* was in store. He tried to keep his vision on the tall hunched gentleman in front of him, but his peripheral vision was filled with horror. To his right was a woman with red hair. She was face down and her skin had blackened and constricted around her skeleton from sun and the elements. To his left was a man whose guts lay strewn about on the ground, all covered with flies and maggots. It was macabre, his worst nightmare come to life. He slammed his eyes closed and tried to block out the images, but a tree root caught his foot, and he tripped and fell, landing inches from a screaming skull. Joel let out a whimper and jumped back to his feet, running to catch up with the others.

Dr. Blunt led them to a swampy area that bubbled and oozed with the smell of carrion and gore. Joel tried to stifle his gag reflex as he looked on from a distance. Codi seemed to be taking it all in stride.

Karl reached for a pole that was mounted near the fence. It looked like a rescue pole found at many public swimming pools. It had a curved end for hooking bodies and pulling them to the edge. He knew right where to place it and with only two attempts, pulled a soggy rotted corpse from the murky depths. It had puffed with gasses and reeked of crap and decomp, but you could still make out the Asian heritage of the person. Joel looked away. Once the carcass had been pulled to shore, Codi took out a small handheld device and turned it on. The Geiger counter immediately started to beep at a high rate. All three men immediately backed away. Joel ran to a nearby tree and tossed his lunch. He could take no more.

"That's him," Codi said as the device in her hand squealed.

* * *

The rental car wound its way back to Knoxville. There was a large splotch on the windshield from the backside of a bird of prey. Joel hit the wipers, but there was no fluid and the nasty white and gray poop smeared the glass. He leaned left so he could see out the small gap in the swiped stain. He was still pale from his farm experience.

"Seriously!"

The sun was done for the day. It had taken almost three hours to get an ERTU, Evidence Response Team Unit, on site to safely secure the irradiated body. The two agents were tired and dirty, and the first ten minutes of the drive were spent in silence, the foul odor of death clinging to their clothes and hair.

"Today has been a day of smells," Joel announced weakly.

Codi was looking at her phone. She glanced over at him with a puzzled expression.

"That lady back in Conshohocken. The CSI one. She smelled like my grandmother."

"You mean the, 'dang, you are a cute one,' lady?" Codi said imitating the woman.

"Real funny."

"I think it was her hairspray, Joel. She smelled like she'd used a whole can of Aqua Net to get that beehive to stand so still."

"Aqua Net. Yeah, that was it. My grandma loved that stuff." The corners of Joel's lips tipped up at the thought, and just as suddenly, they dropped. "And that guy next to us on the flight over. What was that smell?"

"Curry. He smelled like a curry factory," Codi said.

"Yeah, that was intense. Now, I smell like a rotting corpse," Joel added, still leaning to look through the smeared windshield.

Codi did a sniff check on her sleeve and was not happy with the result. "It's going to take some doing to get this smell out of my skin and hair." She continued, "My clothes are a goner. Let's find a hotel next to a clothing store and someplace to clean this windshield."

Joel agreed, and they drove on, looking for a place to stay for the night.

"So were you and your grandma close?"

Joel nodded his answer while thinking back. "She was the one who raised me. Both my parents were career . . . *are* career professionals. She looked after me until I was sixteen."

Codi glanced over at Joel.

"Stroke," he said. "It took her in the night."

She nodded in understanding, remembering how devastating it had been for her when her own father had unexpectedly passed. Then something up ahead caught her attention.

"Look! A Choice Hotel next to a Kohl's."

* * *

Carlo Bustamante was an alias. He had used many. But living in the town of Lagos, it worked. Lagos was a quaint beach town in southern Portugal, famous for its walled town, coved beaches, and laid-back attitude. He was staying in a bright, green-tiled three-story building with white trim, arched windows, and unusually rounded corners. It dated back to the late 1800s and was located just a few blocks from the center of town.

The coastline and town were dotted with hotels and tourists. It made for a good place to blend in, as visiting faces in town seemed to change with the tide, and none of the locals cared about anything other than the income they generated.

His work normally required basements and caves, but he hated them with a passion. Carlo had rented the top floor of the building and played the role of rich bachelor artist. After a few attempts at different legends, he found that, so far, this one allowed him the most freedom.

Carlo's pockmarked face and eyes the color of lead hid a superior IQ. His average height and looks helped make him forgettable. Plus careful management of his identities had so far made it impossible for the authorities to ID or track him.

In reality, he was an artist with a twist. His bomb-making skills were becoming legendary in the black market. And as an artist in mixed-metal sculpture, his reputation in the art world was also growing. Mixed-metal sculpture required him to have a large work area and many pieces of equipment, with frequent shipments to his door of various chemicals and supplies. He kept his cover going just enough to make and sell a few pieces of sculpture to belie suspicion. His current project was a flying horse built with an iron skeleton covered in tarnished copper and brass. The thin copper skin was purposefully molded over the bones to give it a skeletal, otherworldly feel. The next step was to patina the copper to a greenish-blue.

Carlo opened the two cases that had been delivered a few moments earlier. He immediately recognized the contents. This was the last piece of his other latest masterpiece. He pulled the cans of coffee beans out of the boxes and placed them on his workbench. He looked for a can opener and then began the process of opening all nine cans. Planted within the dark roasted beans was a small lead-lined container about the size of a baby food jar. He placed all nine containers in a row and moved over to a machine he had cloned and modified for a very specific purpose.

Carlo applied a recently printed sticker to the side of his creation DJ-FOG 700 and set it to the side. He suited up in protective clothing and began the process of opening each container and grinding the contents down to a micro-fine powder. He then poured the powder into a special container built within the DJ-FOG 700.

* * *

Once the lab turned in its report on the body, Codi and Joel found themselves at a standstill. It was an Asian male, twenty-eight years old, most likely Malaysian or Indonesian. He had no photo or fingerprints of any kind on record. He appeared to have never been to a dentist or a DMV. They checked all the foreign countries' databases they had access to and still had nothing. He was a true ghost. The technician picked up trace elements under his fingernails and would run DNA and chemical tests on his hair and skin. That report would take a week to complete. The radiation was also a mystery. There was no known source or chemical fingerprint on file for its origin.

"I thought all uranium could be identified by its chemical makeup," Codi said.

"That was true, until now," Joel replied. "I'm guessing it will be something our government and maybe others get very concerned about. A new unknown source of radioactive material—that can't be good. Things have just gotten a bit more complicated."

The only thing left to do now was to wait on trace to see if they could shed some light on the case.

"Let's get some coffee," Codi said.

"I know the just the place," Joel said.

CHAPTER TEN

The electro-magnet was enormous but essential for the forty-inch cyclotron. It spun the U-235 and used the electromagnetic field to separate the lighter U-235 atoms from the heavier U-238. Then they would bombard the elements with deuterons, creating more U-238 and a small percentage of Np-239, neptunium. Np-239 has a half-life of two-and-a-half days, at which point it decays to Pu-239, plutonium. Plutonium has a much longer half-life and can be used in reactors and weapons. But the ore being refined here was too flawed to be used in either. The resulting corruption left the final material just below reactor-grade and well below weapons-grade. To purify it would require many millions of dollars in high-tech centrifuges and technology that only major governments possessed. But that wasn't required for what they had in mind.

Dr. Garth Baghdadis used robotic arms to load the radioactive material into a shielded housing. He had thick glasses to match a healthy head of wavy hair. He wore a white lab coat and cowboy boots. Once inside the housing, the material was placed in a lead-lined case capable of blocking all outgoing emissions. After two weeks of round-the-clock effort, they had their first delivery—one-and-a-half kilos of refined ore about the size of an ostrich egg.

The Greek-born, Ukrainian-reared physicist had left his home for the life of a freelancer after a lab accident caused the deaths of three colleagues. The Ukrainian government had covered up the accident and laid blame squarely at the doctor's feet. In an instant, he had gone from the world of science to the world of politics. He knew his days were numbered and his future there, bleak.

Dr. Baghdadis packed his bags and left Ukraine, never looking back. He had found that a man with his talents could make a good living from those with flexible morals and deep pockets. He set his sights on income rather than science and discovery, and the world embraced him.

His current task was the transmutation of surprisingly clean uranium ore into a much more potent element. The needed equipment had taken a lot of time to reassemble, as it had to be brought in with extreme caution and often as individual parts. This was about as black of a site as the physicist had ever worked. But the inside of a mountain was the perfect place to keep a low profile. It naturally shielded both emissions and looky-loos.

His current employer had been slow to listen to his initial concerns and recommendations, and several workers had been irreversibly irradiated. Now they had procedures in place that kept the workers safe and the product flowing.

Dr. Baghdadis had a small crew of trained technicians that ran the equipment necessary for the process. They cycled shifts, and things were finally running smoothly. The bonuses he had in place meant this would be his last job. He just needed to stay the course for the next two years, and then he could walk away to a small-town lifestyle in a warm climate.

The two shielded cases were placed in crates carrying Poudretteite that was mined in the upper tunnels. From there, it was shipped to a gemologist in St. Johns, Newfoundland. The gemologist would take the cases down to the harbor and hand them off to a contact that would load them onto his trawler and go fishing for cod in the Labrador Sea. Once at sea, he would go to a predetermined set of coordinates where the cases would be delivered to a larger vessel waiting under the cover of darkness.

It was a simple but effective system, ensuring the finished product would arrive at its destination without issue. It also allowed each cog in the wheel of the operation to know only their part in it and nothing about the big picture. So, should one of them have a run-in with law enforcment, there would be very little blowback.

* * *

Matt turned off the lamp on his small gray metal desk. It was a throwback from the forties, and if it could talk, it probably had a few stories to tell. The room was functional 1950s government, with a fresh coat of gray paint. The tests had been conducted at a remote military base close to the New Mexico-Arizona border, far from prying eyes. He picked up his laptop and exited. His CO, or at least that's how the lead science officer envisioned himself, called him from the hallway.

"Nice work out there today, Dr. Campbell. I think you have done the world a real service."

He was referring to the FCBT that Matt and his grandfather had invented and built.

"Thank you, sir," Matt said.

"With today's successful firing, we have completed all our tests here. Take tomorrow off before we head back."

"Thank you," Matt said hollowly.

In his mind, his project had run its course, and he was now thinking about what would be next. He'd been feeling less and less a critical piece of the project he built. It was maddening at first, but now he was just apathetic. He had a couple of lines in the water, and he just needed to tend them a bit. Hopefully, one or both would develop into something interesting, but he was done working like this. He needed to get a life, not just be a slave to the system.

Work had always consumed Matt, but lately, Codi had started to infiltrate his thoughts. Working out of the Boston area on a secured base had pulled Codi and him in different directions, each focused on their careers. It became the norm, and it stunted the growth of their burgeoning relationship. He loved her, but careers and relationships always seemed to be at odds, and this was no different. It was a game they were both losing.

Recently, however, things had improved. They seemed to be making the effort it took for a long-distance relationship to work. Each made time in their schedules to get together regularly, and things were better. Matt thought long and hard about her, and he was trying to figure a way to move them into something more permanent. He was no expert when it came to women, and Codi was sure to spook if he pushed too hard. He processed his next move as he watched his boss walk away down the narrow hallway.

He needed to tell her how he really felt. He needed to say the words: I love you. Boy, that was going to be tough. Timing would be everything.

What was he going to do with a day off in the middle of nowhere? It was at that moment, he made a decision—time for a change. But first, a road trip to Roswell to see some aliens.

* * *

Jal Zayid sent the text that would be the Go code for his current operation. He was sipping peach nectar from his balcony overlooking the Willebroekse Vaart River in North Brussels. He could just make out the National Rugby Club grounds in the distance. Jal was a man driven by opportunity. He had watched as terrorism had grown around the globe. Even his home in Istanbul had been a participant.

As a Muslim, he had spent his youth in mosques, following the teachings of the Qur'an. His parents wanted the best for him and sent him to Oxford to study business. While he was away at college, a suicide bomber took out a café across from The Ecumenical Patriarchate Cathedral a few blocks from his home. His parents had been sharing a morning coffee when the bomber walked in and turned the place into a kill box.

Jal tried to find solace in a local mosque in Oxford but seemed to flounder. He dropped out of college and moved back to take over his family's business, only to find his estranged Uncle Taz had drained the family bank accounts and disappeared with the funds. To survive, Jal was forced to sell his childhood home and the family business. It was like cutting off one's heritage. He said goodbye to the life he had known and left on a journey of his own.

With a pocket full of lira and brewing disregard for those around him, whether they were Muslim, Christian, or any other religion, Jal learned how to trade for profit. Information or goods—it didn't matter. He grew cold inside as money became his new god.

He used his newfound wealth to track down his uncle. He was living up the coast from Mersin, a mid-sized Turkish city along the Mediterranean Sea. Jal had gone there with the idea of confronting Taz and negotiating with his uncle. But as he walked up the polished stone walkway to the garden estate, anger flashed through him. This had all been purchased by stealing from him. The large pool, the immaculate home, even the half-naked girls around the pool. He took a moment to compose himself and then rang the doorbell.

Taz seemed weary, as he invited his unexpected guest into his home.

"Uncle, it has been too long."

"Yes. I have often wondered what happened to you," Taz replied, embracing his nephew. "Come, let's take tea by the pool."

Taz clapped his hands, and a young woman appeared as if from nowhere. He ordered tea and biscuits to be brought to them then escorted Jal to a poolside table. A tea setting was placed and the woman poured two cups. Jal fought the bile pressing at the back of his throat, his hatred for his uncle scarcely concealed.

The small talk was mind numbing, and twice, Jal had to check himself when his uncle started to brag. Jal had let on that he was just there to reconnect. After all, Taz was the only family he had left. Taz seemed to accept this reasoning and grew more open as the conversation continued.

After tea, Taz took Jal on a tour of his home, going room by room and speaking with a flourish as he described the furnishings and décor. Jal kept a false smile plastered on his face as an uncontrollable rage burned inside.

"This is my favorite room," Taz boasted.

It was a large, open area with plush seating, recessed lighting, and several display cases prominently featured.

"I have collected a few things from my travels," Taz said over his shoulder as he opened a display case and removed an item.

"This is a sistrum." Taz held up a bronze contraption that had a handle and a small, decorated cage on top. There were two horizontal bars that held loose plates that could slide and jingle when shaken. Taz gave it a wiggle and a ringing sound filled the room. "It's from the early Bronze Age and is considered the first musical instrument. The Museum in Ankara has one, but mine is in better shape." He replaced it in the display case and moved to the back of a leather couch and from the small table behind it, lifted a golden curved dagger encrusted with jewels.

"Sixteenth Century Ottoman Empire." Taz handed it to Jal. "Exquisite, isn't it?"

"May I?" Jal asked.

"Of course." Taz smiled at his nephew.

Jal made a show of pulling the curved dagger from its golden sheath. It was engraved and sharpened to a fine point. He held it to the light, rotating it slowly. "Truly magnificent. Aren't you afraid someone will steal it?"

"I have a very sophisticated security system." Taz motioned to a camera on the wall. "Everything that happens on the property is recorded, all safely secured in my panic room, which is quite impregnable. Plus, the first sign of trouble and I just press this." He lifted a small transmitter that hung on a chain around his neck. "The house locks down, and the guards you met on your way in? Let's just say they will shoot first."

"Incredible, all of this. You have done well for yourself, Uncle." Jal waved his hand around the room, and then slid the dagger back into its scabbard. "You even have your own panic room. Wow."

Taz eyed him for a beat and then nodded. "Would you like to see it? It is quite ingenious. Let me show you."

"If you insist," Jal said to placate his uncle.

Taz walked to a large oil painting on the wall. It depicted the Ottomans routing the Mongrels in open battle. He pressed a hidden button and the painting slid up into the ceiling, revealing a seam on the wall and a keypad. Taz placed his whole hand on the pad and the panel slid open revealing a small room. They went inside.

"One-inch reinforced armored steel. It would take a tank to get in here."

"Impressive," Jal said, as he handed the dagger back.

Taz grabbed the scabbard and pulled it toward himself. Jal held tight to the handle, leaving Taz with nothing but the scabbard.

"Oh, sorry. Here," Jal said as he thrust the dagger into his uncle's torso and left it there, the hatred for the man finally resolved on his face. Taz tried to reach the panic button on his chain, but Jal pulled his arm away and watched with curiosity as Taz slowly dropped to the floor. Jal leaned in close, mesmerized by it all. He had never killed a person before, and the experience was otherworldly. He could see life leaving the body. It was nothing like the movies.

"That's for robbing me of my birthright," Jal hissed.

Taz moved his lips, but nothing came out.

"Enjoy your panic room."

Jal watched as his uncle's eyes fluttered and closed for good. He stood up and looked around. His heart was still pounding, and he willed himself to calm down and think. The room was the size of a small bedroom. There were shelves on three walls with supplies, food, water, first aid and weapons. There was a small bed to one side next to a toilet and a battery-powered lamp. The fourth wall had monitors mounted on it that showed images of the entire complex. Below them were a computer, servers, and storage for the security system. The second shelf on the right wall held four bottles of Black Label Jack Daniels. Jal shook his head at how far his uncle had lost his way. He took the bottles and emptied the contents over his uncle and the electronics. He added any and all paper he found to the mixture.

Jal pulled the dagger from the corpse and used it to sever the right hand. He stepped outside the panic room and struck his lighter. With a flick of the wrist, the lighter landed in the alcohol and paper, igniting it. He pressed his uncle's dead hand against the door scanner and the panel began to close. He tossed the hand back into the room and watched as the oil painting lowered into place, entombing the crime scene. Everything was now sealed behind an impregnable wall. Jal ran to a bathroom and washed his face with shaking hands. He took a moment in the mirror to collect himself before strolling out the front door as if he had all the time in the world.

The incident changed Jal forever. Revenge was sweet, but murder, when required, was no longer foreign to him. He used it carefully and effectively, always preferring a knife.

It wasn't long before he realized there was money to be made in terrorism, the very thing that had flung him down his current path. He embraced it wholeheartedly, too dead inside to realize the irony of it all.

Most terrorist cells were not terribly sophisticated. They had a hatred for the West and enough followers to point and shoot a gun in an ordered direction. He would market to them. He could provide the cutting edge technology and cleverness that would give them the success and credit they clambered for. Because with success, came money and followers.

As a middleman, once the operation was set up, he could wash his hands and move on to the next project. There was no actual involvement for him. He just put A and B together for a nice profit. It was a good way to strike back at the West and stay inconspicuous. It was also a good business model, and business was booming—literally.

After sending the Go code, Jal dropped his phone on the floor of the balcony and smashed it to pieces with his foot. A smile grew as he stepped back inside his current suite. He moved around a lot, living from hotel to hotel, with no one place to tie him down. He believed routine and commonplace were what got you noticed and killed.

The woman across the desk of his rented suite seemed uncurious. She had black hair and all the right curves. She was a mover and a shaker, and together, they were going to make a lot of money. Jal moved back to his chair and sat down across from her. She had all the markings of a Westerner, but like himself, had allegiance to no one.

"It is done," he said.

"The news will say when it's done, not you," came the curt reply.

"You will see. My man is a most ingenious person, and he has never failed me. Not only will it be a success, but the authorities will be left spinning in circles with no clues to follow."

"I suppose."

Dorthia paused for a beat and then suddenly looked Jal in the eyes. This had an unexpected effect on the man. She was an unknown woman of power, much like himself. "We are now fully up and operational," she said. "My guess is two years of uninterrupted supply, but I am thinking more like one if you continue so publicly."

"I paid you handsomely, and I will do as I see fit. I have many sources of technology. You are but one."

"Of course, how you run things is up to you, but this is not a business one grows old in," Dorthia added.

"True, an exit strategy is wise, but business is on the rise. We have just developed something especially nasty in one of my bio labs, and I can't wait to try it. So it is not yet my time. I still plan to ride the camel to the mountaintop."

Dorthia nodded with just a tip of her head. In America, she'd heard the phrase making hay while the sun shines. But to each, their own. She stood and picked up her purse. Jal licked his lips at the figure scarcely contained in the blue silk blouse and black pencil slacks.

"I will expect the same amount every month for as long as it lasts," he said. "Payment on delivery, of course."

She nodded and turned to go.

"Are you sure you need to leave so soon? I have some very good Dotatto figs."

She turned around and considered the loaded offer. Jal was a handsome man. He was almost six-feet in height with brown eyes and well-kept curly hair. He liked the finer things in life, and even though he clung to a few of his Muslim customs, like no alcohol, he was a man with passion. His smile hid his true personality, but Dorthia knew she could handle any man and their eccentricities.

"My flight isn't for another two hours," she said as she stepped back inside the room and closed the door.

She circled Jal like a feline considering its options. Attack or purr. Jal watched her movements with his own predatory eyes. Her impossibly dark green eyes never wavered. Her shiny black hair and her full figure, just visible behind her blue silk scoop-neck blouse.

It was two alphas fighting each other to see who would be on top. Little was said as they stripped their clothes and moved to the bedroom. Jal pressed Dorthia up against the wall as he smashed his lips against hers. Dorthia rotated Jal around until his back was against the wall. This continued for a few minutes as they let tongues probe mouths and necks.

The next hour was filled with cold, hard passion, as each tried to exert their dominance over the other while still enjoying the ride.

* * *

Dusseldorf is situated on the Rhine River in western Germany. It is a combination of modern and historic architecture. Given that, in April 1943, over 700 RAF bombers wreaked havoc on the city, leveling most of the architecture. Any remaining historic buildings were few and far between. It is now considered among the top six most livable cities in the world, with bike and walking paths throughout the city. It has a good combination of tech and financial business to attract sophisticated, intelligent workers.

The Dusseldorf Hauptbahnhof is an older, large, brown brick rectangle with tall vertical windows and a massive clock tower on one end. The railway station was opened in October of 1891, following the nationalization of the German railway companies. The main western entrance was updated in the 1980s with a steel and glass portico, clashing with the rest of the historic design. The Hauptbahnhof boasts close to a quarter-million travelers per day.

Inside is a large open terminal with shops, ticket booths, and plenty of signage. There are more than thirty-four different rail lines intersecting the station. People come and go without much thought beyond their own needs. On Fridays, they often invite live music to perform in the terminal as passengers endure the last workday of the week.

Today, in an effort to be more politically correct, a Middle Eastern band named Nova was performing. To call it a band was a bit of an overstatement. There was a keyboard with canned rhythm and bass playing a repetitive tune. The single member of Nova, Abd al Bari, stood at the microphone playing a traditional Oud. His name had been given to him by his trainer at the Haram Brotherhood, and it meant *Servant of*

Allah. He had undergone a very different training regimen than his other brothers in the fight against the West.

Abd was warbling a classic folk tune as he strummed his instrument. The raised stage held his gear and four rotating colored spotlights, which moved to the beat. The DJ-FOG 700 fog machine spewed mist into the crowd as they passed by, creating a party atmosphere. Children ran and screamed as they played in the fog. The occasional coin was dropped into his tip jar, but for the most part, no one paid the musician any mind. Some travelers were even offended at what they perceived as inappropriate noise.

By 11:00 a.m., Abd was sweating profusely, but he played on. By 1:00 p.m., he was bleeding from his nose, and his ability to follow and sing with the rhythm track was waning. By 2:00 p.m., Abd al Bari was dead.

The effect was much quicker than expected. Within several hours the first victims, mostly children, made their way to the hospital. They were experiencing severe nausea and diarrhea, followed by a high fever. Within a day, the hospitals became overcrowded, and at the forty-eight-hour mark, it was identified as a terrorist attack. The Haram Brotherhood claimed responsibility and followed up with a press release, announcing it as a great blow to the infidels.

Once the press got wind of the gravity of the situation, the panic level escalated. Germany was forced to close its borders and implement martial law in a vain attempt to stop the unstoppable. It took almost a week to identify the source of the radiation poisoning: the DJ-FOG 700 fog machine rigged with highly radioactive particles in the smoke. Once inhaled, your fate was sealed. After a week, there were forty-two deaths and many more expected. The authorities scrambled for suspects and evidence, but their only lead was a dead singer and his band's fake website.

* * *

Dennis Paige was one of the first people to know about the attack. As a Homeland Security agent, he specialized in radiological terrorism and was tasked with finding and stopping it before it could make it to America. He worked under the aptly named Countering Weapons of Mass Destruction Office, which partnered with the National Counterterrorism Center for threat analysis and strategic planning.

Homeland was a complicated beast with many tentacles, but they had somehow managed to streamline their operation and stay one step ahead of the threats. It all had to do with how information flowed and was received. Each office reported directly to an assistant secretary who had direct access to the deputy secretary for quick action and response when needed, along with assistance from any other government departments.

Dennis was forty-ish, round-ish and persistent-ish. He had given most of his life to law enforcement and had developed a work style that required the least possible effort while still getting results. He had tried and failed at his marriage and was now content to just do his own thing, which included putting on some extra pounds. He had considered a dog, but even that was too much of a commitment.

Years back, Dennis had been part of a team that stopped a Russian plutonium core from getting into Miami. The arrests made him with the agency, and now he felt as if he had done his part for his country. Time to keep his head down and save for retirement.

Interpol was working with the German authorities, and the FBI had loaned out some experts from their Counter Terrorism Division on the latest attack. As the day progressed, Dennis kept a close eye on the events at the Dusseldorf Hauptbahnhof as they unfolded: what was known and what was conjecture.

The Haram Brotherhood, who claimed responsibility for the attack, was a group based in northern Iraq. Up until now, it had been involved in small-time terrorist events, including a few suicide bombings in Egypt. This was way out of their league and their first step into the European arena, plus it was way too technical for them.

The group had used an RDD, a radiological dispersion device. The fog machine was custom made to look like something out of a costume store. Inside, however, it was designed to disperse highly radioactive micro particles hidden within the fog. Once inhaled, the victim would succumb to severe radiation poisoning within a few days. The death toll was now up to eighty-seven. Experts were suggesting as many as three hundred persons would die a slow and horrible death within the month.

It was an ingenious and especially nasty act. Dennis read through the report, still wondering how such a backwoods Islamic group could have the savvy to design and pull this off. There had been no identifying pieces used in the fog machine, just custom or readily available parts. It had been built by someone who should be on their radar. Dennis had it on good authority that they were being funded through a Nigeria-based Islamist terrorist group with ties to Saudi money, but that had never been proven. There was a notation at the bottom of one page in the report that caught his attention. "Unknown."

He read up a bit to see what it referred to. The radiation signature of the weapon was from a source that, as of yet, had not been identified. That was strange. Most of the enriched uranium used in terror weapons in the world came from Russian, Ukrainian, or Kazakhstan sources. They were all mapped and their signatures identified, providing a trail for investigators to follow that led from the source to the final terrorist act. He rubbed his temples, as a headache seemed to be mounting. A new or unknown source of radioactive material: this was troubling.

* * *

Carlo Bustamante watched as his Portuguese passport blackened and curled in the flames as it burned in the metal trashcan. A smile came to his face. His radioactive fog machine had been a smash success for his client. It had only been a test run, but they were eager to use him for something bigger. Carlo knew that too much time in one location was bad on many fronts. It was time to relocate. He packed what he needed and donated everything else to the University of Algarve art department. The professor had been giddy when the equipment arrived. A plasma cutter, forge, and a small, computerized CNC machine were the highlights. It did Carlo's heart good to give something back to a community that had harbored him for the last eight months. There, he had produced some of his finest work to date, and it had been used to do some real good in the war against the West. But after the success of his latest weapon, it was time to disappear again. He read the name on his new passport: Carl Savage. It was a good name for a person going to America.

CHAPTER ELEVEN

WASHINGTON, D.C. – FBI FIELD OFFICE – 3rd FLOOR – 9:02 A.M.

Joel walked into the conference room at 9:02 a.m. He was surprised to find he was the last one to arrive. He quickly sat down while clearing his throat in an awkward manner. Sitting at the head of the table was SSA Brian Fescue. Codi was on his right, and a man in a black suit and tie was on his left.

"Morning, all," Brian said. "Thanks for coming in on a Saturday. We have a delicate situation that needs immediate attention. As you know, I had the radiological signature of our body sent out to Homeland and a couple of other agencies. Oh, almost forgot. Agent Sanders and Strickman, this is Agent Paige from Homeland Security."

They each nodded a quick and efficient hello. Brian picked up where he left off.

"As is the practice with this sort of thing, it was sent out. It happens that the signature or fingerprint of the radiation that killed our victim is from a yet unknown source."

"Scary, if you ask me," Codi said.

"Exactly, Agent Sanders," Dennis replied. He leaned forward as he spoke. "The sample you sent to us has a few identifying markers but is not consistent with any known uranium mine. On top of that, we have a signature match to the radiation used in the Dusseldorf attack."

"Wait," Joel interrupted, "you're saying the radiation that was on our body matched the radiation used in the RDD in the German train station attack?"

Dennis nodded. "They are identical. It is a poor attempt at making plutonium. The ore is corrupt, well below reactor-grade, but still very deadly, especially when ingested or inhaled."

"That's why an RDD was used?" Codi asked.

"That's what we're thinking," Dennis said. "The smoke machine spewed and obscured the deadly particles."

"Plus, every person that passed through the area just stirred the stuff back up again," Codi said.

"I'm afraid so. Had they used the material in a dirty bomb it would have been less effective."

"Because it has to be inhaled?" Codi asked.

"Exactly. A bomb sends the radiation into the air, but it scares away anyone that survived, whereas the smoke was non-threatening, and people just moved through it hour after hour."

Joel said, "I read an article in *The New York Times* about a thing called a smoky bomb, instead of a dirty bomb. Seems like somebody else read the article as well."

They realized the truth in Joel's comment.

Brian pushed the meeting along. "Were you able to identify the corpse?"

Codi responded. "Nothing from any database we have access to. He was of Asian descent, about twenty-eight. Most likely Indonesian or Malaysian."

Joel added, "The body was in the water approximately two days. It could have been dumped from the shore or a boat. Or it could have floated down the Richelieu River into the lake."

"That's in Canada?" Dennis asked.

Joel nodded.

"As of now, Homeland is taking over this case," Brian said. "I need you to send Agent Paige everything you have so far on the vic, no matter how small. The last thing I want us to be is the group who held back critical information that could have thwarted another attack. Understood?" He looked to his agents for confirmation.

Codi gave him a blank stare, while Joel nodded copiously.

"And this conversation never leaves this room," Dennis added.

"You think they are targeting America?" Joel asked him.

"That's what I'm here to stop, Agent Strickman. Well, if you'll excuse me."

They all stood and moved to the exit.

Codi left the building with Joel in her wake.

"That guy couldn't stop a donut with a hand grenade," she said.

"What does that even mean?"

"I don't know, but I'm ticked off. If the security of our nation lies with the Pillsbury Doughman, we're in trouble. Come on."

"I think it's Doughboy."

"Not now, Joel."

He paused at the harshness of the reply and let her walk away.

* * *

The two-story gray stone building close to White Bear Lake was perfect for his needs. The town of Willernie, Minnesota was just big enough to get lost in and yet small enough to be a few notches down on the savvy police scale. There were several mosques in town, as the population of the area had shifted to a more Middle Eastern mix. And just down the street was a decent restaurant, Gordy's Steakhouse.

Carl Savage had rented the top floor of the building. It was once a textile factory that had been converted into apartments in the early eighties. In 2012, a financial group purchased the building and reconfigured the space into two industrial floors, each with warehouse and office working space. The first floor was being used by an electrical distribution company.

The multi-use space of the top floor had an area cordoned off for living and an open area for manufacturing. It was perfect for his needs. Once again, Carl assumed his role as a successful artist working in mixed metals. Equipment was ordered, chemicals were sourced, and soon he was working on his next masterpiece: a ten-foot zinc sculpture of three hands interlocking. One was a fist, one a flat open palm, and the third had the index and middle fingers extended. It was a rock, paper, scissors sculpture for a new great park that was being built at the city's edge. He called it, "The Contest." Carl was also focused on a little something special for the West—much larger versions of his previous fog machine. Now that he had perfected the device and had a successful tes, it was time to take his game up a notch.

* * *

Joel's index finger tapped unconsciously on his mouse as he read through a file. He had taken it upon himself to gain access to the immigration files for Canada. He was particularly interested in the time frame of August 1967 to December of the same year. Thomas Richards had last been seen at a diner near Bozeman, Montana. But the message on the wall of the jail cell in Greenville suggested that he was there as well. A simple line from Bozeman to Greenville and beyond led to Canada, an almost certain destination for the fugitive. Now, it was only a question of matching a name or picture to the registrar. The list was massive. This would take a while. He leaned back in his chair and released a slow breath he didn't realize he was holding.

"Hey, sorry about Saturday. I was in a funk."

Joel turned to see Codi standing in his doorway.

"No problem," he deadpanned.

"So what are you working on?"

"Monday morning stuff. I have 'obtained' a list from Canadian immigration covering the last part of 1967."

"You're thinking he crossed over the boarder."

"Hoping is more like it."

"Okay. How can I help?"

Joel gave Codi half the list of names, and they spent a good part of their morning eliminating suspects.

By lunchtime, they were starving and had narrowed their list dramatically. There was one name, however, that stood out more than the rest.

"Lunch!"

Codi and Joel were startled by the voice. Their boss had just stepped into the conference room where they were working carrying a pizza box. They had dozens of printed sheets lined up across the table with some names crossed off and some highlighted. He looked over their organized mess as he laid the pizza on a side table.

"What's with Canada?" he asked.

Codi answered with a smirk, "It's a sovereign state just to the north of us."

"That was helpful."

"We think we might know what happened to Thomas Richards," Joel said.

"The man suspected of killing Agent Daniel Johnson?" Brian asked.

"That's right," Codi said.

"Take a look at this," Joel said to Brian.

"How did you come by this information?" he asked.

Trying to cover for Joel's hack, Codi piped up, "We borrowed it."

Joel looked worried, but his boss just rolled his eyes. Sometimes, cold cases did not require the same level of due process as an active case, especially when the guilty parties were most likely dead. It just required the right information to close it.

"If this pans out, you can always go back through proper channels and make a formal request. Just so it's all by the book." Brian said the last part while looking at Codi.

Joel passed over a paper that had a single name highlighted amongst a list of many others. Codi took a bite of pizza and spoke with her mouth full. "He immigrated to Saskatchewan in September of '67."

"Looks like Thomas Richards became . . ." Brian said as he read the document, "Tom Rich."

* * *

Sterling was a mess, his paranoia spiking. Everywhere he turned, the news carried the story of the recent bombing. They called it a radiological dispersion device, or RDD, but the results were the same—hundreds of people dead or dying. He was sure it was the result of his latest partnership. He had taken door number two, and now, people were dying. What had he gotten himself into? He had jumped at the money without thinking of the big picture.

He accelerated his yellow Lamborghini Urus, a sporty SUV with 650-hp, down wet pavement. The car was a dream. The fastest SUV on the planet, designed to make men jealous and women interested. He took a right turn too fast and had to counter-steer the corner. The slightly reckless driving was helping him focus. He breathed slowly, trying to collect himself. He'd been seeing assassins in every shadow, and it was time to get a handle on things. He paddle-shifted down as the tires squealed around the next corner, just missing a Prius slow to turn left.

But if he really thought about it, what else could his partially refined ore be used for? It was too corrupt to fuel even an old-school reactor. He was in over his head with a partner that would kill hundreds of innocents to forward their agenda. And what was their agenda? Money? Power? Did it even matter? What would happen to him if he so much as became a speed bump of liability in their path? His mind spun with possibilities.

Ahhh! This isn't happening, he thought, the reckless driving no longer focusing him.

His phone vibrated, and Sterling practically jumped. He looked to see it was his wife calling and immediately sent her to voicemail with a practiced motion. The first thing he had to do was keep playing his part. Make no sudden changes or moves that could be interpreted as anything but the good supplier. It was a role he was loath to play. Sterling pulled into a parking stall and killed the engine. He would carefully move his money into an offshore account, and when the timing was right, just slip away. He stepped from his Urus and walked briskly to the elevator, heading up to his Friday rendezvous with Rhonda. He was trying to forget his current situation. He would need something special tonight, and Sterling had just the thing in mind for the young blonde to try.

* * *

She moved like water flowing down the carpeted hallway. Her auburn hair seemed to stream right along with her, leaving a colorful bouquet behind. Her hips moved effortlessly, propelling her curvy figure along. Joel tried not to stare, but there was something about the woman that was intoxicating. Maybe it was her steel blue eyes or her button nose, but he couldn't take his eyes off the woman.

"Joel!"

He jumped at the sound of his name, snapping him back to reality. Codi was coming up behind him, and by the time he looked back over his shoulder his vision of beauty was gone.

"Wh . . . what?" was all he could stammer.

"Conference room in five," she said as she passed by without concern.

The room was empty as Joel sat down, but before he could get comfortable, Brian entered followed by Codi and his vision.

"Joel," Brian said, "this is Shannon Poole of the Royal Canadian Mounted Police. She is stationed here in D.C. as a liaison officer. I thought it might be helpful to go through the proper channels as you make your way up north."

"Please, call me Shannon," she said with a light and positive air.

"Joel." It was all he could get out, as a less than dignified thought coursed through his brain, followed by an embarrassed smile in her direction.

Brian seemed confused by Joel's ineptness, but he continued. "I've gotten approval for her to work this case with us, and I'm sure she'll be invaluable in connecting our two agencies to get closure."

Brian finished his speech, but Joel didn't hear a word. He was well and truly smitten.

Shannon cleared her throat and began. "As you may or may not know, Canada's policing system is, well, honestly, it's a bit of a mess. The Royal Canadian Mounted Police is a national organization much like your FBI. However, there are three states that have their own provincial police force. Quebec has its own called the Surete."

"Like the old name for the French state police?" Codi asked.

"Exactly. So jurisdiction can be like juggling mismatched pieces."

"Got it," Joel said a bit too loudly. Brian shared an anxious look with Codi, who waved him off with a subtle hand gesture.

"As a liaison officer, I should be able to get you what and where you need. We have a good working rapport with the other provinces."

Afterward, Brian left the conference room and Codi was forced to take over. She brought Shannon current on their case, and Joel managed to interject just enough information to be helpful. They showed Shannon to her temporary office just three cubicles down from Codi. Joel helped her get her computer linked in to the network.

"Okay. Tom Rich. We need to know where he went and what he did once he entered your country," Codi said.

"What was the date again?"

"September '67," Joel said.

Shannon nodded and went to work connecting the dots through her government portal.

"If there's anything you need, just let me know, okay?" Joel said, hopefully.

"You'll be the first," she replied in a professional manner and turned back to her screen. Joel stood there stiffly for a second before shuffling back to his office.

* * *

The text left little doubt as to what was needed. *Call me.* It was a number with a Southern California prefix that Codi knew by heart but had not dialed in over five years. Her mother. She picked up the phone and then put it back down. It was an act she had performed many times over the years, known as the "Almost Dialed." Each time, she had been reminded of the way things had ended. The pain and anguish. Codi searched for a term to describe their relationship—estranged. The memory—painful and better forgotten. Codi's fingers hovered over her keypad. *Get a grip, girl.*

She dialed.

The phone rang once and was picked up. There was silence, with a hint of soft breathing.

"Carolyn?"

"Codi?"

"You wanted me to call."

Another beat of silence ensued.

"Yes, thank you. I just need to . . . I miss you, Little Bear."

Little Bear, a nickname Codi hadn't heard since she was seven years old. A jolt of pain and loss shot through her. Her father had coined the term of endearment, and her mother had slowly adopted it. It hurt and brought back memories she was trying to bury. Her face quickly flushed, and she instantly regretted calling.

She tried to concentrate on how good things once were, before her father died and her mother fell apart right when Codi needed her most. Carolyn left Codi to survive on her own. Codi held back a flood of tears as she told herself, *this woman no longer controls you. You control you.* She breathed deeply, trying to steel herself.

"It's good to hear your voice, Carolyn," Codi tried.

"You too. It's been too long."

"Yeah, well the last time I saw you—"

Her mom interrupted. "Let's not go back there. Can we just . . . start over?"

Codi let the question hang for a second, considering the heartache and pain she had suffered through. Maybe things could be different now. Maybe they could put the past behind them.

"Uh, yeah, I'd like that."

* * *

Joel walked into Codi's office and started to pace. Codi stopped typing the email she was drafting and watched him. She had been expecting drama from her mom, but it had been surprisingly easy. She was even considering a trip out to San Diego to reconnect with some old friends and maybe stop by to see her mother. Her mind spun with a million questions and possibilities. She decided to answer a few emails to put it all behind her for now.

"You're gonna wear a hole in my carpet," Codi said, without looking up.

"I don't think she likes me," Joel whispered.

"She?"

"Shannon." He used his eyes to point to the cubicle a few feet away where the mountie was working.

"Are you insane?"

"What? I've tried to talk to her like three times today, and she has been very cold. I'm sure she doesn't like me."

"Oh, dear Joel. Of course she doesn't like you. We are professional agents working a case together. It is not a required thing for her to like you or me. Plus, you gotta give her some space. No woman that is worth your time wants to be hovered over."

"You told me I had to get back into the game," Joel whispered, hoping to not be overheard.

Codi had a brief flashback of her telling Joel those very words. It was right before she executed a personal suicide mission to stop a madman.

"This is not something you can force. It either happens or it doesn't. Give her space and just be your adorable self."

Joel paused his pacing. "You think I'm adorable?"

Crap. Codi had just stuck her foot in it. How was she going to get out of this one without hurt feelings? She noticed Shannon coming their way and immediately stopped talking. Joel started to add something.

"I guess if you consider—"

Codi put her hand up to stop him.

"Hey, it's after five. You wanna grab a beer or something?" Shannon asked, as she popped her head into Codi's office.

Codi and Joel looked shocked for a brief second and then recovered.

"Sure," they said in a surprised, awkward unison.

* * *

Cold River Brewery was a modern microbrewery with a strong pedigree. It had a very robust stout and a smooth pilsner that had won several awards. Codi, in accordance with her new health plan, had an Arnold Palmer. They had been given a corner booth with a view of the restaurant. The back section of the building had a large steel tank for brewing hops. The brewery was well lit and filled with young professionals all looking for something. A way up the ladder or a way to forget the ladder. They ordered some food to go along with their drinks, and soon, the small talk started.

"A mountie, that's really cool. So do you wear the red uniform with that flat brimmed hat?" Joel used his hands to demonstrate the bill on a mountie's hat.

Codi cringed at his question.

"Only for special occasions," replied Shannon.

An uncomfortable silence followed.

"So how does an RCMP become a liaison officer here in D.C.?" Codi asked.

"Simple, you solve a big drug smuggling case and get shot in the process."

"That's kinda how we ended up in the FBI," Joel said, flicking his thumb toward Codi.

"Really?"

"Yeah. Let's see, I got shot, then Codi got shot, then she drowned, and the case got solved. Next thing you know, we're both FBI."

She gave them a puzzled look. Codi nodded to affirm Joel's statement.

With a subtle gesture to Codi's Arnold Palmer, Shannon changed the subject. "So what's with the lemonade? Are you Mormon or something?"

"No, I'm just taking an alcohol time-out. It was starting to become a . . ." Codi searched for the right word. "Crutch."

Joel held up his beer as he spoke. "Dear alcohol, you made me funnier, a better dancer, and good looking. Then I saw the video."

Everyone chuckled.

Shannon turned her beer as she looked at it reflectively. "I know what you mean. I was starting to drink my breakfast and dinner."

Codi looked over at Shannon, who spoke in earnest. "Sometimes, you need to unplug and forget. The mind's only got so many places to hide the bad stuff we see out there."

They all nodded. It had brought the mood down slightly. A drunk thirty-something staggered by singing an off-tune version of "You'll Never Walk Alone." It was a good reminder of what Codi did not want to become.

"So how did you get on the other side?" Codi asked.

"I started drinking better," Shannon said. "Better Scotch, better vodka, and better tequila. That stuff's expensive, so I drank less and less."

Her crazy logic actually made some sense to Codi. "Here's to the good stuff," she said.

They all raised their glasses.

The night moved along, and the three agents soon felt at ease with each other. Even Joel was starting to act normal. Shannon was the first to leave, but Joel and Codi soon followed into the rainy night.

CHAPTER TWELVE

PIERRE ELLIOTT TRUDEAU INTERNATIONAL AIRPORT – MONTREAL – 9:45 A.M.

The flight to Montreal had been uneventful for everyone but Joel's bag. They had been waiting for over forty minutes, and it was still missing. The carousel turned with timepiece precision as the two remaining bags chased each other in a no-win race. Neither one was Joel's. After another delay, the team left the airport on the promise that his luggage would be delivered to their hotel. A short drive in a gray SUV rental had them parking in the guest lot at the national headquarters of the Surete.

The Surete du Quebec is the enforcement division for the province of Quebec. It is a large, modern, glass rectangle on the Rue Parthenais. Once inside the building, they were taken to the office of Inspector Franse Rochelle. She was a short woman with a bobbed haircut and a suspicious mind. She was just cute enough to love and tough enough to be handled with care. She welcomed them into her office and sat with an exaggerated plop.

"You're here about Tom Rich?" she asked.

The estrogen was palpable in the room as three strong-willed women vied for control. Joel had never felt so outnumbered.

"Yes, anything you could tell us would be helpful," Shannon said.

Codi decided to lay their cards on the table. "We know that he immigrated to Saskatchewan in 1967. From there, we tracked his movements to Quebec and a mining operation he purchased."

"Yes. Tom Rich is one of Quebec's historic figures."

This made Codi roll her eyes. The man had murdered an FBI agent.

"He purchased the Poudrette Mine on Mont Saint Hilaire from the founding family. He has made us famous. It's the only source of Poudretteite in the world. His family spends a lot of the money the mine makes giving back to the community. There is even a library named after him. He died in, like, '98, or something. There was a big turnout for his funeral."

"Of course there was," Codi said under her breath.

"His grandson Sterling now runs the mine."

"What kind of man is he?"

"Very similar to his grandfather and father, a pillar of the community, as far as I know."

The trip to Canada was beginning to look like a big waste of time. Sometimes, the bad guy got away with it. It's just how life worked.

"We'd love to talk to him," Shannon said, interrupting Codi's thoughts.

"Who, the father or the son?"

"Both?"

"Well, the father had a stroke three years ago and is unable to walk or speak. They've got him hooked up to a machine, night and day. The son . . . I'll have to make arrangements. Come back tomorrow, and I'll take you up there. Say, 10:00 a.m.?"

They agreed on the time, and Codi and the other two agents stood to leave. As they shook hands, Codi noticed that Inspector Rochelle was maybe five-four with heels on, but the woman carried herself like she was six feet tall.

* * *

The road trip up 116 North had been against the flow of traffic. They watched Montreal dissipate from high rises to urban sprawl. Eventually, farmland opened up to rural countryside. The Richelieu River soon came into view, and the scenery improved dramatically. This part of Canada was picturesque with tree-covered hills and blue, flowing water. A large, green domed mountain slowly grew in size as they drove. Mont Saint Hilaire.

As the guest of a liaison officer who required another liaison officer when in Quebec, Codi wasn't sure what exactly the FBI could do here. But they had come this far, so she would see things through.

Quebec maintained its own police force. The RCMP had jurisdiction on only federal matters here. So the cobbled team of investigators was required—overkill, but required.

A fixed metal sign next to a cornfield indicated the exit for the mine, and the SUV turned right up a gravel road. They were surrounded by tall conifers, which eventually thinned out to reveal a large mining operation. A huge scar of rock had been removed from the mountain over the course of many years. What had started as a quarry mine had turned into an underground mine as environmentalists looked to protect the natural beauty of the area.

Codi took in the sight. Massive power lines on shiny galvanized poles ran to a transformer package next to the main entrance to the mine. There were three mobile offices and a large fenced lot with heavy equipment. A few tractors were in action, including a giant front-loader and a couple of very large earth haulers. Several workers seemed to understand the organized chaos and moved about the complex as if it was child's play.

Codi spied two guards that seemed to have a missile-lock on the agents as they entered the gate. To the right was a giant till pile and to the left a sinkhole filled with impossibly blue water.

Overall, it was a bit underwhelming. They pulled into the lot next to about twelve cars. Inspector Rochelle escorted them up to a gray portable building with white-trimmed windows. It was covered with dust from months of neglect.

Within the first two seconds of meeting Sterling Rich, Codi could tell the man was full of himself. Within the next ten seconds, she could tell he was a liar. This was a person who did as he pleased and rarely considered the consequences. He mostly talked about the mine. His mine. How they mined Poudretteite, a unique pink gemstone that was a thousand times more rare than a diamond. He proudly showed them several samples. Codi flicked her eyes at Joel to get his attention and looked over at the grandfatherly portrait hanging on the wall.

"Is that your grandfather?" Codi interrupted the man's ongoing monologue.

Sterling paused, taken aback by the interruption.

"Yes," he said guardedly. "He started my family's legacy here."

"Do you have any pictures of him when he was younger?"

"I'm afraid not. My grandfather was a very private person. What's this all about, anyway?" he asked with some distaste.

"Are you familiar with the Plymouth Mail Truck Robbery in New England in August 1962?"

"No, why?"

"We tracked the main suspect into Canada and have good reason to believe that Tom Rich could be an alias," Codi said.

A moment passed between all parties before Sterling replied with an outburst. "Are you aware that you have absolutely no jurisdiction up here, agents? I'm only wasting my time speaking to you as a favor to Inspector Rochelle."

"We are sorry we have taken up so much of your time, Mr. Rich," Inspector Rochelle said and started to escort Codi, Shannon, and Joel out of the man's office.

Codi spun back around at the doorway. "Why do you have so much power going into the mine? It all looks like it's new."

Sterling sputtered for a second, and then a darkness filled his face. "We use heavy-duty equipment to access the ore down there. It all runs on clean electricity."

"Thank you for your time, Sterling," Codi said as she turned and left.

* * *

The fourth floor had an alcove that was all windows. It looked over the small town below and the green water beyond. The room had blackout curtains and an entire wall of touch screens that could project individually or all as one. Right now, there was a live-feed of a babbling brook in the forest. It was quite peaceful.

The charming town of Beverly Beach was nestled next to the Rhode River as it drained into Chesapeake Bay. It was twenty miles east of Washington, D.C. Bright Source was a think tank underwritten by DARPA, the Defense Advanced Research Projects Agency, a science and technology division of the Department of Defense, based in Arlington, Virginia. Bright Source came under DARPA's Tactical Technology Office, TTO. Its purpose was to test and innovate systems used to prevent strategic and tactical surprise on land, sea, sky, and space.

Bright Source, or as the other departments in DARPA called it, BS, had been trying to recruit Matt Campbell for some time. With the completion of his last round of tests, Matt was finally ready. He stood and looked out at the view. Million-dollar homes in a small-town environment.

There were five main scientists in charge, and he would be the sixth. They were given a long leash and a great deal of support. They had an advanced lab and access to all sorts of technology. New DARPA projects were run through the brain trust and were often fixed or improved there.

The situation seemed perfect to Matt. After the first twenty minutes into the tour, he accepted the job in his mind. He was now free to push himself creatively again and be much closer to Codi. It was a win-win, and after all he'd been through, it was about time. He picked up his phone and began to craft a text, then paused. What he really needed to do was set up a meeting where he could share his plans with her face-to-face.

* * *

The drive back to Montreal was filled with silence. It had been a colossal waste of everyone's time and taxpayer money. The case that had haunted the FBI for so long was still doing it.

"That guy creeps me the heck out," Franse said, as she passed a slow-moving car.

This surprised both Codi and Joel, as they got the impression Franse and Sterling knew each other.

"Something is going on that he's not telling us," Shannon said.

Joel added, "Did you see the picture of his grandfather? He looks a lot like Thomas Richards, just aged by forty years."

"*A lot like*' won't get you much up here," Franse deadpanned as she pulled back into the right lane.

Codi glanced down at an incoming text: *Call ASAP*. It was Matt.

"We will need proof," Franse said. "If his grandfather was Thomas Richards, that ship has sailed. He's dead. Case closed."

Codi knew Franse was right. The facts tended to add up, but there would be no going after the grandson of a criminal mastermind just because he was related, even if they could track the stolen money, which would be impossible. She slipped her phone back into her pocket.

* * *

Codi slumped on her hotel bed. Loose ends and incomplete endings bugged her. She wanted justice for the dead FBI agent but was not going to get it. Instead, Thomas Richards had thwarted the best police minds and escaped their dragnet. He had established a financial legacy for his family on the backs and lives of others. It really ticked her off. There was nothing worse than having zero control of a situation, and that's what was going on now. The last time Codi had felt this way, she was imprisoned, starved, and dehydrated. Her captors tied her to a chair and tortured her. A tall, freaky-looking Chinese assassin had nearly gotten the better of her. He stripped her of everything she had, leaving her praying for a quick death. Somehow, Joel managed to surprise everyone. He escaped his cell and found a way to save her. It was one of his finest moments, and she would never forget his efforts.

Codi needed a change, a fresh perspective. She stepped out onto her meager balcony and called Matt.

"Hello?"

"Is this stud muffin?"

"Sorry. I don't know who put those two words together, but they don't belong. This is The Stud."

The smile at hearing Matt's voice wiped away her recent negative mood. It was just what she needed.

"So what's up, The Stud?" she asked.

"I have some really big news, and since you are out of the country, there is not much chance of me sharing it in person. So here goes . . ."

Matt went on to tell Codi about his decision to quit his current job. How he was thinking about taking a job closer to D.C. This was a major step in their relationship, and it took Codi a second to let it sink in. It seemed to be happening so fast. There was a beat of silence.

"You're not happy with the idea?" Matt asked.

"Oh. No. I'm thrilled. And if it makes you happy, do it. This will be good for you."

"And for us, too. But don't worry; we can take things as fast or as slow as you want. It will just be easier to do so," Matt added hopefully.

This is what Codi needed to hear. She loved Matt but was happy with the way things were progressing. The distance between them had not been a problem for her. Moving too fast and into something more permanent was not something she was quite ready for. Not yet.

They finished up the call with comfortable low-key chitchat and plans for a get-together to celebrate on the weekend.

Matt stared at his phone, unsure if it had gone well or poorly. With Codi, it was sometimes hard to tell. But he understood being absorbed in your work as well as anyone and, of course, timing was everything in these matters. He decided to assume it went well.

* * *

After she hung up, Codi's attention slowly returned to her wasted day. It was too bad the agency didn't let you talk about your cases with others. That would have been helpful in letting go of some frustration. Now, Matt was going to be living in her backyard. She couldn't get her head around what that might mean in her life right now. She left the balcony, random thoughts spinning their course through her mind.

She sat at the small desk in her room and absently opened a few emails that had popped up since she left off. Thirty percent off bras. REI was having their once-yearly sale. It was sometimes this absurd normalcy that made her feel back in control. She deleted the e-waste and felt a little better for it. The last email was from an unknown sender within the FBI. She opened it and scanned the information. It was from the lab in Quantico.

It was the results from the trace elements search found on their irradiated victim. The John Doe had been exposed to radiation for about eighteen months, based on several hair follicle dissections. From under the man's fingernails were several compounds, including Uranium 238, the less stable isotope of the element, and plutonium.

It had the same signature as the radiation used in the German train station attack. But the thing that stood out to Codi as she scanned the list of other trace elements was the presence of a gemstone: Poudretteite.

* * *

The knock on his door jarred Joel from a fitful slumber. He looked at his phone. It was 12:30 a.m. He had been asleep for only an hour. He cracked open his door.

"What?"

"Joel, come on. We're taking a little excursion. Dress accordingly," Codi whispered through the gap.

"But I still haven't gotten my luggage."

"Okay. Wear what you have."

He quickly put back on his charcoal slacks and white collared shirt from the previous day and followed Codi outside to their rental SUV. Leaning against the hood of the Silver Ford Explorer was Shannon. She was dressed in dark jeans and a black tactical shirt. She looked almost identical to Codi.

Joel paused. "What, did you two call ahead on your outfits?"

The two women shared a knowing glance.

"Took you long enough, Joel. I thought we were going to have to go by ourselves," Shannon said as she got up and went to the driver's side door.

"How am I always the last one to know?" Joel asked. "And can someone please tell me what's going on?"

In unison, the girls replied, "Get in the car, Joel."

"Another reason they sent me to D.C. was," said Shannon, "I was never good at standing on the sidelines."

A realization hit Codi. Agent Shannon Poole of the Royal Canadian Mounted Police was her kind of agent.

CHAPTER THIRTEEN

MONT SAINT HILAIRE, QUEBEC – POUDRETTEITE MINE – 2:34 A.M.

The drive to Mont Saint-Hilare was quiet as the agents pondered their decision to break protocol and go off mission without involving the local Surete Du Quebec. Codi had told Joel and Shannon about the email with the trace Poudretteite results. She gave Shannon the backstory on the radiation match to the German train station attack and the John Doe they found.

It seemed to light a fire in Shannon as she drove through the darkness. Canada would not aid in a terrorist attack on her watch. This was now a federal issue and RCMP had a say in it.

She pulled onto the gravel road off of the 229 that led up to the mine. In the distance, the brightly lit compound fought against the thick trees for dominance.

"Pull over here," Codi said.

There was a small side road off to the left about eight hundred yards from the main entrance. Shannon pulled their rental to the edge of the road. She killed the engine and the lights. Chirping crickets filled the air as the group exited. They would go on foot from here. Joel watched as his partners in black tactical outfits moved into the shadows along the road's edge, his white shirt practically glowing in the dark.

"Joel, come here." Codi hissed.

He moved over to the shadows next to her. Codi reached down and grabbed two handfuls of dirt and began to rub it all over Joel's white shirt. Shannon joined in. A brief moment of ecstasy flashed through Joel.

"This will make you less of a 'Hey, look at me in my shiny white shirt. Aim here,' kinda target."

Ecstasy gone.

"What about after we're done here? This is my only shirt," he complained.

"One problem at a time, Joel." She stood back and inspected her handiwork.

Shannon stepped up and placed one smudge on Joel's cheek. "There. Looking good."

She turned and smiled at Codi. They were ready.

The team split up. Joel and Shannon would investigate the portable offices and Codi would check out the mine. She had a gut feeling that the heavy-duty power conduits would lead her to some kind of an answer.

* * *

The front office door was unlocked. *A worrisome sign.* Joel held it for Shannon, and they quickly entered the rectangular room. The large open space was lit by work lights streaming through dusty windows from outside. Joel could make out four desks and a row of filing cabinets. At the far end was a large table with a collection of coffee cups and a few samples of ore.

"Joel, keep an eye out. I don't want any surprises," Shannon whispered.

He moved to the door and peeked out the small window mounted in the middle of it. The compound was quiet save a few workers moving piles of material. Shannon started to meticulously comb the room for evidence. She went to the large table. When they had visited earlier that day, there were several blueprints laid across it. Now they were gone. She quickly picked up one of the ore samples. It had a pink shiny quality to it. Nothing there.

She moved to the desks.

Joel whispered, "We got company. Two guards approaching, and they are packing."

"How much time do we have?"

"Two minutes, max."

Shannon tore through the desks quickly. They were mostly empty.

"One minute." Joel did the countdown.

She ran to the file cabinets and, to her surprise, they were unlocked.

"Thirty seconds." Joel's voice had raised an octave.

Looking at the empty drawers, Shannon quickly realized that anything of value had been removed since their previous visit. Even the Thomas Rich portrait was no longer on the wall. The room was a bust.

"Fifteen seconds!"

She ran to a back sliding window. "Joel, move it!" Shannon called as she jacked it open.

The door burst open, and two strong flashlight beams searched the dark office—just missing the last of Shannon's body as she dropped from sight.

Crouched by the back of the office portable, Joel tried to catch his breath. His heart was pumping wildly. And there was a very beautiful woman with shiny auburn hair hunched right next to him with her hand on his shoulder.

"They cleaned house," she whispered.

"You didn't find anything?"

Shannon shook her head. Joel processed what that might mean.

"They were expecting us. We should warn Codi."

She nodded and moved off into the shadows, heading toward the mine entrance.

* * *

The entry was massive, a domed portal reinforced with steel girders. Codi kept to one side as she entered. There was room for some very large equipment to come and go through this section. Off to the right was a small changing area with benches and hooks. There were a few clothes hanging up and several cubicles filled with gear. Codi noticed a stack of hard hats and stepped over and collected one. She grabbed a safety vest that was hanging on a peg and put it on.

She stepped back to the left where a giant side-by-side cage elevator stood. It took her a second to figure it out. The right side was for passengers and the left for ore. It had a large bin that could dump material right into one of the large ore haulers. Codi pressed the button on the right control panel. The large cage door rattled upward. She stepped inside and hit the button for the next level down. She could see the newer electrical conduits dropping into the darkness below but wasn't sure how far down they reached.

Once at the first level, she hit the button for the next level, following the pipes down to wherever they might lead. After seven more stops, she found herself deep in the mine. The conduit turned and led off down a passageway to the left. She exited the cage and spotted two large red and white signs: Restricted Entry Authorized Personnel Only.

The electrical conduit continued past the signs along a stone corridor lit with caged LED lights every twenty feet. The passageway was large enough for mining equipment and personnel to pass. But right now it was empty. There was a distant rumbling sound from somewhere down in the mountain. It was extremely disconcerting, as Codi had never liked dark underground places. She pulled her hard hat over her forehead and moved down the path with purpose.

As she rounded a gentle bend, she could see a glow up ahead. There soon appeared a set of large, modern, glass double-doors. Codi took one look and reversed her direction, quickly walking back into the tunnel. Her mind recounted everything she saw. A sophisticated lab of some sort lay beyond the double-doors. There was an electronic keypad for egress and a security camera pointing in her direction. The thing that stood out to her the most, though, was the bright yellow and black sign known as the trefoil, the universal warning symbol for radiation.

As soon as she was out of sight of the camera, she ran. The elevator was still right where she had left it. She stabbed at the top button repeatedly, willing the giant door to close faster.

Once at the top, she ducked under the slowly opening cage and quickly moved to the exit, still wearing the hardhat and safety vest in hopes of not standing out.

As she rounded the corner for the main exit shaft, she ran into two fast-moving subjects. She instinctively reached for her gun but was quickly reminded that she was a guest in this country. She and Joel had been forced to leave their weapons behind in the States.

Just as quickly, she recognized the two strangers.

"Shoot, you gave me a heart attack," Joel said.

"They cleaned everything out. No maps. No files, nothing," said Shannon.

The realization hit Codi. "We gotta get outta here quick."

"What is it?" Joel asked.

"I just stepped in something bad."

Joel instantly recognized his partner's tone. He spun around and headed back to the exit double-time. Codi didn't wait for Shannon's opinion. She tracked Joel's every step. Once outside, they moved counter-clockwise around the compound keeping to the shadows, as pieces of heavy equipment moved in a practiced dance. Scooping, hauling, dumping.

They could see the open gate off to the right and a few workers near the portables. They ducked down behind a stack of old oil drums. It was about one hundred yards through a lit section between the gate and the drums. Codi waited for the right moment before they would try for the exit. She was about to give the signal to run once the large excavator with its long, insect-looking arm out front, passed them. But sudden headlights coming up the road toward the gate had them scurrying back to the safety of the steel drums.

A large-wheel front-loader came up the road and through the gate. Behind it were two guard vehicles. Once through, they stopped and closed the gate behind them. The thing that caught their attention, however, was their rental SUV. The silver Ford Explorer. It was being carried in the scoop of the front-loader. The loader dropped the vehicle from its front bucket, lifted the bucket, and slammed it down repeatedly on the Ford. After several metal-crunching whacks, the rental was almost completely flattened.

"We're in real trouble here," Shannon said.

"I know. We'll never get our deposit back from Hertz now," Codi quipped. "Let's back off and find another way out of here."

Before she could say or do more, five armed guards surrounded the stacked oil drums behind them. "Hands in the air where we can see them!" one shouted.

Codi raised her hands and stepped out to meet them. Joel and Shannon followed. In the background they could see the squashed SUV being dropped into a pit and covered over with dirt. The whole operation had taken less than two minutes. Now the only evidence left was them.

The agents were grouped together, searched, and summarily marched back into the mine, away from any curious eyes. Once inside, they were taken to a small room just to the right of the big elevator. They were shoved inside and a steel door closed behind them. The deadbolt clanked, sealing them in. They were prisoners.

"There goes my probation and my career along with it." Shannon stormed about the small room like a caged animal. Codi and Joel looked over, surprised by the statement. Shannon didn't elaborate. She just kept pacing, her face filled with anger.

Shannon had been sent to D.C. in an attempt to give her one last chance in a place where the RCMP had no authority and only worked in an advisory capacity. She had been reprimanded for taking things into her own hands on a case. Since being reassigned to D.C., she had been following the rules and doing fine, but the boredom was intense. She was better in the field, knocking heads and taking names, rather than writing proposals and politically interfacing with the two countries' police forces. That was a job for a politician, not a real policeman.

"I don't think you have to worry about breaking procedure, Shannon," Codi said.

"You don't know my boss," she replied.

"What do you mean?" Joel asked.

Codi looked at the two agents in a serious way. "These guys are playing for keeps. We're never getting out of here."

* * *

Farid Khadem was finally on the move. He sat in the small inflatable boat as the wind blew through his hair. They had trained him and then put him on hold three different times. It wasn't the false starts that got to him, but if he was going to do right by Allah, he wanted to get on with it—one way or another. His leaders surely knew best, so for now, he would have to be patient, even though many of his brothers had already left.

He thought of the day he would never forget. It was a Tuesday. The Imam himself had called Farid in and given him instructions. He told him God had chosen him, and he would receive the greatest gift imaginable in paradise. They spent almost an hour reading the Qur'an together. It left an inspiring memory and started Farid on a path that was both long and difficult.

Now, ten days later, he was crossing the border into the U.S. The small inflatable bounced as it hit a swell. The Salish Sea was black this moonless night. They had set off from East Sooke on Vancouver Island and were heading to Port Crescent, just northwest of Seattle. It was a mere twelve-mile journey, but Farid was more nervous than he had ever been. He didn't know how to swim, and the small craft seemed undersized for this mission.

America, the great Satan. His thoughts were interrupted by two headlights flashing twice from the shoreline. An older pickup truck waited there idling as Farid trudged through the shallows and ran up to its cab.

"*As-salamu alaykum.*" He offered the common greeting among Muslims.

The driver whispered back, "Welcome to America. Get in the truck."

Once Farid was in the truck and they were driving away, the driver turned to him and smiled. "*Wa alaykum al-salaam.*" The common response of *And upon you be peace.*

Farid's heart started to slow. He had made it. They drove through the night to a small house in the foothills south of Tacoma. Farid then endured three hours of horror—his Americanization. His hair was cut and highlighted. They shaved his beard, and his clothes were tossed. He was primped and cleaned until he didn't recognize himself in the mirror.

He was moved to a basement where his picture was taken. They gave him a phone, wallet, prayer rug, and a Minnesota driver's license with his new name: Fred Kade. He was served a meal of hamburger and fries, along with a Pepsi. This would be his new life for the next two weeks. He was shown to a cot where two others like him would be staying. Both had already been through the process.

Every day, he and his two brothers were drilled and tested until things became automatic. They were allowed time to read the Qur'an and for daily prayers. It gave them comfort and strength to do what lie ahead.

Their Americanisms took hold, and the skills required dialed in. On his last day, Fred was given three hundred dollars cash, a credit card, a backpack with personal items, and a change of clothes. His trainer handed him a small card. "Keep this in your wallet."

"What is it?" asked Fred.

"A social security number. You will need it for the job," his trainer said.

Fred performed his absolutions and morning prayer. He stood before his trainers. The oldest in the group stepped forward.

"From this day forward, Fred, you are an American," his trainer said. "You need to think like one and act like one. If you ever get worried someone is suspicious about you, just take out your phone and pretend to text someone. You will become invisible to the decadent West. I charge you to be brave and give all that you have for your country, family, and Allah. Peace be upon you."

"Thank you, sir," Fred replied correctly.

He purposefully used the Americanism as he shook Fred's hand, rather than offer an embrace. Fred then shook hands with his two training brothers and left in an Uber for the train station. This would be the most important mission of his life.

He watched out the window as the bay and city, built with so much capitalism and corruption, passed him by. He was reminded of his humble upbringing in a small village on the border of Iran and Iraq. His father was a devout and pious Muslim. His knowledge of the Qur'an and the Hadith was great, and he taught Farid its importance. When he turned eleven, Farid was sent off to a local camp just over the border in Iraq for training. He would never forget the look in his father's eyes—so proud. His mother cried softly as he drove away, but what could she understand of a man's needs and desires.

The first several weeks had been more intense than Farid had prepared for, but he would not fail his family's name. He dug deep and persevered. He was taught to shoot and to fight, but mostly to blindly follow orders. He watched as young men around him left for missions and never returned.

He made it his policy not to get too attached to anyone or anything. He was given a test and put in a class where he learned English. It was a crass language with many words that seemed to have double meanings. Just like the lies of the West.

That was when Farid knew he was destined for something great. Great in the sight of his family and Allah.

"We're here." The Uber driver broke him from his thoughts.

"Thanks," Fred said, and he pulled out his phone and tipped the driver. He grabbed his backpack and never looked back as he headed into the Tacoma Dome Station.

"Round trip ticket to Minneapolis please."

* * *

She watched as Sterling stepped out from his downtown Montreal office into the rain and turned right. "Let's go for a drive, Sterling."

He spun at the sudden voice. "I would appreciate a head's up for these meetings," he said with sudden distain.

Sterling looked like he was about to complain further until he saw the mountain of a man Dorthia called Kip step beside her. He gestured with his hand to the black Range Rover parked on the sidewalk.

"You drive," Dorthia said.

Sterling thought about his options and then simply nodded and got behind the wheel. He pulled out into the flow of traffic, and Dorthia watched as the automated windshield wipers chased the rain away.

She was at a loss and could not understand how the RCMP, Surete, and the FBI had all converged on Sterling's business. So much had been invested in this operation, and now she might have to scrap the whole thing. It seemed impossible. Dorthia turned from the passenger's seat slightly toward Sterling and stared. He glanced back at her a few times, feeling like a cat's play toy.

"So let me get this straight," she said. "They asked about your grandfather? Not the mine?"

Sterling nodded his head vigorously. He recounted the visit from the agents along with their questions.

"Who was your grandfather?" Dorthia asked.

"As far as I know, he did a little bootlegging of Canadian whiskey before he bought the mine and made it the family business. That's it."

"And they thought he was the one behind some mail robbery back in the sixties?"

"That's what they were after, but there's no way it can be true."

Sterling suddenly wanted a drink. His mouth felt dry. The mention of Canadian whiskey along with his situation seemed to call for it, a lot of it.

He could picture the bottle of Dark Horse Whiskey sitting back on his credenza, and his lips moved subconsciously with the thought. What he wouldn't give for a shot of the warm, caramel goodness right now.

"So why did they come back covertly . . . just because of some newly installed power lines?"

"Surely they had no authority to do that," Sterling said hopefully as he pulled to a stop at the intersection, waiting for the light to turn.

Dorthia slowly nodded. "Okay." She thought a moment. "I will take them off your hands. You did well to anticipate their return and clean out your offices. We'll keep things just as they are for now. When is your next shipment due?"

"Eight days." Sterling accelerated the vehicle when the light turned green.

"Excellent. Make sure that happens."

Dorthia turned to the large man sitting in the back behind Sterling. He was holding a Glock 19 in silence and was dressed all in black. His look cried out killer. Sterling glanced at the man in the rearview mirror anxiously, as he wiped the perspiration from his head with his sleeve. He was fearful of what Dorthia might say to the man.

"Kip, I want you to take all identifying and personal items off our guests and dispose of them. Clean out their hotel rooms, and then take them on a nice trip up north to see the beauty of this country."

The man nodded. Sterling's death grip on the wheel finally loosened.

"Pull over here. This is your stop." Sterling pulled the car over and got out so fast he nearly got clipped by a passing car.

Dorthia called after him. "Careful, Sterling. We still need you. For now."

* * *

"What do you mean?" Joel asked Codi.

"I mean that there is some radioactive stuff going on down there," she answered.

The air in their prison room had gone stale. It had been several hours since being captured, and Codi, not being the type to just hang out, was trying to connect all the dots. She sat quietly for a moment and then suddenly stood and burst out, "What are the odds that our two cases are connected?"

"We do seem to have a way with that," Joel answered back. "We start off small and go out with a bang. But in this case, radioactive material going bang would be a very bad thing."

"What makes you think they're connected?" Shannon asked.

Joel filled her in on the details of their other case. He didn't mention the part where Homeland had taken it over and pushed them out.

"So these guys are making fissionable material here?" Shannon asked. "That seems unlikely."

"Describe what you saw," Joel said to Codi.

"A hallway with glass walls. There were offices and a large lab. In the middle of the lab was a closed-in cotton candy-maker looking thing."

"And that's where the new powerlines were running?"

Codi nodded.

Joel closed his eyes for a beat trying to recall something. "How big?"

Codi held her hands wide apart to demonstrate. "About the size of a Volkswagen Beetle, only round and slightly taller than a person."

Joel stepped over and sat next to Codi. "Sounds like a cyclotron." Both girls looked intently at Joel, listening. "It was one of the first devices used back in the forties to transform uranium into plutonium. It's an old-school process that uses a powerful electromagnetic field to separate isotopes. That's probably why the ore is so corrupted," he said. "You can pick up a refurbished one from a college somewhere for maybe two- to three-hundred grand. They don't have the ability to fully process the ore, just transmute it. They'd need some very sophisticated centrifuges for that and those things are impossible to obtain unless you are the federal government."

"So are they making nuclear bombs?" Shannon asked.

"No. It's not pure enough to explode, but it is plenty lethal for a Smoky Bomb."

Shannon looked confused.

"An RDD, radiological dispersal device," Codi explained.

"Oh, no."

"Exactly."

CHAPTER FOURTEEN

Carl Savage looked at the small scuba tank he had acquired and removed the valve with a wrench. He set it on a small stand and photographed it from all angles. The photos were digitized into his computer, and using Autodesk Inventory, he stitched the pictures together, forming a 3-

D rendering of the original. From there, Carl sent the specs to his C&C machine, a computerized milling device capable of grinding and forming bulk metal into almost any shape.

He would make four exact duplicates from lead rather than the original steel.

The small, shielded room where he would assemble all of his components was ready. He had built a small box framework and covered the whole thing with sheet lead to block all outgoing Alpha and Beta particles. Now, all he needed was to finish his design and assemble the pieces. He wanted to custom-make as many parts as possible. That way, they could never be traced back to him. The problem with an RDD is that it didn't blow up, so every part and piece was available to the police for analysis. You had to be very careful if you didn't want them following a trail back to your front door. For the RDD in Germany, he had even cloned the steel case the components went in. As of now the authorities were still scratching their heads, trying to trace the smoke machine and its parts.

Once the fissionable material arrived, it would be a matter of hours before his latest masterpiece would be ready. A knock on his door broke his thoughts. He checked the security camera on his phone to see a delivery had been left. Carl opened the door and picked up a single piece of junk mail. It was some kind of direct mail marketing piece. He opened it up to find a brochure for an upcoming music festival, Basilica Block Party Minneapolis, a large three-stage festival centered around the Basilica of Saint Mary. It was going to be their twenty-fifth anniversary with over twenty headline bands. Their slogan was: Twenty-five Years of Praising the Loud. Carl read further. There was a picture from the previous year showing the massive stage in front of the great gray stone basilica. There were twenty-five thousand fans all packed together cheering. The caption beneath it read: *With twenty thousand set to attend already, get your tickets before they're gone.*

Carl smiled at the thought of it all: Christians, thousands of them. He relished the mental image of them screaming, as he picked up a book, *Sculpt Nouveau—Patinas and Metal Finishes.* He placed the flyer inside the book. *A keepsake,* he thought and closed it back up. Carl double-checked the date on his computer, July twelfth. Two weeks away. He opened his email and wrote a quick note to Jal. Instead of sending it, he saved it as a draft. He would be ready.

* * *

156

The runway was little more than a dirt strip with the trees trimmed back just enough to allow the King Air 90 to land. It was a hardy twin-engine aircraft used for smaller cargo loads, perfect for use in the great North to deliver goods to small remote towns. The plane was also popular with skydivers, as it had a large side exit door that could be removed.

Codi, Joel, and Shannon stood along the runway. They were flex-cuffed with their hands behind their backs. They watched as a woman exited the plane. She had the blackest of hair and incredibly dark green eyes. Her hair was shoulder length and just touched the cobalt blouse she wore. For the briefest moment, she glanced over and Codi locked eyes with her. Codi made a quick assessment: This woman was rotten to the core.

The woman quickly returned to business, conversing with one of the men that had escorted the agents to the runway. The taller of the two nodded several times as they spoke. Codi could not make out the words over the idling engines, but the man seemed pleased with his assignment. The woman left for one of the cars and the guard herded them into the back cargo area of the plane. The three agents were forced to sit against the rear bulkhead, shoulder to shoulder. The main guard, plus one, both in black tactical uniforms, followed behind.

Codi could see the sun was just beginning its climb for a new day, very possibly her last day. As the dark sky gave way to an amber glow, the twin engines revved. The two guards with quick draw holsters across their torsos sat in webbed seats attached to the fuselage. They had a perfect view and enough distance to easily stop any escape attempt from the prisoners. They carried the rare, full-auto Glock 18Cs with extended mags, one of the deadliest pistols on the planet.

The drive in the pre-dawn dark had taken only ten minutes from the quarry. The three agents had been stripped of everything except their clothes and were given or told nothing but a few commands in French that seemed universal, especially when used with the end of a gun barrel for emphasis. Get up, go that way, get in, sit down. The business-like proficiency told Codi these were professionals. The fact they were not covering their faces screamed one-way trip.

The plane pulled through the air climbing up toward a single cloud in the sky. The sun broke through the small starboard window in the cargo door. They were traveling north. Codi needed to find a solution to their problem, but the guards remained ever observant. Time was against her, but it might just also be her salvation.

After about thirty minutes, the two guards began an occasional exchange of words. At first, just a few sentences but soon whole conversations. Every time they looked at each other, Codi rubbed her nylon restraints up and down on the edge of the aluminum bulkhead. It was not sharp, but it provided some resistance, grinding away like a plastic pot scrubber on armored steel.

Joel looked over at Shannon who was still in a funk after their capture. Her normally perfect hair was a mess, and her mascara was smudged across her face. To Joel she still looked like the most beautiful thing he had ever seen. He gave her an uncomfortable grin as he tried to inch his glasses up his nose with a head flip.

Shannon was surprised by Joel's inner strength, considering their situation. She had never seen him like this. In fact, the first time they met, she wondered how this bumbling putz had been accepted into the FBI in the first place. She took another look. It hit her for the first time; this man was more than she had previously determined. He was tall and lanky with blue eyes and dirty-blond curls. Yes, he was handsome, but there was something more, something deeper. He was capable and intelligent. She could see that now.

In the past, it had always been her way to be so consumed by her own issues—work, family, and friends—that she always seemed late to the boyfriend party. By the time she was ready, they had given up and moved on. The lack of commitment or interest on her part was not dislike but fear perhaps. It was safer to just be too busy or even aloof. Taking emotional chances was not her way.

It started her senior year in high school. Shannon had agreed to go to the prom with Gary Gilbert. He tried to ask her three different times but seemed to just miss her at every turn. When he finally cornered her, it was the morning of the prom. There had been no time to get a proper dress or good restaurant reservations. The whole experience had been a disaster, leaving Shannon disappointed in an event she had built up in her mind. It left Gary frustrated, and he acted out by leaving some mean things about her on social media. It stung.

The next man in her life came along freshman year of college. She unknowingly became part of a revolving door for a senior who was sleeping his way through the freshman class. She had fallen hard for a man who had no regard for her or any woman. It took six months and a few bad grades for her to turn her life around. She watched two of her roommates continually make poor dating choices. It encouraged her to step back and slow down. There was no rush. In fact, she didn't really need to have a partner in her life. After all, she was doing just fine on her own.

With her busy work schedule, Shannon allowed her dating life to wither. Not that she didn't have time for the occasional tryst. Men were great; they just couldn't get over themselves. They were consumers. Consumers of attention, time, effort, and mostly sex. Frankly, she just didn't have the energy for that in her life right now.

She was jarred from her thoughts when the pilot called back to the guards.

"We're here!"

Codi could feel the plane slow in speed. With robotic precision, one guard backed up the other as they motioned for the three captives to stand. Codi stood with her legs slightly spread to help balance against the slight buffeting of the plane. She had rubbed her flex cuffs against the metal bulkhead for close to twenty different times, but they still held strong. She leaned toward Joel and whispered out the side of her mouth. "They're going to throw us out. Make your body flat in the air for maximum resistance. Aim for water and try to hit it at a glancing blow, like a skipping stone. There's a ten percent chance you'll survive."

Joel nodded, trying to psych himself up for the coming drama. He could have done without the ten percent information, however.

* * *

Codi was beyond exhaustion. It had taken a lot of effort to get here. She had been doing close-quarters combat training for three days. The BUD/S school had been intense and there was no reprieve in sight. It was one of the many stepping-stones to becoming a Navy Seal, and it had taken everything Codi could offer to get here. The sergeant in charge of Survival Evasion Resistance Escape training (SERE) had a hard-on to see how many times he could make the squad fail on limited sleep. Three days, three hours sleep.

For the latest drill, there was a team of four flex-cuffed and gagged soldiers in a small compartment. Codi adjusted her safety glasses with her shoulder. Two armed guards stood in domination across from the prisoners. The chamber smelled like a men's locker room with backed-up toilets. The ceiling was too low to fully stand and the two guards smartly kept their distance from their captives. The guards were wary and alert. At least someone was getting some sleep.

The task was simple. It required the prisoners to escape. They were on their third attempt. The first two ended in a slaughter of Sim Round Blue, a military version of the paint ball bullet. The guards also had a task. They were to swap positions with the prisoners every thirty minutes. It forced them to stay alert and maintain control of their prisoners within close proximity.

After three hours, even the most alert guards lost attention. As they issued orders for the prisoners to swap, Codi used her hip to "accidently" knock her companion down toward one of the guards. As he fell, the guards' attention fell along with the falling prisoner. Codi followed behind him, pretending to trip, as well. It was only a momentary distraction, but it was enough. She swept the legs of the first guard, and he dropped hard, hitting his head against the metal wall. Her other two standing team members used this distraction to get the better of guard two. It was an ugly fight with the restrictions of your hands tied behind your back. Shoulders, heads, and feet were used to knock down and bludgeon the guards. By the time it was over, Codi and her team had immobilized the two guards and cut themselves free. The only problem was the blue bloom on one teammate's chest. The second guard had gotten one Sim Round shot off.

The drill sergeant reamed them up and down for losing a man while they stood at attention on wobbly legs. He paced as he called out his mantra: One, never get captured. Two, resist, but do it smartly. Three, escape is always the goal. Four, sometimes you have to sacrifice. He made everyone repeat it several times until he seemed pacified. Had Codi known that five days later she would break her ankle and have to tap out, thanks to her misogynist teammates, she would have let the man know her opinion of him. After all, they had escaped with one sacrifice, but Codi knew drills were just that—not real.

The drill sergeant left them at attention until one of them passed out. Eventually, after a string of cuss words and a backhanded compliment, he passed them on to the next instructor. The one thing Codi learned from it all was that sometimes, there is no way to get out of a situation cleanly. You have to take your best shot and prepare for losses.

* * *

Yasin Kamran and Ramin Ammar loaded their car for the long trip ahead. They had come to America on student visas and both had earned degrees at the University of Texas, partially funded by the U.S. Government. After graduating, Yasin and Ramin rented a small apartment, outstaying their visa's expiration date. They did some paid research projects and a few for-hire jobs in their field, physics. Two weeks ago, they had nearly been caught while trying to cash a check for some work they had done. The bank would not honor their expired IDs, and the overzealous teller called the police.

They were running out of funds and knew it was time to go back to their homeland in Libya, but their newfound American lifestyle left them hesitant to do so. Poor in Libya is much different than poor in the United States. Ramin reached out to an uncle who had been very helpful in getting his student visa. He asked the man for advice.

Two days later, a simple text to Ramin's phone changed everything. They met with a man called "The Trainer." He outlined a very specific set of instructions. Yasin and Ramin were fearful at first, but the man was very convincing. A stack of cash had sealed the deal. Yasin and Ramin ordered their supplies, and once they received them, they busied themselves with packing their car. This would be a one-way trip ending with a free escort back home where they would be greeted as heroes. It was hard to believe, but what choice did they really have?

Wednesday morning, the two set out for the Gulf Coast. Once in the outskirts of Mobile, Alabama, they stopped at a Waffle House for breakfast. It had become a "go-to" for the two men, and they would miss it.

They drove into the city, and Yasin opened a map The Trainer had drawn pointing to a specific intersection. He navigated as Ramin drove there and pulled to the curb. Yasin removed the container they had purchased on Amazon and opened it to expose its contents to the air. After five minutes, they replaced the lid and drove out of the city with the container. It was a simple action that would need to be repeated many more times.

* * *

The King Air 90 settled as it glided through smoother air warmed by the morning sun. Codi watched as a guard inched toward the cargo door, preparing to eject them. She moved to the balls of her feet, coiled and ready to spring, but the look on her face said she had completely given up. It was important not to show your hand.

"This is your stop," the guard called out with an eager French accent. "There are about a thousand bears down there dying to meet you. Well, actually, you'll be dying to meet them. I'm sure they will fight over what's left, so they can have you all to themselves."

He laughed to himself as unlatched the lock on the far side and moved to the closer side to repeat the action. Once the latch was free, the door popped open violently from the force of the wind, revealing blue sky. It was sudden and intense, causing the plane to flutter from the drag the open door placed upon it.

Codi didn't hesitate. It was now or a quick drop to the ground below. She pounced with all her speed and might. Using her shoulder, she checked the guard mid-torso, sending him right out the open door. His scream was quickly swallowed by the wind and the drone of the engine. With the sudden unexpected exit of his partner, the second guard hesitated just a beat. In his confusion, Codi body-slammed him to the cargo floor. The crushing impact popped Codi's flex cuffs in the spot where she had been scraping. *Finally!*

She rolled to her feet, hands free and ready. The man was quick and recovered instantly, bringing his Glock 18C to bear. Codi had nowhere to go but forward. She dove at the man. The 18C is a fully automatic pistol capable of shooting twelve hundred rounds per minute. The guard had an extended clip giving him thirty ACP 9mm rounds that could be dispersed in just over one-point-five seconds. The first bullet tore through Codi's armpit, burning her flesh and leaving two holes in her shirt as it continued on. The second just missed her ear, causing it to ring so loudly the wind and engine noise died abruptly. Two near-misses. She ducked just in time to have the third bullet sail over her head before she clamped onto the guard's hands.

They swung wildly back and forth, spewing the rest of the bullets like water through a loose garden hose. Joel and Shannon dove for cover as bullets circled the cargo area, stitching a trail toward the cockpit, until it ran dry. Codi hung on for all she was worth. It was much like grabbing hold of a tiger's tail—don't let go.

They struggled, each using their legs to inflict damage on the other. Codi released one hand and gave the man an uppercut. He used her action to wrench the gun free from her single hand. In one continuous motion, the gun came free and arced around making impact with her temple. Spinning stars shot across her vision, and she wobbled backward. He added a kick to her stomach and before Codi could recover, a kick to the head dropped her to the floor.

Joel and Shannon quickly joined in. They still had their hands behind their backs but used legs and shoulders as weapons. The guard parried them away and spun an elbow into Joel's chin, dropping him. Shannon let out a banshee scream as she rushed the guard. He had not quite fully recovered from his altercation with Joel, and the two crashed into the fuselage and bounced to the floor.

Shannon spun on her side and used both feet in tandem to kick the guard in the chest and send him back toward the open cargo hold. He landed in a heap, flipped around and stood. Shannon mirrored his action as best she could. The two combatants stood face-to-face, ready to do whatever it took to end the other. Shannon with her hands still tied behind her back and the guard with both hands free and an empty pistol he held like a club.

Codi blinked and tried to clear her head. She turned to see a blurry image of the two titans. She was still dazed but not willing to give up. She rolled as fast as she could across the floor and kicked the guard's knee. A cracking, popping sound was followed by a howl of pain. The guard dropped half-in and half-out of the plane. He gripped onto Codi and hauled her along with him as the outside wind sucked at his legs, trying to pull him out of the plane.

Codi was pulled head first on her back toward the open hatch. The guard had a vice-like grip around her chest. She had nothing to grab on to. She tried to pry the guard's hands apart, but he was taking her with him at all costs. She swung her arms over her head, hoping to inflict damage, but the blows did little and she started to slide. She tried to grab onto something, anything, to arrest her exit from the craft.

Shannon flipped over and hooked her flex-cuffed hands over the toe of Codi's boot. The strain on her shoulders was immediate and intense, but it stopped Codi and the guard from flying to their deaths. She was inverted, face up on top of Codi. Her heels were on the rim of the doorway, and it was taking everything she had to keep all three of them inside the plane.

"Joel! Wake up!" Shannon screamed. The strain on her shoulders was making her muscles convulse. She would not be able to hold on much longer. Codi had found purchase on a pair of offset bolts that protruded slightly in the cargo floor. She had to hang on with only her fingertips, and it was intense. She wanted to break the man's finger to get him to let go, but if she let go herself it would all be over, possibly taking Shannon along with her.

Joel shook off the pain and tried to lift his head. His view was one of confusion. He could see Codi slipping toward the exit of the plane. There was a man grabbing her around her chest pulling her with him. Half of the man was outside the plane. Shannon was on top of them both. She was straining to hold on, her hands still cuffed and looped around Codi's boots. It was a losing battle. Inch by inch, all three were leaving the plane.

Something inside called, and Joel sat up. His hands were still cuffed behind his back, but he had to do something. He moved into action, but the plane started to tilt in a dangerous direction. Codi would be lost if he didn't do something quickly. He did the only thing that came to mind. Joel rolled over like a beached seal and, with all his strength, bit down on the fingers holding onto Codi. There was a cry and then nothing. The guard was gone. Codi was suddenly pulled back into the cargo area. The tilting plane now started to nosedive, as well. They could hear the engines starting to rev as they picked up speed, heading for the ground below.

It took Codi a second to realize they were still in danger. She staggered to the cockpit and opened the door. The pilot's head lolled to the side as the plane continued to dive and arc left. There were bullet holes stitched across the cockpit and the pilot. Air whistled through holes in the windscreen at high velocity. She climbed into the copilot's seat and screamed, "Does anyone know how to fly a plane?"

She pulled up on the yoke, and the plane slowly started to react. Joel popped his head into the cockpit. Somehow, he had managed to remove his flex cuffs. Codi looked back with a terrified expression.

He shook his head.

"Okay," she said, "get this body out of here and help me! Shannon!"

She was there in a second. Outside the window to her right she could see that one engine sputtered with fire. The sudden fear in her eyes was obvious.

"This plane's going down," Codi said. "If we somehow make it, we will need everything we can grab ahold of in order to survive."

"On it." Shannon knew in an instant what she needed to do. Joel helped her remove her cuffs, and she scrambled off to scour the plane.

Joel pulled the pilot out of the cockpit and laid him back in the cargo area. He then ran forward and strapped into the man's bloody seat.

"Try the radio. See if you can get some help," Codi commanded.

Joel looked over the instrumentation and quickly found the radio. He moved the frequency dial to 243.0 MHz, the emergency channel, and picked up the microphone. It was dead. The radio seemed to be working, but, upon examination, he saw that the microphone had a bullet hole in it. He tried the transmit button on the yoke and called out, "Mayday, Mayday. This is agent Joel Strickman of the FBI. We are in a small plane and going down somewhere north of . . ."

He looked at Codi for an assist. She shrugged her shoulders. Joel realized the hopelessness of their situation. He pressed the transmit button again and continued to call out. It was a wasted effort.

The wing on the other side of the burning engine started to buckle and shake.

"We gotta get this thing on the ground now!" Joel screamed.

Codi aimed for a small meadow next to a lake just visible below. She tried to remember what little she knew about flying.

"See if you can get the landing gear down," she called, sweat rolling down her cheeks. She looked over the instruments and determined which lever controlled the flaps. She set them at thirty degrees. It was something she remembered from a movie, *flaps thirty*. She lowered the throttle until the yoke felt heavy and then gave it just a slight boost. Their speed dropped.

The King Air 90 plunged, leaving a black smoke trail across a perfect blue sky. Codi lined up on the meadow. She knew that if the nose was too low, and they dug in at this speed, they would all be killed. What she didn't know was how to get a plane to go down with its nose up. It seemed impossible.

At five hundred feet above the trees, she dropped the power.

"Hang on!"

Codi pulled too hard on the yoke to get the nose to come up, and the plane stalled. It fell out of the sky like a stone, rapidly losing forward momentum. The tail slid between two trees and was ripped off. The fuselage somehow missed an old growth tree, but the two wings didn't. They ripped away just beyond the engine mounts at almost the same instant. The rest of the plane shot out from the trees, an aluminum-skinned missile traveling at over ninety miles per hour.

They hit a mound and bounced, jarring its passengers to the core. Cody pulled back on the yoke, but there was nothing left to control. It was time to hold on and pray. The plane bounced several times across the meadow before the landing gear snapped off. The body augered into the soft ground. It left a dirt wake as it moved, shooting across the small meadow and into the lake. Suddenly, everything stopped with a giant ball of water and a final jerk that launched everyone forward with a sudden whiplash.

Joel woke to his knees covered in freezing water. His legs were pinned under the instrument control panel. He tried to free himself but was stuck. Steam hissed somewhere outside as hot metal rapidly cooled in the icy water. He looked over to his partner who was not moving. There was a flow of red draining down her left temple.

"Codi! Codi, wake up! Are you okay?"

"That was an unbelievably horrible landing. She should have her pilot's license revoked."

Joel spun to see Shannon standing weakly in the cockpit door, holding a bag. She was a mess, like something pushed out of a fast-moving car on the freeway, but still alive. Joel let out an audible plea. "I'm stuck!"

His words seemed to snap Shannon out of her fog. She wedged the black canvas bag between Codi's seat and the bulkhead and moved to help Joel. She ducked under the rising water and then popped back up a moment later. She said, "It looks like there's an adjustment lever on the other side of your seat. See if you can get it to move."

Joel felt around in the bitter cold water and, sure enough, he found a lever. A few seconds later his seat slid back freeing his legs. He tried to stand, but his legs denied him.

Shannon had moved over to unbuckle Codi from her seat. The water was now up to her chest. She grabbed the unmoving body and pulled Codi free. Joel tried again to stand up, the water temperature forcing him to take quick shallow breathes. This time his legs were wobbly, but he managed to stand.

"Grab the bag. I'll meet you on the shore," Shannon said.

Joel reached for the black canvas bag that was behind Codi's seat and trudged/swam through the water of the sinking cargo hold over to the exit hatch. Shannon pulled Codi with her as she followed right behind. By the time they exited the plane, there was only two feet of air between the roof and the rising water. They swam through the frigid water of the lake, dragging Codi and the bag along with them.

Shannon and Joel dragged themselves and their cargo up the shore, as the last bubbling sounds from the sinking plane died behind them. Shannon carefully laid Codi out on the bank. She plopped down on the ground next to her, too exhausted to move. She took in large gulps of the impossibly fresh mountain air, wondering how she could still be alive. It seemed like a true miracle, and she was grateful.

Codi blinked her eyes and tried to lift her head. A low moan escaped. She would be all right, but it would take some time.

The three agents lay on the shore unable to think or move. They had cuts, contusions, and were generally battered, but they were alive.

Shannon was the first to shiver. It was forty degrees in the sun, but the icy water had lowered their core body temperature to a dangerous level. Hyperthermia in these conditions was a killer.

"We need to get out of these wet clothes, or we are going to die," Shannon said between clattering teeth.

"Sounds like a bad pick-up line."

Shannon and Joel looked over to Codi who had propped herself up on one elbow. She was nursing a bloody bump on her head and a burn to her armpit, but her patented smirky smile was on full display.

"A fi-fire would be go-good too," Joel added.

* * *

Dennis looked at the report that had been forwarded to him. It was the lab analysis on the trace evidence from their irradiated John Doe. He scanned the list of elements and chemical compounds. It meant nothing to him. He would have to get an expert to weigh in on it. He made a note to remind himself to do just that.

Homeland Security, being a newer agency, had newer everything. The offices were modern, and the layout was designed with efficiency in mind.

There were several bullpens with large-screen monitors all showing live feeds. Each represented a specific interest to Homeland.

Dennis' office had a window and a real door with a keycard entry. He had a white melamine desk and two large side-by-side computer screens. He scrolled to the next page on the lab report. The hair biopsy. Eighteen months of continuous exposure. That was interesting. Their vic had been exposed to a consistent source of radiation. That had to limit the possibilities. It must be some kind of ongoing project. Maybe the hidden radiological labs they never found in the Iraqi war. This could be big for him. Imagine if he found and stopped what no one else could.

It was an empty dream, and he quickly refocused on his task, step-by-step detective work. He opened up a map program and placed a dot where the body had been found. Then he did an overlay that showed the currents and speed from the river into the lake. He then calculated backward to the estimated time the lab said the body entered the water. He drew an arc to represent the difference. At the top was the Richelieu River thirty miles into Canada, just below the town of Saint Jean sur Richelieu.

He interlocked his fingers and thought for a moment. He opened another page on his computer. He set it to search for uranium mines in Canada. Dennis was surprised by what he saw. Canada was one of the largest producers of uranium in the world. His idea of Saddam's secret nuclear lab vanished. Was it possible there was a new source from our neighbors to the north?

Dennis picked up his phone and dialed.

* * *

Fred was surprised at his luxury surroundings. The old Tudor-style home was set back off the street, hidden by large maple trees and a six-foot hedge. The town of Maple Grove was just northwest of Minneapolis and had a modern small-town feel. He sat in a white Adirondack chair on the back porch, sipping tea. A large water tower could be seen in the distance with the town's name on it. His room was spacious and not shared with anyone else. He had his own bathroom, and they had a common area with a large TV and foosball table. The two other members of his team had traveled on different days and in different ways, but they had all made it to the home without incident. This was no quick and dirty suicide-vest type of operation. This was highly planned and well thought out. He would be the spear that would stab at the heart of the West. The thought made him smile for the first time since he had been Americanized.

Fred closed his eyes and breathed in the bitter aroma of his Persian tea. He could also smell the afternoon rain that would soon pass through, leaving the town muggy and wet. His thoughts turned to his upcoming job. He was a roadie now. It was a funny word to him. It meant that he was part of the effects company that would be providing lighting, pyrotechnic, and smoke effects for an upcoming concert, a Christian concert. He was now truly in the belly of the beast.

* * *

Joel stripped out of his cold wet clothes, trying to focus on his task and not the two beauties stripping across from him. This was survival, not sexual, he told himself. But if ever he had a fantasy of being naked with two beautiful women in the forest, this was it. Maybe just a quick peek.

They hung their clothes across branches and rocks. Using the blade of her hand, Shannon squeegeed the excess water from her body. Joel and Codi followed her lead. They wrung out their underwear and replaced it. Joel and Codi went to gather firewood, and Shannon dug through the gym bag filled with the items she had collected looking for the lighter she'd taken off the dead pilot, praying it still worked.

The first mosquito must have called all his friends because within a few minutes, a cloud of mosquitoes followed each person. It was a buzzing and slapping nightmare with no relief in sight. Joel's mind immediately went to Zika, chikungunya, and West Nile as he swatted non-stop.

Shannon collected a small bundle of shredded dry grass and used it to expand the lighter's meager flame. Soon, they were all standing around flames trying to bring their core temperature back to normal. The smoke slowed the mosquitoes' relentless attack but only slightly.

Codi waved her hands around her face to discourage the pests from landing. "Don't worry, Joel, your secret's safe with us."

Joel looked at Codi with a questioning expression.

"That lake water was really cold, so no judgment."

"Funny," he said. "Besides I'm a grow-er not a show-er."

This elicited a much-needed laugh from a group who had just come through a serious meat grinder.

"At least you can cross this off your bucket list." She used her hand to include the threesome all in soggy underwear alone in the wilderness. Joel smiled at the thought of his list. It was something Codi had encouraged him to make and do before he died. But never in his wildest dreams would this have been on it. Maybe it was time to rework that list.

After a moment, reality took over as, once again, Joel slapped the back of his neck.

"I'm guessing we were flying about ninety minutes at a cruising speed of about 270 miles per hour," Codi said.

"Almost due north," Shannon added.

Codi nodded in agreement.

"Joel?" she asked, followed by another slap.

"That's about . . ." He did the simple math in his head. "Four hundred miles north of Mont Saint-Hilare."

The information meant little to Codi and Joel, but Shannon suddenly got very somber. "Well that's not on my list," she said.

"What's not?" Joel asked.

"The middle of nowhere. We're in the middle of nowhere—by at least two hundred miles."

CHAPTER FIFTEEN

TORONTO, CANADA – SEVENTY-SECOND FLOOR – 3:54 P.M.

"Agents showing up at the mine, that's troubling," Julian Drexler said. "Where are we on all this?"

Dorthia was standing across the room from her boss. She used the question as an invitation to sit. The modern office chairs were red padded leather with a white stripe accent.

"I gave them a one-way ticket north. Unfortunately, we lost contact with the plane."

He pondered the ramifications of her words. Julian was not a man who accepted mistakes very well.

"Did they crash?"

"That's my belief." Dorthia pulled a tablet from her gray Hermes purse and flicked it on. She pointed to a spot on the map in northern Quebec, truly remote wilderness.

"The plane's transponder placed them right here. If anyone survived, the chances of them—"

"I take no chances. Send in a team and clean up your mess. No one gets out."

"Of course."

"How many deliveries have we made so far."

"Three."

Julian did the rough math in his head. "That puts us just in the black on this thing. Disappointing."

He stood and rapped his knuckles on the glass desk, thinking. "And let's close the mine just to be safe."

"Our client won't be happy," Dorthia responded.

"Screw him. Once this all blows over, we can open it back up. He'll still come running for our product. Besides, I have some other things I could use you on. Get this cleaned up first."

* * *

Of the nearly nine million people that live in Quebec, less than forty-four thousand occupy the northern half of the province. It consists of more than 323,000 square miles, making it one of the least populated places on earth. That's one person for every ten square miles, most of whom live in and around the few small towns that exist along Hudson Bay. The terrain is marsh, water, and forest with granite peaks and valleys, all of it cold. There are very few roads. Most of the country is accessible only by floatplane.

Codi held her hand to her forehead, shielding her face from the sun. They had about two hours before darkness would consume them. This time of the year the sun would set around 10:30 p.m. and would be up again by 5:30 a.m. They'd emptied their canvas bag and surveyed their gear. An eight-inch hunting knife, a small Bic lighter, two water bottles, a roll of duct tape, and a bag of peanuts. There was also a red bandanna, a pair of pliers, a rusty screwdriver, and a handheld flare gun with one cartridge in it. It was better than she had hoped for when she sent Shannon collecting during their crash landing.

"We need to get some type of shelter up. It's gonna be very cold tonight, somewhere in the high twenties. Joel can you gather enough wood for the fire?" Codi asked.

He nodded and went off to start collecting. Codi smiled, looking after him wearing only his glasses, dress shoes, and damp underwear. It was quite a sight. Shannon and Codi worked as a team to drag and stack logs and limbs beside a large fallen tree. They used moss and leaves to make a bed then laid branches over the top. It would have to do.

Joel looked up from his armload of wood to the two incredible women working as a team, one in a pink lacy bra and panties, the other in purple. Both wearing hiking boots. It was a story he could probably never share, but the sight was spectacular.

Just as the sun dipped, they transferred the fire next to the makeshift shelter. Their clothes had dried well enough, so they all got dressed, Shannon and Codi in their tactical gear, Joel in his stained dress shirt and slacks. Soon, they were sharing peanuts and water by the campfire. The illusion of peace and safety was tenuous at best.

Shannon spoke as if she was speaking to herself. "Our best bet is to find a stream, follow it to a river, and follow that to a town. If we are two hundred miles from anywhere, that will take us at least eight to ten days of hard hiking, minimum." She finished the statement with a slap to her neck.

"With no food, compass, or warm clothing, it's going to be a real ball-buster," Joel added unnecessarily.

"That's providing the bears don't get us first," Codi said.

"Or wolves," Shannon added sourly.

Once the sun dropped, a pair of pants and a long-sleeve shirt were no protection from the cold. Even the fire seemed to fail at providing adequate heat. The three shivering agents sandwiched together for warmth, with Joel ending up in the middle.

"Try to keep it in your pants tonight for a change, Joel," Codi said as she squeezed up next to him.

"What! I never—"

The two women started to giggle, and Joel realized he was being teased.

"Don't worry, Joel," Shannon added, "if we are going to die, I can think of worse ways to go."

The smile that grew on Joel's face lasted nearly the whole night.

At about 3:00 a.m., a huffing sound followed by a low growl had all three agents up and stoking the smoldering fire. They listened as a large predator circled them.

"Bear," Shannon whispered as she picked up a burning stick and waved it back and forth in the air. It seemed to have no effect on the beast, which continued to move closer as it circled.

Codi reached for the flare gun and tracked the sound, ready to fire. They moved back-to-back, each holding a weapon—Shannon, the knife, and Joel, the rusty screwdriver. It was a pathetic gesture. After seven very intense minutes, the bear stood on it hind legs and let out a piercing roar. It shook the trio to the core. The bear then dropped down on all fours and wandered off back into the night from where it had come.

"I think I just peed my pants," said Joel.

* * *

Morning couldn't come soon enough. It had been a really miserable night. They had bug bites on top of bug bites. They finished off their peanuts and the water and started on their two-hundred-mile journey south, one step at a time. Joel carried the gym bag and Codi the flare gun. It wasn't much, but it might signal a stray plane or scare off a bear. They took turns calling out to make sure the bears heard them coming. An unexpected meeting might result in an attack.

"Hey, bear, coming through!"

"Joel, were you ever in the Boy Scouts?" Shannon asked.

"Hardly. I was more into computers," he said as he wiped his glasses on his sleeve. "Where did you grow up?" he asked.

Shannon stepped over a fallen log before answering him. "I'm a British Columbia girl. Grew up just over the border in Vancouver."

"The banana belt of Canada," Codi said.

"Oh, believe me, it can get cold there."

"So how did you end up a mountie?"

The silence that followed made Joel wish he hadn't asked the question.

"Wow, check it out!"

They all stopped. Codi was looking down at an aquifer that was bubbling up out of the ground.

"Safe drinking water."

They all knew the dangers of drinking water from a stream or lake. The microscopic organism *giardia* would leave you doubled over and running for the toilet, not something they could afford. Codi grabbed the two empty bottles from the gym bag and started to fill them. The label on the bottle said spring water. Now, it would be true.

Shannon took a long pull on the water bottle. It was crisp and refreshing.

"My parents wanted me to be a doctor," she said. "I wanted to be a doctor. Started medical school and was doing great. The student life at The University of British Columbia was a life that suited me. Parties, friends, study groups, and all-nighters. I loved it."

She passed the water bottle to Joel.

"One night, my roommate Talia and I were heading back from a late study group at the library. She was really something. Tall, blonde curly hair, and an infectious personality. She could turn even the most hateful person into a friend. Just had a way about her. We were on a sidewalk, a lit sidewalk. It was a path we'd taken many times between the cafeteria and the law school. I heard footsteps to the right, and then my head exploded in a shot of pain. Some guy had been hiding on my left. He hit me with a pipe."

Joel suddenly stopped drinking and shared a glance with Codi.

Shannon dug the toe of her boot into the soft earth as she spoke. "I saw some serious stars, but I didn't black out. Two guys subdued Talia and then came for me. I kicked the first guy in the balls as hard as I could and started screaming for help. They must have gotten scared, so they grabbed Talia and ran. I tried to stand but was so dizzy, I couldn't even get to my knees. I wasn't able stop them, to do anything."

"I'm so sorry," Joel said, feeling guilty for asking.

"They found her body three days later. What they did to her . . ." Shannon was too emotional to speak. She took a second to compose herself. "It changed me. I wanted to see those guys caught and fried. I needed justice at any cost."

Codi and Joel shared a knowing nod.

"So did you get justice?" Joel asked.

"They were both killed by a drunk driver two weeks later. I guess it was some kind of justice."

She turned and started back down the trail.

Codi and Joel followed in silence.

* * *

Carl placed the Amazon box on the table. He grabbed a knife and cut the tape that held it together. With both hands, he pulled out a refrigeration device the size of a toaster oven. He set it down and started the process of disassembling it.

He thought back to the job that had started his career. As a young boy in Kazakhstan, he had been a true believer. And an all-encompassing Al-Qaida had taken him into the fold. They trained him and armed him. He watched as many of his close friends martyred themselves for a cause that seemed to be losing ground against a more diligent and focused West. He had just escaped such a fate when he was selected for something else, a mission that would put him in a position to do great harm to the West.

He and six other boys were sent off to school in France to attend the University of Paris-Saclay. It was France's most modern school and the top engineering federal university. The elite school was a perfect match for the young boy who spoke French and Russian. He was given a new background and name, Adrien Brunot. He quickly excelled in his classes, earning a mechanical engineering degree with a minor in English.

With the death of Osama Bin Laden and the splintering of Al-Qaida, Adrien lost his connection to the cell and found himself alone and adrift. He thought of rejoining the fight but was unsure whom he could trust. He considered taking on the West by himself and used his skills to make a water bomb. He placed white phosphorus in a toilet tank in a large bathroom at a soccer stadium. He then filled the tank with O2 from a modified sports bottle and replaced the lid. The next user would flush the toilet, causing the phosphorous to react with the O2 and creating a large fireball.

The residual gas, phosphorous pentoxide, would react with water to create phosphoric acid. Anyone who breathed in the fumes from the explosion would have severe lung damage.

The toilet flushed and the chemical burst into an explosion. It worked perfectly. Three died immediately in the blast, with eight more injured and dying. It felt good to be doing something for the cause again, but the stress of doing it nearly gave him a heart attack. He fled the stadium full of panic and fear. His heart raced until he literally passed out.

When he came to, he was in a dark room with a small lamp glowing in the corner. Next to the light was a man with a gun. "I've been looking for you," the man said.

Adrien gave no reply. As he leaned up on one arm, his heart racing again.

"And you are lucky I found you before the police did."

"Why is that?" Adrien asked, failing to stay calm.

"You and I can do much good together," he said as he put the gun down. "My name is Jal Zayid, and I would like to make you an offer."

He told Adrien of his idea. He could be a freelancer with total anonymity. It would allow him to strike at the West from many angles and sources, something he could never do all by himself. He would be free to design and build as he pleased, without having to get in the trenches or do the actual dirty work. The idea appealed to Adrien. He knew in his heart that he was not a foot soldier.

"I will give you a new name and passport to go with it. We will make a point to change it every eight to ten months so you will remain a ghost. I know you are not interested in money, but you will be paid very well, and you can do with it what you want."

It was the beginning of a great partnership. Jal would get the contracts; Adrien would design and build the mechanisms for exploding. Together they had been a significant, yet unknown part of over twenty successful attacks around the globe. Adrien thought of all the previous names he had donned and then of his current one, Carl. It was the funniest. It sounded like an automobile with a low battery trying to start.

He once again began to photograph and digitize every major component from the refrigeration device. The goal was to make four replica units from scratch with no history or trackability. He used a 3-D printer to replicate the non-metallic parts. It was the last step in his process. He had already designed and manufactured the four steel mixing chambers, the aluminum shell, and the compressors. He stacked four lithium ion batteries on a table. They could run the finished units for up to an hour if there was a power failure.

A heat exchanger of his own design would atomize the mineral oil into a vapor. The small compressor would inject the vapor and the radioactive micro-particles into the chamber where they would be combined. The mixture would then be pushed through coiled copper tubing into the refrigeration unit to chill. The cooled deadly smoke would be disbursed out through a rotating valve, designed to spew it in all directions. Chilled fog would hang lower to the ground than warm fog, like ground mist in a spooky cemetery. It would move and flow with air movement and the motion of bodies, creating wispy trails and swirls. Each finished machine would be slightly larger than a mini-fridge and could cover half a football field. The crowd would go nuts for it.

* * *

The reflection of the surrounding forest exploded as the helicopter dropped over the water. It had taken two additional hours to find the crash site, even with the plane's transponder GPS coordinates. The rubber-stamped sameness of the wilderness was daunting. Trees, lakes, marsh, meadows. Repeat. The Airbus ACH-160 did a touch and go as it was already running low on fuel. Four heavily armed men quickly emerged, crouching low until the Airbus was back in the air.

Black Bellville cold-weather combat boots slogged across to the crash site. Each man carried a Colt C7 assault rifle. A shotgun filled with slugs for the bears was also carried by Machk, an indigenous Cree Indian. He was tall and lanky with black eyes and high cheekbones. His roman nose had been broken in the past, giving it an extra jog. He had an omnipresent green bandana on his head and a keen sense of direction.

Their leader was a massively strong man named Lyle Walters. He had spent the last four years of his life as a free-lance mercenary and was happy to finally be on the payroll of his current employer. Lyle spent most of his free time pumping iron and anything in a skirt in an effort to compensate for his small mind and small penis.

The two other men were French carbon copies of a gun-for-hire: bad attitude, bad social skills, bad breath, all around hard men. They had trained in COS, Commandement des Operations Speciales, the French special forces, and this was not the first time they'd been on a mission of this type. Lyle called them Thing One and Thing Two, after the destructive characters in the Dr. Seuss children's book, *Cat in the Hat*. Their leader had an endearing way about him that worked well in the command structure of a group like this. His guys were loyal and would do whatever was asked, but each knew that just under his outward personality was a killer. A man that was all about one thing—himself.

Lyle surveyed the crash site. He could see the plane's wings and tail back by the tree line. A brown gash in the verdant meadow led to the small lake where it was obvious the plane had hit and sunk.

"Lyle! I got something."

He turned to see Machk waving him over to the meadow's edge. He jogged over. "What you got, Mac?"

"Looks like three people survived. They made camp here for the night and left in that direction." He pointed south. "About a fourteen-hour head start."

"If it was our men who survived they would have known to wait here."

The other two men stepped into the makeshift campsite.

"Looks like we're going hunting," Lyle said to the group.

CHAPTER SIXTEEN

The courtesy call from Homeland had started the day off poorly. Brian had been thanked for sending the lab results on the trace and hair follicles but was then reminded that the case was no longer the FBI's. The man seemed more caught up in who had the authority over the case than actually solving it. Typical D.C. politics, Brian told himself.

It was the call from Anna in Special Projects that put the sour expression on his face. Codi and Joel had not checked in. They had left their hotel room, but there was no sign of them since. Their rental car was missing, and when its LoJack was activated, it returned no signal. His agents had never even checked in at the airport. They appeared to have vanished. Brian did not act surprised. He had experienced Codi and Joel disappearing in the past. It was becoming their thing. Last time, it nearly caused him to quit his job and go look for them himself somewhere in China.

The procedures for a missing or presumed dead agent at the FBI are very specific and do not include the supervising special agent going in the field. He hesitated doing anything due to his trust in Codi and Joel, but he would never forgive himself if he didn't do all he could on his end to help. He picked up the phone. *First things first.*

"Hello?"

"Honey, I'm going to be working late."

* * *

Machk led the group in a quick march. They had fourteen hours to make up, and he wanted to close that gap ASAP. The terrain was consistently unpredictable. One instant, they were be on a game trail, and the next, they were slogging through the underbrush. The last of the snowmelt made for muddy sections that were nearly impassable. Their prey was leaving an easy trail for Machk to follow, and his lifelong hunting and tracking skills were on full display. He estimated they had gained two hours on their prey so far.

"Hey, Mac, toss me some of that water." Lyle chugged the water while still quick-marching. He passed it over to Thing Two and checked their position with a handheld GPS. He sent a pin via his sat-phone to his boss without stopping.

"Hey, One. What you got back there?"

Thing One was bringing up the rear, covering their flank.

"All clear," he called.

"Good to hear."

"I've been thinking, Two," Lyle said as he slowed to close the distance between them.

Thing Two lifted his head to listen.

"Three unarmed, hungry, and dehydrated targets. How would you go at them to make it . . . sporting?"

Thing Two knew Lyle. The man needed a challenge, and three armed and trained killers against unarmed city cops was no challenge, especially when two of them were girls. He mulled over the question as he hurried down the trail. Finally, he said, "I would shoot one, and then the other two would jackrabbit off. We'd at least get our money's worth chasing them down."

"Killing them straight up does seem too easy," Lyle said. "What if we were to wound one? That might give them some real excitement before realizing they had to leave 'em behind. They would still jackrabbit but would feel like they'd abandoned a partner." He tried to picture the moment in his mind. "I wish I could be there to watch when they hear the shot that kills their leave-behind. That would be something."

He smiled for the first time in a week. This was his element. The kind of action that made him feel alive. "After they run," he said, "we could still split up and have a little two-on-one competition."

Thing Two nodded. "I like it. And a thousand-dollar bonus to the team that gets theirs first."

"Good. You and I will take one target and Mac and One the other."

"So who do we shoot first?" Thing Two asked.

"The dude. Definitely the dude. That way we can each get a little something extra before we finish 'em off."

"Momma's sweet cherry pie. I like it." He called out, "Hey Mac!"

* * *

Joel held his hand up against the sun's glare. "I'm getting fried, bitten, and I'm friggin' hungry."

"No whiners on this adventure, please," Codi said as she moved mechanically down the trail. She had gone into beast-mode and had only one focus: one foot in front of the other.

"If we keep moving, we'll have a better chance against the mosquitoes," Shannon said.

"We'll never be able to keep up this pace without some food."

They knew Joel was right. Shannon paused unexpectedly.

"Okay, how 'bout some lunch?"

She moved down to a marshy area and started digging up the rootstocks from cattails. She passed them to Codi.

"Scrape off the outer coating."

Codi took the knife and sliced off the brown outer skin. Inside was a white jicama-looking plant. She cut it into chunks and passed it around.

"It tastes like glue, but it will give you energy," Shannon said. "Oh, and Joel, come here and take off your glasses."

He moved over to where Shannon was by the swamp. She dipped her hands in the black mud and then spread it like sunscreen to cover Joel's exposed skin.

"It might stink a little, but it will cut the sun and help with the bugs," she said.

Joel made a face at the smell, but inside he enjoyed the attention from the strikingly cute mountie.

"There you go," Shannon said as she finished blackening his face.

"Tall, dark, and handsome," Codi said.

"That's the way I like my men," Shannon added.

"Really?" came Joel's reply, his eyes watering from the putrid smell of the mud.

Shannon leaned up close to Joel's ear. "I'll let you know if we get out of here alive."

A jolt went up Joel's spine. He would do everything in his power to make that happen.

* * *

After three days of shivering, poor sleep, and meager calories, the trio was slowing down. Each step seemed more labored than the previous.

They had grown numb to their beatific surroundings. Waterfalls and mossy meadows passed without notice.

"Hamburger, pizza, shredded beef tacos. Hamburger, pizza, shredded beef tacos." Shannon continued the rant, each word in time with a footfall. A marching mantra.

"What are you doing?" Joel asked.

"I'm trying to decide which I will eat first when we get out of here," she answered.

"I took you for more of a grilled chicken kind of girl."

"Not a chance. Hamburger, pizza, shredded beef tacos."

After a few verses, Joel joined in, and soon, a chorus rang out in full voice, as all three sang and clapped their way down the trail. Codi added a little beat-box, and they got a real tune going.

The song finally died out and so did the conversation as each agent wrestled against low energy and starvation to keep moving. They were burning 7,500 calories per day and had eaten just 300 calories for the last two days.

Codi was like an engine. She needed fuel and was the worst off. She had gone into her Seal training mode, where she had only one all-consuming focus. It drove her forward with no energy for anything else.

"Codi! Wait up," Joel called out.

She had gotten so far ahead that they had lost sight of each other.

Shannon and Joel struggled to intercept.

"Sorry, I was on autopilot," Codi said as they approached.

"We need to stay together, especially now that we're all struggling. I'm assigning responsibilities," Shannon said. "It's too easy for one of us to get left behind or wander off because we're not able to stay focused."

Codi and Joel nodded in agreement. Their brains were not functioning at a hundred percent. It would take all three of them to stay sharp.

"Codi, you are responsible for Joel, he is responsible for me, and I got you." Shannon looked over at Codi as she sat down on a rock. "Check in every five minutes to be safe."

"Any water left?" Codi asked.

"Here," Joel said as he handed it to her.

As she reached for the bottle, she paused, looking at something in the distance past Joel's shoulder. Her mouth dropped to a frown.

Joel wondered what it was and looked back over his shoulder and then back at Codi. There was nothing. "You okay?" he asked.

"We got company."

"What? Where?" Joel asked.

"Don't turn around. Keep your eyes on me," Codi demanded. "About three clicks back on that ridge. I caught a reflection from either sunglasses or binoculars."

"Probably a cleanup crew," Shannon said.

"That's what I'm guessing."

"Maybe it's just hunters and a way outta here," Joel said optimistically.

Codi ignored him, her mind now fully alert. "We need to be really smart about this or we won't see another sunrise."

* * *

Sterling watched as the last piece of wall was raised, sealing off the lab. The two workers quickly attached it with steel bolts anchored into the rock. They moved a few feet down the shaft, where blasting caps were positioned in a semi-circle and wires attached. Once back at the elevator, they took protective positions as one worker connected the wires to a detonator. He looked to his boss expectantly. Sterling gave him a nod, and he twisted the handle, releasing a small current down the line to the blasting caps.

A muffled explosion rumbled within the mountain, sending a wave of dust in their direction. After a few moments, it settled enough for them to see again. Sterling walked back down the tunnel. He came to a pile of rubble closing off the shaft. The lab and everything beyond it was now sealed and inaccessible.

He stabbed at the up button on the elevator wondering what would come next. His new partners were extreme, and he was tired of playing the fool for them. How had he lost control? Sterling watched as one of his men replaced the eight-floor elevator control with a new one that went down only four floors, the uranium mine and its transmutation lab effectively gone for now. Except for these two trusted men, everyone else involved in the project had already been relocated by Dorthia, including Dr. Baghdadis

He wondered what she meant by the term relocated. It was time for him to do the same. He handed each man an envelope and said, "Make yourselves scarce for the next six months."

They knew what was expected and exited the mine. Sterling stayed behind, looking at his family's legacy and wondering how it had come to this. He searched his mind for someone to blame but found only himself.

* * *

Lyle lowered his binoculars and allowed the corners of his mouth to rise. They had closed the distance. Their tangos were in sight. Just as they thought, two women and one man. The trio was moving down along a small creek surrounded by two ridges.

"Mac, take One and continue to push them through this valley. I'll take Two and work the ridge and try to get ahead of them." He pointed to a place where the two ridges narrowed.

"See that choke-point down there?"

"Oui."

"That's where we want to converge."

Machk knew immediately what the plan was and nodded. He moved out with One on his heels. They had come a long way in a hurry, but the effort was about to pay off.

Lyle moved up along the ridge, stepping as quickly as the terrain would allow. He was tired of humping through the wilderness and was eager to make contact. The thin air had him deep breathing with every step. He thought back to the last time he hunted a man. It was in the jungles outside Panama City. The man had stolen from his employer and Lyle spent three weeks tracking him down to Panama before he bolted into the jungle. The foot chase lasted just over a day before Lyle caught up to the man. At the time, he was all business, and a simple bullet from a distance ended the pursuit. The act was unfulfilling and left Lyle wanting. He would not make the same mistake today. He would relish the next few hours and make the most of it. Today he would have a little fun before heading back to the four walls of his corporate security job.

* * *

Joel suddenly stopped. In their haste they had run into a large black bear. It reared up in an aggressive posture, growling a defiant warning.

Shannon whispered a command. "Nobody make any sudden moves. Nice and easy, back off, and we'll go around."

The bear stepped forward. This was his domain, and he wanted the interlopers to know it. The three agents reversed slowly away. The bear finally dropped to all fours. It roared once more and then seemed content that he had defended his territory.

"That was close," Joel said.

"Too close," Shannon said. "Moving this fast is going to get us killed."

"So will moving too slow," Codi said, gesturing in the direction behind them.

The situation seemed dire. They were being hunted by more than just one group.

"Here take this and give me the knife." Codi handed the flare gun to Shannon. "Keep moving downstream, and I'll catch up as soon as I can." She spun around with the knife and ran off before anyone could protest.

"Is she always like that?" Shannon asked.

"Most of the time, but it seems to work out. At least so far," Joel deadpanned.

* * *

It was time to put some of her BUD/S training to good use. Codi took some mud and moss and covered her face and hair in it. As quickly as her legs would take her, she ran to the top of the ridge. Just before reaching the top, she paused to catch her breath. She heard footsteps coming her way and ducked under an outcropping to hide, listening carefully as they moved past her. Two bodies, she told herself while moving out of cover and back onto the trail to follow. She stayed back far enough to avoid being seen, hoping they were more focused on their targets ahead rather than behind.

The two men were in a hurry. Each carried a Colt C7, the cousin to the American AR15. They moved like pros and seemed to have a destination in mind. Codi paused at a gnarled tree trunk. She could see the two ridges of the valley narrowing up ahead and knew immediately what was about to happen. She turned and sprinted after the two killers. Joel and Shannon were in real trouble.

* * *

The bear was angry. It had been disturbed and forced to defend its territory. It circled the valley aggravated, still ready to pounce. Machk and One dropped onto the small game trail that paralleled the stream. They closed the distance on their prey. Machk guessed they were mere moments away from a sighting. A sudden thrashing to his right revealed an angry predator in wait. A large black bear charged. In their hurry Machk had not been concerned with bear safety and his shotgun was stowed over his shoulder. He reached for it and flipped it around as the bear swatted One as if he was a toy soldier. The bear turned to Machk and rushed forward.

As the beast launched, Machk just managed to pull the trigger. The blast was ear splitting as a one-once lead slug was sent down the barrel at 1800 fps. It hit the bear right in the solar plexus, causing a mortal wound. The bear swiped once more before it died two feet from its intended prey.

Machk stepped to the side, still shaking from the near-death experience. He gathered himself and ran to One who was lying in a heap by a nearby stump. Machk rolled him over to see a large gash that had opened him up, chest to crotch. Gore poured out of him, and Machk backed away in revulsion. One moved his lips like a fish out of water trying to speak, but even that fizzled out as his eyes glazed over. There was nothing more Machk could do. He stepped over to the bear and knelt beside it. He had hunted a lot of animals, even a few men, but never had he come so close to dying. It was a sobering thought. He gave the bear that had almost ended him full respect.

"Maskwa, I am sorry," he said, using the Cree word for Big Bear.

He touched the animal's ear in a show of respect. Mother nature was, at best, unpredictable. She rarely showed favoritism and was almost always dispassionate in her moods.

Machk stood and jogged on after his quarry. If he had time later, he would come back for the pelt.

* * *

The shotgun blast echoed through the valley, galvanizing Shannon and Joel into a sprint. It seemed close by, and they had no defense from armed mercenaries. The canyon walls were closing in on both sides and the game trail became more precarious, with rocks and boulders strewn across it.

Joel tried not to become hypnotized by the female form running in front of him. It was amazing. He wanted desperately to say something personal, but with certain death so close, now was not the best time. So he did what Joel did best and just blurted out. "If we get out of this, I'd like to ask you out on a date," he called to Shannon.

Shannon kept her pace. She didn't look back at Joel but could imagine the look on his face, hoping and waiting for an answer. She took a full ten steps before answering. She figured good news was worth waiting for. "If we get out of this, I'd like to go on a date with you," she called back.

"Really?" Joel almost stopped, forgetting their situation.

"Yes, Joel. Now quit chatting and run!"

Joel picked up his pace, along with the corners of his mouth, just in time to stumble on a root that stuck out in the trail. He went down in a tangle of legs and arms. Shannon stopped and stepped over to help him up.

"Eyes on the trail, not on imagining how good I'm gonna look in my red strapless sundress, okay?"

Joel nodded as he stood and together they continued down the trail.

"Because I'm going to look amazing," she called back.

* * *

"Fescue." Brian picked up his phone and leaned back in his office chair.

"Brian, this is Agent Dennis Paige over at Homeland. How are things?"

"Good?" Brain deadpanned. This guy was unbelievable. *One call he reads me the riot act, and the next, he's acting like we're buddies.*

"Nice. Hey, look, I need a favor. As I understand it, you have Shannon Poole from the RCMP working with you. I need to borrow her for a quick trip up to Montreal to interface with the Surete."

The coincidence struck Brian like a toddler smashing into a clear glass door. *Something was going on in Quebec.*

"Sorry, no can do." The words felt good in his mouth. "Shannon and the two agents you met with last time you were here are missing." *Those words, not so much.*

"Missing?"

"Yes. They went to Montreal three days ago and haven't been seen since."

"I thought I told your agents to stay away from my case."

Brian paused to bite his lower lip. *Calm down and play nice*, he told himself.

"This was an entirely different case. They sent you everything we had on your radiation victim and walked away from it."

"Is it possible their case is somehow connected to mine?" Dennis demanded.

"First of all, you might want to call it *your* case, but you wouldn't have a case if not for my agents. Second, they are working on a cold case, so I doubt it has anything to do with yours."

Brian didn't like the man's insinuation. However, he had a creeping suspicion that if Codi and Joel were involved, he had probably just lied to the man at Homeland.

A brief pause took over the conversation.

"I'm sorry about your agents and my outburst."

"I understand. Keep your eyes open while you're up there, will you?"

"Will do. Thanks."

When Dennis hung up, Brian banged on his desk. *What on earth was going on?* He was going to get to the bottom of this.

CHAPTER SEVENTEEN

Codi stopped at a tree situated one hundred feet from a solid granite vantage point on the ridge. The area was the size of a small porch overhanging the valley floor. The two hunters had taken up residence there with both of their rifles pointed down to a small clearing next to the stream. They were waiting for Joel and Shannon to clear the trees, so they would have an easy shot when they crossed the clearing.

Codi needed to do something and quick. There was no cover between her and the hunters. One hundred feet totally exposed, it was a suicide mission. A shot reverberated through the canyon below. She watched as both men popped up to get a look at what might be happening down there. It sounded like a shotgun blast. This was as good of a distraction as she would get. She stayed low and moved forward on the balls of her feet. Fifty, thirty, then twenty-five feet. She dropped to a prone position as both men looked at each other. She heard the one on the right call out to the other. "Get ready. They're coming into position." They both crouched back down into a kneeling firing position and took aim as two targets moved through the open meadow below. As the men lowered and focused on their targets, Codi made her move. She pushed forward, bee-lining for the one that was closest.

Her last couple of steps must have been heard as the man started to turn around. Codi jumped feet first driving her knife into the first man and landing both feet into the side of the second one. She landed hard on the rocks jarring her side and elbow. Her whole arm went numb with pain. The second man flipped over the edge of the precipice, his hands grabbing for purchase that would never come. The first man grunted as the knife sunk into his back.

He pulled himself up and tried to lift his rifle in Codi's direction. His right arm shot with pain from the knife that was sticking in his back and the rifle fell uselessly. He stood and pulled a pistol out of his holster with his left hand while his right arm dangled. He was not as competent with his left hand and struggled to release the safety and rack the slide one-handed.

Codi quickly got to her feet and threw a loose rock in the man's direction to slow him down. She followed the rock with a sweeping leg that caught the pistol just as it was pointed at her. It skittered off the rocks and over the side. She reached for the rifle, but the man anticipated her move and kicked it over the side, as well.

"Well, what do we have here," the man said with a grimace. "A wildcat all ready for skinning."

He said the words as he removed a large hunting knife from its sheath. He moved it through the air like a practiced knife fighter. Though he had use of only one hand, he still seemed exceptionally dangerous.

"Come and get some, pretty lady. I'm gonna put this inside you and twist ever so slowly." He demonstrated the knife twist and then gestured to his crotch. "Then I got something else to put inside you, just as your last drop drains out. I bet you'd like that, wouldn't you?"

Codi was between the man and the edge of the overhang. There was no way out but through him or a long fall down. The man pressed his advantage. He crouched in a fighter's stance and closed the gap between them. Codi kept her hands up like a boxer probing for a weakness or opportunity. She moved right. He countered. She tried left with the same result. She had her heels backed to the edge. She was in real trouble.

"Be careful, don't want you falling and missing all the fun," he said with a smile that never reached his dead eyes.

He slashed with the knife and Codi ducked. He swiped again and caught her on the wrist bone. Blood leaked out with every heartbeat. Codi tried to control her mind. It was starting to panic. She lowered herself just a bit more and waited. The man lunged stabbing straight at her. Codi let the knife come. She slipped her head sideways just enough and parried with her left hand. The blade skimmed off her cheek, missing her eye by a half-inch. She used the back of her right fist to connect with the nerve just above his elbow and force the knife up and into empty space. This made the man take an extra step forward that he wasn't prepared for. She slipped under his armpit and behind him. As she passed him, Codi grabbed the knife that was still in his back and recycled it. Out, then up, and back down into his neck.

The man spun wildly slashing his knife through the air. Codi ducked and stepped back. She was now standing on the safe side of the precipice. They had exchanged places. He teetered on the edge of the rock but found his balance and spun back around. He took another step toward her. Knife still raised and ready.

"Would you just die, already!" she said.

As if some great goddess of the forest heard her, a painful, bloody grimace passed across his face. He stopped and dropped to his knees. His gurgled breaths coming more and more shallow, as he doddered.

"What, no witty banter?"

"Your dead, bit—," he sputtered through blood-soaked teeth, just before dropping his knife and falling face-first to the ground.

Codi watched him die without remorse. She tore off the bottom of her shirt and wrapped her wrist, then collected both knives and headed diagonally down the ridge. This wasn't over yet.

* * *

A shot sent splinters from a tree just over Joel's head. He ducked reflexively but kept moving. It was just a question of time now.

"We got to split up," he called to Shannon. "I'll cut across the stream. You stay on the trail."

Shannon ran on as Joel cut left. He high-stepped it across the stream and back into the cover of the trees in record time. He scowled as he glanced over his shoulder while panic-climbing the hill. He could just make out a glimpse of a man with a green bandana and a gun following Shannon. *Dang.*

He waited to catch his breath and then turned back toward the trail. Shannon was now in serious jeopardy. A surge of terror hit Joel hard; he had to do something.

Joel had lost someone he cared deeply for on a previous case, and it had gutted him. She had been a light in Joel's life, and they had built a strong relationship before a coward and traitor from MI-5 ended her life. He could not let that happen again.

Shannon ran until there was no more run left in her. She needed to find a place to hide. On the left of the creek, she found a low spot covered in foliage. She jogged off the trail and dove into a thicket of bushes. Her lungs heaved in gulps as she tried to catch her breath. She squirmed into a prone position and dug in, pulling the flare gun out and taking very careful aim as she waited.

* * *

Machk jogged down the game trail with his head on a swivel. He was alert to his surroundings, not wanting a bear or some other unwanted pest blindsiding him. About twenty feet ahead, he noticed a scuff in the dirt and slowed his pace. He followed the spoor to a thicket of blueberry bushes. He paused and raised his weapon. A flare suddenly shot right at him. He used the butt of his gun to deflect it like a foul tip, and it sputtered off in the distance. He quickly re-aimed his rifle at the thicket.

"Come out real slow, or I'll end you where you lie."

Shannon slowly got to her feet and dropped the empty flare pistol. Her eyes shone with fierce intensity. If only looks could kill. She stepped forward with her hands at her side.

"Where's your boyfriend?"

"We split up. He ghosted me," Shannon answered.

Machk looked around quickly for the missing man. He had missed the fact they had separated, and it surprised and worried him. He had been so caught up in closing the gap that he had become careless. Not good. No doubt Lyle and Two would clean things up. He looked back at his prize.

"I got you all by myself."

"I doubt you can handle me all by yourself," Shannon countered.

The challenge seemed to have no effect on the man, as he remained focused on his task.

"Down on your knees. Interlock your fingers behind your head."

Shannon complied.

"Now, put your forehead on the ground."

Again, she did as she was told. The awkward angle would make it extremely difficult for her to do anything. The man lowered his gun and leaned it against a tree. He pulled out his pistol and racked the slide. He moved to an angle that put Shannon between him and the trail.

"If you move, I'll shoot you. But I'm happy for you to call out all you want. Yell to your boyfriend. Tell him what's up. Go ahead."

Shannon squinted up from the strained position. The man seemed serious. So she screamed. "Joel, get out of here. Don't try to save me. *Run!*"

Machk let her call out. This was just what he had wanted. It would be like calling a rutting elk with a doe bugler. He would come running. All Machk had to do now was wait.

Joel heard Shannon's call. He was torn. It was definitely a trap, and his only weapon was a rusty screwdriver. He continued to move down the trail, worried sick about Shannon. He was not a good hunter and definitely not very stealthy, but his choices were limited. He tried to go from tree to tree, hiding behind them as he moved forward, closing in on the sound as she screamed for him to do just the opposite.

Shannon's call suddenly stopped and so did Joel. What did that mean? Had she been killed? Joel quickly picked up his pace, panicking.

"Stop right there!"

Joel froze. He dropped his screwdriver and raised his arms. His head turned slightly to the right. A few feet off the trail was Shannon, slumped over on the ground. No, not slumped, bent. There was the man with the green bandana on his head, pointing his pistol right at Joel. His black eyes stared with glee.

"So predictable. Now, slowly come over next to your girlfriend and assume the position."

Joel walked next to Shannon and bent down, interlocking his fingers behind his head and placing his forehead on the ground.

"You okay?" Joel whispered.

"You were supposed to get away."

"Yeah, about that . . . sorry?"

"You really are adorable, you know that? Stupid but adorable," Shannon said.

Joel smiled at the comment, supposing it would be his last compliment.

Machk circled the two captives. He let them speak. It was of no consequence to him. His partner would have reveled in this moment and probably taken his time with the woman, but Machk had no such designs.

A simple bullet in the back of their heads would do. He pointed, cocked his gun, and squeezed the trigger.

* * *

It felt like déjà vu because it was. Brian put the call out to establish a team to locate and track down the missing agents. The only difference was the mountie. He needed to combine the two agencies' resources. A call to RCMP in D.C. had set things in motion. Now, all he needed was for them to get at it. An older gentleman named Isaac reported to Brian three hours later. He had a tight-fitting black suit that revealed a slight stomach bulge. He had thinning brown hair and a nasty scar from his right ear to his nose that spiraled in the center.

Brian showed him to the room where he would be working. It had a small round table in the middle surrounded by metal chairs and long tables along two walls. The front was all glass. The people who worked there had nicknamed it The Fishbowl. It was bare-bones, and there was no place to hide, but as a work environment, it was perfectly functional. A short rap on the door was followed by one of Brian's own agents entering the room.

Brian made the introductions. "Special Agent Gordon Reyas, this is Inspector Isaac Cumberland."

"Isaac is fine."

They shook hands.

Brian continued. "Okay, Isaac, we will have a couple more agents here tomorrow to get things started, but you two represent the two departments involved. Gordon, I expect you to keep me apprised of your progress, as I expect you will do the same to your boss, Isaac." They both nodded in reply. "I have sent what little we have to your inbox, Gordon. Please copy Isaac and help him get logged in. I don't have to tell you time is critical when agents go missing. So let's get on it and get 'em back in one piece."

"Knowing Codi, she's probably out there killin' it, boss," Gordon said.

"I hope you're right."

Brian couldn't help but think about his situation and the call he had received from Dennis at Homeland. If the two cases were somehow connected, then Codi, Joel, and Shannon could be in real trouble. Radiation and terrorism were a dangerous combination, one that often left bodies in its wake.

* * *

Codi had come a long way in a short amount of time. She had heard Shannon crying out and had zeroed in on the source. It was now only a matter of going into absolute stealth mode to close the last fifty yards to where she was being held. When Joel arrived on the scene, he had been a great distraction to help her get even closer. The man who held them seemed efficient in his mannerisms. Codi knew she had run out of time.

She was at least twenty feet away when he pointed his pistol at the back of Joel's head and started to squeeze the trigger. Codi's arsenal consisted of two knives, but the killer had two guns. A pistol in his hand and a rifle slung over his shoulder. She noticed a shotgun leaning against a tree next to him, but she would never make it.

Codi picked up a stick from the ground. She chucked it to her right. And prepared for the longest knife throw of her life. The man suddenly stopped his action and turned to the sound of the stick. Codi flung the knife with all her force. She quickly followed behind it sprinting straight at the man as she cocked the second knife for another throw.

The man sensed her presence and spun toward her. The first knife impacted him in the chest. Unfortunately, it hit him hilt first and just bounced away harmlessly. Codi had closed the distance significantly as she flung her second knife. It caught him in the shoulder. Machk grunted with the impact but didn't even take a step back. He acquired the new target charging his way and pulled the trigger.

His gun arm suddenly exploded in pain as a large limb bashed it, sending the bullet flying errantly. He turned just in time to see the limb make a second contact with his head, and then all went dark.

* * *

"Nice work, Joel. I think you killed him," Shannon said.

Joel stood holding the limb in his hands. Rage was still etched across his face, and he was hyperventilating. Shannon took the limb from him and tossed it away.

"Remind me to never get on your bad side," she said.

"I don't have a bad side," Joel said numbly.

Codi stood back up. She had dived to the ground in a desperate attempt to dodge the gun's bullet. She dusted herself off and walked over to them. She was still covered in mud and twigs from earlier.

"He's right. No bad side." She smiled at her savior as she bent over to check the vitals on the downed man. "Looks like you only mostly killed him, Joel. Help me get this guy tied up. I don't want to take any chances."

"Is he the last one?" Joel asked.

"For now." Codi picked up his gun and put it in her waistband. She tossed the C7 rifle to Shannon and the shotgun to Joel. *Finally, they were armed.*

Codi pulled off the man's backpack and handed it to Joel. He rummaged through the contents, passing out energy bars and water. He pulled a larger packet from the bottom.

"Freeze-dried beef stroganoff for dinner!" It was the second most beautiful thing he had seen all day.

"Looks like a good place to camp for the night," Shannon said, using paracord from the pack to tie up their prisoner.

Codi gathered firewood. Tonight would be a feast for more than just the mosquitoes.

* * *

Special Agent Gordon Reyas set up his things in The Fishbowl. First on the list was his computer. It was not the first time he'd been asked to work with agents here. A couple of cases ago, Agent Sanders and Agent Strickman had gone missing, and he had been assigned the impossible task of finding them. They had been kidnapped and replaced with lookalikes at a Chinese airport in broad daylight. In the end, his team had struck out. It wasn't until Codi and Joel pulled a self-rescue that the team even knew what country they were in.

He plugged in his computer and adjusted the monitor.

Isaac had settled in, and they were both searching traffic cams around the hotel in Montreal, the last known sighting of the three agents. Isaac had arranged for two RCMP inspectors to interview staff and inspect their rooms. Because it fell under the umbrella of federal, there was no need to involve the Quebec Surete, only to inform them.

"Bullet?"

Gordon had been staring at the scar on Isaac's face, and he couldn't help himself. It just . . . came out.

"Ganglion cyst." Isaac paused and turned to Gordon. "Had it removed. It had made quite a home in there. But I do have a bullet hole."

"Seriously?"

"Yep." He rolled up his sleeve and showed him a scar on his right forearm."

"*Argh.* It seems everyone in this department has a bullet hole except me."

"Consider yourself lucky. But if you really want one, it's pretty easy to get one. Just go out there with a greenie and don't pay attention to your surroundings. The problem with that method is you can never plan where the bullet will hit."

"Greenie?" Gordon asked.

"First time officer. Cost me this." He held up his arm. "And it cost him his life."

Gordon suddenly felt stupid for asking.

* * *

A low groan caused all three agents to turn in unison.

"Goldilocks is waking up," Codi said.

"I think you mean Rip Van Winkle because Goldilocks was the bed and chair girl, and Rip Van Wink—" Joel stopped mid-sentence as Codi gave him her patented stare-down.

She stepped over to the man and nudged him with her toe. "You in there?"

The man tried to focus on her, but he was a real mess. There was no bleeding from his head, just a large bump where Joel had hit him. He tried to speak, but his words were garbled.

"Take it easy. You need a few minutes," Joel said.

The prisoner tried to sit up but couldn't. Shannon had hog-tied him with his feet and hands behind his back. She felt it was fitting based on what he was about to do to them.

They waited until he seemed to stabilize.

"Who do you work for?" Codi asked.

The man seemed confused by the question.

"Who. Do. You. Work for." She said it like she was talking to a toddler.

"Lyle, my squad leader," he said with some difficulty.

"Who does Lyle your squad leader work for?"

Again, he seemed confused.

"What do you do for the mine?" Shannon asked getting impatient with Codi's tactics.

"We don't work for the mine," he said.

Codi kicked him.

"We work for Callard Industries based in Toronto."

"Who comes into the forest without bug repellant?" Joel had searched the entire pack and came up empty.

Codi shot him a look of: *not now, Joel.*

"I don't have a problem with mosquitoes," Machk said.

"What? How is that even a thing?"

"Joel!"

"Sorry."

They continued to press him, but Machk got weaker with each question, and his knowledge of what was going on with this mission was almost nonexistent. He knew nothing about the radiation room Codi had seen or what they were doing with it. They had been tasked to get rid of three plane crash survivors who knew too much, nothing more.

"Get some rest. If you want some water, drink your spit."

She left him and sat next to the fire. They settled in for the night, each taking turns on guard duty, but for the first time in several days, each enjoyed a full belly. The mosquitoes still seemed determined to still get their share. It was another night spent slapping and swatting.

* * *

Chaos was the order of the day, and it was like a big soft comfortable quilt on a cold rainy day to Brian. He watched as his precious darlings, Tristian and Abigale, scampered back and forth. They were screaming one second and laughing the next. It reminded him of a cat with a laser pointer how quickly their attention changed direction. He could watch them all day, but it was past their bedtime. "Tristian, Abbey, it's time to get ready for bed."

The words immediately started a flurry of reasons why they were not going to do it. His wife Leila watched with an endearing look. She had been around long enough to know a good thing when she saw one, and she had a very good thing in Brian. He tried his best to wrangle the now uncooperative minors.

Finally: clothes off, in the tub, teeth brushed, and in bed for storytime. He selected a family favorite, *Where the Wild Things Are*. It reminded him of an attitude he often had to deal with at work and at home. *Off to bed without any supper.*

A vibration caused him to look at his phone. He knew immediately something bad was happening. It was a code the FBI used to alert and recall all agents. Something big was going down. Storytime with dad would have to wait.

* * *

The first rays of sunlight streaked through the smoke as it rose through the trees. The fire's flames flickered and danced. It had been a harrowing several days, but the team had come through it. Codi sat up and brushed the dirt from her shirt. She was eager to finish her interrogation of the prisoner. There was a lot more going on here, and she hoped he had more answers. During the night, she had certainly thought of more questions.

Joel had taken the third watch around 4:00 a.m. and was stoking the fire, hoping to cut down on the smoke that was burning his eyes.

"How's he doing?" Codi asked him, gesturing toward the prisoner.

"He hasn't moved for some time," Joel said as he stoked the fire.

"You look as bad as I feel," Codi said as she stood and tried to stretch.

"Well, I feel so bad I don't care how I look," Joel replied.

"I'll second that," Shannon said as she moved closer to the fire, warming her hands.

Codi couldn't agree more with that sentiment. She went over and tapped the sleeping prisoner with her toe. "Waky, waky. No eggs. No bacy." Nothing. She knelt down to inspect him.

"Well, that ain't good."

"What is it?" Shannon asked pulling a stick from her matted auburn hair.

"I think he's dead."

Joel and Shannon came over to look. Codi checked for a pulse or some sign of breathing. She shook her head. They all stared at the tied up body lying on the ground.

"Better him than us," Shannon offered.

"I must have hit him too hard," Joel said somberly.

Codi stood and placed her hand on Joel's shoulder. Shannon did the same on his other shoulder. They took in the dead body and their situation.

"Head injuries that don't bleed can be deadly," Joel deadpanned.

"Looks Native American to me," said Codi.

"He was their tracker," Shannon added.

Joel nodded.

"And he would have killed us all if we hadn't stopped him." Codi paused. "You did what had to be done."

"Rest in peace, dirt bag," Joel said as he reached down and cut the cords that bound the man.

"We've still got a long way to go. Leave him for the bears. It's what he would have done to us."

* * *

Lyle woke to a red blur. One moment he'd been crouched down, aiming his rifle at the male target down in the valley, and the next he was plummeting down the mountain head over heels. Then everything went black.

He surveyed his surroundings. He was wedged next to a large rock. It had stopped his downward progress and most likely saved his life. There was a good-sized gash on his head that had bled into his eyes and dried blood where his head had made contact with the rock. He wiped away the excess from his eyes with his free hand. His vision improved. The gash was deep but not life threatening. He was lying on his side, jammed between the rock outcropping and the slope of the hill. It looked like morning so he must have been there all night. His mouth was as dry as desert sand. He would need water soon.

One arm was pinned underneath his body. He tried to wiggle it free. A shooting pain in his leg sent him rigid with agony. Lyle looked down to see the jagged edge of his femur protruding through his pants. He could see red mixed with the white of his bone. A compound fracture. He would need an air evac out of this place. He reached for his pack to access his sat-phone and call in the cavalry, but with just one hand available, he was too pinned to access it.

He needed to extract himself from the gap he was currently stuck in. He started to wiggle like a worm in an attempt to free himself. Inch by inch, he was moving, but the pain was excruciating. A huffing sound followed by a low growl froze him mid-wiggle.

He stayed motionless and tried to identify the source moving only his eyes. A large black momma bear padded around the rock sniffing the air and was now staring straight at him. Lyle slowly reached for his pistol with his free hand, but his holster was empty. It must have fallen out during his tumble down the mountain. A moment later, two cubs joined their mother. They appeared nervous at seeing a human right there on the ground. The mom nudged Lyle's shoe with her paw.

"Now, momma, you don't want any part of this. I'll mess you up real bad if you screw with me. So just take your little cubs and turn right around."

She let out a soft roar and then nudged one of her cubs forward. Lyle reached with his free hand and picked up a rock and held it in an aggressive manner. The cub retreated.

"Ha, bear! Get out of here, bear," Lyle yelled, trying to scare them off. The momma bear moved quickly to her prey and swiped her paw. Lyle swung the rock at her like a club and threw it, but it bounced off harmlessly. She leaned in and bit down on his arm. There was a sickening crunch followed by a high-pitched scream. She shook it, and a popping, tearing sound preceded his arm being ripped out at the shoulder. Lyle

moaned a deep guttural sound that sounded inhuman. Blood poured out of his shoulder socket, but the bear's actions had loosened him out of the crevasse. He wiggled and lifted his torso up, freeing his other arm. Lyle pried himself up and stood on one leg. The momma bear had given his arm to one of her cubs, and it was tearing flesh from bone, eagerly devouring the sweet meat.

Lyle slowly stumbled back away from the bears, blood squirting down his side. He was feeling light-headed, and his body felt heavy. In a sudden burst, the momma bear took a few steps forward, closing the gap on Lyle. She swiped a paw, and his intestines spilled to the ground.

He dropped, unable to go on, sobbing between cries of pain and anguish. He tried to put his intestines back in with his only arm. The other cub joined their mother, feeling braver now. She showed it how to open a living carcass and what parts were most tasty. It was a lesson quickly learned. Soon, all three were feeding on the soft parts of their prize to the sound of human shrieks.

Lyle eventually succumbed to the loss of key internal organs but not before he lived a horror show of his own making.

CHAPTER EIGHTEEN

CHICAGO O'HARE AIRPORT – PRIVATE TERMINAL – 9:04 A.M.

The chartered flight was the first in a carefully planned exit route. Sterling had collected everything that mattered most to him—his Audemars Piguet watch and his cash. He left Montreal, his wife, and his mistress behind and landed in Chicago at the private terminal. From there, he swapped passports, assumed a new identity, and boarded a flight to LAX. Once in Los Angeles, he took an Uber down to Long Beach, where he boarded a cruise ship to Mexico under his new name. When the ship docked, he took the tour of Ensenada and never returned to the ship. From Baja California, he paid cash for a flight to Mexico City. He changed passports and names once again. He looked down at his new moniker printed on the French passport. Sterling processed the kind of man he would now be. He was free from his family's legacy and free from the day-to-day drudgery of the mine. As Stuart Chauvette, he could be anyone, but greed and narcissism were not easily discarded. From Mexico City, Stuart purchased a ticket to Bora Bora in French Polynesia. The flight put him on the island in just under seventy-two hours after leaving everything behind in Quebec. As he stepped off the jetway, he relaxed for the first time in six months. It was a feeling he would love to get used to.

"Monsieur Chauvette, right this way. I have a carriage waiting."

Sterling's panic level spiked and flowed throughout his body. Standing next to a silver Hyundai at curbside was the man of his fears, Dorthia's large bodyguard Kip, and he was smiling. The man had done nothing but scare the living crap out of Sterling each time they met. He was at least six-eight and had to weigh 280 pounds. His neck was as thick as Sterling's thigh. And his quiet death stare had been polished and perfected.

"Please," he said as his smile quickly became serious. Sterling slumped into the back seat as the man played chauffeur. They drove away from the airport, coconut palms lining the two-lane blacktop.

Sterling was at a loss as to how he had been so easily tracked, let alone beaten to his destination.

"We are pleased with your carefully planned disappearance and encourage you to lay low for the while."

The driver spoke without taking his eyes off the road.

"We are, however, going to need to reopen the mine at some point. So we have some choices for you. There is a bag by your feet. It has one million dollars' worth of French Pacific francs."

Sterling glanced down at the floorboards and saw a brown leather backpack. He tapped it with his toe, and it seemed full. The driver handed him a legal envelope.

"Here is a bill of sale for the mine. I will need you to sign and date it. Or you can promise to come back to Quebec in six months or so and run things for us again."

Sterling took the paperwork and quickly signed and dated it. He handed it back to the driver. For the first time since leaving the airport, the man took his eyes off the road. He scanned the document.

"Good. I'll have it notarized. You don't need to be there for that."

He continued to drive in silence, and Sterling started to sweat.

"So, where can I drop you?"

"Ah, the St. Regis," Sterling said with trepidation.

"Nice choice. Very exclusive. I love the bungalows there. Make sure you try the coconut Mahi and pak choy."

"I will, thank you."

The casual banter actually started to relax Sterling. Maybe things would be okay. He rolled down the window and looked out at the lagoon with its breathtaking views and indescribable shades of cerulean. The warm salt air blew across his face. He smiled at the thought of an extra million dollars cash. He hardly noticed the bullet that plunged into his heart and definitely not the one that followed into his brain .

* * *

After morning prayers, Fred dressed in black jeans and a tee-shirt with an E-Fex logo on the breast. He was given a laminated badge on a lanyard that he put around his neck. He rode with one other crewmember in a panel van with a larger version of the same logo on the side. They drove east through the city, across the river, and then northeast. They passed several small towns, coming to a stop in an even smaller one. The driver asked them to wait in the van, as he pulled to a stop. Fred watched as he walked up a ramp from the gravel driveway to a metal door attached to a two-story gray brick building.

"My name is Fred," he said to the other crewmember, in the forced silence that permeated the van.

"Ben," the other said as he gave a brief nod.

"I guess we will be working together."

"For the betterment of Allah," said Ben.

"Yes, of course. We have been most fortunate to be selected for this honor."

Ben's eyes broke with his partner. A casual conversation in English was a construct that he was still struggling with since entering the United

States. They sat in silence for a time, each still getting comfortable in their new skin.

After a few minutes the driver returned and waved for them to follow. They exited the van and waited by a freight elevator that opened to the parking lot. Their driver struck a match to light a cigarette in a twitchy fashion. Once in the car they rode it up to the second floor where it emptied onto a small landing. There was an open door leading to a workshop of some type. Fred and Ben followed the driver inside. He pointed to four wooden crates on the floor.

"Take these to the van."

Inside, Fred saw three large sculptures of hands in different positions. They seemed symbolic, but the meaning was lost to him. The driver spoke with the man who seemed to work there, as Fred and Ben loaded one of four large crates onto a hand-truck. They rolled it to the elevator and returned for the rest.

Within a few minutes they had removed all four boxes and loaded them into the panel van. The driver flicked his spent cigarette onto the gravel parking lot as they piled back into the van and headed for the highway.

***

The familiar sound was a warning to Codi, and it was headed their way. "Take cover!" she shouted.

After all they'd been through, there was no hesitation. Each agent scampered from the game trail by the stream to the cover of a rock or tree.

The slow drone of an engine crossed overhead getting lower as it flew past.

"A floatplane!" said Shannon.

"It's landing!" Joel yelled hopefully.

As soon as it passed, Codi bolted into a sprint following in its path, Joel and Shannon close behind.

Their game trail had led them to a creek that became a stream. The three agents followed its sandy banks making good time. They were armed and fed and things were looking up. Twice, they had to work their way around feeding bears and a small waterfall, but the terrain was starting to flatten out. It was a good sign.

Codi slowed. Her endurance was not what it had been. Several days of living on the edge had taken its toll. It was amazing how impactful the lack of sleep and food was on the human body. The trees up ahead started to open up. She stopped abruptly. Joel and Shannon finally joined her, each staring at the sight ahead. A small pristine lake with glimmering blue water was set against stoic fir trees. Parked on the sand bank was a red and white floatplane with the name Norma Jean written in black cursive. They could hear the sound of hot metal contracting as a cool breeze pushed across the lake.

"I don't see anyone," Codi whispered. "Spread out and take it slow."

They moved like a team, keeping in sight of each other, ready for action, taking every step with care.

As they neared the plane, the sound of rustling brush came from their right. Joel tensed. Codi dodged out of sight. A figure materialized through the brush.

"*Freeze right there!*" Joel screamed, pointing his shotgun at the man.

An old man in a red flannel shirt paused. "Jeez! You scared the crap outta me," His voice was as rough as sandpaper. "What is wrong with you, boy?"

The old man appraised the couple. They had a haggard look about them, even desperate. The young man had dried mud all over him, and his street clothes were ripped and tattered. The woman's auburn hair looked like she had combed it with a Dust Devil.

"This ain't some adult Lord of the Flies thing, is it?" the old man said. "Cause I don't wanna play."

He reluctantly raised his hands. He wore blue jeans and boots with a belt holding a 356 revolver in a hip holster. The man had to be seventy if he was a day, his face mottled with liver spots. His curly hair had long ago gone gray, and his green eyes were slowly milking over with cataracts.

"Sorry," Joel said sheepishly. "We thought you were one of them." He lowered his gun. Shannon did the same.

"One of wh—"

Codi popped out from a bush just behind him, her gun still leveled. "Can we ask who you are?"

The unexpected voice from behind him gave the old man a jolt. "Stop doing that! You know, sneaking up on old folks could be considered elder abuse."

He paused, quickly reading the seriousness in Codi's eyes.

"My name's Grif. I forgot my flyin' bottle. It's a must when you have a prostate as big as I do. So I had to make a pit stop, okay? Was on my way to Lac Maurel for some fly fishin'."

Codi lowered her gun.

They filled Grif in on the details of their plane crash but nothing more. He soon relaxed and offered to fly them over to Kuujjuag.

"It's a small Inuit town on the Koksoak River. There's a dirt airfield, and you should be able to catch a ride back to civilization. First Air and Air Inuit both fly in an' outta there."

* * *

Dennis rode in the back of the black Expedition, listening to the French officers in the front seats chat. With his high school French, he was only able to pick out an occasional word, which helped little to understand them. So he looked out the window at the amazing countryside that tracked a pristine river.

After he got the report back from one of his experts, he put all the pieces together with a little help. The trace mineral Poudretteite found under their irradiated man's fingernails could only have come from one area: Mont Saint Hilaire. There was a mine there, a nature reserve, and a river. Each could contain trace elements of the rare mineral. Dennis had worked with his boss to put together a team of Quebec authorities to assist him with checking out the area. They decided to start with the mine and work out from there.

A short brassy woman named Inspector Franse Rochelle met him at the airport and was currently doing the driving. They had linked up with five other Surete officers and one academic. The route to the mine had been relatively quick as the two vehicles turned off the main road and headed up the narrow blacktop to the entrance. The main gate was closed and there was no obvious work going on. Franse honked the horn several times and then got out of the SUV.

"Collin, cut the lock," she called over the comms.

A tall lanky man in full tactical gear exited the rear vehicle. Dennis stepped out and stretched his legs.

"Did you know this is not the first time I have done this?" Franse said.

Dennis gave her a curious look.

"I took two FBI agents and a mountie up here about four days ago."

Dennis held his tongue, but his face flushed with anger at the thought that Brian had lied to him. He forgot everything he'd been told about them going missing. They were working on his case after he'd been told point blank that they were not. He would get to the bottom of this when he got back to the states and make sure they never worked another case again. He managed to stay calm on the exterior and asked, "What did they discover?"

"That whatever they were looking for no longer existed," Franse replied.

"What's the meaning of this? We're closed!" a voice shouted, as a man in a security uniform with a rifle approached the gate.

Officer Collin stepped back from the lock and raised his C8 close quarters combat rifle.

Franse put her hand on her pistol grip and called out to him. "I am Inspector Franse Rochelle of the Quebec Surete. We have a warrant to search the premises. Lower your weapon and open the gate, or we will cut the lock and enter by force."

"I'd like to see that document," the guard replied.

She stepped forward and handed him the paperwork through the bars of the gate. She waited while he inspected it.

"I'll have to make a call. Wait here," the man said.

"Not going to happen. Drop your weapon now, or I will have them fire on you, and I will cut the lock myself."

Franse maintained a serious expression, determined to bluff the man. Several more officers exited the vehicles and all pointed their weapons at the guard. He suddenly lost all color and dropped his weapon.

"You'll have to cut it. I'm not letting you in."

Collin moved back to the gate and cut the lock. He swung it open, and two officers subdued the guard with flex cuffs while the others entered and secured the perimeter. Dennis and Franse strode to the portable offices and cleared each one. They were empty of people and all files. Someone had stripped them clean. They moved across the open area to the mine opening. One of the team carried a handheld Geiger counter instead of a weapon. He was dressed more like a professor than a member of an assault team. His name was Doctor Hodges, and he had been borrowed from the physics department of the University of Montreal.

"Anything?" Dennis asked the doctor.

"Just normal background radiation so far."

"Let's try the mine."

Doctor Hodges nodded and they moved inside. The team cleared each level, slowly working their way down to the fourth and bottom level. The Doc followed behind testing and taking readings. He carefully checked every shaft and spur but came up empty.

"No unusual amounts of radiation here. There are trace amounts, but everything is within accepted levels," the Doctor said.

"What do you mean, trace amounts?" Dennis asked.

"Radiation can be found in many things. And this mine is no exception. However, it would take a tremendous amount to irradiate a person like the one in the file you showed me, and I'm not getting anywhere near high enough levels to do that. The source of the radiation must be from somewhere else."

Dennis nodded at the doctor's statement, convinced they had to look elsewhere.

"Okay, let's go check out the nature preserve."

* * *

Matt tried to process his new life. He was giddy and grateful. It was a weird combination for him. He had accepted the job offer with Bright Source. He would need a new place to live that wasn't too far from the office and within striking distance of D.C. His head spun with possibilities. He needed someone to share his mood. He was desperate to call Codi and share his decision but afraid she might feel pressured with him living so close. He needed to tell her how he felt about her. She was the one for him. He just needed the right time and place to do it. Plus, he had to break the news in a way that wouldn't blow up in his face. He hated feeling out of control, and with Codi, that was often the case. He paced the hotel room he was temporarily staying in, his happiness waning. Matt pushed Codi from his mind.

He broke one of his own rules and dialed.

"Wow, this is a first. You voice-calling me during business hours. What's wrong, do you need bail money?"

"Nothing, just catching up, bro."

"Okay. I'm on my way to pitch a new client. Go," the voice responded.

The pressure made Matt anxious, and he said the following sentence like one word. "I took a new job near D.C. with a company that's a think tank for DARPA named Bright Source."

Matt hadn't talked to his brother, James, in close to six months. It wasn't that they didn't get along; it was more of *I'm too busy with life to pause.* Matt's brother was three years older and a decade less mature. He had a mischievous way about him and seemed to attract women without effort. He had the same brown curly hair as Matt but with brown eyes to match.

They'd grown up in Plano Texas and were the terror of the neighborhood, each trying to outdo the other's shenanigans. As they grew older, Matt took to school and learning whereas James was the class clown. Their personality traits had served them both well. Matt followed in his grandfather's footsteps, graduating from MIT with a full ride and a year early. James dropped out of college and started his own business. It failed within the first two years, but he learned some valuable lessons. Now he ran a successful ad agency in the Midwest based in Saint Paul, Minnesota.

"So Mom's coming up to celebrate my birthday, and I think you should join us as well. Bob and Cameron will be there. Plus, there's a big concert going on, and I can show you some of my favorite places. Now, I know you're too busy with your new job and all to come out, and I don't expect you to, but I wanted to invite you all the same. So don't worry about it—"

"James!" Matt interrupted. "I'd love to come."

There was a moment of silence as James thought he'd misheard.

"Wait a second, did you just say you would come?"

The two brothers laughed and spent the next few minutes catching up. The timing couldn't be better. Matt would fly out to Saint Paul on Thursday, and they would have the whole weekend to celebrate. It was going to be epic.

* * *

The floatplane was cramped with four, but it managed to skip across the water and take flight. Joel hung on with both fists. He was not too happy to be back up in an airplane so soon after crashing in one. Grif was excited to have a captive audience and spent most of the flight northeast telling stories about his solitary existence. Two-and-a-half hours later, Joel couldn't feel his legs, but he did feel like he could write an entire book on the old man's life.

"Kuujjuanq," Grif said, pointing. "Used to be Fort Chimo. The U.S. ran an air base back here in the forties. Now it's home to about two thousand. If you like fishing, camping, and exploring, it's all done here."

A settlement on a large river was just visible ahead. There were only scattered pine trees, for they were nearly too far north for them to grow. As they made their approach to the airfield, Codi could make out a single paved road cutting through the village. She stretched her neck and looked out the windscreen as the little town grew in size. It was a collection of simple clapboard and steel buildings. The one identifying feature was color. The town was a museum of color—every color. It was an HOA's nightmare. But it was magical to Codi. Set alongside the tundra were dark browns to bright blues and reds, even purple.

They flew over the rainbow kaleidoscope and bounced across the bumpy runway. An uninterested herd of muskox grazed in an adjoining field, paying little attention to the plane. Shannon and Codi had to help Joel out of the back of the plane. It took a moment for his legs to start working again.

They thanked Grif for the ride. Eager to be back on his way, he waved and goosed the throttle, leaving them in a blast of propwash.

The air smelled clean and cold, and the blue skies seemed vast. This was a place of extremes. Minus twenty in the winter and forty-five in the summer. They walked past a sunflower yellow church with its weathered white cross and found a small general store. It was painted blue and white with a front porch overlooking a dirt parking lot. A weathered sign read "Northern Store." As they approached the front door, a man leaning on the porch railing drinking a St-Ambroise Beer called out, "No guns inside."

The three agents paused, not knowing what he was talking about.

"Mama don't like guns inside," the man said.

He gestured to a galvanized tub by the entrance. There were at least twenty different guns lying in the tub. Pistols, rifles, shotguns.

"Okay, gotcha. Thanks," Joel called back to the man.

Codi, Joel, and Shannon had no badges to prove who they were so decided to play it cool. They placed their weapons inside the bin and pushed the front door open.

Inside, the building was crammed with everything. Aged pine was the material of choice. It was on the walls, floors, and the shelving, which held canned food, fishing supplies, and engine oil. The store seemed to be a gathering place for the town, as several groups were hanging out, chatting. They noticed the newcomers but seemed indifferent to them. There was a small café in the back with ten four-top tables. To the left was a sales counter next to a DVD rental shop.

"Wow, I didn't think these things still existed," Joel said, looking at the shelves of DVDs.

"Try being homebound in arctic snow for five months every year," Shannon said. "These videos are worth their weight in gold up here."

"Can I help you?"

A plump woman with bronzed skin and suspicious eyes stepped to the counter.

"Can you direct us to the provincial police station?" Shannon asked.

"We don't have a police station up here, only the town elder."

They gave her a quick rundown of their plane crash and Grif's help in getting them there.

"Oh, you poor dears! Thank goodness you ran into ole Grif. Come on back and let me get you fed. I'm Mama Cass, like the singer."

As she stepped from behind the counter, she dropped twelve inches in height. She'd been standing on a raised plank. The woman was maybe four-feet-tall with boots on. Codi saw no resemblance in the Inuit woman to the 70s singer for the Mamas and the Papas, but her smile and eagerness to help were endearing. She took them to a table and served them coffee and water. She came back a few minutes later with plates filled with food.

"Muskox stew, wild berry cobbler, and smoked whitefish. There's more if you need it." She turned her head. "Stony!" she called to someone. "See if you can find Doc Redfern and bring him here."

A middle-aged man in rubber boots and a slicker nodded and headed out the exit. Joel seemed to be holding his coffee cup with reverence. "Can I ask you about this coffee," Joel inquired. "It's delicious."

"When you live up here certain things are a must, and good coffee is one of them. I use a mix of Arabica beans. Grind them fresh every morning. The water up here, as you can imagine, is spectacular. I heat it to 195 degrees and use a French press. Pretty simple, actually."

"I think Joel is in love," Codi said.

"Seriously, this is very good coffee," Joel added.

"Thank you." Mama Cass tilted her head in thanks and left the three to eat.

The food was amazing, and Codi had to admit the coffee was really good. They ate in silence, each too hungry and beat from their recent events to speak.

The front door opened with a kick and a tall hunched-over man with long gray hair stepped in. He was wearing a 9mm Glock in a belt holster and a sour expression. His tan shirt was covered in embroidery and his cowboy boots clicked across the worn wood floor. He stepped over to the table and stood next to Joel. "Hello," he said. "I heard you had some recent trouble." He had a natural suspicion in his voice, saved for all outsiders. "I'm Doc Redfern. What is it you're in need of?"

Codi was amazed at the speed of information in a small town, especially one without cell service.

Shannon introduced herself and the two FBI agents. She gave the man just enough information to be helpful. His eyes seemed to enlarge with each sentence, as she told about their crash landing and their harrowing escape from the wilderness.

"As you might imagine, we don't get too many problems up here. Six months ago, I had a marijuana bust and, of course, there's the occasional suicide. I have a satellite link at my place. You should be able to get a call out on our radio phone."

They finished up their meal and thanked Mama Cass. The group made a quick march over to Doc Redfern's place. It was a purple and yellow home with a recent add-on room to one side. There was a clinic sign above the door and a large gray satellite dish on the roof. Inside, it was warm and smelled like bleach. Doc led them to a small room in the back that was set up for communications. He flipped a few switches and adjusted a dial.

"We can do text and Internet pretty good here, but speech can be tricky, depending on about a hundred different factors."

He held up a handset with a button on it. "You have to push to talk. Who's first?"

Shannon contacted her boss in Toronto and got him up to speed. The connection was poor, and it was a struggle to communicate. He promised to get a team put together on the mine and send a plane to pick them up. Codi was next. She called Brian and got about what she had expected. The connection was even worse than Shannon's had been. She had surprised him with her call, but he didn't seem surprised by her recent events. He listened and had her repeat things several times as the signal seemed to waver in and out.

"While you guys were off backpacking in the forest," he told her, "we've had some serious intel come across the channels. We've been asked to pause all current cases and help out on something a little more timely." It took two times repeating the message, but Codi could read between the lines. Something serious was going down, and he couldn't talk about it over a radio phone.

Brian ended with, "Be safe and I'll work with Shannon's boss to get you expedited passports and a plane ticket back here." Something, something, then, "we need you all, ASAP." The final words turned into a shrill tone, and Codi quickly pulled the headset away from her ears.

"That sometimes happens," Doc Redfern said. "We should be able to get a signal back in twenty minutes or so." He switched off the squelching radio phone. "So who would like a hot shower?"

Three hands went up.

CHAPTER NINETEEN

In 1993, the Royal Canadian Mounted Police headquarters in Toronto was divided into four separate sub-units: East, West, North, and the airport. Once they landed, Shannon took Codi and Joel to her former office on Atwell Drive. It was a large single-story structure made of modern slump stone and concrete. They were led to a back room with temporary tables and chairs. Several laptops were set up, and a large monitor was connected to the wall. There was hot coffee and tea and a change of clothes for all. The coffee was bad, and the clothes didn't fit well.

"Nice onesie," Codi said, looking at Joel's front-zippered jumpsuit. It was one size too small, and it stopped at his shins and rode up his crotch.

"Paint it orange and give me a shiv," Joel added, turning like a klutzy runway model.

Codi and Shannon's outfits were not much better. They were matching summer dresses with a red and white checked pattern. Shannon's was a bit too small and Codi's just the opposite.

225

"I think these were confiscated in a drug bust," Joel said, sniffing at the funky smell of the material.

They sat in folding chairs in a semi-circle and were greeted by Assistant Commissioner Stanley Cogswell. He was a competent no-nonsense man with seemingly no agenda, just a genuine desire to help.

Codi was surprised by his tactics. She appreciated his concern and was hoping they would not become the latest political hot potato. When things went wrong, the higher ups were always looking to blame someone.

Once the introductions were made and cards dealt, the meeting took an unexpected turn.

Stanley dialed his phone and placed it on speaker. The clicks and buzzes before it started to ring told Codi it was an international call.

"Fescue." The voice put a smile on Joel's face as his boss answered.

"SSA Fescue, it's Assistant Commissioner Cogswell again. We have our agents in house and in reasonable condition."

"That is very good news, sir. Codi and Joel, I'm glad you could find the time to join us," Brian jabbed.

Codi rolled her eyes, but Joel suddenly felt uncomfortable in his own skin, his eyes darting back and forth. *What had he done wrong?*

Stanley looked around, unsure what to say next.

Codi, Shannon, and Joel debriefed the team on their last several days. Shannon kept one hand on her skimpy skirt in an attempt to keep the meeting PG. At some point, an officer brought her a blanket and she relaxed.

"We've been authorized to brief you on a situation that has come up," Stanley said, changing the direction of the conversation.

"If you don't mind, I have an update, sir," Brian said, interrupting.

"Yes, yes, please, by all means," Stanley said.

"Twelve hours ago, the CIA obtained credible evidence that a major threat is in motion directed at North America."

He let a second pass so everyone could process his words.

"We have been asked to mobilize all our resources and shelve any cases that are not top priority to lend assistance. Homeland is in charge of the investigation, and judging by our past experience with them, they won't hesitate to do what they think is right to stop the threat."

Codi and Joel shared a look that contradicted Brian's politically correct words.

"First of all, how are you three feeling? If you're too wiped out by your adventures, I get it. But if you still have something to give, we could really use your help right now."

Codi took a second to get a visual confirmation from each of her partners.

"We're good, sir."

"Excellent."

"What is the nature of the attack?"

Brian took a moment to collect and organize his thoughts. "A terrorist group known as The Haram Brotherhood, the cell that attacked the Dusseldorf Railway Station, was linked with purchasing two hundred pounds of Semtex out of Czechoslovakia. Now, I don't have to tell you what that could do in a crowd."

Codi and Joel had experienced the plastic explosive on a previous case. It was nasty stuff.

"We have tracked it to a dock in Riga, Latvia. The freighter the CIA targeted was bound for the U.S. They did a complete search and came up empty."

"So the stuff's in the wind?"

"That's the theory. What do you know about RadNet?" Brian asked.

Joel didn't hesitate. "It's a division of the U.S. Environmental Protection Agency. They use hundreds of radiation air monitors mounted on towers all across the country. It runs twenty-four hours a day, seven days a week, and collects real-time measurements of Beta radiation. I thought their main focus was to track environmental radiation in the air, rain, and drinking water?"

"Good, Joel. What most people don't know is that two years ago, they upgraded the sensors to also detect Alpha radiation."

"Let me guess, that's the radiation given off by nuclear fissionable material?" Shannon asked.

"Right. Twice since the upgrade, RadNet has been instrumental in detecting an Alpha radiation anomaly. That information was sent to Homeland Security, and they ended up stopping a major threat against the U.S. It would take a very shielded and sophisticated operation to not leak radiation and give yourself away to RadNet."

"What's that got to do with the missing Semtex?" Codi asked.

"Three days ago, we got a brief hit in Mobile, then Atlanta, and yesterday, Charlotte. The NSA has uncovered some chatter they believe points to something big this Friday night."

Joel pulled up a map of the U.S. on one of the laptops. He zoomed in to the east coast.

"It looks like they're headed to D.C., Philly, or maybe New York City with fissionable material," he said.

"Or even up to Toronto or Montreal," Shannon added.

"What do you mean by brief hit?" Codi asked.

"It was like somebody took the lid off a jar of cookies. We got a clear hit and then nothing. We've searched the area with Geiger counters and combed traffic cams. Nothing so far. It's a level of sophistication that's making a lot of people very anxious," Brian said.

Codi put the two seemingly separate events together. "If they have the Semtex and now the radioactive material, that would make a very nasty dirty bomb, and we have only two days to sort it all out."

The statement hung in the air for a moment as everyone considered the ramifications. Brian asked Codi again about the lab she'd seen in the mine. It was a possibility that needed a follow-up. Apparently, Homeland and the Surete had gone through the mine with a fine-toothed comb and came up empty. But Codi insisted she'd seen a radiological lab with her own eyes. They would need to give the mine another look.

They finished up the call, each party anxious to get back at it.

"Well, I'll leave you now," Assistant Commissioner Stanley Cogswell said. "Please keep me informed of any progress, or let me know if you should need anything in the way of support." He stood and left the team to do their job.

They set up their mini task force of three in the back room with computers on folding tables and chairs. A package arrived from the FBI liaison in Toronto containing new phones, IDs, badges, and a company credit card. They immediately paused and took Shannon with them for some much needed shopping and eating.

Two hours later, they looked like real agents again and were back on the clock. Codi tried to hide her disappointment at being given a seemingly fringe assignment in the midst of all that was going on back home, but a chance to bring down the mastermind responsible for their kidnapping and attempted murder would have to do.

"The owner has disappeared," Joel announced, staring at the computer screen.

Codi and Shannon leaned over to get a better view of Joel's screen.

"Are you talking about that douchebag at the mine?" Shannon asked.

"Yeah. He was last seen leaving his office four days ago and then nada."

"Joel, see what you can dig up on his whereabouts. Codi and I are going back to Mont Saint Hilaire for a look around."

"Try to stay on the ground this time," Joel said.

* * *

She sipped a Pinot at one of her favorite bars in the city. The Four Seasons on Yorkville Avenue was a mixture of classic and modern with a generous use of earth tones and light to help make any weary traveler relax. The green and white bar opened up to a small café with saddle leather booths and chairs. The swiveling barstools were designed with comfort in mind, sporting armrests and supportive backs. The mirrored back wall made the collection of fine spirits look as if each had a monozygotic twin. It also allowed her to keep an eye on the room behind her.

A young man from Amsterdam was sitting next to her nursing a vodka tonic. They had just passed the small talk phase, and things were getting interesting for Dorthia. He was in his mid-thirties, the CEO of an up-and-coming tech company, and his body language screamed take me to bed. It was just the kind of message Dorthia was looking for that night.

A vibration on her phone interrupted her whisper into the man's ear. She could tell he was getting aroused. Dorthia paused and looked down at the message.

Leaving Toronto for 6 weeks. Keep things moving along. Will check in. I'll handle things with our client.

It was from Julian. This was not the first time he'd done this, and each time, Dorthia moved a little closer to taking over his business. He had once ruled his business with an iron fist, but lately seemed to be lacking the hardness it took to squash the competitors and turn a profit no matter the circumstances. She'd noticed it in small details at first and then in a couple of deals that had been more reckless than she would have liked. Perhaps age did that, but whatever the reason, she relished the independence it gave her, and most of all, the power.

She texted a single letter: *K*

She set the phone back on the bar, contemplating the situation.

"Is something wrong?" the man next to her asked.

Dorthia looked over at his impossibly blue eyes. He had told her his name was Hans, or Henrick . . . . some H word.

"No, everything is perfect, actually." She gave him her best man-eating grin. "Let's get out of here."

* * *

The small blue Hyundai Elantra turned left from Market Street and passed the famed Liberty Bell. They had seen many sights throughout their trip. America was enormous. She was a sleeping giant, and Yasin was glad he would be on his way home when the giant awoke.

Over the last week, Yasin Kamran and Ammar Ramin had made it a competition to find and eat the most American food they could in each town they stopped in. They studied Yelp reviews and even made a few detours to satisfy the quest. So far, Carolina BBQ was the winner. The Geno's cheese steak they each ordered was less than spectacular, and Ammar could feel his stomach start to turn from the greasy food. Yasin turned right on Walnut and pulled to the section of curb that was highlighted on the map. Ammar grabbed his backpack and pulled a small thermos-type container from the main pouch. He opened the lid and held it up to the open window. They made small talk as they waited the required five minutes. Ammar replaced the lid, and the two men drove back out into traffic. Next stop: New York City. Then the real fun begins.

* * *

Julian stepped into his home and hit the lights. He punched in the alarm code as he called out, "Maria!" He waited impatiently for his housekeeper to reply. Strange, he'd talked to her at the airport, and she said everything would be ready for him. He pulled his luggage along the polished stone floor past the modern kitchen and across to the living room. He needed a drink. He could see the indigo lake through the picture windows as dusk approached. He'd bought the 4,800-square-foot home on two acres along the shore of the Lagunas de Ruidera in southern Spain three years ago. It was his go-to and get-away-from retreat.

"Maria!" he tried a bit louder. Nothing. Julian moved to the bar and reached for the Balvenie single malt Scotch whiskey. It was aged thirty years and had an unusual depth and complexity. His taste buds yearned as he poured the glass. The light in the room suddenly popped on and Julian turned as he spoke. "There you ar—"

The sight of Maria gutted like a fish and hanging from the balcony, stopped him cold. Jal Zayid and another man entered the room. The other man was dressed in a simple black Kurta with white baggy pants. He had a black and white checkered Kafiya on his head and there was blood on his clothes. Maria's blood. He had a smile parting a full beard that was more like a dog's snarl. Julian's mind flashed through his current situation and how he might turn the tables.

"Can I pour you a glass?" he asked, trying to act casual.

"You know we do not drink," Jal replied.

"Yes, of course. My apologies," Julian said as his eyes flashed to a curved knife that was stuffed into the stranger's belt.

Jal stepped forward and made himself comfortable on one of the sofas. "This is one of our clients from The Haram Brotherhood."

As Jal spoke, the man never moved his eyes, which were locked onto Julian. It was very unsettling.

"You and I have helped put them on the map," Jal continued.

Julian tried to take back some control of the conversation. He took a sip of his Scotch. "I take it this dramatic entrance has a purpose?" He gestured to the filleted corpse of his housekeeper.

"We had an agreement, Julian. You were to provide us with twelve shipments of processed ore. As I understand it, you have closed down the operation after only four."

"Your grasp of the situation is very up-to-date. So you should also know why we did it. We have only temporarily suspended operations not ceased them. As soon as the authorities bugger off, we will be back in business, as promised. In fact, I'm in final negotiations as we speak to acquire the mine, so I will have total and complete control over the operation. No more screw-ups from an unseasoned and unreliable partner. My man in Toronto is handling it as we speak. All I have to do is give the word, and we can be back up and running within a few days."

"Your man. Don't you mean woman?"

"You should know," Julian replied.

"Yes," Jal said, remembering their tryst in Belgium.

"The good news is the Surete has been over the place with a fine-tooth comb and found nothing. I expect our delay to be very short, indeed," Julian added.

"As I see it, this whole thing has too many moving parts, too many people at the top. It was destined to fail. It is good that you are cleaning house. We are doing the same."

He let the statement hang in the air before continuing. "We propose a one man, one contact operation. Something that can be controlled."

"I can work with that," Julian said. "You know, you could have just called."

Julian took a large sip of his drink and set the glass on the bar. As he moved to sit down on one of the cream-colored sofas across from Jal, a sudden movement caught his eye. Before he could react, a small knife plunged into his stomach. The pain was searing and instant. He dropped to the couch and grabbed at the wound trying to apply pressure, as blood oozed through his fingers. Jal sneered and sat back down.

"There we go. I told you we could wipe that smug attitude off of his face," Jal said to the man from The Haram Brotherhood with a genuine smile.

"I can get you anything," Julian gasped, realizing the stab wound wasn't too deep. "What is it you want?"

"I want you to die. But not too fast." Jal leaned closer to Julian. "We put a little something on the blade of that knife. It is a new formulation one of my labs has developed."

Julian's face suddenly ghosted white. He gritted his teeth to an intense burning sensation that was spreading throughout his body.

Jal continued. "There is a snake that exists on only one island in the world. Funny enough, the island is called Snake Island. The snake is the cousin to the fer-de-lance, a most deadly snake. This snake, the Golden Lancehead, has some of the most toxic venom in the world. It contains both hemotoxin and neurotoxin. You see, when you live on an island you soon consume everything on the ground, so if you don't evolve you die. The Golden Lancehead evolved to hunt birds, and this island has millions of them."

Julian tried to follow Jal's story, but he was losing his ability to focus.

"Now, as you can imagine, if a regular snake struck a bird, it would fly off and die too far away for the snake to get it. The Golden Lancehead had to become so venomous that the bird could barely get ten feet away before succumbing to the venom. Quite ingenious. We took some of that venom and did a little reconfiguring at my lab, and this new stuff we have is supercharged. It's crazy powerful." He leaned back and relaxed with his arm up on the couch.

"Go on, lift up your shirt and check it out."

Julian was starting to sweat and shake. It felt like acid was coursing through his bloodstream. He lifted his shirt with trepidation to inspect his wound. The area around the small stab entry point was blackened and had spiraled outward like a crazy spider web the size of a dinner plate. It was a sickening sight.

"Yes, I give you fifteen more minutes at most. You got a timer?"

"Please, Jal. I'll do anything."

"I think I have a timer on my phone. Hey, Google, set a timer for fifteen minutes."

Google confirmed the request.

Julian tried to speak, but the pain was becoming all-consuming.

"Now, the next few minutes get a little painful as your guts start to liquify."

As if on cue, a burning sensation like no other had Julian screaming in pain and clutching his torso.

"Now, it's a race to see if you die from heart failure or organ failure first. What's your guess?"

* * *

The meeting had been going on for close to three hours. Dennis was only allowed to listen in, not participate. They had tracked the radiation signatures through RadNet in a pattern that led to New York City, a city of over eight million people. It would be a daunting task. The people in charge from the National Counterterrorism Center had divided the city into a grid and were in the process of assigning teams to each section. Dennis's boss had been less than thrilled to pay for his trip to Canada that resulted in a big fat zero. It would cost Dennis dearly. To quote his boss, "While you were out chasing rainbows, we were tracking the bomb right into the heart of New York City."

He had assigned Dennis to one of the many search task forces being assembled to protect New York City. It was a demotion, but at least he was still part of the operation. The man in charge of the meeting finally sat down after introducing a woman, Assistant Director Miriam Fuller, a petite brunette with a perfect-fitting suit.

She stood. "Two hours ago, a RadNet sensor in Queens alerted us to a possible Alpha radiation leak. As some of you know, we have been tracking a recurring signature from Mobile, Alabama, up the east coast to New York."

She pointed to the big screen on the wall that showed a line from Mobile to New York City. The screen flipped to a new image of Queens where the radiation was last detected.

"As of now, our worst fears are confirmed. Someone or some group is moving radioactive material into the city or through the city."

Dennis leaned back in his chair and processed the information. He was sure this was just the tip of the iceberg. Whatever they had planned must be big. He looked around him. It was a government smorgasbord of three-letter acronyms. Each department head seemed determined to get his name attached to this case. It could be a career maker. But this was a case that he had brought to their attention. If not for him, they would have nothing.

The speaker continued to drone on and Dennis half-listened, still upset at the situation. There would be over twenty-five hundred police and other agents scouring the city to find that match in the haystack before it ignited and burned down the whole farm.

He was effectively now second fiddle to a bunch of power hungry politicians who knew nothing of true police work. He'd followed the evidence, and it had not delivered. Now, he would use his best asset and follow his gut and outthink them all. If he were a terrorist and wanted to make a statement in New York City, where would he go? *Times Square.* He would detonate the bomb there. It was time for Dennis to call in a few markers.

* * *

Once on the ground in Montreal, Shannon and Codi met up with Inspector Franse Rochelle again. They drove out to the site. It was beyond silly to Franse, a third trip to this stupid mine. This time, however, they had backup. A car with armed agents followed their lead.

Franse told them of her last fiasco with the man from Homeland Security.

"Please tell me you're not talking about Agent Dennis Paige?" Codi asked.

"Yes. The man is so full of himself there is no room to hear even the most important words," Franse said.

This was an evaluation Codi could agree with.

"I worked with a man like that in Vancouver," Shannon said. "It was incredibly painful. The amount of effort to get things moving in the right direction was ridiculous."

"How did you deal with it?" Franse asked.

"Didn't have to. Somebody did me a favor and shot him."

"What?" Franse was appalled.

"Just in the leg. He got a promotion and was moved to a different division."

Franse seemed to calm at this revelation as she turned off the main highway.

"When I got shot, I got disciplined and sent to D.C. to liaise," Shannon said.

"Friggin' double standards," Codi said.

"At least it's better than it used to be," Franse said.

"Doesn't make it right."

"No."

They drove on in silence.

Franse was happy to see that the guard on duty at the gate was a Surete policeman.

He opened the gate and let them in. Seeing the mine again brought back a level of anxiety Codi hadn't expected. Franse passed out flashlights and the three stepped through the mine entrance.

Codi reached for the button on the cage elevator.

"Wait a minute. Something's not right," she said. Codi inspected the control panel. There were four indicated levels and an open and close button. That was it.

"This is not the same panel that was here before. There were eight levels, not four."

She pressed the button for the fourth level and they all got in. They exited on the fourth floor. Codi pressed the button to the third floor and watched as the car rose.

She leaned over the protective gate that prevented anyone from falling into the shaft and looked down at the darkness beyond, her flashlight doing little to illuminate the void.

"That's why Homeland never found anything," Codi surmised. "All the evidence is four floors below us. Come on."

She climbed over the railing and started down the steel maintenance ladder mounted to the side of the shaft. It took some time and effort, but eventually, all three woman reached the eighth floor tunnel. It was as black as a moonless night at the bottom of a well. Only the beam of their flashlights cut through the gloom. Codi hated the claustrophobic feeling she got in dark tight places. She tried to slow her breathing and press on.

"This way." Codi pointed her light down the shaft to the right and the three agents moved into the maw of darkness. She followed the electrical conduits that had led her to the lab before.

After a few minutes of walking they came to a large pile of rubble blocking the way.

"Looks like they collapsed the tunnel," Inspector Franse said.

There was no getting past it.

"Shoot. It was on the other side of this." Codi took out their portable Geiger counter and turned it on. A slightly elevated clicking could be heard. "Definitely higher count down here."

"But that could be caused by a lot of factors," Franse said.

Codi knew she was right. This was proof of nothing.

"We need to get some people down here and break through this," said Shannon.

Franse took a closer look at the pile. "It's going to take some serious effort to get through all this rock and see what's on the other side or if anything's even still there."

Codi knew they were wasting valuable time. Especially with Friday only one day away.

CHAPTER TWENTY

RCMP AIRPORT DETACHMENT – UTILITY ROOM – 6:26 A.M.

Joel looked up to see his two partners enter the back room. They carried their disappointment like Halloween masks on their faces. Both agents felt like they had just wasted a day that they could ill afford to waste. Joel tried to change the mood.

"So I was able to track Sterling Rich to Mexico. He changed passports in Chicago."

Codi and Shannon moved toward Joel to see what he was yammering on about.

"Flew to LAX and took a cruise ship out of Long Beach to Mexico. Here, look at these surveillance photos." Joel clicked on the screen, and it showed the same man, Sterling, at each destination Joel mentioned.

"Only he never went back to the ship. That's where the trail goes cold, in Mexico."

Joel had been searching through hours and hours of security footage and traffic cams, hacking the occasional ATM trying to track and follow

Sterling's trail. He'd gone to his hotel room late and had come back to the office before sunrise.

Codi and Shannon tried to refocus. With the possible attack set to take place that night they were even further behind now. The mine was essentially a bust and there was not enough compelling evidence to get the Quebec authorities to authorize an emergency operation to open the collapsed shaft. It would be weeks before that happened. The clock was ticking on a terrorist attack, and they were spinning their wheels in Canada. Hopefully, the authorities back home were having more luck.

"So he got off the cruise ship in Mexico and disappeared," Codi said, trying to care.

"He's somewhere. I just don't know where, and if he's careful or changes passports again, I may never find him."

"Or if somebody put him in a box and buried it in the ground," Codi added. "Is it just me, or does it feel like we're three steps behind this thing at every turn?"

"So what was the good news you said you had?" Shannon asked Joel, hoping to change Codi's state.

"That was the bad. The good is I was able to break through the Callard Industries shell and have traced it through two more shell corporations and found this." He cast his monitor to the big screen on the wall for easier viewing. Shannon was slow to remember the name of the company the hunter/tracker had given them in the forest before he died. Her expression opened up as the name came flooding back.

The screen had a home page with a logo, information tabs, and many pictures of buildings.

"RelCom based here in Toronto. The CEO is a Julian Drexler. It looks like a legitimate holding company for a lot of commercial real estate."

"So . . . one of their divisions employs mercenaries . . . and tried to kill us," Shannon said.

Codi stood. "Let's go pay Julian a visit. But first, how 'bout some breakfast?" Her cell buzzed. She looked down and answered it on the second ring.

"Breakfast for two, can I help you?" she said in an overly cheerful voice.

"That sounds nice, but it's almost lunchtime out here," Matt replied, though a good breakfast burrito sounded good to him. "How's your case going?"

"Like a hot knife through armored steel."

"That bad?" he asked.

"If it was any worse, I'd be doing the crime, not solving it."

"Well, I'm sure you'll get a break soon. Just wanted to let you know you are missed and that I'm going to Saint Paul to visit James for his birthday weekend."

"I didn't know your brother was born. I was sure he hatched."

They spent the next couple of minutes talking. Codi was genuinely happy for Matt and excited for him to reconnect with his family. She looked up to see Joel waiting by the doorway. "Hey, I gotta run, but have a blast. I'm sure I should be back by Monday, and we can catch up. I want to hear all about the debauchery."

"I'll take pictures. If you happen to get to Minnesota, look me up.

"Will do. Miss you."

"I miss you too, Codi . . ." Before he could say more Codi hung up. Her stomach was now calling.

* * *

A soft tap on the door stopped Dorthia from her typing. She closed her laptop and looked up to see Kip. Her smile spread as her trusted sidekick walked into the room. "Got your message. Nice work in Bora Bora."

"He was too clever for his own good," Kip answered.

241

She nodded in agreement as he handed her the signed document that gave her ownership of the mine. She filed it in a desk drawer and locked it. Dorthia stood and moved to the other side of the desk. The view from the seventy-second floor of the CN building held little sway for her. It was Julian's thing. But until she had completely taken over, some things would remain as is. She sat on the corner of the desk.

"So what do we know from up north?"

Kip moved closer to the large glass and steel desk and sat down. "Lyle checked in once they found the crash site. He confirmed three sets of tracks leading away. That was the last time they made contact. I sent a second team in, and they have reported no sign of our first team or any survivors. I would never make assumptions, but my guess is they fed the bears."

Dorthia looked up and eyed him carefully, wanting to accept his assessment.

"Four highly-trained and armed Mercs went into the forest and were eaten by bears?" She waited for an answer that would never come. "Let's keep our ears open to any hikers found or rescued just in case. Have your second team do another search grid."

Kip nodded his agreement, glad to be done with the matter for now. He, too, was at a loss as to the first team's whereabouts.

A buzz on the desk phone was followed by, "Dorthia, there's a man named Jal here to see you. I know he doesn't have an appointment, but he says it's important that he speak with you."

The message caught Dorthia off guard, and she pondered the ramifications of this meeting.

"Send him in," said Dorthia. She nodded to Kip, and he assumed his place in the corner while she returned to her desk chair.

The doors opened and the tall, handsome Arab entered. His cold brown eyes scanned the room. He had curly hair and wore a perfectly tailored beige linen suit.

"Jal, good of you to come. I see you have shaved your beard," Dorthia said without getting up.

"Not at all, I had local business to attend to. Looking too Muslim in this part of the world is problematic," he said with a genuine looking smile that never reached his eyes.

He took the seat across from Dorthia. There was a hint of the spark that had briefly existed between them, but the burning flame seemed to have extinguished.

"Who's the muscle?" Jal asked while hooking a thumb at the large man standing in the corner.

"Things have become complicated," Dorthia said as she looked him in the eyes. "Authorities have been to the mine more than once. We have been forced to suspend production for the time being."

Jal paused to consider his next words. He needed to move the conversation in a direction that put the onus on someone else. He was a master at steering the ship without ever touching the controls.

"I am aware of the situation. I just hope you are aware of mine. My clients are, shall we say, difficult. They seem to overreact to the slightest things. They won't like having their supply cut off. In fact, they are demanding repayment and restitution."

There was no truth in his words, but Jal saw an opportunity.

"I can assure you, Jal, that—" Dorthia started but was interrupted.

"*No!* I can assure you, Dorthia, they came to my place of business, and they did horrible things to your boss. I am lucky to be here." He paused and shook his head at the memory, pretending to be disgusted. "And they will do much worse to you if this venture is not successful."

She picked up her cell and dialed an emergency number only she knew of. It rang with no answer.

Dorthia hung up. Her face had gone wan. She looked like she'd lost control for the first time in her life. "Julian, he's . . ."

"Dead. And we will be next if we are not very careful."

Kip moved in Jal's direction at the perceived threat, but Dorthia held him off with a gesture of her finger.

"Okay. So how can *we* be very careful?" She stalled, waiting for her mind to regain some control.

"You now have sole control of the mine, is that right?"

Dorthia was shocked that he could possibly know this bit of information.

"Yes," she replied, hesitantly.

"That is good. We will want to work with just one person. There were too many moving pieces before. What is the position on the mine as of right now?" he asked.

Dorthia leaned back. She could recognize a negotiation when she heard one, and this was Jal negotiating.

"We've had four shipments sent and delivered." She clasped her hands together as she spoke. "Once the authorities got wind of the operation, we closed it down and sealed it off. They have been to the mine, inspected it, and come up empty. All we have to do is lay low for a bit and wait for this to blow over. Then we reopen, and we're back in business."

She said the last part with a flourish of her hands.

"That is all very reasonable, but what should I tell my clients?" Jal asked.

Dorthia thought for a moment. "Tell your clients the next shipment will be heavily discounted as a show of good faith and for their patience."

He considered her words. His ploy had worked.

Dorthia leaned forward. "Jal, this is a marathon, not a sprint. Everything is still in place for an efficient reboot. Tell them we will be back in full operation by year's end. I will reduce the cost per pound for the first two orders. Say, thirty percent off?"

He nodded thoughtfully. The thirty percent could go right into his pocket. "Things are about to get very hot," he said. "Perhaps, it is just as well we take a break."

Dorthia didn't like the sound of that. *What was about to get very hot?* she wondered. It was none of her business, but the thought of more cops looking their way was never a good thing.

Jal smiled and stood. "You know how to contact me. *Ciao.*" He turned and left the room.

Dorthia stared longer than she needed as she contemplated her next very careful move.

* * *

Joel stabbed the elevator button to the seventy-second floor of the CN tower. They listened to a watered-down version of "Straight From The Heart" by Bryan Adams. Joel's shoulders had developed a tic, exacerbated by a lack of sleep and too much caffeine. He stepped back as the doors opened to their desired floor. A man in a beige linen suit nodded to the group as he waited for them to exit the car. Codi appraised the stranger's cold brown eyes. Something registered with her, but she dismissed it for more pressing matters.

Four doors down on the left was a double-door entry with a RelCom logo on it. Joel held the door open for Shannon and Codi.

"May I help you?"

A young male receptionist was sitting at a desk, guarding the entrance that led to four offices and another large set of double doors.

"I'm Inspector Shannon Poole of the RCMP, and these are Agents Sanders and Strickman of the FBI. We'd like to speak with Julian Drexler, please."

"I'm sorry. Mr. Drexler is out of the country on business. I'd be happy to set up an appointment for you when he gets back in late August."

Codi had heard enough. She moved for the double doors.

"Hey, you can't do that! This is a private office!" he called.

"He's right, you know," Shannon echoed.

Codi didn't hesitate.

"I'm calling the police," he said as he reached for the phone on his desk.

Joel put a hand on the receptionist's hand and pushed it back down. "Don't make me shoot you."

The receptionist's face suddenly drained of color, and he stopped all resistance.

The truth was, Codi and Joel had still not been issued weapons, as they were not within their jurisdiction in Canada. Only Shannon was packing.

Codi pulled open the large door and froze. There was a woman standing in front of a large steel and glass desk talking to a giant of a man. She looked back at Codi, and in an instant, they recognized each other. The woman reached for her purse, and Codi slammed the door shut and moved to the side as three shots rang out, puncturing holes in the door just where she had been an instant before.

"It's the woman from the plane!"

Shannon pulled her Colt out of its holster and moved to cover. Joel ducked behind the desk.

"Is there another exit to that room?" Shannon shouted to the receptionist, who looked like he had just peed his pants.

"Exit? Room?" He shook his head, eyes jacked in fear. "*No!*" he screamed and ran for the only exit.

"Stop, or I'll shoot!" Shannon cried.

He never stopped and never heard her words. Panic had completely taken over. Shannon let him go and retrained her gun on the door. She said, "Joel, call 112. We could use some help."

Codi dropped to the floor and pressed her ear to the crack at the bottom of the door. She stayed there for a beat then held up two fingers. She changed them to a finger gun.

Joel translated to Shannon. "Two people both armed." He looked around for some kind of weapon. He pulled out the desk drawers and came away with a screwdriver. *What's with the friggin' screwdrivers?*

He grabbed the phone and dialed 112 as he crouched behind the desk.

"They're making a move," Codi hissed as she stood next to the door. Her stance was like a coiled spring, ready to attack.

The door slowly opened on oiled hinges. It was the most intense silence in Joel's life. There was nobody there. Shannon started to stand, but Codi waved her back down just as a huge man in all black dove out of the office, stitching 10mm bullets across the room with his Kimber Eclipse. The sound of the powerful handgun was deafening, as massive slugs punched their way through everything they touched.

Shannon ducked and blind-fired her much smaller Sig Saur P320 from behind the desk. Joel dove to the floor next to her. She finished her first clip and reloaded in a snap.

Codi had nowhere to go, so she made like wallpaper, hoping to remain undiscovered. Shannon's blind shots, however, were working their way to her current position. Codi had one option, and she took it without hesitation. She sprinted straight into the open office door. There was no time to react or course correct. She ran face first into the woman from the plane who was running out of the office, hoping to escape behind Kip's barrage of bullets.

They smacked faces so hard that they both fell in a dazed, tangled heap, each bleeding from impact cuts.

Kip had been stunned at the sudden blur of a person going back into the office. He turned to fire. It was a brief delay but enough for Shannon to reengage. Her last two shots found her target. The big man shuddered at the impact. He turned back and drained the rest of his weapon at Shannon. Bullets chipped and fizzed past her, shredding the desk, which gave little resistance to the weapon. She dove toward Joel, sure that they were goners. Her ammo now expended, there was no escape from the onslaught. The impact flattened Joel to the floor. Shannon's chest planted squarely in his face. There was no time to enjoy the moment. As suddenly as the fusillade began, the bullets stopped. Shannon popped up and peeked over the destroyed desktop. The man was reaching to reload. It was now or never. She jumped up and ran at him. His hand came back empty. He was also out of ammunition. Shannon suddenly put on the brakes. This changed things.

"Joel, I could use some help," she called, but Joel was already up and circling.

"On it."

They moved in opposite directions. Kip smiled and flipped his Kimber in his hand to use like a club. Joel held his screwdriver like a knife as he closed on the big man. He was a mountain, but even mountains could be toppled.

Codi shook her head and extracted herself from the woman. She spied a Berretta Pico 380 ACP on the floor. The woman must have dropped it. Codi moved for it. Her legs suddenly went out from under her, and she hit the floor hard. She flipped over quickly and got back on her feet. The woman had done a leg sweep and was now also standing—each equidistant to the small gun lying between them. Codi knew better than to go for the gun. That was a good way to get a kick in the head. You needed to play the man, not the ball, in this case. She mirrored the woman's movements, each trying to suss out the other's level of skill.

Joel made the first move, jabbing with his screwdriver. The man parried it away and used his foot to kick Joel back down the hallway. It nearly caved in his ribcage; the force was so intense. Joel struggled to get his breath as he tried to stand back up on wobbly legs.

Shannon held her gun in its regular position using the barrel for quick jabs. She hit him twice in one of the bullet holes that seeped blood from his torso, but it seemed to have no effect on the man. He swung his large pistol like a club, trying to take Shannon out with a single blow. He was surprisingly quick for a big man, and the loss of blood only seemed to make him angrier.

Codi took a step back, baiting the woman. She lunged for the gun and Codi countered with her knee, making contact with the side of her head. The woman seemed undaunted and grabbed the Berretta. Codi followed her kick with an elbow to her back and grabbed the woman's gun hand in a death grip. They rolled about the room, heads butting and kicking in an ugly struggle, each with their hands clamped on the pistol.

Joel stood, gasping for air, his cracked ribs aching. He couldn't fully extend his body without shooting pain, so he slouched. He spied a fire extinguisher on the wall and grabbed it. He pulled the pin and hobbled back into the fight.

Kip could feel the burn in his chest and stomach from the bullets he now carried. He used them to fuel his inner fire and was determined to end these two interlopers. He had disabled the one attacker and was now focused on the second. He swung his pistol, keeping the woman at bay. Each time making the arc a little slower and wider, hoping to draw her in. She had delivered several jabs with the point of her gun as if it was a knife. They hurt, but they were nothing compared to the burning inside.

Kip took another strike from the woman but used her forward momentum to stop his big swing short and drop his weapon on her wrist. There was a cracking sound and a yelp, as her hand involuntarily released her weapon. He grabbed the damaged hand and flipped her into his body. Once in his grasp, there would be no escape. He slowly and methodically began squeezing the life out of her. She kicked and squirmed, elbowing him in his bullet wounds. He grunted, but his giant paws stayed tight around her neck. He was too powerful. She was growing weaker with each passing second. Her punches and kicks were losing their fervor. She tried to pry his fingers off her neck, but she soon lost all strength. Her arms dropped, as her body stilled. Kip held just a bit longer to be sure.

"*Hey, jerkwad!*" Joel shouted, gritting back the pain.

When the man turned to the source of the voice, Joel pulled down on the plunger, releasing the contents of the fire extinguisher. A stream of light yellow chemical powder shot into the man's face. He dropped Shannon and turned to wipe the burning chemical from his eyes. Joel levered the extinguisher in the air and dropped it with all his might onto the man's temple. The mountain toppled, hitting the floor hard with a bounce. He lay motionless on the ground in a cloud of yellow smoke. Joel moved to Shannon and shook her.

"Hey, wake up." There was no response, nothing. Her face lay motionless covered with a light dusting of the yellow chemical. Joel had been in this situation before, and it had been almost too much for him to bear. He had lost the love of his life. She died right in his arms, and he'd been powerless to stop it. Now, here it was happening again. There was a rise of bile in his throat as panic set in. Once again he felt powerless as he held the lifeless body of Shannon in his arms. Joel started to sob and abruptly stopped himself. This Joel was a different man than he had been before. Besides, the pain in his ribs hurt too much to cry. He was stronger now, more willing to do the hard stuff, just as Codi had taught him. To never give up. To keep going, no matter what. He forced himself to focus. To look at the situation with intelligent eyes. She wasn't breathing, there was no pulse—CPR.

He laid her down on the carpeted floor and began the process, setting aside his own pain for now. He pushed air into her lungs and began the thirty compressions recommended for cardiopulmonary resuscitation. He remembered his trainer's words: *lather, rinse, repeat. Over and over until they revive or help arrives.*

Joel was true to his training and kept at it, every breath he took accompanied by a shot of pain in his diaphragm. *He definitely had some cracked ribs.*

Codi gripped the pistol, fighting to keep it from pointing in her direction as they struggled on the floor. She finally rolled under the woman and used her tucked feet to launch her away. Codi watched as the woman flew back still holding the gun. Her head hit the corner of the glass desk, making a cracking sound. The woman slumped and twitched for a good minute. Codi stood on shaky legs and stumbled over to check her pulse: just unconscious. She flex-cuffed the woman's hands behind her back and picked up her weapon. She walked back into the lobby to find Joel bent over, working on Shannon whose skin had taken on a waxy look.

"Come on, Joel. You got this," she said.

She checked the man lying on the carpet next to them. He had a pool of blood spreading around him. She checked his vitals. Finally, there was some good news. The man was dead.

Shannon suddenly lurched into a sitting position, a cloud of yellow chemical dust streaming behind her head. She took in a large breath, shocking Codi and scaring Joel. She took another huge lungful of air as her eyes bugged out, and she tried to recall how she got there. Joel grabbed her in his arms and held her tight.

"Thank God, you're okay," he said with yellow-coated lips.

"I . . . I can't breathe," Shannon squeaked.

"Oh, sorry," Joel muttered, as he released his python-like grip.

They shared a smile, and he moved a stray lock of her auburn hair out of her face.

"What's that on your lips?" Shannon croaked.

"The same thing that's all over your face and hair, fire retardant."

She looked around, taking in her surroundings.

"You killed the mountain with a fire extinguisher?"

"With a little help from your gun, yes."

Codi left them to see how her prisoner was doing. She had regained consciousness and was sitting up with her legs crossed. She immediately requested her solicitor and started the blame game, citing that Codi didn't have a legal right to come into her office in the first place. The woman threatened and accused her with the promise of a lawsuit and jail time. Codi was tempted to finish what she had started before the corner of the desk stopped the fight.

Armed policemen rushed into the room, guns drawn, trigger fingers itchy. Backup had arrived. Whoever said *better late than never* had never been in a gun battle.

Surprisingly, Dorthia's solicitor arrived at the same time they did. She must have called him before the gunfight broke out. He was a short, well-polished man in a custom suit, who immediately took charge of protecting his client's rights. That was the end of any information they might be hoping to get. The police carefully escorted Dorthia out.

"Well, that was a bust," Codi said. "We almost get killed, and for what?"

"We did find the guys who tried to kill us," Shannon added hoarsely. Her strength had still not returned, and she was rubbing a sprained wrist.

"Yeah, but how does that help with what's going on back home?"

"Maybe this doesn't have anything to do with it," Joel offered.

"Maybe." Codi wiped the blood that was dripping off her eyebrow.

They sat there chatting and nursing their injuries. The EMT's checked out Shannon thoroughly, wrapped Joel's cracked ribs, and put a butterfly bandage on Codi's forehead. They recommended that all three go to the hospital to get checked out. Codi dismissed the idea and glanced at the clock on the wall. It was 10:00 a.m. Friday morning. They were running out of time, and there were no clues left to follow. Maybe they should get back to D.C. and try to lend a hand. Toronto was a dead end.

* * *

"You going to be okay?" Codi asked Shannon, as Joel told one of the inspectors his version of what happened. They were sitting on the shredded desk in the reception area. Police and investigators scurried all around, taking samples and removing Kip's body.

"Yeah, I feel lucky to be here," Shannon told Codi.

"You can thank Joel for that. I had my hands full with the evil witch of the North," Codi said.

"I plan to thank him—properly."

Codi gave Shannon a sideways glance.

"Don't worry, I'll be gentle."

That put a smile on Codi's face. Her partner was the perfect match for Shannon, and she only wanted the best for him. Shannon just might be that. She let out a long breath as she picked up her phone to check in.

* * *

The warehouse was filled with gear and equipment for the concert. There were pipe-and-drape, staging platforms, lighting grids, and even a couple of electric lifts. Fred and his team removed the industrial smoke machines from the wooden crates. They were about the size of mini refrigerators but inordinately heavy. Each had a textured black coating and an ADA Fog–1250 logo on the side. The manufacturer had put casters on the bottom to help the crew move them from event to event.

Fred powered them up and followed the instructions they'd been given to connect them via Bluetooth. He opened the corresponding app on his phone. A quick snapshot of the QR code on the back of each machine, and the app automatically synced his phone with the machine. Now, he could control all the features of the machine. It was quite simple, just three buttons: Green for power on, Red for smoke on, and Blue for cold smoke on. What Fred didn't know was that once all three buttons had been activated the machine could not be turned off. It had a battery backup that would run it for a full hour, even if unplugged.

Fred tested the first two buttons and was rewarded with a strong burst of fog spewing into the air. They'd been instructed not to test the third button. That was for concert use only. Once all the machines had been synced and tested, Fred and Ben powered them down and loaded them into the van. They finished up by loading a dozen black cases that held rotating projector lights. They climbed into the van, and the driver pulled out.

The Basilica of Saint Mary is located on its own city block. It was completed in 1913 and has been a gathering place for Christian-minded parishioners ever since. It has two tall granite gothic spires that flank a giant oculus supported by a colonnaded portico. The grand copper dome of the cathedral reaches 138 feet in the air and is topped with a bronze cross.

A large, temporary fence had been placed around the main entrance and parking lot. There were workers loading and building three raised stage platforms. Security was setting up metal detectors, and scaffolding was being erected to hang lights, all in preparation for summertime's hottest church party.

They backed the van into the staging area and unloaded. The driver left with one crewmember to reload and return.

Fred and Ben stacked the black shipping cases next to the other stage lights. They then worked together, rolling one smoke machine at a time into position.

The venue was designed with the two main stages facing each other with space for an anticipated crowd of twenty-five thousand in between. There was a smaller stage positioned opposite the basilica. Food and swag shops were set up in a perimeter arc around the security fencing. It created a large border that would house and help contain the screaming fans. With standing room only, it would be one massive mosh pit. There were three entrances for the concertgoers and one for the staff. Each entrance would have metal detectors, wands, and pat-downs.

Set within the crowd area were four twenty-five-foot-high lighting towers. Each was set one hundred feet apart, forming a square. In the very center was a raised platform for sound and engineering. Workers were hooking up mixing consoles and lighting effects boards. Fred and Ben hoisted one of the heavy machines up to a small platform that was attached to tower one. It was mounted ten feet in the air and would allow for the cooled smoke to fall and spread throughout the crowd. It would be a very dramatic effect. It took an hour, but they got the other three machines mounted, secured, and powered up to towers two, three, and four. When they finished, they stood back to admire their handiwork. Now, all they had to do was return for the concert and turn them on. Fred and Ben were feeling more comfortable in their surroundings. They followed a couple of the roadies to the craft service table for a snack.

CHAPTER TWENTY-ONE

It had taken two hours, but with a little help from Shannon and a promise to send a detailed incident/shooting report, they were allowed to leave the crime scene. Joel stabbed at the button for the down elevator.

"So what's the update?" he asked Codi.

"The consensus is New York City. They're sending everyone available there to help out. It's going to be utter chaos."

"How did they determine that?" Shannon asked.

"Something about a RadNet trail leading right into the heart of the city," Codi replied.

The doors opened with a soft ding, and they entered the car. Joel pressed the "L" button.

"We've been ordered to go to the hospital, get checked out, and come home. Brian agrees that there is nothing more we can do from this end."

"We should go to New York and help," Joel said, holding his side as he spoke.

"I tried that option but got shot down. We are officially off this case."

"At least we solved our cold case," Joel mumbled.

The three agents were so exhausted that they didn't have the energy to complain. It was what it was. Silence filled the car as it came to a stop halfway down. The doors swooshed open. A tall handsome man with a briefcase stood there for a second before he entered the car.

Codi looked at him for a moment before turning to her two partners. It was nothing . . . or was it? A small glow bloomed into a lightbulb inside her head. She glanced as he entered and hit a button to the parking levels. The doors re-closed. Her face took on a thoughtful expression.

"Codi, you okay?" Joel asked, looking at her with concern.

"Yeah. Humor me for a second, will you?"

The doors opened to the lobby, and they got out.

"Shannon, bring your badge, we're going to make a quick stop by security."

They followed the lobby guard's directions and found the door marked *For Employees Only* in the sub-basement. After a brief conversation with the man at the desk, they were given access to the building's security footage. It took no time for Codi to find what she was looking for. All three watched as a tall, handsome man in a beige linen suit exited RelCom and headed right for the elevator. The three agents came out of the elevator, and he went in. It all seemed so harmless, but they had just missed catching him right in the middle of it all.

Codi reversed the footage and froze it on a frame that clearly showed the man.

"Joel, do your stuff."

Shannon got permission to use one of the terminals in the security office. Joel went to work, tracking the man's movements out of the building. It took only fifteen minutes, but Joel had pieced a puzzle together from various security and traffic cams. The mysterious man had left the office building and walked three blocks to a Hilton Hotel.

Joel printed out the man's picture, and they thanked the guard for his help and left the building.

A short dash later, they were in the lobby of the Hilton. Joel heaved in painful breaths as Shannon tracked down the manager. His ribs were on fire, and he just wanted to lie down. It took some convincing, but the thought of harboring a terrorist in his hotel had the manager on their side.

* * *

Jal entered his room in a huff. He dumped his gun next to his half-packed suitcase on the bed. He had planned to kill Dorthia in her office, but her bodyguard made that impossible. He would have to deal with her in a different way. He thought for a second, trying to calm his mind. It was still possible that she could be of some use to him. A reopened mine could provide for many more attacks on the West, and that meant money in his pocket and happy clients. He paced the room as he considered the right course of action. With the promises and guarantees he had made to his clients they would give no wiggle room on delays. It was also something for which he prided himself and his business, as well.

He thought of several ways he might spin the current situation. And when given all the facts, his version of them, that is, The Haram Brotherhood would respond favorably. After the incident in Spain, he'd convinced them that he was still in control and would come through.

Right now, his first job was to ensure tonight was a smashing success and eliminate any evidence that might point in his direction. He went to the slider and opened it, stepping out into the sunshine on the small balcony. It warmed his face. He used it to center his thoughts. He wondered how he'd gone from being an anonymous middleman to point man. He'd always been the clever one, the brains behind the scenes. *Connect A to B, take a profit, don't get involved.*

Jal added up the pieces. He had put the whole plan together. He had conceived the smuggling route into the United States. It had been his idea to Americanize the martyrs to help them fit in. He had set up the training and the safe houses. He had sold The Haram Brotherhood on the method and the location of the attack. He had selected the train station in Germany as a test. It was his idea to use the radiation in a fog machine. He had put together the one-man-band's website, and through back channels, got him his first and only gig. He had planned the red herring. He had done it all. The idea bloomed in his head. To say he was just the planner and organizer would be to sell himself short.

Somewhere, he had crossed over. It was no longer just about putting A with B; it was the true cleverness of his plan. If he really thought about it, The Haram Brotherhood was nothing more than a paying client. The real genius was him. The real threat came from him. He was the terrorist, and he would stop at nothing to see it through.

The thought hit Jal like a bolt of lightning. He stopped his pacing as pride filled his face. He nodded his head slowly at the realization: there was more to this world than just money. He could leave a lasting legacy. A swath of death and destruction that would make 9/11 look like child's play. *That* was a legacy to strive for. It wasn't about which side was right or wrong. It was about being the smartest man in the room, the country, and the world. It was the most important thing he could do, and it was all within his grasp. Tonight would be glorious.

As he stepped inside from the balcony, Jal now knew what his next steps must be. A soft sound at the front door grabbed his attention. He watched as the doorknob started to turn. Jal looked to his pistol on the bed. He would never make it in time.

The manager turned the doorknob until it was open and stepped back. Shannon was the first to enter, as she had the gun. Well, not her gun, as that had been confiscated because of the shooting, but the lead inspector had been kind enough to lend her another one with the promise that she would not shoot any more people with it.

Codi and Joel entered the room on her footsteps. It was empty. Codi did a quick reaction inspection. There was a half-packed suitcase on the bed and an open slider leading to a small balcony.

"Outside," she called and moved through the slider.

The sun warmed the south-facing side of the hotel and Codi had to squint to see. She caught movement to her left. Jumping from balcony to balcony just a few meters away was the man they were looking for. Codi didn't hesitate.

"We got a rabbit!" She leaped to the next balcony, matching the man's movements as he tried to flee. At thirty-eight stories up, it was difficult to concentrate, but Codi forced her mind to forget the height, focusing on the railing in front of her as she leapt. Twice, the man looked back. She was gaining on him.

The corners of the hotel were reserved for suites. They had larger balconies that tracked around the corner of the building. Jal launched himself over the next railing and onto the larger corner balcony. He landed hard and both ankles jarred with pain. He ignored it and desperately pulled on the slider. To his amazement, it opened. A quick glance back had his pursuer just ten feet behind him. He ducked inside, making for the exit door.

Shannon had fled back to the hallway once she saw which way the man was fleeing, calling over her shoulder, "Joel!"

"I'm on it," he yelled back, as he dialed her on his cellphone. The manager, who had let them into the room, looked like he was going to have a coronary. Shannon sprinted left. Her cellphone started to ring.

"Hey, Siri," she said, "answer the call and put it on speaker." She ran down to the corner of the hallway listening to the play-by-play instructions Joel gave through her cellphone's speaker in her front pocket. Her borrowed gun was out and ready. Joel stayed on the balcony, relaying information to Shannon. With his injured ribs, he was in no condition to chase anyone.

"He's at the corner. Looks like he went inside. Codi followed him in."

Jal knew what was behind him, but he didn't know what was on the other side of the slider. In an instant he made a decision and turned left into the suite. Once inside, he ducked behind the blackout drapes. He waited as a shadow on the other side of the sheers ran past the window on the balcony. The woman slipped inside and immediately started to clear the suite. The moment she moved out of the room, he slipped back out onto the balcony.

Codi entered the living room and took a quick inventory: nothing. She yanked open the bedroom door and moved inside to investigate: nothing. She quickly ran back into the main room and headed for the door. As she pulled it open, Shannon had her gun sighted and aimed in her direction. Codi knew immediately what had happened.

"Come on!" she called as she ran back inside.

She could hear Joel's voice coming from Shannon's pocket saying, "He's back outside on the balconies, and he's coming my way!"

Shannon turned and ran back out door and into the hallway. Codi popped back out to the balcony. The man was now caught between Joel and Codi. He desperately tried the slider next to him, but it was locked. Joel was on the man's balcony and was holding one of the patio chairs in a threatening manner. The look on Joel's face said anger, but Codi was sure it was pain from his cracked ribs.

"Come on, you jerk wad," Joel screamed to the man. "Bring it!"

Codi hopped onto the balcony next to the one the man was on to close the distance. She was now three meters away from him, and he was three meters away from Joel. Shannon popped out onto the balcony next to Joel and raised her weapon. Joel dropped the chair in a sigh of relief. "Oh, thank you," he said to her.

"Hold it right there," Shannon shouted to the man. "You have nowhere to run!"

The man disregarded her and looked over the railing. It was a long way down.

"You'll never make it!" Codi called out.

He climbed over the railing and lowered himself. Codi sprinted for him, jumping from one balcony to the other like a high hurdler.

He hung from his hands, rocking his body back and forth. Just as Codi reached him, he let go.

A cry from below was followed by silence. Codi leaned over the railing to see what had happened. She quickly climbed over the bar and followed the man's path.

"Are you crazy?" Joel yelled. "Get back up here."

She swung out and then back toward the building and let go.

Joel and Shannon watched as Codi disappeared from view. They dashed for the hallway and the stairs to the next floor down. Shannon grabbed the manager's master key card that was still in his hands as they ran past. He seemed at a loss for words or action.

Codi landed on top of the man as he tried to stand on a torqued ankle. She used her leverage to subdue him and spun him over. He spit at her and tried to kick her. Codi dropped her elbow across his nose. He howled as blood spouted out of his nostrils.

"Do that again, and I'll knock your teeth out," she said.

The man tried to sucker punch Codi, and she kicked him in the mouth. Sure enough a tooth flew across the balcony. The man lifted his hands up in surrender.

"Enough!" he whimpered.

"What's your name?"

He held his hand to his bleeding nose. "You have no right to treat a Canadian citizen like this."

"I'm not from Canada. Now tell me what I want to know, or I will smash in the rest of your face." She lifted her foot again ready to strike.

"Jal, Jal Zayid." He looked at her with rage-filled eyes. "I will kill you for this."

"Get in line."

Codi played a card that wasn't in the deck. It was a last ditch attempt, but she had nothing to lose at this point.

"We know who you are, Jal, and we know what you've been up to," she lied. She let the words sink in.

"You know nothing."

"We know about your involvement in the last attack."

The man looked slightly dumbfounded. How could this be?

"What we don't know is where the next attack will be. Luckily, I have you here to tell me."

"I have done nothing. I will tell you nothing." His expression solidified.

"I hate blanket statements, don't you? It leaves no room for negotiation." She kicked him in the ear, and when he reached at the pain she grabbed his hand and twisted until he flipped on his stomach. She forced him up to his feet and slammed him into the railing. She let go of his hand, and he used it to catch his balance. She grabbed his feet and flipped him up and over the railing. He gripped onto the edge with both hands, stunned at the suddenness of it all.

"I have no need for a man without answers, so goodbye, Jal Zayid. The world will not mourn."

"Are you insane! You can't do this."

Joel and Shannon ran down two flights of stairs to the next floor down. They sprinted to about where they saw Codi go over the railing. Shannon started opening doors. The first one was a young couple having some type of argument. Shannon didn't have time to say anything; she just went to the next door.

"Sorry," Joel called out.

The third door opened to an empty room. Shannon could see two bodies out on the balcony, and she ran over and opened it. She realized what was happening and immediately raised her gun.

"Stop right there, Codi. This is not how we do things here."

Codi spun to see Shannon pointing a gun at her. Joel quickly entered behind.

"Help me!" the man called out. "This woman is crazy. She is trying to kill me!" He was bleeding and struggling to hold onto the railing with sweaty palms.

"Come on, Codi," Shannon said. "We'll take him in. He has rights in this country, and I can't be a part of this."

"Yes! I have rights! You must help me!" Jal ordered, his white knuckles starting to tire.

Both women yelled back, "Shut up."

Codi said, "Joel, can you and Shannon find me some handcuffs to subdue this prisoner for transport?" Codi tilted her head at Joel as she said the words.

Joel picked up on her intention.

"Yes. Come on, Shannon, you can't be a part of this. We need to find some handcuffs."

Shannon was pissed. This was not how they did things in Canada. She looked at Joel and then back at Codi. Her face had reddened and her eyes narrowed. She held her ground. They had been through a lot together, but this was not okay.

Joel stepped in front of the gun. He reached for it. "Shannon, please."

She turned and stormed out without a word.

"No! Don't leave me here alone with her," Jal screamed. "You don't need to find handcuffs. Just use a lamp cord. I won't fight you. Please."

It was the last thing Joel heard before he closed the slider and ran to catch up with Shannon.

She paced back and forth in the hallway. An older couple with matching luggage hurried to their room when they saw the gun she was holding.

"We don't know anything about this man. He could just be an office-to-office salesman, selling . . . friggin' pencils." She stormed a bit more. "Codi has no right to come here to my country and disregard our laws."

Joel let her vent. She was right. But in this situation, so was Codi. And after all they had been through, he trusted Codi's instincts.

Codi reached for the man's hand and started to pry it off the railing. The man looked down, and a wave of true fear showed across his blood-soaked face.

"Last chance before we see if you can fly."

"You will get nothing from me. But the whole world will know my name by tomorrow. I will live on in history, and you will be forgotten."

"You're lying." Codi reached into his pocket and pulled out his phone. She held it up to his face to engage the facial recognition and the home page appeared. She quickly changed the password to her liking and scrolled to his contacts list. There were no contacts, but there were three numbers: two incoming calls and one outgoing.

Jal watched as his phone was taken from his pocket. Before he could do anything, the woman used his facial recognition to open the phone. He had one last play, and it was a big risk. The moment she seemed distracted by the phone, he swung out and let go on the way back toward the building. The fall was sudden and quick. He tried to catch the next railing on the way down, but his hands failed to hang on. The attempt sent him cartwheeling, and he went past the next floor headfirst. The following balcony caught him in the shoulder. He managed to get his leg over the railing. It was a sudden and violent stop, but he had self-arrested his fall.

Jal climbed over the railing and limped through the unlocked slider into the room and out of sight, grateful that Allah had spared him. Everything hurt and he probably needed a doctor, but freedom would require quick action.

The move had surprised Codi. She climbed over the railing and carefully dropped one level at a time after him. When she reached the floor their target had dropped to, there was nothing but smeared blood on the railing and slider. She ran to the hallway—it was empty.

"That's it. I'm not doing this any longer." Shannon stormed back into the room and out to the balcony with Joel in tow. It was empty. No suspect, no Codi.

* * *

The full might of the Department of Justice dropped on New York City. With over twenty-five hundred agents and department heads there to make a name for themselves, it was utter chaos. Fifty grid sections had been designated, each with a team leader in charge of a hundred officers, all connected with a unique radio frequency for each team. The team leader could connect to the main base of operations where the frequencies were monitored. Each team was given a mobile tactical office. They were fed a constant stream of traffic camera footage from their grid area and on-the-street check-ins from the collection of officers. It was a massive undertaking that had come together surprisingly well.

Dennis pled his case and called in a few markers to get the grid section E-12, which included Times Square. He made sure to set up his command trailer just under the enormous curved LED display on the NASDAQ Tower. His team was spread out, each one people-watching for something amiss.

It was a busy Friday and tourists from across the globe had spread throughout the city. They all strived to mark their journey with a photo or the purchase of something from the myriad of stores that lined the square. Characters of all types panhandled for photos as a way to pay their bills. There were several Spiderman characters walking around, a Batman, Disney heroines, even Super Mario. Dennis stepped out of the command trailer as an Elmo walked by with a cup of hot coffee. It smelled good. He would go get himself one. This was a real mess, as bodies mixed and moved to an unheard beat. He started to doubt his decision to take on such a busy section of the city. It was overwhelming.

The air was already hot and sticky as the sun rose in the east. It smelled like sweat and warm seawater. The first incident happened when two officers converged on a couple of girls wearing hijabs. They were convinced they were guilty and had gone in too rough. Several tourists were taking videos and live streaming on social media. They found nothing in their backpacks and had to let them go without a plausible explanation.

It was only going to get worse, Dennis thought.

* * *

Jal limped through the slider into the room. He could hear the shower running in the bathroom and noticed a Toronto Blue Jays hat and jersey lying on the bed. He pulled his bloody shirt off and wiped his face, then donned the new shirt and hat. He kept his head down and exited the hotel via the back stairs. He dumped his old shirt in a trashcan and joined a group of tourists on the street where he flagged down a cab.

Jal tipped his driver as he closed the cab door and walked into the air charter terminal. He climbed aboard his Cessna Citation and used the small bathroom to finish cleaning himself up. Fifteen minutes later his jet was moving down the runway.

Once in the air, he changed clothes and wrapped his ankle. His shoulder was throbbing, but nothing there was broken. He'd been lucky. Jal always kept a backup bug-out bag in his jet, but today was the first time he'd ever used it. The confrontation with the authorities had made him angry. His nose pulsated with every heartbeat; it was probably broken. And he was missing a tooth. His mind kept flashing to the face of the woman that had caught and beat him. He would make her pay for the abuse. *Something that would leave her screaming.* The thought helped him to relax.

The tooth could be replaced, the nose fixed, and his wounds would heal. Jal sat next to a portside window as the jet turned and headed south. He would soon be in America, a place filled with the promise of the dead and dying. It was a dream come true, and it was game time.

He dug through his bag, popped three Advil, and grabbed a new burner phone. He reviewed the next several hours and all that still needed to happen. A quick text told him everything was on track. He would need to clean up just one more detail before tonight if he was to make sure things went to plan. He selected a passport from a small stack. UK, with the name Robert Fischer. It would do nicely. He fingered the gun in the bag and decided it would be too risky with customs. He selected a pen that was sealed in plastic that disguised a needle-like blade coated with his new favorite toxin. It was perfect.

Once on the ground, Jal cleared customs with ease and rented a car. He headed east on I-35. At a glance, America seemed like just about every other major world country. Major freeways, lots of traffic, and most people more concerned with themselves than what was going on around them. It was the perfect storm for a man like Jal. He could slip in, do his business, and be gone before anyone was the wiser. Next stop: an old friend.

* * *

Assistant Commissioner Stanley Cogswell had come through big-time for the team. He'd arranged a plane to take them all back to D.C. Shannon suspected he'd received several disturbing calls about a shootout and other unconfirmed and frankly hard-to-believe allegations. He most likely just wanted to be rid of the trio. Let America have them for a while. Codi, Joel, and Shannon had become exactly what he feared, a political hot potato.

The tension in the jet after the altercation in the hotel was high. Codi and Shannon sat at opposite ends of the jet. Codi had given Joel the burner phone taken from the suspect, and he was tracking the three numbers on it. Joel had suddenly developed the habit of frequently checking his watch. It was 12:31. Time was nearly up. The attack was scheduled for today. The question was when.

Since losing their only lead, Codi had been all business. She tried to hide her frustration and guilt from the screw-up with anything that would move things forward. The three numbers were thin as far as a lead, but they worked with what they had.

Shannon was pissed for two reasons. Besides Codi, she was heading back to being a liaison officer in D.C. It was her worst nightmare of boredom reborn. She was a good field officer and a sharp detective. Maybe she should consider giving up policework and doing something else. The politics were never going to be in her favor.

Joel tried to focus on the case and not on the intense tension in the jet. It was nearly unbearable. If he had a knife, he could cut it and still feel uneasy. He decided to let sleeping dogs lie, as it were, and push on. He got on the phone to Special Projects.

"Special Agent Reyas."

"Gordon, I need a favor, and I need it right away."

"Joel? Not going to happen. Do you have any idea what's going on around here? The DOD and the DOJ are all over us, assigning this and that, trying to stop a terrorist attack on U.S. soil."

"I know all that. It's why I need your help."

"For real?"

"Yes."

Codi moved next to Joel to listen in. It took some doing, but Joel finally convinced Reyas to track three phone numbers and names.

Ten minutes of absolute silence on the plane later, he got a return call.

"I tracked the numbers. One is to an air charter service, and the other two must be burners as there are no names attached. I called the air charter service and your guy just landed in the Twin Cities. The second number is to an Islamic section of town outside Paris. The third one is no longer active," Gordan said.

"What does that mean?" Joel asked.

"It means that they have smashed the phone or pulled the battery or SIM card. I can't track it. All I can tell you is the last time it was used was within thirty feet of cell tower A12b34c, located at the corner of Stillwater Road and Trim Place in Willernie, Minnesota."

Shannon's curiosity got the better of her, and she joined the two agents on the call.

"Can you spell that for me?" Codi asked.

Gordon did. "It's near the Twin Cities," he added.

Codi had a flash of concern at the mention of the Twin Cities. Matt was celebrating his brother's birthday there. She pulled up Willernie on her phone and relaxed slightly as it was a good forty miles or so away from the city. She quickly sent a text to Matt. *Where are you right now?*

"Where was it used the time before that?" Shannon interrupted. Joel and Codi looked over at the unexpected comment. Shannon had moved to a closer seat.

"Hmm . . . Just a minute. The same place!"

Joel said, "Contact the air charter service and see if you can get someone at the Twin Cities airport to grab Jal, or whatever name he's using now, if it's not too late. Thanks." He hung up.

"Take a look at this." Shannon had Jal's phone open to the email page. There were no messages sent or received, but in the drafts section there was a note. *Everything will be ready on time.*

It was an ominous statement.

"Sometimes criminals use this method to communicate," Joel said. "They each have the same email address but never send anything, just changing the note in the drafts section."

"Clever," Codi said. She and Shannon shared an, *I'm sorry and you are forgiven* look as Joel ran to the cockpit holding his side and called to the pilot.

"Reroute us to Willernie, Minnesota," he called out.

"Where?"

CHAPTER TWENTY-TWO

Brian answered the phone on the tenth ring. Things were hectic. He was overseeing eight different teams, all reporting in every hour, each trying to find a path worth following. Something, anything that might get them closer to the impending attack that was now due to happen.

"Fescue."

"Listen, we have a lead."

"Codi, I don't have time for this. You and Joel are not the priority."

"We are tracking a man that could give us a time and location of the attack."

Brian paused with an audible sigh and then spoke. "We got three more hits on RadNet. Yesterday, Charlotte followed by Philly, then New York this morning. We are sure it is today. There are over twenty-five hundred authorities canvasing the city. We'll stop it. Whatever it is you're chasing up there is not part of this," Brian said.

"Is it just me or does it sound like they're herding us?" Joel said. "A terrorist group clever enough to hide their radiation signature except for a few moments in each city? Think about it."

"I agree, Joel, but we are not the ones running the show."

"I know this guy is involved somehow," Codi added.

Brian recognized the tone in Codi's voice. She would not let this go, and he didn't have time to deal with it. "Look, I trust your instincts. Follow them, but don't call me back unless you're dead or this thing is on the other side." With that he hung up.

"Wow, that's a first," Codi said. "The boss is really stressing."

"Big time," Joel added.

Joel, Codi, and Shannon knew what was at stake and each hoped they had what it took to see this through. After a brief debate, they agreed it was too convenient that there was a radiation signal in just certain cities for just a few minutes. It sounded more and more like someone was leaving a false trail meant to throw them off. Every law enforcement official with ADD was going for the shiny object. The only other possibility, Joel shared, was that it was a plan to get as many authorities as possible in one place before they lit the candle. That idea was almost too scary for them to consider. Codi thought about telling Joel to back off on the late-night conspiracy theories he'd been reading on the Internet. In truth, they could only deal with what was right in front of them, and right now, that was Jal.

* * *

After setting up everything in the morning, Fred and Ben were taken back to the safe house. It had been an interminable delay as the two young men waited for their call-up. Fred stepped into the living room, sipping on pear nectar. Ben was sitting on a green upholstered couch with a brown and white afghan. Fred sat in the middle of the couch with a relaxed plop. He gazed at the window as dust motes danced against the sun's rays. Their trainer entered and stepped over to them.

"Allah prepares those who prepare themselves," he said.

The boys nodded in understanding.

"You have been through your training. You know what to do and how to do it. Failure will be met with a quick and decisive bullet and a long torturous stay in Jahim."

The thought of an eternity in a burning hell sent fear through Fred's spine.

"Success, on the other hand, will welcome us all to Jannah, where there will be seventy-two virgins waiting on your every need."

This brought a smile to Fred's face. He looked over to see Ben nodding in uncertain agreement. Fred had never had a woman before, let alone seventy-two. His mind drifted. It would be glorious or perhaps a complete disaster.

"Fred and Ben, it is time."

The words pulled Fred from his thoughts of seventy-two women.

Fred and Ben both knew what this meant. Standing, they embraced their trainer, grateful for his guidance. "*Allahu akbar*, brothers," he said for the first time since they'd arrived.

They replied in kind.

Ben and Fred left for their rooms to pray and perform their ritualistic cleansing before leaving the house for the last time.

* * *

By 1:00 p.m., everyone was on edge. Dennis had requested radio checks every fifteen minutes, but with fifty officers under his command, they'd become more trouble than they were worth. He'd spent the morning hopped up on caffeine and anxiety. All of the screens were starting to look the same, and the air had long ago gone stale in the trailer.

"I'm going to get some fresh air," Dennis said as he stood and stretched. "Keep on the screens, and let me know if you see anything suspicious."

"Will do," came a voice from behind him as he exited.

The air outside was no better. The humidity had risen, along with the body count on the streets. Dennis moved among the masses, all flowing to each one's determined destination. He purchased two hot dogs from a street vender and climbed up the TKTS red stairs in the middle of Times Square. They were designed to be a viewing gallery for tourists, where they could sit and relax while taking in the sights and people who made Times Square so interesting. They were built on top of, and named after the TKTS Broadway ticket booth, where you could purchase tickets to any available show, on or off Broadway. The stairs gave bench warmers and tourists with tired feet a haven where one could get an elevated view of the over one million people that passed by each day.

He handed one of the hotdogs to officer Roulston, a middle-aged sergeant in the NYC Police Department, who was posted at the top corner looking out at the faces below.

"Here."

"Thanks. Got any mustard?"

Dennis gave him a perturbed look. "Anything?" he asked before biting into his dog.

Sergeant Roulston shook his head in response, his mouth already full. The two men stood in silence eating and watching. He had the authority to clear out the streets if things got real, but his boss had made it very clear that that was a last resort. Any panic or injury to the public was squarely on his shoulders.

Dennis realized he'd taken on an impossible task, and his boss, the man who had reassigned him to this section of the grid, must have known it, too. He would end his career here, dying to stop a threat that would be nearly impossible to spot, or be consumed by it. Or, worst of all, finishing his days doing paperwork in the backroom of a satellite office in Des Moines. It was a lose-lose scenario, and worst of all, he'd asked for it. How he had not been smart enough to stay in the shadows of this mess was a question he didn't know the answer to. But here he was, and Dennis was sure that all he had left was to do his best.

Movement to his left caught his eye. A seven foot-tall Statue of Liberty moved into the crowd. She had a patina finish and held a plastic replica torch in her right hand. As far as costumes went, it was very good. She seemed to be scanning the crowd, interested in the others around her. There was a bit of a jitter and nervousness to her as well. Dennis locked in on her immediately.

"Ten o'clock," he said with a subtle gesture of his chin.

Sergeant Roulston located the target.

"That outfit could hold a whole lotta something bad," he said as he started to move in her direction.

He progressed slowly, as if there was no rush, stepping down the red glass steps and onto the concrete. Dennis followed him and moved to the right, so they could come at the suspect from two different directions. He called in their discovery to the command trailer.

"This is Agent Paige. I have a single person of interest wearing a Statue of Liberty costume mid-plaza. We are closing in to investigate."

"Copy that. Standing by. A costume would be a great place for a vest bomb. Proceed with extreme caution," came the response over his earpiece.

When the two officers closed to within thirty feet, their target picked up on their deliberate movement toward her through the crowd. She stopped and looked both of them over. Dennis froze in place.

"She's made us."

Dennis slowly reached for his gun but didn't pull it out. There were at least forty people between him and the suspect. He raised his left hand as a signal for the perp to stop. The last thing he wanted was for the suspect to detonate her vest in the middle of this throng, but the evidence all pointed to this possibility. He needed to give her a way out. A way to save herself. Dennis backed up a couple of steps. Bodies of all sizes and shapes moved past, oblivious to what was happening just a few feet away. Sergeant Roulston missed Dennis's move to back off. He continued forward still closing the gap. The statue's eyes glanced back and forth in a panicky twitch, just before she turned and ran.

"She's on the run! Officer Roulston and I are in pursuit. Heading east on West Forty-sixth," Dennis called in.

A crackle of radio chatter replied. "Copy. Be advised, suspect is heading east on West Forty-sixth out of Times Square wearing a Statue of Liberty costume."

The two officers ran through the maze of bodies, trying not to get anyone hurt, but it seemed like everyone in town was getting in their way while the tall lanky costume seemed to have an open path. Once they were around the corner on West 46th Street, the tourists seemed to thin out. More patrol officers on foot quickly joined. The narrow one-way street was lined with parked cars and delivery trucks. Dennis could see the possible terrorist about half-a-block ahead. She had a long stride and was putting distance between them.

Two patrol cars pulled to a stop at the end of the block and officers exited the cars. They moved down the street obstructing the path of the runner. The Statute of Liberty stopped for the briefest moment to weigh her options. Forward, two policemen were closing on her. Backwards had the same problem. To the right, an open door awaited.

Dennis was already starting to get winded as he and Sergeant Roulston closed the distance. The suspect fled into the open entry of Saint Mary the Virgin Cathedral and disappeared.

Sergeant Roulston was the first officer to reach the doors of the church. It was a tall, gray stone façade built over a steel beam skeleton in 1895. It stands as a beacon for the Episcopal Church. He pulled his gun as he stepped inside. Dennis followed behind.

"Suspect has left Forty-sixth and entered a church," Dennis called in.

A voice over the radio from one of the other officers added, "She's gone into Saint Mary's."

"All units, be advised . . ." The radio dispatcher updated the situation.

A tall, arched, cobalt blue ceiling was decorated with gold stars. The polished marble floor that divided the pews was littered with patina clothes and a crowned rubber mask. The Statue of Liberty had shed her skin.

Sergeant Roulston updated everyone on the situation. Dennis moved down the along the pews, his pistol drawn and ready. They quickly cleared the main chapel, helped by the two officers who had arrived from the other street. The huge open room with parallel arches flowed to an iconic crucifixion statue at the front above the altar. The church spanned the entire block with entrances on both sides. Dennis exited out the back onto 47th. Five policemen stood on the street. "Did anyone come out this door?" he asked them.

"No, sir," one of the officers replied. "We closed in from both sides of the street as soon as we heard."

Dennis stopped to think.

"Okay, you two wait here. Anybody comes out that door, you detain 'em, got it?"

They nodded their heads in unison.

"Come on!" Dennis and three officers turned and headed back into the church. Sergeant Roulston and one other officer were still inside looking around.

"There's got to be another exit or they're hiding somewhere," Dennis said.

"I got a man on the main entrance to make sure they don't double back," Sergeant Roulston added.

The six officers spread out and started to scrutinize the church. Every cupboard was searched and each room cleared.

"I got something," an officer called out.

Dennis moved in his direction. There was a service exit out the right side of the building with access to an alleyway and the church's dumpster. The officers poured out into the alley and began eliminating possibilities.

As Dennis investigated several boxes next to a dumpster at the back of a TGI Friday's next to the church, he detected movement. "Come out very carefully with your hands where I can see them," he said.

He kept his pistol trained on the possible terrorist. A tall lanky man with a large forehead stood on unstable legs. He was wearing a black cat suit that was a size too small. His eyes were jittery and painted with teal eyeshadow around the sockets. He had an involuntary tic that seemed to fire off at random intervals.

"P-please don't shoot me." He started to sob.

"Where's the bomb!" Dennis demanded.

"Bomb? What bomb?" he squeaked through quivering saliva-coated lips.

Two officers immediately tackled him to the ground and restrained him. They emptied his pockets. There was nothing that might indicate he had a bomb, just a small plastic bag with an off-white powder.

"You gotta be frickin' kidding me. Drugs!" This was no terrorist. Dennis turned and left without another word.

"Get him outta here," Sergeant Roulston said as he followed behind.

* * *

"Please return to your seats and fasten your seatbelts. We are on final approach," the pilot announced.

They exited the jet and rented a car. Shannon had convinced the pilot to refuel and wait for them. Her argument was that he had been ordered to take them to D.C., and he hadn't yet done so. Joel received a callback from Agent Reyas. Jal was in the wind. He called up the local authorities and had them put out an APB on him.

Shannon had given her gun to Codi, as she was no longer allowed to have one in the U.S. It was a peace offering that seemed to have calmed the last currents between them. Joel was hoping to find at least another screwdriver somewhere along the way.

They drove up the 61, hoping they weren't wasting their time. Joel had tried to convince Codi and Shannon to let him send a message in the email draft inbox, in hopes of setting a trap. Codi was adamant that if they said the wrong thing it could be a warning to the man, and he would vanish before they could find him. The silence as they waited in anticipation of what might come next was getting to Codi. She was sure they were on to something, but there were so many unknowns, it was maddening.

They stopped at the corner of Stillwater Road and Trim Place in Willernie and got out of the mid-sized rental. It was late afternoon, and the sun was finishing its descent for the day. Codi felt a buzzing and checked her phone. A text from Matt read *getting the James tour and then heading for the Tilt Pinball Bar downtown… miss u.*

"So what are we looking for?" Joel asked, as he exited the car. Codi slipped her phone back in her pocket satisfied Matt was okay.

"A sign: 'terrorist work here' or 'terrorist wanted, apply within?'" Shannon said.

"Got it," Joel answered with a smirk.

Codi looked around. The town was small and had a very Americana feel. But on closer look, there were many signs in storefront windows written in Arabic.

"America is changing," Joel said.

"It has always been changing. Think about the Native Americans. We have built this nation on change, a few simple statutes, and colonization. Most immigrants are just trying to better themselves. If people looked at you suspiciously every time you left the house, you would want to move to a neighborhood that was filled with others like you. That's why this happens. Immigrants congregate by nationality and religion. It's all thanks to the rest of us not welcoming them here."

Joel was surprised by Codi's strong opinion.

Codi continued. "We've been doing it for more than three hundred years. The Protestants, the Irish, Africans, the Italians, the Mormons, Chinese, Mexicans, now Middle Easterners. The American Dream is not for everyone."

Codi paused to look up at the sign for Gordy's Steakhouse. There were several two-story buildings in sight, but most of the small town was single-story single-purpose structures.

"So they either live or work nearby, or they came here to make a call." Joel said in an attempt to get things back on track.

"Let's see if anyone who lives nearby knows anything," Shannon said.

"Yeah, maybe there's a nosey neighbor."

The three agents spread out and did the work most cops and salesmen hate—door-to-door. It took twenty minutes, but Joel ran into an old woman that knew of a man that had moved there within the last month. It was a paper-thin lead but worth checking out at this point. He called the team, and they met back at the rental car.

"According to a neighbor, an artist named Carl Savage moved into the loft of that gray brick building over there three weeks ago." Joel said, pointing.

"Artist?"

"That's what she said. Also said he looked Middle Eastern."

"So does half the population around here. Anything else?" Codi asked.

Shannon shrugged her shoulders. "I got nothing; although, it does fit the timeline."

"Okay, let's check out this Carl. Then go to the sheriff's office and see if maybe they can help."

"Depending on the type of artist, that could make a really good cover," Joel added hopefully.

* * *

Fred had finished Wudhu, the ritual washing and prayers to prepare him to enter paradise. He changed into his final outfit and looked in the mirror. He was saddened to see a reflection he barely recognized. He had made it a point not to look at his reflection after his Americanization. He preferred to remember himself as he used to be, a true brother in the fight against the West.

"Farid Khadem," he said to remind himself of all that he represented and stood for. His heritage and traditions. His family's name was at stake. He would make them proud this day.

As Fred, he was forced to look the part, to fit in. He would play this masquerade just long enough to bring about their blessed destruction. It was a great sacrifice but not as much as it would soon be. He tried to focus on the task ahead of him. His hands were trembling, but he would not falter. Allah would be proud this day and welcome him home.

"*Allahu Akbar*," he mouthed before turning and leaving his room for the last time.

There were no words spoken as Fred and Ben rode in the van to their destiny. They pulled over to a loading curb and exited the van. Security had officially finished setting up and was staffed and ready. Everyone, even employees, now had to pass through their gauntlet. They each had their E-Fex shirts on and a lanyard around their necks with a picture ID and backstage access. Fred went through first, feeling confident in all their preparations. A loud beep sounded.

"Whoa. Hold it right there," a guard called.

Fred felt the bile rise in his throat as panic started to climb his spine. He froze, his hands to his side. He noticed that he was still clutching his cellphone in his right hand. *Stupid.* He showed it to the guard. "Sorry." He stepped back through the detector.

He set the phone in a small bowl, and it was passed over to the table on the other side.

"Okay, try that again," he was commanded.

Once through, Fred watched as Ben glided through the process with no problems. He rolled his eyes at his partner, acknowledging the *faux pas*. They moved to the center of the of the audience area and took their stations by tower one. There were no fans or bands here yet, just roadies all doing final prep and checks before things started. Someone was up on the main stage talking into a microphone. *Check, check, check.* It seemed odd to Fred. He opened the app on his phone and watched as it synced with the four fog machines. They were ready.

Check!

* * *

One hundred, eight Trim Place was a tall brick box. It had square windows and a galvanized rain pipe running down the front. There was one entrance on the right and a small freight elevator in the front. It was built for a business, but there was no signage anywhere.

Codi opened the metal door at the end of the ramp leading from the gravel parking lot. Inside were a small open area and a counter in front of many stocked shelves. A single bell dinged and a woman in a pink hijab and a teal abaya appeared from the back.

Joel quickly realized this was an electrical supply business, as he spied rolls of wire and breaker boxes on some of the shelves. A little closer inspection revealed the name of the business. Huge letters on the front of the countertop: *Willie B's Electric Supply.*

"Hi," Codi said in her nicest voice. "We're supposed to meet Carl. Is he here?"

The woman pointed to a circular staircase in the corner. "Carl."

Codi nodded her thanks, and the three moved up the staircase to the floor above. At the top was a small concrete open area that led to a blue door on the right with a black welcome mat. To the left was the small freight elevator. Codi noticed the security camera above the door as she rang the buzzer on the wall—nothing. She rang again and tried knocking on the door. It moved ever so slightly under the pounding of her fist.

She shared a look with Joel and Shannon.

"Here, let me. I'm not bound by the same rules down here as you. Sound familiar?" She kicked the door during the final comment, and it swung open.

Codi and Joel were on her tail as she stepped into the room. It was a cavernous industrial space with equipment and tables set about in an orderly way. The kind of decorating an engineer would do—all function and no form. Parts and pieces lay out on tables and were stacked on shelves. In the front were three large zinc covered hands, each in a different position.

"Rock, scissors, paper," Joel said as he examined the quality craftmanship of the sculptures. "He's good." Joel looked through the names of some of the chemicals on a nearby table. "There's some nasty stuff here."

Codi glanced over to a small cage-like structure toward the left of the room. It was five feet square and had a furniture pad thrown over it. She went over to investigate. She pulled the pad off to reveal lead sheeting mounted to a wire cage.

"Lead sheeting," she called out as she pulled one of the walls open and looked inside. There was an industrial grinder for reducing material to a fine powder. She took out her Geiger counter and flicked it on. It squawked immediately. That got everyone's attention. Codi quickly slid the wall back closed. The alert died down to an acceptable level.

Codi verbalized a swear word out of frustration, as the reality of their situation hit.

She backed away from the box. "Joel, see if you can get ahold of the local authorities."

"Tell 'em we have a body as well," Shannon said.

Both Joel and Codi turned at the statement. Shannon was standing in the back right corner of the room. There was a man on the floor with a small wound in his abdomen. Joel stepped over and quickly turned away at the sight.

"Somebody has been covering his tracks," Codi said. She got a subtle nod from Joel and Shannon.

The victim's face was blackened and puffy with bulging red eyes. Shannon lifted up his shirt to inspect the wound. There was a small incision with radiating black streaks covering most of his torso. She processed the sight. "Some kind of bioweapon or virus, maybe? I've never seen anything like it."

"Virus?" Joel's face turned pale. "Is it contagious?" He didn't want an answer.

Codi leaned over the body to take a closer look.

"Codi, I don't think you should do that!" Joel warned.

"I've seen this before. It looks like venom."

"Venom?" Joel checked his rising panic and moved back toward the body.

"Yeah, my dad and I were doing some bouldering out in Pine Valley when I was, like, eleven. There was a guy that had lost his way hiking and got bit by a Mohave Green." Both Joel and Shannon looked at Codi with confusion. "A particularly nasty rattlesnake. When we found him, most of his skin was blackened and puffed out, just like this."

Joel's eyes scrunched at the thought of it.

"Joel!" Codi said.

"What?"

"Phone call."

"Oh, yeah." He picked up his cell and dialed 911.

CHAPTER TWENTY-THREE

SAINT PAUL, MINNESOTA – I-94 WESTBOUND

The drive over on I-94 from Saint Paul had taken less than twenty minutes. Thursday had been spent with family. Friday was show and tell day. James took Matt and a couple of his old high school friends on the trip. They stopped by his offices and then did the town before hitting the freeway west. They pulled up to the Tilt Pinball Bar, a hip place lined with old pinball machines on 26th Street. It was famous for its splashy 70s graphics, bar food, and beer selection.

Jimmy exited the car and leaned on the roof, looking over at Matt. "Okay" he said. "We got two hours before we head over to the concert. Who wants to make a little wager? They have Black Knight and Twilight Zone."

"I'm game," Matt said, interlocking and flexing his fingers.

As kids they'd been all about the arcade in their small town. Matt had programed his own electronic pinball version back in high school, but nothing beat the analog feel of the silver steel ball. The foursome found a table and started to eat, play, and drink the afternoon away. It didn't take long for things to get a bit rowdy. The conversation seemed to start and end with women. It then circled back around again, each one touting their greatness, followed by the absolute disaster females had wreaked upon their lives. Matt did most of the listening, as his experiences seemed to conflict with the others. As the blood alcohol level rose, so did the boasts and dispersions.

* * *

The three agents sifted through the industrial space looking for anything that might give more answers. Shannon had found a cellphone sitting next to a SIM card and battery. They tried to activate it, but the owner's face was so bloated and distorted the facial recognition would not work.

Joel checked the time; it was 3:50 p.m. The day was getting away from them. Codi dropped a small scuba tank she'd been inspecting on the table with a thud.

"What have we got so far?" she asked.

Joel stopped what he was doing and stepped over. "We have a source of radioactive material that is only dangerous as an RDD."

"So they discover uranium in their mine and find a way to transmute it into lousy-grade plutonium."

Shannon joined in. "That makes it a lot more valuable on the open market. Uranium on its own is not that useful."

"Plus, they have an unknown, untraceable source. That makes it even more valuable on the black market," Codi said.

"Right. So they sell it to whom?" Shannon asked.

"I'm guessing that guy we almost caught in Toronto," Joel said.

"Maybe. With a little work we should be able to ID him," Shannon added.

Codi leaned her elbows on the table. "We know The Haram Brotherhood took responsibility for the attack in Germany."

"That attack was pretty sophisticated, and from what I've read, the Brotherhood is not," Joel said.

"And we are pretty sure that guy made the RDDs," Codi said, while gesturing to the corpse in the back of the room.

"He has all the equipment for it, so, yes. And somebody went to a lot of trouble to kill him in order to sever any connection he had to the attack."

Shannon nodded. "Covering their tracks. The last question is where they're going to attack."

"New York. That's what everyone is banking on," Joel answered.

"So why build here?" Codi said with an open raised palm.

"Freeze!"

Two policemen rushed into the room with their guns raised. Codi and Shannon hardly reacted. Joel shot his hands in the air. Then he looked at his partners and slowly lowered them. "We're federal agents," he called out as he did so.

"Show me some ID and be real slow about it," one of the policemen called.

Joel did and they hesitantly put their guns away. The sheriff stepped in a moment after that. He was short and balding with a rapid gait that said *I own this place*. He was packing a well-formed beer belly and a fair amount of anger.

"What's the meaning of you Feds coming in here and killing a citizen without any kind of warning or heads up?" His lifelong cigarette habit had made his voice deep and course.

Codi stood right up to him. "We didn't kill your citizen. This guy was dead when we got here."

The sheriff looked over at the obviously bloated corpse.

"Look, Sheriff," Codi said, "we are under a severe terrorist threat. We got radiation readings here, and this man is suspected of building the bomb they are planning to use. So unless you have some information as to why you had a terrorist bomb-maker in your town and didn't do squat about it, I recommend you back off right now. We don't have time for this. There is an imminent attack, and we could use some help."

Codi was hopped up on adrenaline and needed to let it die down a bit, but this yahoo had gotten her worked up. The sheriff was taken aback by her outburst. He blinked for a beat and then cleared his throat. "Name's Gilbert. What can we do to help?"

Codi took a calming breath and asked for a few things. There was no time to seal off the scene or wait for forensics; they would have to do with what they had. A couple of minutes later, they were gathered around a workbench. Joel had a working laptop and there was a map of the area spread out on the weathered wooden surface. One of the deputies had pulled a work light over and a few bottles of water. To say it was a command center would be hyperbole in the highest form.

"We know a few things," Codi began.

She and her team were joined by Sheriff Gilbert and two of his deputies, Paulson and Tamber. They were both in their late twenties and were still shell-shocked from the sight of the grotesque corpse and the telling-off Codi had given their boss.

"One, an attack is planned for today. Most east coast law enforcement thinks it is taking place in New York. They might be right, and if that's the case, there is nothing we can do here. But we believe everything going on out there is a diversion for whatever is really planned.

"What is really planned?" asked Deputy Tamber.

"Honestly, we don't truly know," Codi confided.

"What makes you think the attack isn't happening in New York?" the sheriff asked.

"We chased our suspect from Canada to here. We believe he is tied to the attack in Germany and is now in the process of cleaning up after himself," Codi said, gesturing to the dead body.

Sheriff Gilbert nodded, looking around for a camera, wondering if he was on some kind of sappy reality show.

"We think it is a type of RDD, or dirty bomb," Joel said.

Both deputies raised their hands as if to ask a question.

"Radiological Dispersion Device. The radioactive material they have is not fissionable."

Again the deputies looked confused. Codi was beginning to think the sheriff kept them around so he didn't have to look dumb.

"It won't blow up. But if the material it is ingested or breathed in, it is deadly," Joel added.

"We don't have time for CSI to clear this room," Codi said. "What we need is for you to help us go through this place and look for anything that might give us some kind of clue about the attack."

The two deputies nodded without moving.

"Well then, let's get to it," the sheriff ordered.

Twenty minutes later, they had found nothing.

"Hey, boss! I have something." Deputy Tamber pulled a cutout of a printable sticker from under the inkjet printer. On closer inspection, they could make out the letters ADA Fog–1250.

Joel looked up the information. "It's an industrial smoke machine for big live events."

Deputy Tamber held up three more.

"There are four."

The news hit the three agents like a jolt of electricity.

"What?" Sheriff Gilbert asked.

"That's the same way they dispersed the radiation in their last attack in Germany," Codi answered.

"You mean the train station?"

Codi nodded curtly. "Joel, can you pull up a list of live events. What is that?"

Shannon had been shaking out all the art books on a nearby table and a scrap of paper fluttered to the floor. She picked it up.

"Praise the Loud," she read, holding a brochure.

"Did you say praise the loud?" Deputy Paulson asked.

"Why? What is it?" Shannon replied.

"Well, there's that big concert at the Basilica of Saint Marie this weekend."

"That's right, the Basilica Block Party. It's their twenty-fifth anniversary," the sheriff added.

Joel drilled down on the information and spun the screen around so the others could see the website's caption: *Basilica Block Party - 25 years of praising the loud.*

"A Christian rock concert with thousands of participants," Joel said. "That can't be good."

They all knew this was it. A terrorist's wet dream. Kill thousands of rock-and-roll-loving capitalists and Christians all in one place.

Codi's face flushed as she tried to remember what Matt's plans were after they finished at the Tilt Pinball Bar. If he and his brother were going to the concert, she needed to put a stop to that immediately. She sent a second text and tried calling but got no answer.

Joel scrolled through the website for more details.

"It is a two-day event starting tonight at 5:15." Joel checked his cell. They had thirty minutes.

"That's on the other side of the river, at least a thirty-five-minute drive this time of day," Sheriff Gilbert rasped.

Time had run out.

* * *

"All units, repeat, all units be advised we have a RadNet alert indicating alpha radiation at the corner of Eighth Avenue and Forty-second Street." Dennis looked at the map, which indicated the grid he was responsible for. It was two blocks from his section. This was it. After a day of chasing their tail, it looked like it was game on. He sent half his force to the area with explicit directions.

The phone in the trailer rang, and he picked it up before the first ring stopped.

"This is Paige."

"Dennis, this is Director Fuller. We got a break. Our terrorists just made their first mistake. The intersection where the RadNet sensor is located has two traffic cams. During the time of the radiation detection there were twenty-two cars that passed through. I'm sending you the list with pics. If one of them pops up in your grid, take 'em down."

"We're on it," he said to the *click* of her hanging up. Dennis quickly relayed instructions. Within moments, one of the techs in the command trailer had the list printed out and stills from the traffic cams up on several of the monitors. Dispatch linked the information to all officers in the field, and the search was on.

It took five long minutes, but the first car was pulled over and thoroughly searched. One by one, they identified the suspects and then eliminated them. With only seven vehicles left to identify, a call over the radio grabbed their attention.

"All units, we have a blue Hyundai Elantra, license number x-ray, bravo, hotel, 3, 7, 6 evading arrest. Be advised; they are to be considered armed and dangerous. Last seen heading east on Fortieth Street."

"That's it. Pull up a map." Dennis watched and listened as police across the city closed in on the vehicle.

He positioned his men to move in the instant the terrorists were close to his grid. He placed a mental finger on the map and followed it based on the radio chatter as it moved and swerved across Manhattan.

"They're going to cut up Broadway off of Forty-first," Dennis told his team. "Get some men in that area and a spike strip if we have one. And get everyone else to clear out the Square." Dennis dashed from the trailer. He knew it in his gut. They were heading directly for Times Square. As he stepped from the trailer, a sudden chill in the otherwise hot and muggy day went up his spine. The sun was starting to set, and the neon and LED glow of Times Square was taking over.

Police started calling for people to clear the streets, and a general sense of fear swept the crowd. For the most part, they were leaving, some with a panicked sprint, others as casual as a Sunday stroll. Dennis jogged to the intersection where Broadway dumped into Times Square. People were everywhere. He guided several officers to redirect the exiting throng. Two more officers blocked the street with their cars. He could hear sirens closing in.

He scanned the street. Right in front of him, just five cars away, he saw them. Two Middle Eastern men driving a Blue Hyundai. The moment they were spotted, they slammed on the gas and careened off two parked cars as they tried to force their way forward. Horns honked, sirens wailed, people screamed, and police converged. The sound of metal on metal filled the air, as the blue car scraped free and shot toward the two cop cars blocking the street. They smashed through the police cars and slammed into a hot dog stand. The car was damaged beyond drivability. Before they could exit, twelve highly motivated law officers had the car surrounded, guns drawn and ready.

Hands went up, and the two suspected terrorists exited the car and lay on the ground. The police quickly took control and searched them from head to shoes. There were no bombs, no detonators. Dennis looked in the car and saw two backpacks and a small thermos on the passenger side floorboard.

"I got something. Let's get RERT and the bomb squad in here."

The bomb squad arrived first, followed by the EPA's Radiological Emergency Response Team. Dennis ordered his team to establish a safe perimeter. Sergeant Roulston radioed for a translator, as the two men didn't seem to understand English. Pictures were taken and sent to base for an identity search. His superiors and their bosses were on their way. Each vying for a photo op next to the captured terrorists.

Twenty minutes later, RERT had removed and emptied the backpacks. They had nothing but personal belongings inside. They opened the thermos.

"It's a Lead Pig," an agent said.

Dennis looked confused.

"It's a lead-lined jar designed to safely hold radioactive material," the RERT agent added. "Looks like it has about . . ." He shook the jar while looking inside. "Two ounces of radioactive material inside it."

Sergeant Raulston stepped over. "According to the interpreter, they say it's Cesium 137 for a science project they're doing." He handed Dennis some paperwork. "Here are the receipts for all of it, purchased through Amazon."

"You gotta be kidding me. They bought radioactive material off Amazon?" Dennis said.

"Yeah, I checked, the Lead Pig, the Cesium 137. You can order this stuff all perfectly legally."

Dennis's phone vibrated. "Paige," he said after stabbing the green button.

Director Fuller's voice was almost robotic. "We have an ID, Yasin Kamran and Ammar Ramin, both here on expired college visas."

"Does it say what they were studying?" Dennis asked.

A moment went by before Director Fuller answered, "Physics."

Dennis could feel a migraine coming on. Was this the source they had tracked from the Gulf Coast all the way to New York? It seemed weak to him. Two ounces of radioactive Cesium in a dirty bomb would maybe kill a dozen people. *There had to be more to it, right?*

The U.S. criminal justice system had just spent a lot of taxpayer money chasing a science project. The media was going to eat this up, and his bosses would be looking for a scapegoat. He felt his legs go weak.

* * *

After too much of everything, they paid their bill and walked out of the Tilt Pinball Bar, mostly in a straight line. Each one with a silly grin plastered across his face. James led the way as the group joined in with the flow of concert-goers, all heading to the same venue. Two blocks over and six down delivered the four musketeers to the back of the security line. Matt reached for his phone but came up empty. He did a double-check with the same results. "Hold up we gotta go back!"

What are you talking about? James ordered.

"I left my phone back at the bar," Matt answered.

James lifted his left hand up as he dialed his phone with his right. He spoke for a few seconds, before hanging back up. We are good. They are holding it for you. You can grab it after the concert.

This seemed to appease Matt, and he stepped back in line with the other three.

"Okay, quick announcement before I get any more hammered . . . here." James passed out tickets for everyone. "You are all now responsible for yourselves. If we get separated, meet back at the Tilt Pinball Bar afterward. And somebody besides me will need to drive us home. His statement was met with instant objections."

* * *

Codi was impressed. The sheriff drove like there was no tomorrow. Which, for some in the Twin Cities, might be true. She had still not heard back from Matt and was now seriously concerned. Their relationship had been growing, and for the first time in a long while, Codi felt secure. Matt was a good person, and she was lucky to have him in her life. A sudden panic hit her. What if Matt and his brother James were going to the concert? It was an unthinkable scenario that she had no time for right now, but she sent him a quick text, *Stay away from the concert*! She turned back to the call with Brian and filled him in on their situation and what they needed.

He used the margin and the shoulder with sirens blasting the way. It was a two-car convoy with Deputy Tamber driving the trailing vehicle. Codi sat next to Sheriff Gilbert with her phone pressed to her ear, listening to it ring.

Joel and Shannon were in the backseat trying to get someone with horsepower to take them seriously on a Friday evening. The last thing they needed was for the sheriff to put out an APB and risk tipping off the terrorists. The smart ones listened to police scanners. This had to be done just right.

"SSA Brian Fescue."

"You took my call. I'm impressed," Codi said.

"Please tell me you are dead—"

"Listen carefully," Codi interrupted. "We are driving a hundred miles-an-hour on a crowded freeway."

Brian felt the back of his head start to pound. He was instantly regretting letting Codi follow her instincts.

She had prevented the sheriff from sending out a general broadcast until they had more information. They didn't need the public or a bunch of local cops panicking. Or worse, a mole working on the inside thwarting all their hard work. There were just too many unknowns. They needed to go from the top down.

Joel was having trouble getting through to the officer in charge at the Minneapolis Police Department. He had been put on hold again and was getting nowhere. The sheriff grabbed his radio mic and started to transmit a warning.

"Hang on just a bit longer, Sheriff," Codi said.

They were running out of time and options, but she needed to do things right or she would have a giant cluster on her hands with no way of controlling the outcome.

Brian listened to everything his agent said and realized that Codi might really be on to something. He had heard about the calamity that was going on in New York and was feeling helpless and directionless before her call.

Even the National Counterterrorism Center and the FBI's Joint Terrorism Task Force had come up empty. He was glad to have been kept at arm's length from the fray.

"Tell Joel to hang up," Brian said to Codi. "I'll take care of things from this end. Call you back."

"What'd he say?" Sheriff Gilbert asked.

"Drive like our life depends on it," Codi answered.

He nodded and pushed them even faster. They were starting to make up time.

"The Waze app says twelve minutes," Shannon called out from the backseat. She double-checked her pistol, given to her by the sheriff and slid it into her waistband. Codi did a slicing motion across her throat and Joel hung up his phone. He and Shannon shared a concerned look. Things were about to get real dicey.

* * *

Matt lifted his arms as the guard moved the wand around his body. After a couple of seconds, he waved him through. He stood watching as his hyper-ticklish brother was squirming at the thought of the security wand touching him. *What a dweeb*, he thought, a half-smile plastered on his face. This was life, and he wanted to soak it all in. His mind flashed to Codi for a second. She would have loved coming along. His vision of her only slightly distorted through his buzz. *Codi could drink them all under the table and still run faster than a speeding bullet and jump the tallest building . . . Wait that was a TV show? Phew, the tequila was strong at that bar.*

"What?" James asked.

"Oh, nothing. Just love watching you squirm." Matt said as he tried to clear his head.

"Not funny. I don't make fun of you for being a brainiac."

"Yes, you do. What's the phrase you used to call me? My brother, the VRS," Matt responded.

"That's right, Virgin Rocket Scientist. Well, not anymore."

Matt's half smile transformed into a full-blown grin.

"Come on, let's get some beers, R.S."

* * *

The Minneapolis Office of Emergency Response is located at 25 37th Avenue NE. Their tenant is to mitigate and respond to any known disasters or acts of terrorism for the surrounding metropolitan area. The staff of three works out of the third floor of the civic center. The open-air concept room is filled with thirty beige utilitarian cubicles all supporting various city support functions. Next to a well-used maintenance closet sits a pudgy four-foot-eight woman with perfectly coiffed hair and a sardonic expression. Valerie Wallace had just packed her things up for the night and was looking forward to a quiet night binge-watching TV with her four-legged best friend, Crunch, a seven-year-old Collie-Golden mix with a love for chewing ice. Through her thick coke-bottle red-framed glasses, she spied the blocked number with suspicion. Valerie picked up line two and answered with a patented wearied greeting. "Office of Emergency Response, this is Valerie."

"This is Supervising Special Agent Brian Fescue with FBI Special Projects in D.C. We have an EAR and need to be put in touch with someone at the city that can make things happen fast."

Valerie sat up straight and adjusted her glasses. An EAR, or Emergency Action Response, was serious. She had trained for this situation. More than a hundred hours at the local community college and some training clinics the city had put on. Her throat abruptly went dry, and she tried to speak, but nothing came out.

"Hello?"

"Sorry. I can help you." She quickly processed the situation. "I'd like to add our captain of special weapons and tactics to this call. Please stay on the line."

A brief pause ensued that included some ridiculous hold music, *The Girl from Ipanema*. It seemed fit for a spa, not the Office of Emergency Response.

Codi looked at her phone. Then up at the semi that was parked on the shoulder up ahead. She unconsciously stepped on a brake pedal that didn't exist on her side, as the sheriff swiped left, just missing the truck along with the car in the lane next to them. Joel gripped the seat and held his breath.

There was a clicking sound and the music died. "You still there?"

"Yes," Brian answered over the lazy song.

Valerie made quick work of the introductions. "Captain Scherer this is Supervising Special Agent Brian Fescue with the FBI."

Brian got right to it. "Captain Scherer, I have one of my most trusted agents in your area, and she is on the phone with us."

Codi didn't let Brian finish. "Captain, there is a high probability that the concert at the basilica is a terrorist target."

Captain Scherer stopped in his tracks. His wife and three kids all looked over to him expectantly. They were only twenty-five feet from the security line at the concert.

"We need to build a wall around it without the terrorists knowing and get as many people out as safely as we can."

"Agents, can you hold for one second, please."

Codi was now getting very frustrated with the infrastructure of Minneapolis.

Captain Scherer put his hand over his phone and turned to his family. "Shelly, take the kids, and go home now."

"But what about the concert?" his wife asked

"Dad!" Their teenage daughter, Gina complained.

"Do as I tell you—now."

Shelly, realizing his tone, gave a short nod and turned their family back toward the car. She glanced back over her shoulder one last time with true fear in her heart.

He pulled his cell back up to his ear. "Okay. What do you need?"

CHAPTER TWENTY-FOUR

SAINT PAUL, MINNESOTA – BASILICA BLOCK PARTY – 5:19 P.M.

Sheriff Gilbert slammed on the brakes, double-parking his car on the main roadway. Everyone scrambled out and dashed through traffic as they crossed the busy street. Horns and screeching brakes announced their arrival. Captain Scherer stepped to the curb and made quick introductions. He led them to the SWAT command center that had just arrived, and a large group of officers gathered nearby. The captain had managed to get twenty-six officers, both SWAT and regular police. It took five precious minutes for Codi to lay out a viable plan and disperse the officers. They had no idea what to expect inside, but time had run out and only quick action would do.

The venue was set up with a tall temporary fence around the whole area. There were three ingress and egress points, plus a fourth entrance for staff and performers. Just inside the fencing, several booths and food trucks were stationed around the perimeter. They sold everything from t-shirts to burgers and ice-cold beer. The officers spread out and immediately closed the venue to any newcomers. They went to work escorting audience members that had not yet made it to the main viewing area away from the scene. It was now only a matter of moments before social media leaked their presence and actions. That alone could start a panic and force the terrorists into premature action.

Once set up, the command center raised its antennae array and started jamming all cell and radio signals in the area. It made communication almost impossible, but the same applied for the terrorists and social media. Codi, Joel, Shannon, and the sheriff followed Captain Scherer into the crowd. There were easily over twenty thousand people packed together, listening to a warmup band finish their set on stage three.

They pushed their way through the crowd, separating as they went. Each with their own assignment—find the terrorists in the massive crowd. It would be easier to find Jimmy Hoffa's grave.

Deputies Tamber and Paulson helped other officers take apart the outside fencing and pull it aside so people could easily flee the venue from any direction.

Fred checked his phone. It was five minutes until he and Ben were supposed to start the fog machines. From here on out, he would embrace his true self, Farid Khadem, son of Mohamad Khadem. True and faithful follower of Allah. He moved to tower one and took his place just inside the cordoned-off area. Ben did the same, moving into position at tower two. Farid opened his phone app. Everything seemed to be in order. Once the main band started playing, he would release the fog and make sure it kept flowing. Farid said a silent prayer to himself and tried to focus on the mission. Sweat was soaking through his shirt in spite of the evening's cool temperature. He started a silent chant—*Allah Akbar, Allah Akbar.*

The warmup band finished playing to a cacophony of cheers and claps. A low rumble was heard coming from the main stage as a solid base note moved up the scale. The audience moved and shifted to face it. The Minneapolis skyline framed the huge stage. A local DJ stepped into a refocused spotlight. The sound climaxed, and he grabbed the mic and called out. "Give it up for the Painted Pigs! One of my favorite local bands. Okay, for those about to rock!" He paused and held the mic out to the crowd. A giant cheer went up. "Behold the party twenty-five years in the making—The Basilica Block Party!" Another roar from the audience. "This is a place where Christians from all denominations can get together and Praise The Loud!" He paused for another yell-out from the crowd. He waited until it died down and then announced the first main act. The throng went wild as rock and roll lights danced everywhere, and the band took to the stage. Giant screens on either side of the stage came to life.

James, Matt, and their two friends had made their way into the audience about thirty feet from tower one. It was not a mosh pit here, but not far off, as people were still shoulder-to-shoulder. There was the faint smell of weed in the air, and a few clouds of vape fog hovering here and there. Families were commonplace and several dads held smaller children on their shoulders.

Matt put his arm around his brother and pulled him close. "Thanks, this has been a good break for me."

James looked his brother in the eye and gave him a sincere nod.

Even though years had passed, the bond between the two brothers was still strong.

Codi pushed through the bodies, her vision robotically panning left and right looking for something out of place.

Joel struggled to part a path as he aimed for the stage. His ribs ached, and he was fighting through the pain. The music started back up, and the roar from the crowd was deafening. The band was one of the major headliners for the venue, and people pushed forward making Joel fight for every inch. He tried calling out, "FBI, I need to get through." But no one seemed to care.

Jal watched from a back corner of the large crowd. He was disgusted to be sandwiched in with so many Christians. He nearly shook in revulsion. But he used his mind to focus on what was coming. He could see one of his men standing in the distance on a platform next to one of the towers and the other at the far tower. There were large smoke machines mounted to the towers just above each man's head. He scanned the other two towers to see the same machines mounted in the same way. It was a glorious sight that made him proud. With a successful operation, he conservatively estimated ten thousand spawn of Satan dead or dying within the week. It would be the greatest attack ever on the West and would make 9/11 look like a dress rehearsal. But most importantly, he would be the one behind it all, and no one would know it. The thought made his current predicament all worthwhile, and for the briefest moment his nose no longer hurt. All he had to do now was wait, watch, and observe. If all went as planned in the next few minutes, he could exit the premises and be on Canadian soil within the hour.

Farid glanced at his phone for the third time in a minute. He was watching the timer count down. When it hit zero, he pressed the three buttons in sequence on his app. It felt as if a giant weight had been lifted from his shoulders. He had accomplished his mission. Now all he had to do was guard the tower, while he watched thousands of vile Westerners bathe in a cloud of death.

Nothing happened.

He pressed it again. Same result. He closed the app and reopened it. Still nothing. He glanced over at his partner and gave him a wave. He seemed to be having the same issues. In an instant, the thought hit him like a jolt up the spine. They were being jammed.

Codi was the first to see him. A young man with darker features standing on a raised platform next to one of the lighting/speaker towers. He was dressed like a roadie and was pressing buttons on his phone. He looked very concerned. She watched as he signaled to another man at the other tower. Her eyes took in the scene and quickly spied the large metal box mounted to tower one a few feet above the man's head. She then noticed the same boxes mounted to each of the other towers. There were four. That must be it. Codi gave a quick shrill whistle and waved, trying to get her team's attention.

"Shannon," she screamed out.

Shannon and Captain Scherer turned and looked her way. They were about thirty feet away and moving to the far side of the crowd.

Codi used her hands to point to the towers and then held up two fingers indicating two suspects. She made a box shape with her hands and pointed up. It took a few seconds, but Captain Scherer and Shannon got the message and started moving for the other suspect by tower two. Codi turned back toward her suspect and started pushing her way through the throng. The man turned and looked right at her. In the second that passed, she knew he was one of the terrorists, and he knew she was looking for him. He dove under the stanchions and bolted into the crowd.

Jal saw one of his men jump down and run off. He watched in horror as the woman who had ruined his nose chase after him. *How was this possible?* He immediately reached for his phone and hit the override button to start the smoke machines. He waited and watched—nothing. The only weapon he had was a pen in his back pocket that disguised a thin blade inside, much like an ice pick. Without missing a beat, Jal pulled out the penknife and moved through the crowd toward the nearest tower. Hopefully, it still had enough venom on it. He would not let his operation fail.

Sheriff Gilbert had seen Codi signal to the other officers. It took him a minute, but he soon figured out that the towers must have the RDDs. He pushed his way over to tower four. There was no one suspicious there, but he wasn't about to leave it unguarded. He would protect it from further tampering.

Codi dropped her shoulder and rammed her way after her suspect. The man was quick as he scampered through a sea of bodies, but he was blazing a trail that Codi used to her advantage. For every person he had to push aside, she gained two feet on him.

Codi dove at the man, horse collaring him and crashing into a group of men holding beers and laughing. They all went down in a tangle of bodies. Codi pulled away from the scrum and slammed her elbow on the back of the suspected terrorist's neck. She twisted his arm up behind his back. The man yelped and stopped resisting. She grabbed a flex cuff and hooked it around his wrists.

"Codi?"

A familiar voice cut in, just above the music. She tracked her eyes to its source. Matt was on his side trying to get untangled from another man. There was beer on his shirt and a stunned look on his face.

She placed her foot on the back of the terrorist's neck, pinning his head to the pavement. "Matt? Didn't you get my text? What are you doing here?"

He stood up. "Partying with the guys, why?"

"Hi," James said weakly, as he stood up next to Matt.

"James, happy birthday. I'm Codi. Nice to meet you. Look, guys, do me a favor and get this dirt bag to an exit and hand him over to a policeman. And don't go near those smoke machines." She hooked a thumb back toward the nearby tower.

Before they could answer Codi leaned over, grabbed Matt with both hands, and planted a kiss for the ages on his lips. It didn't last long, but a jolt surged through Matt that left him feeling woozy and suddenly very sober. Sparks flew from his lips to his amygdala, as neurotransmitters in his bran released dopamine. He took on a lost but very satisfied expression as Codi pulled back and looked him in the eyes. "Sorry. And I love you." And then she was gone. Off to assist Shannon and Captain Scherer.

Matt stood there motionless for a moment, unable to speak. Once again, Codi had gone and done it. She said the words before he could. Like a tornado, she burst in, caused all sorts of chaos, and then was gone. He couldn't decide if he was mad or happy. Then the realization took hold. *She said the words! I Love You!* It was like a dream.

Finally, Matt placed his foot on the dirt bag's back, re-pinning him to the ground.

James had the strangest look on his face.

"What?" Matt asked.

"Your girlfriend's friggin' gangsta. And she's totally hot. Holy smokes!"

Jal pushed through a family of four and noticed a sheriff standing next to tower four as if on guard. He carefully slid within the rocking crowd, keeping his eyes toward the stage, making sure the sheriff didn't notice him. Once he got next to the stanchion, he waited.

As soon as the sheriff looked to the left, Jal slid under and came up behind him. With a practiced flick, he slid his knife up into the base of the man's skull and used his other hand to carefully lower him to the ground. Jal pulled the man's pistol and slipped it into his belt, the crowd around him completely unaware.

Jal climbed the tower and quickly took a deep breath and held it. He pressed the manual buttons on the box, first green, then red, and finally blue. Smoke immediately started spewing into the air. It flowed outward and down. Nearby fans started clapping and shouting. It was magnificent. Jal paused for just a beat to watch as everything he had planned came to fruition. It was his proudest moment. The crowd loved the smoke effects, but it would bring their demise. He quickly climbed down the tower and away from the deadly fog. He moved for the other towers.

"Sorry, man, you can't be here."

Joel had finally slipped over the retaining wall that separated the crowd from the cameras, lights, and stage. A giant of a man in a yellow windbreaker quickly moved in his direction. "FBI, I have to get on that stage," Joel said while holding up his badge, but the man didn't seem interested.

"There's no way I'm letting you do that. Now take your little badge and get back in the crowd before I throw you out on your ear."

The guard had seen every trick in the book and nothing was getting past him tonight. Joel pulled his gun discreetly so the man could see he was serious. "This is a matter of life and death. I have to get to that stage."

The guard held his hands back realizing this guy might be the real thing. He let Joel through.

Shannon pulled her weapon and called to the man on the raised platform. He was so busy trying to get his phone to work that he had not seen Captain Scherer and Shannon surround him. In a sudden flash of fear, he dropped his phone and raised his shaking hands to the sky. His eyes were as big as saucers. Captain Scherer kept him covered while Shannon escorted him to the ground and hooked him up. She cuffed his wrists and ankles, taking no chances, before doing a thorough pat down. Captain Scherer climbed up on the tower and pulled the power cord on the fog machine. Immediately, smoke started to spew out. *It must have a back-up battery and a fail safe,* he surmised. He tried pushing the power button, but again, nothing happened. Fog continued to flow out of the machine. A quick inspection of the box revealed it was put together with specialized screws. It would take a specialty tool just to open it. He tried to push it off of the platform where it sat, but it had been bolted down—*Argh.*

He kicked at the black box with both feet. His progress was slow, but after several attempts, the box started to wobble and finally broke free. It crashed to the asphalt below where it sputtered and died.

Three more to go.

Joel ran up the steps and over to the lead singer of the band, who was mid-song on a soulful ballad.

". . .that's how *you know it's love.*" The singer suddenly stopped. "Dude, I'm performing here. Get off my stage."

The crowd quieted, watching the drama unfold. Joel grabbed the mic from the long-haired androgynous singer and turned to the audience. "Sorry to interrupt. I am FBI Agent Strickman, and we have a slight emergency. We need everyone to slowly evacuate the premises."

The crowd started to boo him.

"This is not part of the show. Please, very carefully head for the exits!"

The crowd quieted down.

"For your own safety, please exit slowly, now."

They seemed hesitant, but one by one, people started to move for the exits, the not so distant memory of a Vegas country music festival in the back of their minds. Joel continued at the mic encouraging them to not panic. He could see fog coming from one of the back towers. He knew if he panicked the masses, there would be even more casualties. So he said nothing about the deadly smoke as it began to spread out and down.

Codi saw the fog coming from the back tower. She could see the silhouette of a man climbing back down and heading to the next tower. She changed directions and ran to intercept. The crowd was thinner this far from the stage, but it was still slow going. She kept her gun out of sight but readily available.

Shannon looked at the spreading cloud of death from the back tower.

"I gotta stop that other fog machine. Keep an eye on our perp," Shannon yelled. "It's killing those people." She started to move for the fourth tower.

"Agent Poole!" Captain Scherer called out, as he stepped from the tower.

Shannon stopped and turned back, just as a fist flew to her face laying her out cold.

"Sorry, dear. My town, my responsibility." Captain Scherer made sure he laid her gently on the ground. He turned and sprinted through the crowd toward the deadly cloud.

He screamed as he ran. "Keep away from the fog! It's poisonous!" This started people panicking, and they rushed away from the expanding cloud.

Jal climbed the third tower and pressed the three buttons that would trigger the fog to flow. He now had two towers spewing deadly smoke into the evacuating crowd. He might just salvage his operation. Someone had warned people to stay away, and his heart sank as he saw people move away from the brume. He needed to get the other two towers working and fast. There were many more people in that area.

Joel encouraged the crowd as they moved at an agonizingly slow pace to the exits. Someone in the audience screamed, and a panic started. Luckily, most of the people near towers three and four had cleared by the time they started releasing their payload. He pleaded with them to walk, not run, to the nearest exit, which by now was multiple places as the police had pulled down huge pieces of the fencing around the venue. They stationed themselves around the perimeter, encouraging fans to get clear.

Jal paused to look at the path to the next tower. Heading right for him was the female FBI agent. Without hesitation, he pulled his gun and fired.

The bullets flew at Codi. One nicked the top of her collarbone. Another one hit a nearby fan's calf. He screamed and fell. Codi instantly dropped to the ground. In one move, she barrel-rolled and came back up into a sitting position with her gun drawn and pointed in her target's direction. Panicked concertgoers ran in all directions. By the time she had a clear shot, the man was gone. She jumped to her feet and ran, ignoring the pounding pain in her shoulder.

Captain Scherer climbed the fourth tower and unplugged the fog machine. Again, nothing happened. Fog continued to flow. He kicked and kicked at the black box, until it, too, broke lose, crashed, and died.

Codi moved through the thinning crowd, her gun covered with her other hand but ready for action. She used a technique she called *one of these people does not belong here*. Scanning from person to person, eliminating innocents as she went. A flash of dark hair moving with a group to the south caught her attention, and she sprinted in that direction.

Matt could see the fog spreading in his direction. He and James grabbed their prisoner and started escorting him toward the exit. Several shots fired within the venue sent a flash of concern through him for Codi. He hoped she would be all right. It caused the crowd to jack-rabbit, and he and James almost lost their prisoner as a bunch of scared concertgoers charged through them. He would be glad when they got this guy delivered for safekeeping.

Shannon cracked open an eye. Her head rang and her jaw was on fire. She sat up slowly and looked over. The terrorist she had caught was still double-cuffed and lying on the ground. She moved over and cut the flex cuffs on his ankles and helped him to his feet. She pushed him ahead of her as they moved for the exits. She noticed her suspect had peed his pants. She held little blame for a young boy brainwashed and converted to such an extreme mindset. But she would not have hesitated to shoot him dead in order to stop his actions. He was one of the lucky ones. She looked around for the man who'd slugged her, but he was nowhere in sight.

Captain Scherer climbed the third tower and kicked at the black box with both feet. His progress was slow, but after several attempts, the box started to wobble and finally broke free. It crashed to the asphalt below where it sputtered and died. His feet were throbbing, and he was sure there was a broken bone in there somewhere. He climbed down and ran for the next tower. He would stop the terrorists no matter the cost.

Joel could see that most of the audience had dispersed. From what he could tell, there were no obvious casualties. The fog was still spreading from one of the towers, but nobody was left in that area. He held out his hand and dropped the mic. No one saw, but he'd done his job well. A little pat on his own back was in order, plus he'd always wanted to do that. He climbed down off the stage and out the back exit.

"Dude, you killed my set!" the singer complained to him.

"You're welcome," Joel replied as he walked right past.

Codi pushed through the exiting crowd, focused on a man thirty feet ahead moving to the south. She did a quick glance back. The area was almost emptied. This was good. She could just make out Joel up on the stage. The crowd was beginning to thin out. She pressed closer. The man moved out of the concert grounds and passed a food truck with a giant pink taco on it. Codi followed him across the street and up the sidewalk. He kept with a small group moving across the street. He glanced over his shoulder, and in an instant, bolted at the sight of Codi.

She gave chase. "Stop! Federal agent!" she yelled.

He didn't.

Valerie stepped to the sidewalk. There were people everywhere: some running, some crying, some just standing there. She had gotten the word out, and emergency services were all reacting to the event. Ambulances, fire, more police, and RERT were all arriving. It was a mess, but most people seemed to be okay. Her boss had finally called her back and was heading there to meet her. Most likely to take credit and make sure there was no blame headed in his direction.

She moved to the police commander and introduced herself. She handed him a box containing ten handheld Geiger counters.

"Use these to determine who in the crowd might need medical attention. We'll need to isolate them and start ERPT."

He looked at her with a slightly confused expression.

"Emergency Radiation Poisoning Treatment."

"Oh, right."

The last fog machine died as it hit the ground. Captain Scherer climbed down the metal tower. Other than his foot in extreme pain from kicking at all the boxes, he felt fine, but in his heart, he knew he was in real trouble. The amount of fog he'd been forced to breathe in . . . he stopped thinking about it and sat on the ground. He looked around. Across, at the other tower, lay the body of the sheriff who'd come with the two FBI agents. *God rest his soul.* Captain Scherer was the only living person left on the grounds. They had evacuated everyone. Hopefully, the concertgoers were spared the effects of the fog. He picked up his phone to call his wife but remembered they were jamming the area. It was an action that had probably saved thousands of lives. The phone suddenly slipped from his fingers. They seemed too weak to hold it. *Strange,* he thought. He suddenly felt incredibly tired and decided to lie down for just a moment until his strength returned.

Jal dashed through a parking garage. He moved between rows of cars, making himself a difficult target. He knew he would not be able to lose the agent that was dogging him. He needed something that would turn the advantage his way.

Codi kept up with the terrorist, waiting for him to tire and make a mistake. She was slowly closing on the man as he ran out of the structure and down a back alleyway. She raised her weapon to fire just as he turned into the backdoor of a restaurant.

She barged through the door recklessly, not wanting to lose her mark, and crashed into a metal trashcan that had been overturned in the doorway. She scrambled back to her feet, ignoring her battered shins. She ran through the restaurant amid shouts from the owners. Once out the front door, she spied the man now running across the street and turning the corner. She pushed harder after him, her lungs pushing oxygen in and out at a rapid pace, and her legs protesting her effort. As she came to the corner, Codi did a quick peek to make sure she wasn't being targeted. The man threw an elderly lady to the ground and jumped into her car. He hit the gas and sped away. Codi spun around and looked for a solution, anything. Next to the bike rack was an old school 2-stroke Vespa GTS. She didn't hesitate.

Jal watched as the female FBI agent shrank in his rearview mirror. *Finally.* He turned down another street and headed for the airport. He kept his speed and actions within the law so he would garner no attention from passing police, most of whom were still busy at the concert. He let his actions of the day replay in his mind. The operation had been brilliantly planned and executed right up until the last minute, when everything came crashing down. He had managed to get the RDDs going, but the crowd had dispersed too quickly. It was a total disaster and would take months, maybe years, of planning to rebound with something as grand. He let his mind peruse future possibilities. Once the mine was back open, he could start over. For now, he would need to lay low.

The little Vespa had good power, and Codi had no trouble catching up to the beige Toyota Avalon. She stayed several cars behind to keep from being seen, biding her time, until she could make her move.

As the traffic thinned Codi's luck ran out. The Toyota suddenly burst forward. She'd been made. She hit the gas and chased after him.

Jal weaved in and out, passing the few cars on the road. He was surprised that the woman was able to keep up. He made a sudden left turn onto a one-way street, weaving and dodging as cars narrowly missed him. Car horns screamed in protest, and the woman chasing him seemed to be having a tough time of it.

Codi had to slow as several out of control cars skidded and raced in her direction. They were all so worried about hitting the Toyota they didn't even see her on the Vespa. She had to swerve all over the place to stay in the chase. It was near death with almost every car or truck coming her way.

A small pickup truck made an unexpected move, and Codi had no time to maneuver. She kicked off the foot pegs into the air as the vehicle drove through her Vespa like it wasn't even there. She heard a crunching sound, followed by squealing tires as she tucked into a ball. Her back clipped the roof of the truck, sending her spiraling like the spin-dry cycle on a washing machine. She wrapped her arms over her head just before she hit the pavement and rolled to a stop, scraped, battered, and bruised. Her shoulder stung and her head was spinning.

Jal was mesmerized by the sight in his rearview mirror. The FBI agent was flung through the air when a black pickup truck flattened her moped. A sudden horn blast broke him from his reverie. He turned just as a delivery van t-boned him. The impact was sudden and jarring. It flipped the Toyota on its side, up against a light post at the intersection that mashed in the roof in a V-pattern. The light post shuddered as the glass exploded, and then the whole thing crashed to the street, sounding like a canon fire. The Toyota remained on its edge, passenger side down, balanced precariously. The smashed vehicle was half in the street and half on the sidewalk. Fuel and coolant spilled from the wreckage. Other cars pulled to a stop, not wanting to get too close.

Codi forced herself to sit up. She dragged herself toward the smashed Toyota, pulling out her pistol. Several bystanders screamed and ran for cover. She couldn't see any movement, but that meant nothing. This man had tried to murder innocents without regard. She would have him in custody or in a pine box.

Jal never lost consciousness, but his head had taken a big blow from the collapsing roof. He had fallen onto the passenger-side door. He could tell through his disorientation that the car was on its edge. He used his feet to kick out what was left of the windshield and crawled out. He tried to stand, but his head spun so much he fell back down. He could see the FBI agent staggering in his direction. He crawled toward the sidewalk and spotted a gap underneath the car between the curb and the street. He grabbed his gun and wormed his way in. He wiped the blood that was dripping into his eye and sighted down the barrel.

The bottom of the car was facing Codi as she approached. She could see fluids leaking onto the street but still no sign of the driver. She stayed focused with her gun held level as she weaved past several stopped cars with scared drivers hiding inside.

A siren could be heard in the distance, along with the sound of steam escaping a rip in an over-cooked radiator. A sudden volley of gunfire made Codi duck as bullets flew in her direction. They were rushed and inaccurate shots. Codi stood back up and continued forward. She could just make out a figure lying prone in the gutter behind the teetering car. He had crawled into the space where the car angled up from the pavement to the sidewalk. She could see him pointing his weapon at her, but she didn't care. Another round of bullets shot in her direction. Codi didn't even flinch this time, she just kept moving forward.

Jal shook his head trying to clear his mind and steady his shaking hands. He had a clear shot on his target, but he was still dizzy and suffering from the crash. He gathered himself and took very careful aim. The woman stopped walking, making herself the perfect target. Jal pulled the trigger.

When Codi was fifty feet from the car, she paused. Two shots rang out followed by a clicking sound. One of the bullets whizzed dangerously close to her ear. Codi took aim and replied.

She purposely put her bullets into the pavement, sending chips of asphalt and sparks toward the car. The third bullet did the trick and the growing pool of gasoline ignited. Within a few seconds, it spread, following the liquid trail heading for the gutter. She could see the man squirming, trying to crawl back out from under the car as the fire chased him.

The first scream was normal, but it quickly changed to a high-pitched, haunting squeal. The man flopped and flailed, trying to get free from under the car and escape the fire as his skin sizzled and burned. Codi watched impassively for a second and then stepped up to the tottering burning car, careful to avoid the flames that were starting to grow. She shoved against the undercarriage with all her might. The vehicle wobbled and tipped back over onto its mangled roof. There was a crunching and popping sound as metal met flesh and bone, smashing it to a pulp. The high-pitched wailing suddenly stopped. She stood for a brief second listening to the flames crackle and pop before moving back across the street.

There was an advertisement on a vacant bus bench beckoning her: *Been injured in a motorcycle accident? Attorney Ben Callister will fight for you!* She sat down slowly, considering giving the attorney a call. As she sat, her body blocked out the attorney's phone number. She leaned her head back with a slow exhale. For the first time in two weeks, Codi relaxed.

EPILOGUE

Codi and Joel were in a solemn mood as they stared through the glass. The room had been hastily cordoned off from the rest of the hospital. It was one of the few times she would allow herself to set foot inside one. There were ten bodies neatly lined up in two rows of five. There were tubes and life support machines everywhere. Some people had IVs; some did not. The outcome for most was good, but two bodies off to the right held their attention the most.

It was a father and his six-year-old daughter. They'd been exposed to a deadly amount of radiation and were not expected to survive the day. Though the body count was relatively low, considering everything, it hit the two agents hard. Codi let the past events weigh on her, trying to think of how she could have done more. There was always that possibility in her mind. *If only I . . .*

She caught herself and stopped, knowing thoughts like those could be destructive. She said a silent prayer for the dead and dying and promised to always give one hundred percent. There would always be evil in the world, and someone needed to stand up to it. She considered herself lucky to be one of the people that could do that job. This had been a close call, and even though the body count was low, it would still carry a heavy burden.

She reached over and put her hand on Joel's shoulder. There were tears streaming down his cheeks. He tried to wipe them away in embarrassment. Codi pulled him to her and gave him a comforting hug.

"You did good out there—saved a lot of lives."

Joel nodded but was too choked up to reply.

"By the way, nice mic drop," Codi whispered in his ear.

Joel pulled back. "You saw that?"

Shannon walked into room 401. She could hear the rhythmic sound of an artificial lung. There was a small viewing area with a few upholstered chairs and a floor lamp. A large glass window held the view into a hi-tech hospital room. It was a barrier to keep the contamination at bay. Inside the viewing room was a woman and two children, one of them a teenager. The woman had red eyes that had cried until there were no tears left. The voice on the speaker was weak and breathy.

"Give us a sec, hun."

She nodded almost imperceptibly and pulled her children with her out of the room.

"I understand we got him." The whisper of a voice was timed with the outgoing breath of the lung machine.

Shannon nodded at the man she didn't recognize. The chart said it was Captain Scherer, but he was so deformed, it was impossible to tell. His face looked like someone had taken a blowtorch to it. His torso was all lumpy beneath the sheet. There was no hair left anywhere, and his lips and nose were almost gone, leaving skeleton-like teeth staring at you. Severe radiation exposure was a cruel and punishing death.

"You saved a lot of innocent people," Shannon said.

Captain Scherer grimaced as he spoke, the tubes in his mouth making the words hard to understand.

"Sorry about the jaw."

The corners of her mouth turned up, tracing a straight line to her twinkling eyes.

"I never did catch your first name," Shannon said.

"Tim." It seemed to take all his effort for this last reply.

Shannon placed her hand on the glass. "Tim, I'm Shannon. God bless you."

She was suddenly filled with emotion and fought hard not to totally lose it. A single tear moved down her face. Shannon nodded her appreciation and then turned and left the room.

Outside, Shannon breathed in gulps of fresh air before turning for the black Suburban parked at the curb. She stepped into the passenger seat and closed the door.

"How was it?"

"Don't ask."

Brian nodded.

Shannon spoke reverently. "He saved my life."

There was a moment of silence in the vehicle.

"If that ever happens to me, promise you'll take care of it quick and painlessly," she said.

"That goes for me, too," Codi added.

SSA Brian Fescue pulled the car into the street and accelerated away. He had flown in several hours earlier to help mop things up and support his agents who had truly gone beyond the call of duty. The figures were still coming in, but besides Captain Scherer, there were only ten cases of radiation poisoning being treated. Two were expected to live. The team had saved countless lives and had stopped not only the attack but also the man behind it.

Joel and Shannon were in the backseat holding hands. Codi glanced back, and a smile spread across her face.

"What?" Joel asked.

"Nothing, just happy for you, that's all. Besides, I think Shannon has something planned, now that this whole thing is behind us."

Shannon and Codi shared a knowing look. "Remember, be gentle," Codi said.

"Not quite behind us," Brian interrupted. "The President is asking for a meeting. So we're on the jet back to D.C."

"No, thanks. Been there, done that," Codi replied. "You take this one, Boss. The rest of us have more important things to attend to."

"More important than the Pres—" Brian started to protest but could see Codi was determined.

"Fine," he said. "Where can I drop you?"

Codi looked down at her phone. There was a text from Matt. *Meet me at the Hotel Ivy when you're done.*

"You can drop us off at the next intersection. I need a drink, the good stuff."

* * *

Dennis stepped into his new office. It was exactly three square feet bigger than his previous spot and one floor higher. He noticed the same nameplate on the door that he had before. The fallout from the last week had been intense. Higher-ups hiding from the press and lowers just plain hiding. He watched as two of his direct superiors were given reassignments to lesser posts. A few supervisors had been given the boot and the blame, but he had somehow escaped with his career intact and a minor promotion. It meant twice the work for a ten-percent raise.

Now was not the time to complain, however, and he set the box down he had carried up from his old office and started to unpack his things. He had no pictures of family; he'd burned that bridge long ago. Just a few souvenirs from a life as a detective and his favorite coffee cup, a large brown affair with black lettering: *Sorry No Habla Stupido.* He went back to work. He had three detailed reports to write and a staff meeting to run, all before ten.

* * *

Farid shivered in his cell. He'd been taken on board a plane to a facility that was built underground. He now lived in a small concrete cell with no windows and a solid door. It had a small one-way viewing port and was painted to match the rest of the room—gray. He was allowed very limited sleep and an occasional meal of unrecognizable food.

He was taken into questioning every few hours and verbally abused under harsh lights until he was a blubbering mess. On day four, he had finally broken to the capitalist scum. Through tear-filled eyes and intense anguish, Farid told them everything he knew. It was a welcome relief to get it out. Now, they could kill him, saving him from further torment.

But the men in charge had no such plans. Within a few hours, FBI teams were dispatched to the two U.S.-based training facilities Farid had divulged. They took several more suspects into custody and were working their way up the chain of command. In the end, it was a big win for justice. And something they could share with the press to help mitigate the New York fiasco.

* * *

Codi cracked open her eyes to a blurry cup of coffee. She sat up, stiffly. Everything hurt. Matt's impossibly green eyes stared at her with a happy twinkle.

"I could get used to this," Codi said, while grabbing the cup and breathing in the robust aroma.

Matt sat on the bed next to her, his trim torso and strong biceps on full display. He glanced at the recent scabs and bruises that covered the most amazing body he had every seen. He knew right then and there, he could never do better. Codi was the alpha and omega for him. Now, he just needed to get the courage to tell her. Maybe he would start out slowly.

"Now that I live closer," he said, "we should set a schedule like Thursdays at my place and Sundays at yours."

Codi glanced over to Matt with a skeptical eye. It made her neck hurt, and she winced.

"I'm not big on committing to a boyfriend schedule, especially with all that we have going on right now." She let the retort hang for a second.

Matt suddenly panicked at his boldness.

"I was thinking more like my house Sundays and your house Thursdays."

The tension in Matt's face eased.

"And that's what, a girlfriend schedule?" he asked.

"Exactly," Codi said as she took a sip of her coffee.

"How 'bout if we meet in the middle?" Matt countered, his flirtatious attitude clear.

Codi set her cup down and smiled, looking Matt squarely in the eyes.

"Perfect." She leaned forward halfway and Matt did the same, meeting in the middle for a passionate kiss.

With lips still pressed together, Matt finally got the words out. "I love you."

"I know," Codi replied through the side of her mouth.

Matt pulled back. "Jerk."

"Shut up and kiss me."

IF YOU LIKED THIS BOOK

I would appreciate it if you would leave a review. An honest review helps me write better stories. Positive reviews help others find the book and ultimately increase book sales, which help generate more books in the series.

It only takes a moment, but it means everything.

Thanks in advance,

Brent

INTERESTING FACTS

For more facts, go to my website and see as well as read these details.
brentladdbooks.com

The Plymouth Mail Truck Robbery

What the press dubbed "The Great Plymouth Mail Truck Robbery" was, at the time of its occurrence, the largest cash heist of all time. It is still, to this day, unsolved and an embarrassment to the Justice system. Vincent "Fat Freddie" Teresa, a Boston mobster, claimed in his book, My Life in the Mafia, that John "Red" Kelly was the man who planned the robbery. He allegedly received a generous eighty cents on the dollar when the money was laundered.

Poudretteite Mine

Poudretteite is an extremely rare mineral and gemstone that was first discovered as minute crystals in Mont Saint Hilaire, Quebec, Canada, during the 1960s. The mineral was named for the Poudrette family because they operated a quarry in the Mont St. Hilaire area where Poudretteite was originally found. It is still mined to this day.

The Body Farm

The Body Farm, or Anthropology Research Facility (ARF), and Bass Donated Skeletal Collection are utilized year-round for research and training by the University of Tennessee faculty and students, as well as by students and professionals from around the world. It is a site designed to achieve excellence in research, training, and service in forensic anthropology and closely-related fields. For over three decades, the Forensic Anthropology Center has garnered an international reputation for research on human decomposition.

Uranium Mine

Canada is one of the largest producers of uranium. The ore is transmuted through a complex process to create plutonium. Major governments around the world identify and track the source of the ore and the methods used in the process for obvious reasons. Enriched uranium is extremely valuable, whereas mined uranium is not.

RDD - Radiological Dispersal Device

Radiological Dispersal Device, also known as a dirty bomb, is any device capable of dispensing radioactivity. Most use explosives to force and disperse radiation. Rogue nations and/or terrorist groups use these weapons mostly to produce psychological rather than physical harm by inducing panic and terror in the target population. An ingestion or breathing in of the radioactivity would be the only way to really inflict casualties.

Basilica Block Party

For over twenty-five years, The Basilica of Saint Mary in Minneapolis has been home to the largest Christian rock festival in the U.S. It is America's first basillica, and the annual concert helps maintain the building and the voluteer programs for the year. Some of the biggest names in Christian rock perform, and over twenty-five-thousand fans participate.

Radioactive Amazon

At the time this novel was written, you could order radioactive materials through Amazon. Things like Trinitite, Cesium 137, lead sheeting, and Lead Pigs to hold them in, are also available.

ABOUT THE AUTHOR

Writer Director Brent Ladd has been a part of the Hollywood scene for almost three decades. His work has garnered awards and accolades all over the globe. Brent has been involved in the creation and completion of hundreds of commercials for clients, large and small. He is an avid beach volleyball player and an adventurer at heart. He currently resides in Irvine, CA with his wife and children.

Brent found his way into novel writing when his son Brady showed little interest in reading. He wrote his first book, making Brady the main character—*The Adventures of Brady Ladd.* Enjoying that experience, Brent went on to concept and complete his first novel, *Terminal Pulse: A Codi Sanders Thriller*—the first in a series, and followed it up with *Blind Target.* Now the third book, *Cold Quarry,* takes his beloved characters down another rabbit hole.

Brent is a fan of a plot-driven story with strong, intelligent characters. If you're looking for a fast-paced escape, check out the *Codi Sanders* series. You can also find out more about his next book and when it will be available if you visit his website, BrentLaddBooks.com